EBOLA

ODYSSEY

ANTHONY C. FABIANO

LtCol USMC
(Retired)

Ebola Odyssey

By Anthony C. Fabiano

ISBN 9781937592875

Published in the United States of America

This book is a work of fiction. Names, characters, places, and incidents are the products of the author's imagination or are used fictitiously. Any resemblance to actual persons, living or dead is purely coincidental.

Dedication

To all of those who have worked diligently to bring about stability in some of Africa's most violent regions, your efforts have not gone unnoticed.

Chapter 1

"Help me!" the mother who could not have been more than sixteen yelled. She had pushed the shopping cart four miles to the clinic. Her only child, unresponsive was crumpled within the cart. She delicately lifted her three-year-old daughter and walked past all of the patients who had waited hours to see the American doctor. Blood dripped in steady streams from the child's nose and ears.

"In here," Featu ordered as she assessed the child. "Bring your child here." She allowed the mother to carry her into the operating room, which was no more than a wooden table shielded from view by three white shower curtains attached to the ceiling. The clinic was small, extremely small. Actually, it was an old car repair facility, but no one had cars anymore in Liberia. Most vehicles were destroyed during the latest civil war. Rusted metal signs that denoted a wide range of auto part suppliers hung on the wall. The building was far from sanitary. The removal of the signs was on her list of things to improve – around item sixty on the list of over two hundred.

"Will my child die?" the mother asked. Tears flowed down her face that washed away the dirt. The young mother trembled. "My poor baby."

"Did she fall?" The American doctor named Sam from Long Island asked as he quickly moved across the room. He left his other patient as he observed the commotion. The mother did not respond to his question.

"Ahhhhhhhh," the young mother wailed. She chanted several times, "My poor baby...my poor baby." Blood dripped out of every major orifice. The tall, lean American doctor looked intently at his new patient and quickly realized what was at stake. His instincts took over as the horror of the situation drove him to move backward with the utmost urgency.

"Shut it down!" The American doctor screamed. "Shut the door now!" He moved like a leopard across the room toward the outer door. He slammed it shut and shifted the lock into position. "Shut it down."

"What's wrong?" Featu inquired. She was younger than the doctor by about thirteen years, yet she had more experience in treating gunshots than most emergency room nurses. As a teenager, Featu helped the missionary where she lived treat government soldiers wounded in battle against rebel factions.

"No words." Sam directed. "Shut it down." He paused a moment, "Just shut it all down," He looked at his assistant and added in a blunt manner, "Do what I ask." The stern response surprised Featu. They were lovers in the off hours, something that started three months ago. The tone of his voice shocked her as she was in love with the white American doctor. Featu obliged and closed the half-rusted steel garage door. She disliked the rusted metal as it was unsanitary; however, she obliged. Sam insisted that they keep the steel door to protect the medical supplies that were in high demand on the black market. All of the windows had metal bars installed.

"Move the daughter to the other corner of the room and do not allow the mother to leave," Sam demanded.

"Is it dangerous?" Featu moved in close and pressed her soft cheek against his face. She whispered in a soft voice. "I'm scared." She trembled.

For a brief moment, the doctor thought of how he had fallen in love with her. His nurse of the past ten months and lover for the past three months, Featu had a seductive sense about her. Her body was chiseled and firm, results of daily hard work. She was from the Mandingo tribe, who were close to the border between Liberia and Guinea. She was close to six feet tall and walked several miles one way every morning to the clinic. Featu would have passed as an international model with her looks and poise.

"Yes, extremely dangerous," Sam said as he looked into her eyes and added. "It is something that will kill us all." He grabbed the satellite phone and used the makeshift ladder to climb to the roof. Adequate phone reception was impossible. As he stood on the roof, he dialed the international number that he had memorized for the man who worked at the UN and mentored him at Columbia Medical School. In his haste, he forgot the time difference, but this could not wait. Sam spoke loud into the phone to leave a message. "Doctor Abuja, this is Sam Levowitz in Liberia. We have a situation here. I fear that we may have a new Ebola outbreak."

In Monrovia, the capital city of Liberia, the man who wanted to deliver Liberia out of chaos walked back and forth. Adolphus Urey was promoted to Minister of Defense after the last office holder left Liberia over corruption charges. Urey was Liberian by birth; however, ninety percent of his life was spent in America. His father was the Minister of Finance in the prior Samuel Doe regime in the 1980s. After Charles Taylor took over the government, the entire cabinet was purged, and Taylor pulled the trigger personally on Urey's father. At that time, Urey was a young boy and relatives smuggled him out of Liberia. The long travel brought him to America where he was raised and educated at Harvard on a full scholarship. After Taylor was removed from power, the UN sent five thousand troops to stabilize the nation. Once it became safe, Urey returned to his native land.

As he prepared to enter the President's office, Urey rehearsed his comments in his mind. He looked at the inscription on the wall, '*The love of liberty brought us here.*' The motto of his nation had tested the strength of its people for over one hundred and fifty years. Urey was determined to maintain peace in Liberia – wherever the threat came. What he did not imagine was a large-scale prison break of former child soldiers in neighboring Sierra Leone that would threaten Liberia again.

The Defense Minister wasted no time and handed the Liberian President several photos. Their neighbor to the north had a major security breach as eighty former child soldiers had escaped from a prison in northern Sierra Leone. Both knew the ramifications if these dangerous men entered Liberia. The photos were taken along a known diamond smuggling route. During Sierra Leone's bloody civil war, over a billion dollars of rough, untraceable diamonds were smuggled into Liberia for sale on the world market. Remote surveillance stations were erected to keep track of any movements along the known smuggling routes that fed into UN headquarters. "Are these current?" The President asked. After Urey nodded approval, the Liberian President added, "This could be disastrous."

"These men are former RUF." RUF stood for the Revolutionary United Front and was the rebel army that thrust Sierra Leone into a bitter decade long civil war. Urey pointed to the picture. "These men... they have murdered before. We must stop them."

"Have any been captured?"

"Few," Urey responded. "Some tried to return to their villages and were beaten to death by mobs." The brutality inflicted by former child soldiers in cross-border raids resonated strongly in the minds of locals. In the next single photo, Urey showed the Liberian President the face of a man – one of the most wanted terrorists in the world. "This man is Al Qaeda."

"Are we certain?" Liberia's President asked, and Urey nodded.

"What are the Americans planning?" Defense Minister asked.

"Too early to say," The Liberian President replied, "We have a long relationship with the United States, and I am certain they will not abandon us in our time of need."

"We don't have long until the rainy season," Urey looked out the window. The skies were clear, yet the biblical West African storms would arrive soon. Twenty-two feet of rain would arrive in a short time period.

"The Americans are sending one of their best operatives," The Liberian President replied and added, "with utmost haste."

At the same moment in the northernmost mountain range of the lower forty-eight states, a Park Service Ranger stood over the edge of a deeply fractured crevice and peered into the abyss. He shouted several times and received no answer. The ranger held the rope tight around his waist and yelled loudly again. Over twenty minutes had passed since he helped lower the volunteer from Seattle Mount Rescue team into the dangerous ice opening. Alongside the ranger, three hikers, one male, and two females, sobbed vehemently. They waited impatiently for a response, any response that their friend had been found. They yelled down into the abyss. A crackle in the radio was inaudible, yet it was enough for the ranger to understand as he pulled the rope through the climbing device. Slowly the volunteer rose from the ice opening with a teenage female hiker strapped to his back with a thick strand of rope. Even though she weighed only a hundred and twenty pounds, she was pure dead weight. Drool emerged from the mouth of the teenager as she remained unconscious from the fall. The volunteer used all of his strength to grip the rope and pull their bodies forward. Time was critical, seconds mattered. The evacuation helicopter had already landed on the slope two hundred yards down the mountain. The volunteer grunted as he yanked the last ten pulls out of the rope.

As he emerged, the other hikers screamed in excitement. The ranger took over and placed the victim on a sled and pulled her toward the helicopter at a breakneck pace. The volunteer did not hear the words of thanks from the hikers. He panted heavily, like a boxer who finished the tenth round of a prize fight. His knees crumpled, and he fell to the ground. Tom Russell removed his hiking helmet and goggles. Even in the cold of Mount Rainier, sweat dripped from his forehead. The water nearly froze as it fell to the ground. Russell looked out over the skyline and the majestic view of the Seattle skyline as a backdrop. Russell's vacation from his day job was over and the two weeks of volunteering with the most elite mountain rescue team came to an end. Russell had to go back to his day job as an operative for the Central Intelligence Agency.

Russell stood five feet, ten inches and was solid muscle. He was almost 35 years of age and had kept his body in top physical condition. For the CIA, Russell's expertise was Africa. His light skin, brown hair and blue eyes easily made him stand out among the locals. However, he had been effective from his assignments in Libya, South Sudan, Congo, Zimbabwe, and most notably Liberia. And most recently, he had returned from an operation to stop an international poaching ring on the border of Rwanda two months ago – battered, bruised, and with two bullet holes in his left side. He underwent three surgeries in Cape Town, South Africa. As soon as he could fly, he was airlifted by a military cargo plane back home to heal.

Russell had joined the Central Intelligence Agency directly out of the military, a rare practice. While the military possessed a robust intelligence operation, few, if any, were direct hires as CIA field operatives. Russell's superiors were awed at his abilities. Tom Russell was pulled into the CIA and thrust into several deadly situations. Russell was an unusual breed and was hand selected for some of the most dangerous African operations.

Russell looked up at Mount Rainier, a formidable climb for any hiker and then peered down at the call number. There was a dozen missed calls in the past thirty minutes. He hit the redial to the CIA Operations Center. He looked out toward the distant mountain range and thought about an additional climb in Oregon as he still had three days left on his leave of absence. He hit the return dial.

"Russell here," he said as he spoke into the satellite phone. Russell looked around to make sure no one could listen, but then he chuckled to himself as he remembered that he was two hundred meters from the summit of Mount Rainier.

"When can you travel?" The desk officer asked in a robotic tone. Russell grimaced and bit his tongue. He was not upset that he did not receive any get-well cards from his superiors. It would have been nice to hear after several months of being out of commission that someone was concerned about his health. Russell knew that he was expendable, and he was told numerous times that if captured, the Agency would disavow knowing him, especially since a majority of Russell's operations were deep cover.

"Two days." Russell responded flatly, "Is that agreeable?" The desk officer on the other end placed Russell on hold for over a minute. When he returned to the call, the desk jockey agreed to the timetable and provided comments on the logistics associated with Russell's travel back to Africa.

Russell concluded the call and tossed the satellite phone into his pack. He hated the Langley desk officers. He understood that they were needed to support the CIA's clandestine missions. However, on his most recent trip to Langley, Russell discovered that none of the desk officers assigned to support him had ever been to Africa. Russell mused that this specific desk officer he nicknamed wonder boy had never been out of the states. More than likely, wonder boy spent his time in the bars around Washington, D.C. and thought that he was hot shit as he worked at the Central Intelligence Agency. Russell theorized that wonder boy would brag across a bar to some lady how he had just saved the world. Most of the desk officers assigned to manage Tom Russell were not pleased with the latitude superiors provided Russell to continue his climbing while they attempted to contact him for urgent missions.

After a four-hour hike back down Mount Rainier and a two-hour ride home, Russell was exhausted; however, the clocked ticked, and he still needed to clean his gear and prepare everything for storage. He did not know how long he would be out of the country. A projected operational timeline had never been provided any Africa plan, as it was a high adventure - high risk - anything can go wrong type of place. He cleaned his gear with utmost haste and hung the climbing ropes across the staircase railings to dry. He did not know how long he would be gone and cleaned out the fridge. Everything went into the trash.

Russell had a female acquaintance, someone he shared dinners and drinks. His recent love affair lasted past two months. Russell found few women who would put up with his quirky sense of humor and nonchalant nature toward relationships. This relationship was the longest in the past four years. The only thing that she knew about Russell was that he made a lot of money selling his share in a technology startup business. His bank account, physique, and good looks made him a prime target for single women at any bar scene. Five years ago, Russell was listed as Seattle's most eligible bachelors. He kept his personal life secret. Russell saw a few reminders of his current girlfriend's presence as she had left a jacket, scarf, and worse of all - feminine hygiene products in his bathroom.

Russell had someone he cared about, but it was complicated, especially since she was a career Israeli Mossad agent while he worked for the American CIA. Russell fell hard for this Mossad agent. They had a brief romantic interaction that results in a child. Russell made attempts to keep in touch; however, he had not heard from her in eight months.

Russell completed a detailed inspection of his house before he set the alarm code. He left a cardboard box on the doorstep, which contained the remnants of his recent relationship. Russell had no patience for breakups, so he texted that he had to leave the country unexpectedly. Hopefully, he would never see her in a bar when he returned. Russell turned to look as he entered the cab and hoped he got everything. From notification of mission until the time of his departure from Seattle: fourteen hours had elapsed – time was critical.

Russell found a quiet spot at Tacoma International Airport and phoned his longtime mentor, Colonel Frank Kitson Jr of her Majesty's army who now worked for MI6.

"Kitson here," replied the man with a thick British accent.

"Colonel, this is Tom Russell." The friends had not spoken in nearly eight months since Russell's last mission in Africa. "Just wanted to give you a heads up that they are sending me your way." Kitson worked with MI6 and had served throughout Africa. Russell and Kitson formed a tight bond after several highly volatile African operations. They had each other's back countless times, especially when their survival chances were minimal.

"Already heard that they would send in the best," Kitson replied. "We have moved some assets to be in close proximity." Kitson knew better not to give out any location details as he did not see a signal that Russell's phone was encrypted. Anyone close to Russell could pick up the communication with less than sophisticated listening devices. "Once you get settled, we'll get connected."

"Confirmed," Russell said, "See you soon." He was not surprised that Kitson was on top of things and knew he was on the way back to Africa.

"Don't get cramped up on that long flight," Kitson said added sarcastically, "young man,"

"Never too old," Russell said and completed the call. It was something Russell and Kitson joked. Russell had a deep respect for Kitson. Russell spent the next twenty-six hours bouncing around airports from New York to Brussels and finally on his final leg of his journey toward Liberia.

Colonel Frank Kitson, Jr. retired from Britain's army and now worked for British Intelligence, MI6 division. Kitson was twice Russell's age, yet he did not show it. Kitson had over two decades of experience in Africa. Most

9

notably, Kitson had served in Rhodesia during the late 1970s uprisings. As a former British colony, many of her Majesty's soldiers were sent into the warzone and immediately became embroiled in a tug of war between outdated colonial policies and the new budding desire for freedom wanted by many Africans. The white colonists comprised only ten percent of the population, yet they had an octopus-like grip on nearly all business activity in and out of Rhodesia. As part of the negotiations, Rhodesia would be divided into two new countries, Zambia and Zimbabwe and the white supremacist majority would be removed from all government positions to allow for fair elections.

As a young lieutenant, Kitson was charged with peace enforcement and led a team of eighteen soldiers into the African bush. He set up a small compound, yet he instinctively knew they were watched. New orders had arrived that informed the young lieutenant to force all rebels to turn over weapons and surrender to the new government. Kitson looked at his men. He knew they would be butchered if they went after the rebels. The next morning Kitson donned his crisp military dress uniform; walked five hundred meters without any weapon outside of the compound; set up a table with two chairs; and laid out a silver tea set. Kitson mixed some of her Majesty's finest tea. After his preparations were complete, Kitson sat and waited. For six hours, he sat still in the brutal sun, yet he did not move. As the sun began to set into his eyes, he noticed movement on the ridgeline. A heavily armed African walked to the table. Four hundred of his devoted followers who were also heavily armed watched from the ridgeline. Kitson ignored the large rebel presence on the hill and focused his attention on the rebel leader as he walked toward him. Kitson reached out and shook the man's hand. Unbeknownst to Kitson, a reporter for the London Times traveled with the rebels and took a momentous photo. The headline over top of the front-page article back in London read *"Young British Officer Captures Rebels with Her Majesty's Finest Tea."* For his actions, he received the Queen's Medal.

For the next thirty years of his distinguished military career, Kitson traveled the world. He even served in Northern Ireland as part of a special MI6 team - these two years were summarily absent from his official military record. After the horrific 9/11 terrorist attacks, Kitson volunteered to serve in Afghanistan. After his yearlong deployment, Kitson returned to London and found his true calling as a professor at the Royal Military Academy located in Sandhurst where he taught both Prince William and Harry. Kitson was called back into service by his lifelong friend the Price of Wales and future King of England. Prince Harry had accepted an assignment in Afghanistan and Kitson was requested by his old friend to accompany the young prince with the task of keeping him out of the spotlight. All of the British newspapers understood the significance and agreed to Kitson's demands. Reporters regularly were allowed to take photographs of Prince Harry in action, yet no one could publish the stories until Harry was safely out of Afghanistan. Everything worked fine until an American liberal journalist heard about Harry and leaked the news. Kitson mustered all of his resources to get Harry out of Afghanistan immediately. After Afghanistan, Kitson took an assignment in Liberia where he met Russell. The two became instant companions. Kitson proved invaluable as Russell's mentor.

In New York City, an advocate for the eradication of the world's most deadly virus spoke into the microphone. "Mr. Secretary-General, if there were a new Ebola outbreak in Africa, we cannot contain the spread with current resources." The Ghanaian doctor looked at the Secretary-General of the United Nations. The doctor clicked several slides in the presentation and pointed a pen laser to the massive twenty-foot projection screen in the United Nations General Assembly main conference room. Delegates from around the world watched with mild interest. Many had taken off their headsets and watched the wall clock progress toward noon. Lunch would be served in a banquet hall and today's special menu was from Bolivia, which was a favorite among the delegates. In a moment, many delegates would move with lightning speed to get their spot in the buffet line. The clock clicked close to noon.

The doctor had four more slides on the potential outbreak zones of Ebola as it spread into West Africa. Not even the representatives from Liberia, Nigeria, Sierra Leone, Cote De Voire, his native Ghana, or the other remaining eight nations that make up the Economic Council of West African States (ECOWAS) seemed interested in the presentation. Most had thoughts of getting in line for the buffet. As the clock ticked past noon, the delegates began to stand and depart quickly. Headsets, vital for interpretation, were tossed to the side as the voices on the other end continued the translation of the Ghanaian doctor. The disruption became louder and louder. The doctor raised his voice. As he looked at the Secretary-General, the two men connected eyes and the doctor knew that his time was up. "In conclusion Mr. Secretary-General, if we do not halt the spread of Ebola in the Central African Republic, it could spread to other regions. The worse possible scenario would be a massive outbreak in West Africa whereby the nations will be vulnerable dealing with the aftermath."

"Thank you, doctor, for your very informative presentation," replied the Secretary-General as he motioned to his assistant. He continued to speak as he handed a note to his assistant. "Your focus tracking this deadly disease has been noteworthy, and we must commend you for your lifelong dedication." The assistant looked at the note written that stated, 'Ebola not an issue, don't waste our time scheduling this before lunch.' The assistant read the note and bowed his head in disgrace as he backed away from the Secretary-General's seat. As Doctor Abuja from the nation of Ghana looked at one of the most important leaders in the world, he noticed a majority of the UN's General Assembly had already departed.

The cold steel office buildings in New York City were nearly three thousand miles away from Africa. Flags from around the world waved in the stiff March breeze as Doctor Abuja walked out into the street. He was far from his native Ghana and wished he was there right now to bask in the warm sunlight. The spring months in the West African region produced a warm climate based upon the proximity to the equator. March was considered one of the driest months of the year for those living in this region. The rain would come in another two months to combat the harsh dryness. Doctor Abuja kicked past large size pieces of ice that littered the sidewalk from the recent winter storm. The city crews could not keep pace with the back to back storms. Even with the focus on the United Nations zone, mountains of ice were stacked all around. The chilled breeze from the Hudson River tore through his overcoat. His bones hurt from the frigid, minus ten-degree temperatures. He hunched over as he lunged his body forward in the stiff wind.

Doctor Abuja was fifty-two years old and had lived in New York for the past seven years as the United Nations coordinator for global response to infectious diseases. Doctor Abuja was a graduate of Columbia Medical School and a resident professor. He had a lifelong commitment to track outbreaks around the world. He was well respected; however, Doctor Abuja was not a good diplomat. When the Hanta virus broke out in Algeria last year, he briefed the General Assembly and incorrectly projected the disease would spread beyond the desert borders into Libya. His forecast caused a political stir with Libya's flamboyant leader. Doctor Abuja was chastised by the international media for incorrect projections and lost credibility.

Doctor Abuja lifted his feet above the treacherous ice and carefully placed each foot down. Even with a slow pace, he slipped and fell. Papers exploded from his briefcase and flew into the chilled air. Pages of aerial views of the Central African Republic flew into the March afternoon. Doctor Abuja scrambled across the sidewalk and watched pages float into the street. He lifted his hand into the air as several taxi cabs ran over the documents. Horns honked as the cab drivers saw a man crawl toward the street's edge. Pedestrians looked down as an African man rolled on the pavement screaming into the air. They could not see the well-dressed suit under the wool overcoat. Some thought that this man must be homeless and mentally challenged. Four policemen responded to the cries and circled around Doctor Abuja. In this heightened security zone of New York, the policemen rested their hands on their pistols – ready to move in a moment's notice. Doctor Abuja picked up his cell phone. With the preparation for his speech, he forgot to check his message. As he listened to the voicemail from his star pupil who worked in the remote jungle where the borders of Liberia, Sierra Leone, and Guinea intertwined, Doctor Abuja felt a tightness in his stomach as if he was just punched. He grabbed his papers and ran as fast as he could down the icy street. He yelled and waived for a taxi cab.

Several thousand miles away from New York in the Mali desert, Al Qaeda's senior operative in Africa demanded respect of the men crowded inside of the tent. The night was cold, and no fire was allowed. He knew the American CIA drones would track heat signatures and launch missiles. Kamal Abdullah pulled several goatskins over his shoulders as he watched. Each recruit shouted and waived their arms. Kamal remained silent.

As the son of a prominent Cairo physician, Kamal Abdullah was groomed to follow in his father's path. After his mother died, Kamal's father married a French woman. To appease his wife's religious beliefs, Kamal's father became a non-practicing Muslim. His betrayal to Allah disgusted his only child. During his college years, Kamal secretly joined the Muslim Brotherhood, one of Egypt's most notorious paramilitary groups. Kamal embraced Islamic fundamentalism. Three weeks before Kamal was supposed to graduate medical school, he murdered his father and his new wife. The Muslim Brotherhood provided him sanctuary and helped him escape Egypt. Kamal found a path toward Al Qaeda, and he received his indoctrination training at a remote desert terrorist base on the border between Yemen and Saudi Arabia. His medical skills were needed, and he was sent to the Tora Bora region of Afghanistan. Kamal remained in close proximity to Osama Bin Laden. After the Americans destroyed the cave complex with a massive bombing campaign, Kamal moved with Bin Laden to northern Pakistan where he received further specialized interrogation training. With his medical background, Kamal excelled at the brutal tactics. Kamal conducted over a dozen interrogations that resulted in death. He was emotionally cold. His brutal skills made him the perfect terror weapon. Kamal rose within Al Qaeda's ranks and was assigned to handle high priority missions.

Kamal waited for his followers to finish. He looked into the faces of the men who embrace the caliphate, which was Al Qaeda's distorted vision of spreading their harsh imperialistic view of Islam. Kamal pushed the new recruits that he broke out of the infamous Magbruaka prison where some of the many RUF rebels were sent to live the rest of their lives under lock and key. Sierra Leone courts ruled many of these men who at the time were boys remained a threat to the world from the sheer violence they bestowed during the civil war. For the past fifteen years, they were incarcerated, until Kamal set them free on a late-night raid.

"The American CIA watches for us everywhere." Kamal pointed his finger upwards. "Their satellites are always watching."

"Curse the Americans." The followers chanted again, "Curse the Americans."

"America protects Israel, and they will all pay dearly," Kamal spoke loudly. "The weapon that we have will expedite our caliphate."

"Death to America." The followers shouted. "Death to Israel."

"Your sacrifice will ensure our success." Kamal looked into their faces and chanted a prayer. In front of him, he unrolled several clothes that contained vials filled with infected blood taken from a victim of the hemorrhagic fever who had survived. Kamal lifted his hands toward the sky over the vials. Kamal chanted, "Allah is great." He repeated again and again. "Allah is great."

Chapter 2

"What do we tell her?" Featu asked her boss - the American doctor who was named Sam. Featu looked at him intently and waited patiently for a response, yet he did not answer. Featu moved closer. Her body was thin, but not frail. She had a way about her that drove the American insane with passion, yet he had to focus on his patients. Sam stepped backward from her and looked at the sealed off area in the clinic. He attached plastic sheets to the metal beams. In this area of the building, mechanics had once overhauled engines. Plastic sheets sealed the windows as well. He had made a makeshift laboratory in order to test blood samples. To keep everyone away, he had used red spray paint to draw a skull and crossbones design on the rusted metal door. Sam had hoped the image would keep anyone away. Word spread like wildfire that a deadly disease had arrived at the clinic. No other patients had arrived to be treated.

Sam picked up a vial of child's blood and held it up in the air. He looked at the world's deadliest virus inches away from him. As an intern under his mentor at the CDC, he had extensive training for infectious disease management. However, in Liberia, he lacked the proper protective wear. He worried that they would become infected as well and checked their blood regularly. He looked back at Featu. They were intimate, and he dreaded that he would have infected her.

"What do we tell her?" Featu repeated. She grabbed Sam's arm tighter to gain his attention.

"We tell her nothing," Sam said as a matter of fact. "She will be dead within forty-eight hours."

"She wants to move next to her daughter." Featu looked at the two makeshift beds that Sam made out of plywood. There were no mattresses.

Pillows were made out of old rags. Sam had brought two of his own blankets from his upstairs apartment and gave them to his patients.

"We can slide her closer," Sam said. He inspected the boards. "The daughter has about another hour to live." He put on the makeshift mask and rubber gloves that he scrounged out of the old bin of leftover equipment. The mask was a welder's helmet with face shield. He needed that just in case any blood shot in the air. If he got any of the contaminated blood on his mouth, nose, or eyes, he would more than likely get the virus.

"Do we let her suffer more?" Featu looked very concerned. Sam observed several tears from Featu's eyes. She quickly wiped them away. Sam did not respond as he pushed through the plastic sheets that hung downward.

As he entered, Sam looked at the mother and pushed the makeshift bed closer to the daughter. He was careful, yet boards wobbled. He pushed his right knee against the base to straighten out the wood. The mother already reached over to touch her daughter's arm. She slid her hand down toward her daughter's limp hand. She grasped it with all of her might. Sam observed how much strength she still possessed.

"My little angel." The mother said in a whimpering voice. "My sweet angel... why God. Why?" Sam looked at the mother and with one of his own shirts wiped away the sweat from her forehead.

"She'll be fine," Sam reassured her. "The Lord watches over us." Sam was raised with religion in his Gold Coast home, yet he fell out of attending services as it seemed more of a who's who of Long Island royalty that looked their best in Sunday mass. Sam looked at the blood drip onto the floor. Sam had observed the horror of violence as completed his internship at New York City General Hospital. As an emergency room doctor, he treated many gunshot victims. During his internship, the number of homicides spiked in Manhattan as a dramatic heat wave strangled the

East Coast for five weeks. Sam had served in one of the most violent periods in the city's history. Patients were lined up outside as there was no more room left in the emergency room. Sam had not been in any place of worship ever since. He questioned if God existed as such horrific violence raged in New York City that summer.

As he watched the dying mother, Sam sensed something religious about her. With his gloved hand, Sam rested his on top of the mother's forehead and recited a prayer that he had not spoken in years. The child whimpered and had a frail breath. Featu plugged the child's nose with cotton to prevent the blood from leaking into her mouth. Sam wiped away the blood that dripped from the corner of her eyes. The amount of blood had increased significantly in the past hour. Sam rolled her to the side and observed even more blood. The bottom of her pants was drenched in blood. She now bled out of every orifice. Sam assessed that she had just a few more moments to live. The infected blood gushed out at a blistering pace.

A few inches away, the young mother was in excruciating pain both physically and mentally as she watched her daughter die. She screamed aloud, a frightening shrill that struck Sam's nerves. Tears riveted down the side of Sam's cheeks. Death was horrific. Death by Ebola was by far the most horrific event known to mankind. Sam pulled the syringe from his pocket. The syringe held all of the morphine left in his clinic. The amount he withdrew would be more than enough to knock the mother out and into unconsciousness. Within a few seconds, she stopped breathing. With the thick gloves, Sam checked her pulse and felt nothing.

"She's gone," Sam said to Featu who shook her head in acknowledgment. Featu cried as well. Sam pulled the table apart and dragged his patients out of the room as he grabbed ahold of the plywood sheet. The mother slid to the floor. Sam wrapped a blanket around her. He tied her to the wood with a makeshift knot and pulled the body. Behind the building, Sam had already staged stacks of wood in a large pile.

Locals wondered what had transpired in the clinic. Rumors started, and many stopped as they passed to stare at the clinic. They watched Sam build a large pile of wood. From the commotion of Sam, a crowd had formed. They stood on the other side of the road and pointed. When Sam emerged again, they observed a strange sight as a man with a welder's helmet and rubber gloves dragged two bodies out of the clinic. Sam gently lifted the bodies on top of the logs. The site of Sam as he placed the bodies on the pile of wood alarmed the locals.

Sam picked up the plastic container next to the generator and walked back to his patients. Sweat dripped from his face, and he held off the urge to wipe his face with his gloved hands. He looked down and saw blood on the rubber gloves. He would worry about completing decontamination later. The midday sun was brutal, and he felt the sun beat on his body. Sam was beyond thirsty, yet he continued. The thirty-foot walk back to his patient felt like what a convicted murderer felt as he walked to death row. It was a long walk, and now Sam served as the executioner.

"I'm sorry," Sam said as he leaned close to the mother. "May the Lord have mercy on your soul," he said aloud. Sam doused the body with all of the liquid from the container. The smell of gasoline pierced the air. He stepped back about four feet and turned. Some of the gasoline got onto her face and must have stung severely. Sam watched in horror as he saw movement. The young mother lifted her right arm, she was not dead. What Sam did not realize was the morphine that he purchased on the black market was not morphine at all but sugar water. Sam acted quickly and ignited a cloth wrapped around a stick doused with gasoline. Sam stepped closer and laid the flame on the body. Flames emerged and burned rapidly. The logs were completely dry from the drought and helped fuel the flames. Sam turned and observed a crowd of about forty locals who watched. He felt their stares. He looked down as he stumbled back to his clinic – a vision of hope once for this remote community – now a death scene for the world's deadliest virus.

In the deep jungle inside near the border between Liberia and Cote d'Ivoire, an area where neither any military personnel nor police were present, tribes have long held justice here and exacted punishment on violators that dated back hundreds of years. Modernization had not arrived. Here, tribal justice prevailed. In the center of the remote village, the tribal elder listened. A young woman, no more than fifteen, was being accused of not being a virgin. Her father died eight years ago in a tribal clash along with half the male population. Her grandfather was ordered to watch over her, but he became ill and never left his hut. Rumors surfaced that the young girl was wicked and sought the affection of married men – all of it was not true.

She stood and watched the older women in the tribe pick up rocks, large rocks. They picked up rocks the size of footballs and held them in their arms. The tribal elder watched the commotion brew as more came to watch what may become a stoning death. Another witness was called and made more outlandish accusations that the girl practiced voodoo. The tribal elder listened patiently, yet he knew the accusations were wrong as the day in question was the day, he saw the girl working in the community garden. He rubbed his hands against the armrests. The massive wooden chair was carved from the gigantic tree that once rested in the center of the village. The tree was about a hundred and forty years old. Father after father passed down the importance of that tree to build an alliance as men climbed to the top and remained there for days to spot invading tribes. Until the alliance of peace was made among the five tribes in the area, war was commonplace. The tribal elder clinched his hands tightly to the chair arms as he heard the witnesses. Intricate carvings of lions and elephants zigzagged under his grip, images that his grandfather carved.

The tribal elder announced he would take a moment to arrive at a determination. The moment translated into two hours as he fell asleep in his hut. He returned to the scene only to see more had arrived to watch the deadly stoning. The women held heavy rocks in their arms the entire time.

Patiently, they waited for the decision. No one spoke for a long time. The dead silence was only interrupted by a fussing infant strapped to a mother's back yearning to nurse on her mother's breast. Some held their rocks in one hand and infants in the other to watch. The tribal elder could have chosen the easy decision of death, yet he wanted to send a stronger signal and exiled the young woman from the village. Fatima walked out of her village with her head bowed and eyes on the ground. She had been given a second chance at life. The village watched. As Fatima was out of sight, ear piercing shrieks erupted from the village women that signaled someone in the village had died. Fatima was dead to them. She walked out into the unknown.

In the northeast corner of Liberia, close to the Sierra Leone border, the well-dressed man looked out over the ocean. Foreigners frolicked in the waves that crashed onto the crystal white beach. Robertsport was the bastion of relaxation from the horrific living conditions that resulted from the most recent Liberian civil war. White skinned people sat in newly constructed wooden chairs under the shade of palm trees. Young local boys brought drinks back and forth from the bar. The Robertsport bar was owned by Anwar who also operated the Cape Hotel in Monrovia. Like many of the Lebanese in Liberia, Anwar controlled a major stake in the limited hospitality industry. Robertsport became the primary rest spot for most foreigners in Liberia. Anwar provided a daily shuttle with armed escorts for those who wished to get out of the grime of Monrovia. Once word of the Hawaiian-like vacation spot of Robertsport became known, the number of foreigners who wanted to partake spiked significantly. Anwar saw the opportunity and overhauled an old beach shack to make a bar. The new bar was remodeled in three short days as Anwar handed out twenty dollars a day for each worker, a month's wage for many. Over sixty men lined up each day to have a chance at work. All were paid in American cash that each laborer hid in a safe place as theft was rampant.

Anwar watched the local boys as they served the foreigners. They moved at a fast clip. The patio furniture was chained to cement blocks so it would not disappear at night. Anwar allowed several of the boys to sleep in the beach hut to protect the alcohol at night. Across from Anwar sat the Liberian Minister of Defense.

"More and more of them keep coming, but nothing gets fixed." The Minister commented as he pointed his glass toward them. "The cleanup from the war will last a long time."

"And these foreigners will need protection," Anwar said. "With the UN arms embargo, my security men are not allowed to carry anything beyond a stick. It is not enough."

"They will be butchered." The Minister paused for a moment to reflect. "The last war showed us how brutal things can become."

"Too brutal," replied Anwar. After a sip, he added. "Seems like a lifetime ago. Do you know the smell of death that still haunts me?" Both men knew that he was talking about the pile of dead bodies that were stacked outside of the American Embassy which was less than two hundred yards from Anwar's hotel in Monrovia.

"Let me talk to the President about a waiver for your men to have weapons to protect these foreigners." He picked up the paper bag full of cash that Anwar had placed on the table. It had a good weight to it and would be worth the Minister's efforts.

The Minister motioned for his trusted assistant, Ike and he handed him the paper bag. Staples were pressed against the paper and Ike knew better not to inquire about the contents. Anwar and the Minister continued their discussion. Ike held the paper bag tight to his chest as he walked to the renovated mansion that overlooked the beaches. Ike had moved into the mansion after his previous boss, Colonel Frank Kitson Jr. of the British Army, had left Liberia in hot pursuit of a Hezbollah gun runner.

With short notice, the CIA had sent on their best African operatives back on a mission. As he flew halfway around the world, Russell was exhausted, yet it was something Russell had gotten used to in his line of work. As a CIA operative on call, he had to travel at a moment's notice. Russell became adept at travel. During the sixteen hours of flying and eight hours of layovers, he kept his mind active. He had limited information on his mission and would have to link up with Kitson once he arrived in Africa. Langley informed him that this would be a joint British and American mission, equating to MI6 and the CIA playing nicely together. The direction came from the nation's leaders as they were briefed on the emerging situation in Liberia. Russell came out of Roberts International Airport and looked at the mob of locals who waited patiently for their family and friends returning from America. With his diplomatic passport and credentials, he passed quickly through security. The only bag he carried was on his back. Any equipment that he needed was already sent ahead via an Air Force military cargo plane the previous night out of Antwerp from the CIA's safe house there. Russell waived to the local policeman. The man had raised a sign above his head with the word "Russell" printed on it.

Russell looked out the back-seat window as the vehicle sped toward Monrovia, the primary scene for most of the horrific warfare that consumed this West African nation for fourteen years. The siren from the police car rang out in the afternoon. Russell mused to himself that if no one knew the CIA was coming, they sure did now. He would have to inquire with the embassy on why they sent a local police car instead of a hardened vehicle from the embassy to meet him. But then again after his last mission in Liberia, Russell was persona non-grata by the U.S. Ambassador.

Russell wore his sunglasses as he exited the vehicle and walked into the Cape Hotel. The front lobby had not changed; however, Russell observed that the owner, Anwar, had installed several more security cameras in the corners of the room. Russell remembered how paranoid Anwar was of Hezbollah operatives in West Africa. Anwar was a Christian

Druze who came from the mountains to the west of Beirut. Hezbollah terrorists murdered half of his village in 1984, a year after the American Embassy in Beirut was blown up. Civil war raged throughout the mountains surrounding Beirut. Artillery was moved in. His village resisted Hezbollah from using their location to shell Israeli positions in fear of what the Mossad would do to them. Anwar's family was massacred, yet he escaped. A few months later, his nephew Tareeq arrived – his family massacred as well. Anwar was the brains behind the Cape Hotel, and Tareeq was the good-looking face of the operation that was needed.

Russell made a quick change of clothes and headed out to the beach in front of the Cape Hotel that was the most pristine beach in Monrovia. The Cape Hotel was adjacent to the old U.S. Embassy. The new modern American Embassy was located several hundred yards further up the hill and overlooked the highest point in Monrovia. In the old embassy compound, there was a helicopter pad that served as a primary means of evacuation during the last civil war. As dead bodies were piled outside of the U.S. Embassy, the Americans evacuated. The air was ripe with death. Driving outside of the compound would have been suicide as warring factions fought for power. The only means of evacuation was by helicopter. As part of his previous education on Liberia's last civil war, Russell had watched video footage of helo after helo evacuating the staff. The U.S. Embassy in Liberia had the unwelcome status of being the most evacuated embassy in the world.

Russell dropped a towel on a lounge chair and walked over to the patio area that Anwar built on the public beach. Russell mused as he knew there probably was no building permit or city zoning board to review. Construction projects in post-war Liberia were usually approved via bribes. The ocean water resembled bath water, yet it refreshed him. Russell watched as several of Anwar's local security thugs walked along the beach to keep locals away from the manicured sand that Anwar had shipped in.

The beach was an open area, yet technically closed to locals as the foreigners enjoyed the plush accommodations at the Cape Hotel.

"Are you back for long, Major?" Tareeq inquired as he walked over to the cabana that Russell claimed as his place of solitude.

"It's Lieutenant Colonel," Russell responded and added. "I was promoted." Russell could not develop a random cover story in Liberia as many of the locals would remember that he came to Liberia as part of a U.S. military mission to help capture Charles Taylor. The exploits of his team's mission became something of a legend.

"Well…Colonel it is." Tareeq replied. "The usual?" Tareeq handed Russell a drink menu, but Russell waived him off with his right hand. Russell looked at Tareeq up and down and wondered how Tareeq could do it. Tareeq wore a vintage white suit along with a white tie. His shoes were entirely white and without any blemishes. Tareeq had movie star looks with his tanned face and perfect smile. He was a welcome contrast to look at compared to his Uncle Anwar who was much shorter and a lot heavier.

"Absolutely, a nice gin and tonic please," Russell replied. He developed a deep thirst for some type of alcohol after his travels, and the gin and tonic helped remind him of Africa. Russell was impressed that Tareeq would recall his favorite drink. What Russell did not realize was that Anwar installed advanced facial recognition software and developed a database on all of the Cape Hotel guests. Anwar expanded his operation from just lodging into the intelligence business. The waiter ran off with his order as Tareeq sat down in a chair.

"How long has it been?" Tareeq asked. He already knew the answer but wanted to generate conversation to see if there was anything further, he could tell his uncle.

"Four years," Russell said as he looked around. He took a stiff drink as it arrived. He remarked to himself that it was less than forty-five seconds from the time of order to have a drink in his hands.

The local man panted heavily from his sprint. There were very few jobs in an apocalyptic, post-civil war Monrovia and his job was one of the best. The unemployment rate was nearly eighty percent. At a snail's pace, the international community assisted the Liberian government in getting on its feet. Without the Lebanese businessmen who returned after the civil war, the unemployment would be higher.

"You know I missed this place," Russell said as he waived his glass in the air for another drink.

"No," Tareeq said surprised. "You missed Liberia?"

"The people, not the place." Russell posed. "This place will always be a shithole. It's the people that made it a better place."

"And worse," Tareeq replied, "The wars had stopped for now, but there remains a lot of criminal activity. You cannot go out by yourself at night." Foreigners were easy robbery targets.

"What about the casino?" Russell asked. He already knew that Hezbollah controlled the casino in Monrovia and heard rumors that a prostitution ring was run out of the casino as well.

"We don't go there anymore," Tareeq replied. "New management." Russell left that alone. Tareeq looked at his new guest and asked, "What about your girlfriend that you had here? Did you ever see her again? She was a French doctor with the UN… right?"

"Yes, she was a doctor," Russell replied. The real truth was she was an undercover Mossad operative for Israel. "But I have not heard from her in a while." He looked at Tareeq and wondered if Tareeq knew that the Israeli Mossad agent got pregnant with Russell's baby and that Russell has only seen his son several times because the grandfather wanted Russell dead for impregnating his daughter.

"Probably for the best," Tareeq said. Russell did not have a reply as he looked out over the ocean. Tareeq walked away quickly without giving any excuse for his immediate departure. Russell saw the reason. Four local boys splashed in the waves in front of the manicured beach and obstructed the picture-perfect scenery. One of the guards who was afraid of the water yelled from the edge of the ocean at the boys. Tareeq yelled at the guard to go into the water and physically remove the boys from the pristine sunset the Cape Hotel visitors were getting ready to enjoy. Russell thought to himself how very little had changed in Liberia as the rich and powerful still had a stranglehold on everyday life.

Several blocks away from the Cape Hotel and in a dirty part of the city, the white men who lived in the building rarely ventured out. It seemed peculiar to the locals that white people would live in this part of town. The locals knew there was something was strange about them. No one went near that building. Inside of the main room, maps were strewn across the walls as well as photos of any foreign intelligence operative within a two-hundred-mile radius. The men in the room were well equipped with smuggled machineguns and two wooden boxes of grenades stacked in the corner. These men knew fighting well. Widespread violence erupted across Africa as rogue elements fought for control in the ungoverned regions. African governments were inept at controlling the spread of violence, and some governments even sought out an alternative – mercenaries. Several nations hired a lesser-known international criminal empire called Voctrad. After the downfall of the Soviet empire, KGB officers fled with large suitcases filled with gems, gold, and priceless artifacts. Voctrad was born out of the chaos that ensued from the Soviet Union's epic collapse. To solidify their position in the world's black market for weapons, Voctrad actively recruited the best Russian soldiers. The organization branched out into selling all types of weapons stolen out of the former Soviet stockpiles. Many came from the elite Soviet Special Forces unit, called Spetsnaz.

Voctrad quickly gained a foothold in Africa's mercenary activities. Assassinations, targeted bombings, and weapons smuggling ensued as the primary means to gain wealth. Voctrad's tactics were brutal. In Ethiopia three years earlier, an uprising was squashed. The heads of the entire male population of a village, nearly three hundred, were jammed on wooden stakes at the village's entrance. When the rebel factions came to investigate, they were trapped in a crossfire and eliminated. In Sierra Leone, Voctrad controlled much of the blood diamond smuggling into neighboring Liberia by using human mules to carry the diamonds over the mountains. Those who refused were shot on the spot. In the Congo, Voctrad controlled the illegal smuggling of uranium to rogue nations such as Iran and North Korea. Where any conflict existed on the African continent, Voctrad had a controlling interest. With far-reaching international resources, their criminal empire sold sophisticated weapons on the world's black market.

"If we control the diamond smuggling out of Sierra Leone," the former East German soldier spoke while he pointed at the map, "we can make millions." He paused for a moment and suggested, "We just need to kill off some locals to show who is boss." He pointed to the smuggling routes toward the northern border between Liberia and Sierra Leone. "We can strike them here."

"Good," Checkov replied. "We can send the diamonds to Beijing." Checkov was cunning and knew how to smuggle rough, untraceable diamonds out of Africa for clients who lived in nations that did not sign the Kimberly Accord that required knowledge of the diamond's origin. Once the rough diamonds were smuggled out of Africa, they were polished into brilliant pieces and sold openly in jewelry shops. No international agency had been able to stop the practice, and the demand for less expensive "blood" diamonds kept the flow active.

Checkov had served with the East German police and then transitioned into the special branch of intelligence under the KGB. All of that was well before the fall of the Soviet Union and German reunification. Checkov looked at his men. Each of them bore the tattoo on the left side of their neck of the double lightning bolt – a link to their Nazi SS heritage. On all of his men, Checkov did deep background checks to make sure bloodlines to the infamous organization existed. His grandfather served as a driver for Adolph Hitler and a bodyguard for Heinrich Himmler in the last days of the fall of Berlin. When the Soviets arrived and formed East Germany, his father joined the KGB and helped execute those attempting to flee East Berlin. When the Berlin Wall came tumbling down, Checkov knew that he and his men had to get out of Germany before the CIA found them.

"What of the special equipment requested by Hezbollah?" another of Checkov's men asked.

"We have confirmation that they found what we need in a Siberian warehouse." Checkov looked at the photo of the machine and then lit a match. He burned the photo. "What Hezbollah wants to do with this weapon will change the world order, and we must be ready to pounce." The flame flickered and consumed the photograph of a 1960's era piece of metal that resembled a crop dusting machine. The machine was never mass produced by the Soviets, yet the prototype had been tested in the remote area of Siberia on a prison camp. The weaponization of the world's deadliest disease had been accomplished and lost in history as the Soviet Union collapsed. Checkov knew that he was on the verge of something very horrific - a disease borne from monkeys and spread like wildfire with no known cure – worse, a disease that could be weaponized.

Chapter 3

The three brothers between the ages of twenty-two and thirty sat still, quietly still as Kamal paced back and forth. They were devoted to the caliphate – Al Qaeda's plan to take over the world within the next one hundred years. What interested Kamal was not only the brother's devotion to his cause but the tattoo letters etched in their arms. These brothers knew how to kill. Each brother bore a tattoo that contained only three letters - RUF. In the midst of the Sierra Leone turmoil, cross-border village raids to kidnap young boys were commonplace. RUF soldiers raided the brother's remote village and captured them. At the time of their indentured service, the boys ranged from eight to thirteen years of age. Once they arrived at a diamond camp, each boy had been given doses of heroin and other potent drugs. Along with the other child soldiers doped up on drugs, the brothers brutalized their victims. Rapes, murders, beheadings, and butchering body parts became commonplace. Along with many other child soldiers, the three brothers were ruthless killers.

"You will find me a sacrifice," Kamal said as he pointed to each of them. His eyes were wide open as he spoke. "Get me someone we can infect with the virus." Kamal walked back and forth. He planned the mission for months and thought about every detail. The brothers watched intently as Kamal paced. "Allah will show us the way." Kamal paused for a moment and spoke again, "Allah will praise us for our devotion. Allah will help us capture the disease and Allah will help us unleash the horrors of an epidemic onto the world."

In Monrovia, Russell waited patiently until after the U.S. Ambassador had her morning coffee before he knocked on the door. The receptionist looked up with surprise when she saw the most hated person ever to return to the U.S. Embassy. Russell led an elite team into Liberia to find information on the whereabouts of Charles Taylor. In the middle of the night, rebel forces closed in on seizing Monrovia. Charles Taylor escaped Liberia in a private jet with his son Chucky and two million dollars in cash. The despot had friends high up in the Nigerian government and sought refuge. Taylor's ultimate plan was to escape Africa for Argentina, where extradition for war crimes would be impossible.

Russell had recommended to senior leaders at Langley for a potential solution to capture Taylor. The plan hinged on forcing Taylor to escape Nigeria for Cameroon. Russell passed his request for a private jet onto Langley. As the CIA planted false information into the Nigerian government about the imminent plan to capture Taylor within Nigeria, Taylor was tipped off and made his way to the Cameron border. Russell waited patiently and captured Taylor as he left Nigeria. As the CIA plane returned to Liberia, UN officers were present to arrest Taylor for crimes against humanity. Across the tarmac, a U.S. military cargo plane waited to fly Taylor directly to the Netherlands to face trial in The Hague. The havoc of an unsanctioned CIA operation in Liberia caused a major rift between the CIA and the State Department.

"The country ban that I placed on you Mister Russell was temporarily lifted." The U.S. Ambassador stated as she looked down at the classified file in front of her.

"I never knew that I could not return," Russell said nonchalantly.

"Make no mistake about it," The U.S. Ambassador lowered her glasses to stare directly at Russell, and she continued, "You are not welcome in Liberia." The career diplomat had served in many at-risk locations. She did not have a good liking for Tom Russell. She was assigned to Liberia after the Taylor regime was toppled and the UN stood up a mission to bring stability. Russell kept his cool and did not provide any expression.

"Were you briefed Madame Ambassador on the threat?" Russell added politeness in his tone as he did need her assistance: first, to get his weapons that were shipped to the embassy and second, to look at fresh satellite imagery downloaded in the embassy's secure vault.

"Yes, indeed." She paused as she read more of the confidential file. "We have heard about the former child soldiers who escaped prison and were recruited by Al Qaeda."

"Some speculate that Al Qaeda operative named Kamal broke them out, and they are headed to Liberia to team up with Hezbollah and former KGB operatives." Russell pointed to the photo of Kamal.

"Al Qaeda in Africa is not a large enough threat. We have more issues with poverty and disease. War has left Liberia with the large UN presence here."

"But now we have reports that the Russians, Hezbollah, and Al Qaeda are working together."

"The Russians are here to harvest timber, but that is all."

"We have documented that Voctrad was formed by a bunch of former KGB thugs."

"I think some of your friends in Langley are out of touch with reality on what is happening in Liberia. I have never heard of a criminal enterprise code-named Voctrad. And the thought that Hezbollah would be teaming up with a fictitious gang."

"There is a global threat if a virus can be weaponized."

"In my years, I have never heard of an attempt to develop a weapon to deliver a virus." The Ambassador looked at some old Soviet photos.

"Not just any virus, but Ebola." Russell interrupted her, and he sensed immediately that was not a well thought out decision on his part.

"As I was saying Mister Russell," The Ambassador stated loudly. "None of that makes sense." She stared back and added. "I've never heard of weaponized Ebola." Russell mused internally how the Ambassador called him Mister Russell and not Lieutenant Colonel or Special Agent or CIA operative. Russell sensed that the Ambassador wanted to put him in his place.

"But Hezbollah is here," Russell interjected.

"Yes, we know that they send some of their fighters when they get banged up from fighting in the Gaza Strip." The Ambassador waived her hand in the air. "My security chief gets a list of the names as they land at the airport and we coordinate with the UN to keep tabs on them."

Russell did not want to create more angst from mentioning the satellite photo of a large ocean container ship with a dozen speedboats alongside parked off Liberia two weeks ago. Analysts in Langley traced the boat's origin back to Damascus, and the manifest had sixty additional Hezbollah operatives that were not onboard when the boat was inspected in South Africa.

"I'm sure that it is all nothing," Russell quipped, "probably a big ghost hunt." He looked out the window to give the impression that he did not want to be there. "But Langley sent me here to check things out."

"Indeed." The Ambassador put down the papers and looked Russell in the eye. "Make no mistake that you WILL check in with my security officer on a routine basis. And if you find any issue of Ebola in Liberia, you WILL inform me immediately."

Russell nodded and left the room. The security officer waited for him and handed him a card with all of the vital embassy phone numbers.

Russell walked out of the office and tore the card up. He did not want to litter and tossed it in a trash can. He greeted the Marines as he departed the embassy. They had no idea who he was or his rank in the Marine Corps Reserves, and Russell wanted to keep it that way. He thanked them for what they were doing in Liberia and walked out of the U.S. Embassy.

Back at the Cape Hotel, Anwar sat in the lobby sipping thick black coffee and watched his guests. He upgraded his fleet of vehicles and hired new escorts to drive visitors around Monrovia. It was still the Wild West-type of place where non-locals, predominantly Caucasians, were targets of robbery, kidnapping, or even murder.

"My friend, Tom Russell" Anwar shouted as he stood and hobbled over to greet Russell as he entered the Cape Hotel. "How are you? Is your room ok?" Russell had already spotted four listening devices in his room. He thought about pulling out the devices, but that would have made Anwar more suspicious.

"Everything is great." Russell put his arms up in the air and said. "The place looks great. You should be commended how beautiful the hotel has become."

"Yes, indeed," Anwar replied. "Many, many hours of work. My passion is to serve others."

"And protect them from the dangers on the streets." Russell pointed out the window at the private security detail. The UN restriction on weapons in Liberia remained in effect; however, Anwar was able to receive a special exemption as his team provided escort duty for many foreign diplomats that traveled around Monrovia and to Robertsport for the beaches.

Most of the visitors would come for several meetings and spent most of their time shopping for souvenirs in the shops or looking for rough diamonds on the black market. The knowledge of illicit 'blood' diamonds came to light in the early 1990s when massive amounts of rough diamonds flooded the market. With the Kimberly Accord, the origin of the rough diamond had to be identified, and the hope was to curb the flow of conflict diamonds. The global diamond market attempted to be more legitimate; however, in remote parts of Liberia, men labored for hours to find diamonds in the mountain streams. These diamonds were sold in shops that only locals know about. What the diamond buyers did not know was many locals were still kidnapped and disappeared to work for Al Qaeda to fuel terrorist operations. The foreigners smiled brightly as they purchased rough diamonds at severely discounted prices on the black market and smuggled them out, yet they never realized how their purchase impacted freedom.

"My security team practices twice a week outside of Robertsport," Anwar said. He poured Russell a cup of coffee. Russell watched the thick, black glob flow into the glass.

"I remember the place." Russell took a sip and gagged for a moment. He continued to drink as not to insult his Lebanese host. Russell spoke after he composed himself. "The beaches are beautiful and not many visitors during the week." Russell looked around the room to make sure no one was within earshot. "A perfect place to train."

"Would you care to teach them some of your tricks?" Anwar asked.

"Actually, I need to borrow someone for several days as I need to go up country," Russell said as he sipped more of the hot mess. He hoped that his stomach would hold its contents.

"Really," Anwar replied. "Up country?" He wondered what Russell was up to and he continued. "That can be considered a very big place." He paused for a moment and looked closely at Russell. "I see, something special for my friend. I have a former soldier in mind. He is from Gio tribe and is very loyal." Anwar patted Russell on his shoulder as he departed and Russell thanked him again for his hospitality.

The Cape Hotel was very active in the evening with dignitaries from many nations who vied for dinner seats at the world-renowned Piano Bar atop the five-story hotel. Cool breezes fluttered from the open balcony doors. The room could hold only ten tables as a large portion was devoted to the grand piano. The large man had learned to play at an early age. As a boy, he spent hours practicing and mastered the piano. The young pupil survived the civil war and caught Anwar's attention. The piano player was called 'Play it Again Sam' by everyone although that was not his name. 'Play it again Sam' played the famous Casablanca song "As Time Goes By" at least a dozen times every night. He mastered the tune.

Dinner at the Piano Bar was one of the best meals Russell had in a long time. The fish was fresh off the morning boat, and the hot spicy Liberian pepper sauce was something he forgot how much he missed. His mouth was on fire, and he doused the flame on his tongue with a stiff gin and tonic.

"I'll have what he's having," Kitson said as he sat down.

"Are you sure?" Russell smiled as he replied back to his longtime friend and mentor. "If I recall Colonel, you had a hard time digesting the hot sauce."

"Maybe in the past," Kitson replied, "but in my two years in Sierra Leone, I became used to more hot things."

"We're a long way from home," Russell replied.

"Indeed, we are." Kitson looked down at his drink for a brief moment. Russell had not seen his friend since his wife died last fall. Russell made the jump across the pond, otherwise known as the Atlantic Ocean, to attend the funeral. Kitson was married after he graduated from Royal

Military Academy at Sandhurst. His wife Sandra had held down the household while he was off around the globe serving her Majesty's interests. Sandra became gravely ill from a malignant brain tumor. Kitson rushed back from Africa after the diagnosis and remained by her side for the four months until the end. MI6 never pushed him to return to Africa until his personal life was back in order.

Russell was very impressed by the attendees at Sandra's funeral, especially from the Royal family. Prince Charles and both of his sons attended. Russell had a brief moment to talk with Prince William's new bride Kate while she waited for her husband to pay his respects. She tended to her baby boy named George, who would be the future King of England, after his father and grandfather, of course. Russell rarely heard Kitson say much about his background and his accomplishments. They went to a bar after the funeral. Russell was brought into an old English tradition of speaking of the great things the dead accomplished in their lives. At one point, Russell observed a slightly inebriated Prince Harry at the end of the bar away from the rest. Russell was in his full-dress blues, U.S. Marine officer uniform. When he approached Prince Harry, the prince called Russell "Sir" and was very respectful. After probing why Harry was upset, the prince relayed how Kitson saved his life on four different occasions in Afghanistan, and he was beside himself for Kitson's pain. Russell departed Britain with a new appreciation for his close friend and mentor.

The Piano Bar was lively as a new cadre of foreigners had arrived. Several wore tailored suits which seemed out of place in one of the world's poorest nations. Russell listened intently as they spoke and thought that they were French. Russell watched several of the new arrivals and waited for them to pass before he spoke. "We have no room for error on this one," Russell said as he sized up his old friend. He did not know if Kitson had been on a mission since his wife's death and surmised that he had not. His job in Sierra Leone was comfortable with a posh office and routine inspections of police officers and remote military bases. The UN had pulled all international peacekeeping forces out of Sierra Leone three years ago, yet Great Britain still saw a need to keep a residual force in its former colony for stability. "Have you seen the reports?" Russell inquired.

"Let me change out this candle," Kitson said as he motioned for the waiter and requested another cocktail. "Can you please get us a new candle as this one appears to be broken?" Kitson winked at Russell as he handed the candle off. The waiter looked down at the candle with a confused look. He did not know what to do and stood idle for a moment. He was purposely told by Anwar to position that candle at the table of the American. Kitson continued, "Now that we have some alone time for eager listeners." He finished his drink in one large gulp and said. "If the reports are true, this is something that could kill millions."

On the other side of Monrovia, Checkov watched the pretty young girls across the room at Wave Tops, a bar operated by several foreign contractors. Wave Tops was located on the fifth floor of a building that rested on the Marshall River. Checkov watched the young women who drank heavily. They celebrated a birthday of one of the girls. She was in her early twenties and from Denmark. Checkov watched the young girl as her friends fed her drinks. Across the bar, Checkov saw a regular to Wave Tops, a diplomat from Spain who could barely stand. The man pushed through the crowd and stumbled down the stairs. Checkov laughed to himself as he knew the drunk Spaniard would more than likely kill a local as he drove back to his fully secured compound. There was no drunk driving enforcement in Monrovia. Checkov walked over to the edge of the balcony. It would be subzero back in his native Russia, and he had no plans to return. He was a wanted man by Interpol. On the deck of Wave Tops, Checkov basked in the sun.

"Her!" Checkov said to the closest goon who stood next to him. "Get me her." Checkov pointed to the young woman who just had her birthday. Two of his men followed her toward the restroom. Tonight, she would experience what became the beginning of several days of horrific sexual torture until Checkov got tired of her and put a bullet in her skull. People routinely disappeared in Africa, especially young pretty foreign women. Any thoughts that if the young women traveled in packs, they would be safe was a fallacy as evil men hunted them like animals.

Several hundred miles to the south in Nigeria, an Israeli Mossad operative waited patiently at a café for her contact. Francesca Wazley was a Colonel in the Israeli Defense Force, yet she rarely wore a military uniform as her real job was a Mossad international spy. Francesca looked at her reflection in the glass of water. Her appearance had been dramatically changed after six weeks of plastic surgery at a world-class facility in Palm Desert, California. Francesca came to the United States under a French passport and left under a Portuguese one. She had spent several days at Joshua Tree National Forest that reminded her of home. There were two places the unusual fork-shaped trees grew based upon the climate – one was the high desert outside Palm Springs, and the other place was Israel.

"No more for me." Francesca waived off the waiter.

"But if you need more to drink, you must go to the restroom first." The waiter replied. Francesca did not look up and placed an American ten-dollar bill on the table.

"Did anyone follow you?" The Nigerian woman asked. She smelled bad. Her hair resembled a large bush. The local woman was her first contact in Nigeria.

"Do you know who I am?" Francesca stated. She nodded.

"There was another kidnapping. This time it was forty girls who were on a field trip." The contact talked fast. She was visibly nervous and scared. "All of those girls were taken by those bastards." She breathed deeply for a moment and said. "The horror…the horror."

"Are they alive?" Francesca inquired. She was patient with the woman. "Do you know anything more?"

"No… no… I ran as fast as I could." The woman said, "It was my fault. They should not have been there." Francesca already had the brief on her contact that she worked in the school. "They said if I did not help them that they would kill my baby."

"Who?" Francesca asked. "Who was threatening you?"

"I don't know." She cried and repeated herself. "I don't know." Francesca spent another ten minutes trying to obtain some useful information from the woman; however, the lady was overcome with guilt and was impossible to understand.

Francesca looked at the coded text on her phone - mission was a go. The Israeli Prime Minister had promised the Nigerian President that they would help fight Boko Haram who kidnapped young girls as wives. Francesca walked down the streets of the Abuja. She had noticed local men watch her as she passed. Francesca had that type of impact on men. With her brilliant white teeth and slim figure, she fit the cover story of an international model on a photo shoot.

Chapter 4

By the end of the day, Francesca had changed her appearance drastically. The female Mossad agent was adept at rapid appearance changes and skilled in espionage. Even in Africa, she had the innate ability to blend into the international community quickly. She had put her hair in a bun and donned a white doctor's jacket as she walked into the Nigerian hospital. Francesca was a certified doctor and leveraged her background to infiltrate Doctors Without Borders. No one knew that she was an Israeli spy.

After she graduated from Tel Aviv Medical Center, Francesca applied with the Mossad and received her first assignment in Paris. She was asked to clean up a site where an informant was killed. When she arrived, she found the informant still alive, though barely. Knowing that he would die anyway, the man pulled the pin on a grenade and tossed the explosive device across the floor toward Francesca. The blast ripped a large hole in the left side of her abdomen. She crawled out and scrambled across the street as Parisian police arrived. For three days, she waited as an elite Mossad team extracted her. In the meantime, she used her surgical skills to repair the nine-inch abdominal wound. She removed the shrapnel and attempted to suture thread she pulled from her shirt. When that did not work, she pulled apart several bullets and removed the gunpowder.

Francesca realized that she had only moments before she would pass out and die from blood loss. If she did not stop the bleeding, all was lost. Before she went unconscious from the extreme blood loss, she poured the gunpowder over the wound. She ignited it with a match - fire sealed the wound. She grimaced in pain, yet she did not utter a sound. Six days later, Francesca awoke in a Tel Aviv hospital with her father next to her bedside. He never told her that he was the one who assigned her to the Paris mission. Francesca's reminder of her inaugural Mossad operation was an eight-inch-deep scar on her left side that was her only identifiable feature.

"I was told you are Christian," Francesca said as she looked at the priest, a man who witnessed much violence in his lifetime.

"Yes, I am." The local priest said. The chapel was small and built out of cinder blocks and a tin roof.

"And you support Jews as well?" Francesca had researched her contact. She knew the answer.

"Your country has been very gracious." The priest said. He was from a remote village in the Congo. The military moved into the area and took control of the local uranium mine. The priest's village was saved by Israeli commandos who had secured uranium from the despot army general and sold on the black market. Twenty years had passed, yet the priest remained loyal to Israel.

The priest felt overwhelmed with grief from the recent abductions. He looked up and cried aloud, "The girls…the girls were taken. They were waiting for us. They knew that we were coming." He held his head in his hands and sobbed violently. "We must find them."

Francesca drove to the village that was nestled below the monastery. Francesca strolled along the dirt path adjacent to the river. She regularly took photos from the posh camera slid loosely over her shoulder. She kept the camera loose for a purpose. Children played in the water as mothers slammed clothes against rocks. Across any available flat surface, clothes were spread to dry in the afternoon sun. Francesca smiled at a few children and asked to take their photos. She handed them several coins that brought an entourage of larger boys. Francesca observed the man behind her. She knew he would come, yet she had no idea what he looked like. With a quick grab and fleet of foot, her camera was stolen from her shoulder. Children yelled and pointed toward the man as he ran away. Several tried to chase the athletic man. Atop of the hill, he jumped on a waiting motorcycle. Francesca instinctively knew this man had connections to the underground black market. The motorcycle sped toward the crowded market, and Francesca took off in a dead sprint. She gauged the distance and terrain. Francesca could not keep up the pace, pulled her Desert Eagle from her back holster, and waved it at a kid on a motorcycle. The boy did not flinch and quickly gave up his motorbike. Francesca surmised that waving pistols must be a common occurrence in Abuja. She smacked him on the side of his head with just enough force to knock him down without killing him. She jumped on the running motorcycle and was in hot pursuit.

Francesca was adept at motocross racing as one of her Mossad training requirements. She quickly gained ground as the motorcycle hummed loudly at full throttle. Twisting in and out of pedestrian traffic, Francesca came alongside the thief in less than thirty seconds. The man looked astonished as she came up alongside. She smiled and blew a kiss at him and with her right leg kicked the side of the motorcycle. The market stall filled with fresh fruit exploded as the motorcycle crashed. Francesca walked over with her massive pistol raised with both arms, ready to fire.

"Please do not kill me?" The thief pleaded.

"I need information." Francesca leaned over and placed the barrel of the gun against the man's forehead.

"Are you willing to pay?"

"How about I let you live?" She stated in a firm voice.

"That is not good enough. We all die young in Nigeria." The thief pleaded. "No one lives long here. You must pay. Everyone pays." The man tried to negotiate. Francesca respected that even in the face of death, the man attempted to negotiate.

"I need to know everything about the kidnapped girls." Francesca had a very short timetable. She looked at the thief and smiled. "You can keep the camera, but I need information."

43

In the remote mountainous region along the Liberia and Sierra Leone border, the Al Qaeda camp was full of activity. Kamal sat on a log as he watched his new recruits fight with sharp knives in hand to hand combat. Some were stabbed. Some bled. One died as he failed to block the knife that caught him in his chest. Kamal looked at the pictures of the CIA operative in Monrovia. His appearance had not changed. It took him five days to make the journey by remote roads through the jungles and out of the Central African Republic. The three brothers remained by his side, and they continued terrorist indoctrination along the journey.

"And you are positive that he arrived in Liberia?" Kamal asked.

"Yes. Yes." The Liberian police officer said. He had traveled ten hours to bring the photo to his terrorist leader. Kamal made sure that all of his men were intensely indoctrinated into the caliphate. This man was loyal.

"Are you positive that he stays at the Cape Hotel?"

"Yes. Yes," the man replied. "I drove him there."

"Infidels," Kamal said. He paused for a moment as he looked at Russell and continued, "Many infidels stay there." Kamal looked at the other surveillance photos of the Cape Hotel. He saw women almost totally naked as they lounged by the beach. He saw photos of the Piano Bar packed with many drunks who huddled around a piano singing at the top of their lungs. The infidels enjoyed themselves, and that angered Kamal. He tossed the photos into the dirt. "We shall burn it to the ground." Kamal stood and shouted for everyone to listen. The men stopped their training momentarily to listen to their prophet. "Our enemy is the alliance of America, Britain, and Israel. They are the unholy ones, and they will perish in utter destruction." Kamal continued. "We will unleash the most horrific disease known to mankind. Allah will ensure that we survive."

A far distance from Monrovia and deep in Liberia, Russell sat in the backseat of the SUV as one of Anwar's security detail drove further into the African bush. They traveled only in the daylight hours. The roads were too treacherous during the night based on the horrific road conditions as well as bandits. A log could easily be placed in the middle of the one lane road to stop all traffic. It was not uncommon for bandits to extort money for traveling the roads. The kidnapping of foreigners was commonplace as local bandits asked for ransoms. Russell did not want to get into a gunfight as it was hard to estimate how many bandits could be on a team and what weapons they carried. Even with the UN embargo on weapons, aged AK47s made their way across the border from Sierra Leone and were sold on the black market. They stayed the night at a hotel if that was what it could be called. It was a four-bedroom cinder brick place on the side of the road that used to be a school. Russell insisted that they remain in the same room and he barricaded the door with two chairs.

Early in the morning and before sunrise, he pushed the driver to get moving. No bandits would be awake this early in the day. Russell had a tight timetable. Every minute of the day would be precious. They still had two hours to the remote clinic and needed to travel all the way back to civilization. It would be a long day. Russell kept a close watch on his GPS and directed the driver in the final turns around the village to bypass anyone. They arrived at the clinic at precisely seven in the morning. Russell observed no movement in the building and walked up the stairs. The boards creaked and signaled someone was coming, yet there was no movement.

"Hello," Russell spoke out loud as he knocked on the door. He heard nothing. Russell pulled the pistol out from underneath the back of his shirt. He put the muzzle in the doorway and slowly opened the door. The apartment was small and possessed a bed, table, and a bathtub. There was no bathroom, which was common in Liberia as centralized plumbing was a luxury in the post-war environment. Russell looked on the bed and saw movement, but not what he was looking for. A local woman laid naked on the bed face up. Russell looked at her completely nude body for one moment and let out a cough. The woman was startled.

"Don't shoot," Featu said as she grabbed a white sheet and wrapped it around her thin body.

"Where is the doctor?" Russell lowered the pistol as he quickly realized she was not a threat. "Doctor Levowitz?"

"Sam?" Featu asked, and she recognized his last name as she only heard it pronounced several times. She did not know much about his life in America. She only knew Sam in Africa, the man that she fell in love with. She looked up and said, "The doctor is downstairs." Featu looked at Russell defiantly and added, "We run the clinic together." She added as a point of fact, perhaps to put credibility to why she was in the foreign doctor's bed. Russell already had reports that Sam had started a relationship with his nurse at the clinic four months ago.

"Get dressed." Russell turned his face. He kept his hand tightly gripped on the pistol just in case he heard something, anything that could be deemed a threat.

"Who are you?" Sam asked when Russell walked into the clinic.

"Tom Russell," Russell said. "I was sent here by your government to make sure you are alright." Russell made up the lie. He was sent to find the doctor who could stop Ebola. Langley had a complete trace on all phones to include satellite phones out of West Africa. The hunt for any information around Ebola was pushed to the next level.

"As you can see, we have no patients," Sam said as he turned and pointed to the empty clinic. "We are taboo." The plastic sheets still hung from the ceiling.

"Ebola?" Russell asked. He already knew the answer. Langley had been tracing all calls out of Liberia, and when Sam called Doctor Abuja, the CIA had retrieved the voicemail.

"We cannot do anything here," Sam said. "No one comes here anymore." He walked along the clinic and looked at the empty beds. Sam was reflective. "We have no medication, not even experimental drugs. We have nothing here to help." Russell sensed that Sam was indeed upset.

"Do you know what form of Ebola was contracted?" Russell asked. That question surprised Sam, and he looked at Russell with a very inquisitive stare.

"And who did you say you worked for?" Sam inquired. "Our government?" He paused and looked directly into Russell's eyes. "What does that mean?" Russell heard something outside. Sam heard it as well and turned quickly.

"Wait here," Russell said. He went outside and saw his driver getting into an altercation with several local men. Russell looked across the road and saw several dozen men walk with a man who looked much older than the rest. Russell assumed that man was the village elder.

"Burn them!" The eldest man shouted as they walked closer. "Burn them all."

"Stop!" Russell screamed in the air. Several men ran toward the clinic. They had plastic jugs in their hands, and Russell surmised that the contents were gasoline. Russell pulled out his pistol and fired two shots in the air. "Now that I have your attention." He looked at the men and leveled the pistol at the head of the village elder. "No one will be burned today; do I make myself clear?"

"Fire!" Featu shouted and ran out of the clinic. "Fire, the back of the clinic is on fire." Russell thought for a brief moment of shooting the village elder but lowered his weapon. His mission was to get Doctor Levowitz. Smoke filled the room, and Russell found Sam getting water to put out the fire. The back of the room was already engulfed. Several men must have sneaked around the backside. Russell knew from his prior experience in Liberia that many men were superstitious of going outside at night. The locals believed in the heart men, those evil witchdoctors who would cut out hearts. Most Liberians were afraid of the night that was the time heart men came out, or so they believed. Russell understood that was why they attacked the clinic at first light.

"Run… get out of here!" Russell shouted as he grabbed Sam. Both coughed hard from the thick smoke and Russell pushed him to the floor. He pulled his arm as they crawled out of the building. Outside a large crowd had gathered to watch the commotion. The village elder must have informed everyone that today they would destroy the clinic and burn the deadly disease. Sam and Russell coughed for several moments as they sat on the ground next to the SUV. Russell watched Sam's facial expression. Tears flowed from his face as he watched everything, he worked so hard for be destroyed.

"Everything is gone," Sam sobbed.

"You cannot stay here," Russell told Sam and Featu. The crowd remained agitated well after the building was completely destroyed. "They will burn you next."

"Our work is done here," Featu said as she slid her arm around Sam to comfort him. "We cannot remain here." She pleaded to her boss and lover. "There are many others in Liberia who need our help." She grabbed his hand and said, "We must go now."

"Are you tested?" Russell asked. He had kept his distance from them as not to get too close. "For the Ebola?"

"We are clean," Sam said as a matter of fact. "I've tested our blood twice a day for the past week since Ebola arrived." Sam looked at Featu and back at Russell quickly. "We are clean." Sam was considered very knowledgeable by the CDC in understanding deadly diseases, and his area of expertise was Ebola.

"Are you certain?" Russell asked.

"The test is crude but effective," Sam replied. For a long moment, they stood in silence as they watched the building's cement block wall collapse as the wooden support beam disintegrated from the fire. The fire raged high into the air.

Russell had an intelligence update that the one man in the world who fully understood how to wage war against this untreatable virus had arrived from America. Doctor Abuja's airplane landed at Roberts International Airport in the afternoon. Russell held the door as Sam and Featu climbed into the back seat. He observed that they held hands and slept most of the way back toward civilization. As they got closer to Monrovia, Russell directed the driver to go toward the beaches at Robertsport.

At the Coconut Grove Casino outside of Monrovia, Anwar sat across the table from his arch nemesis, a bald, fat old man named Hassan who was Lebanese. Hassan had fought against the Israelis as a very young man in the 1973 Yom Kippur War. At the age of fifteen, he was expected to fire a weapon; know hand to hand combat; and master explosives. Hassan was assigned a group of fighters who formed the Lebanese Brigade. They helped launch the attack with the Syrians. Many to include Hassan had infiltrated the area as peasants. The world watched and waited for Israeli to retaliate. Under Golda Meir, the Israelis pounded the Egyptian tanks with bazookas and held off the Syrians. Within days, the Israelis pushed the Syrians back across the border. Hassan escaped with few survivors of the Lebanese

Brigade to Damascus. The Israelis were relentless to teach a lesson and pounded Damascus with artillery for twenty-eight days until the final cease-fire was blessed at the UN Security Council and received favorably within Tel Aviv. Syrian President Assad was furious at the attack on his homeland and unleashed his anger on the Lebanese Brigade as he blamed them failing him. Assad ordered every last one of the Lebanese shot. Word spread quickly on Assad's orders as the men in uniform respected one another. Before the shots were fired, many had escaped on a container vessel destined for South Africa. Those who remained behind and attempted to return home were captured near the border and imprisoned. Eventually, they were executed.

In South Africa, Hassan spent his young years working as a trained assassin for the Apartheid leadership to eliminate dissent among the locals. After the fall of that regime, he went to Libya. In early 1983, he found his way back to his homeland to find Beirut in shambles from civil war. Hassan moved to Liberia in the early 1990s with permission from Charles Taylor to bring Hezbollah fighters injured in battle for some much-needed rest. When Charles Taylor was kicked out of Liberia, Hezbollah remained.

"Your American friends are causing us troubles," Hassan said as he sipped tea from the cup. The afternoon was busy at the casino with a busload of Chinese workers from a remote work camp unloaded at the front door. Hassan watched the video monitor as he spoke. "We need to remain together on our path to independence."

"Does the path still mean the destruction of Israel?" Anwar inquired. He looked at the bald man in his late fifties who chewed cashews by the handful and drank his thick tea. Hassan refused to drink at the casino, not out of want, but out of necessity as a significant amount of Hezbollah's money was laundered through the casino. With the surge of foreigners from the UN soldiers, international aid organization workers, and Chinese laborers, the casino business ballooned.

"We have had this discussion too many times my friend." Hassan waived his hand in the air as if to dismiss the thought. "How long have we known each other?"

"Ten, maybe twelve years," Anwar replied.

"And we let you operate here," Hassan said as a matter of fact. Anwar had paid the politicians and anyone else that needed to be taken care of. His liquor was smuggled in on UN planes out of Brussels. His food was brought in on speedboats from Ghana once a week. There were few avenues to obtain good meal choices for his foreign dignitaries. The scraps from their meals were heartedly consumed by the staff. Nothing went to waste.

"Liberia is not yours to control," Anwar responded. He was playing with fire, and he knew it. Anwar felt more confident in the last month with the hiring of his own security team. He had no reliance on the UN or Liberian police for security assistance. He controlled the Cape Hotel, and it was his kingdom as an oasis in the armpit of a fourth world county that slowly emerged, at a snail's pace, from fourteen years of civil war. "Do you remember who saved you when Taylor lost control of Monrovia?" Hassan reminded Anwar of the help from Hezbollah fighters who neutralized an entire rebel battalion that attacked the U.S. Embassy. As the fighters closed in on the Cape Hotel, Hezbollah snipers fired from the windows in the Piano Bar with precision. Bodies were piled up and burned. The smell of smoldering corpses still haunted Anwar to this day.

"The Americans know you are here." Anwar needed to change the subject. "It is just a matter of time."

"This man Russell?" Hassan tossed a photo on the table. Anwar looked with surprise at the photo taken in the United States. "Your American friend is CIA." Hassan judged Anwar. "You didn't know?"

"No," Anwar responded coldly. He took a drink from the glass of twenty-five-year-old scotch. "Your friend Russell and his sidekick, the old

British Colonel, have been very busy in Africa. We have reports that they murdered one of our operatives Rajik Nabee in South Sudan. We have heard about their activities in the Congo and Zimbabwe. These are very deadly men. And you call them your friends?" Hassan turned away from the monitors and finally looked Anwar in the eyes and said. "The next time I see Russell and Kitson, I will have them killed."

"What does this have to do with me?" Anwar said. "My nephew and I have done nothing wrong."

"Anwar, Anwar, Anwar," Hassan said as he toggled his right index finger back and forth in the air. "You must remember that the homeland needs us." Hassan looked at the foreigners and back to Anwar. He spoke very clear, "Israel must be destroyed. Obliterated. It is our land after all."

Chapter 5

In Nigeria, Francesca waited patiently as she watched the road below. The harness that she had rigged in the tree held her weight and that of the sniper rifle. Francesca kept an earpiece in her left ear that was remotely linked to a listening device two hundred feet away. Based on her calculations, she would have one shot as the truck made the corner before it vanished down the mountain. It was a calculated risk to put a bullet in the head of the driver in a moving vehicle at over six hundred meters. Francesca had few options. The Boko Haram camp was heavily guarded, and she was alone. The pressure was on for the terrorist group from the government and the media. Daily newscasts of parents who pleaded for their daughters' release pummeled the airwaves. Boko Haram leaders typically moved the girls into the deeper, ungoverned territories. More importantly, sixty men desired the young virgin brides.

A random dog barked near the listening device as it chased a bird. Other animals could be heard. Francesca rested her head against the stock of the sniper rifle. Rest was not an option. Her eyes remained open. She was diligent. Her recent missions were more for short periods of time. With her son at home, she took shortened assignments. Mossad leadership was pleased Francesca brought a level of high energy - high impact - immediate results that no other Mossad operative, male or female, could provide.

With one eye tight on the scope, she let her mind wander. Francesca thought of her American lover and father of her son. She missed Tom Russell. They had a very unusual relationship - one built on lies and deception; however, their passion was unrivaled. Francesca had never experienced such high impact emotions in her life. Her rambunctious, passionate escapades with the American CIA operative had caused a lot of concern in Tel Aviv, especially with her father. Francesca's father was a Brigadier General in the Israeli Defense Force. Most of the Mossad was made up of career military professionals. Brigadier General Wazley had distinguished himself as being extremely deadly in hand to hand combat. He was adept at killing with bare hands. The last time Russell saw his son's grandfather, he tried to kill Russell. During a dinner party hosted by Francesca's father, Russell gave his view on how he thought the Gaza Strip should be a free trade zone and that was the tipping point. A shouting match ensued as Russell was not about to be pushed around by an overbearing father. It turned worse as several punches were thrown and Russell knocked the general across the room. Russell vaulted over a railing and plummeted forty feet down an embankment while Francesca's father was in full pursuit. Russell spent several days at a CIA safe house outside of Tel Aviv and was smuggled out of Israel in a fishing trawler. Russell was told by very high-level officials at Langley to never visit Israel again and never have contact with Francesca or his son.

Francesca listened intently while her eyes remained closed. A sound like a shotgun could be heard in her earpiece. Francesca quickly grabbed the weapon and looked through the scope. Another sound erupted. It was the truck that backfired as the driver slowed the vehicle down as he prepared to navigate the treacherous upcoming turn. As the truck moved into her view, Francesca fired two shots. The first one shattered the windshield and glass ricocheted inside. The second bullet hit the driver on the left side of his face. The passenger tried to take the steering wheel from the slumped-over driver. Francesca fired again and hit the passenger in the shoulder. He jumped out of the moving vehicle and rolled to the ground out of the way of the rear tires. The truck bounced against a rock and rested precariously near the edge of the cliff. The wounded terrorist hobbled toward the truck and tried to fire his weapon with one arm. Francesca shot him in the head. She could have been more cautious in the shot and aimed for the chest, but she wanted to send a signal to Boko Haram. Like a mountain lion, Francesca sprang down the embankment. She switched the rifle to carry it on her back and pulled out her Desert Eagle pistol. With one shot, she blasted off the lock on the back of the truck. Without haste, she opened the door to see the wide-eyed faces of young women who were previously held hostage for the past thirty-eight days.

"Go!" Francesca screamed. "Run!" She paused as she looked back toward the main road. A car just turned the corner. "Get out...run." The occupants of the car were shocked at the site in front of them. In the back seat, men moved to emerge out of the rear windows with their AK-47s raised. Francesca aimed at the vehicle's windshield and unloaded the magazine of twelve remaining rounds into the vehicle. The vehicle zigzagged and crashed. She patiently walked over and reloaded a full magazine on the way. The four men in the vehicle were injured, but not dead. They moaned in pain. Francesca placed the barrel of her fifty-caliber cannon against the forehead of the driver and blasted his brains out. As she aimed at the rear passenger's head, her phone rang.

"Red scorpion here." Francesca gave her call sign.

"Does utopia fall?" The interrogative question raised Francesca's interest. The desk agent on the other end of the line gave Francesca a code word that changed with every mission to know that she was not in a compromised situation. Even with a secure satellite encrypted phone, the Mossad still communicated in riddles.

"Not when it rains," Francesca replied.

"It has poured north of your current position, a place you frequented and met an American."

"Understand, ready to deploy." Francesca ended the call. She kept her eye on the terrorists as they continued to moan. Within several seconds, she put bullets in the front of their heads. The massive caliber of her pistol sent brain matter all over the ground. With the blood, she wrote on the side of the car 'you are next.' The truck was mostly emptied, except for four girls who were scared to death from the gunfire. Francesca reached her hand into the back of the truck and motioned for them to escape. After they emerged, the kidnapped girls ran as fast as they could toward freedom. Within an hour, Francesca was at the airport and boarded a private jet.

At the pristine Robertsport beach, Sam held Featu tight to his body as they rested in the hammock. He needed the break from the tragedy. The warmth of Featu's body enticed him. The warm breeze gently pushed the palm tree branches back and forth above them. Featu snored slightly in her deep sleep. Sam kept very still. He looked over at the young boy he hired to tend to the hammock by pushing it back and forth. Sam and Featu made love in a deep romantic fashion the night before. The room in the back of the clinic had no air conditioning. The incredible lovemaking had increased their body temperatures. Neither of them got a good night sleep as perspiration dripped from their bodies. The fan in the bungalow was cranked at full blast but did not provide any comfort in the night's heat. Featu calculated in her mind that they had sex for three months and thought that she might be pregnant. Featu could not bring herself to mention her fear of pregnancy to the American doctor. She cherished the moments they had together.

Sam looked up at the sky and saw a commercial plane begin the decent toward Roberts International Airport. The plane would pass along the coast right above them at two thousand feet and glide into final approach to the airport some twenty miles away to the south. He recognized the American Airlines mark on the plane's tail. He wondered who would arrive to help or was the plane coming empty to take away the fleeing foreigners. He had heard from Abuja that there was a mass exodus of foreign workers, those who made a career working for UN organizations. There were so many of them. Each with a different abbreviation making the understanding of the alphabet soup list of UN organizations.

"Doctur Sam," Ike asked. "U cum wiff Ike." Ike looked down at the two as they lumbered back and forth. The boy grabbed hold of the hammock and used his weight to stop the movement. Ike pointed to the large mansion on the cliff. The walk up the hill was steep. Featu was still in a somewhat daze, and Sam held her hand tightly to provide an extra pull up the steps. Sam looked up at the mansion as they approached the top of the stairs. It was massive. Ike pointed them toward the patio.

"Thanks for coming." Russell stood, and he offered his hand. "You look a lot better than we last met."

"Thanks for saving our lives," Sam said. He held Featu's hand tightly. "Whose place is this?"

"The Minister of Defense." Russell paused, "He is a longtime friend." Russell knew that the two of them would be very tired from the lack of sleep as he was the one that had the air conditioning unit disabled. He needed leverage. "Would you care to stay here for a few days?" Russell pointed to the large house. "There is plenty of room and only a few of us."

"Absolutely," Sam replied as he looked at Featu. They were exhausted. There was a small clinic in Robertsport that they could sleep in, yet it had no air conditioning. Featu nodded hesitantly. She was not used to special treatment.

"Ike will bring your items up." Russell nodded to Ike. "Why don't we go inside and get you settled." Russell inspected the room after Ike spent several hours getting the room ready. The guest bedroom on the third floor had not been cleaned in several months as no one had used it. The Defense Minister's bedroom was on the second floor and above the library where he stored his weapons. The windows of his room were bulletproof glass that was able to take up to a 50-caliber round. The tunnel underneath the library was linked to an old sewage line and expanded. It traveled down the hill, and the escape door was covered in overgrown weeds. There were more precautions that the Defense Minister installed in his mansion that would soon save their guests lives.

After a deep sleep, Sam and Featu awoke and took a steaming hot shower. The water pressure was something that Sam had not seen since he left the states. For Featu, it was her first life's experience taking a shower with a high rate of hot water pressure. And they embraced tightly as hot water poured over their nakedness. Afterwards, they opened the closet to see all of their clothes neatly hung. There were several additions to the closet. Featu glided her hand across half a dozen dresses that were quickly purchased by Ike down the street. Ike informed the seamstress of the size of the female guest to the mansion by moving his hands to demonstrate Featu was slender and almost six feet tall.

"Welcome," Kitson remarked as the guests entered the dining room. Kitson introduced himself as the British liaison to the UN, yet he did not provide much information on his true mission in Liberia. The guests looked upward. Three sets of chandeliers filled with candles hung above the twenty-foot table. The flames flickered and provided enough illumination for the massive room. "How about a spirit before dinner?" Kitson waived to the table filled with all types of alcohol.

"What are our options?" Sam asked.

"Well in Africa, we Brits enjoy gin and tonics to ward off mosquitos," Kitson replied. Sam looked at the table, and fifteen bottles of Gordon's Gin were lined up in perfect formation; purchased during Kitson's recent trip to the UN base in Monrovia. Liquor in the local markets was four times more expensive than at the UN base as cases are flown in daily on the UN resupply airplanes.

"Sounds perfect," Sam replied.

"And my lady?" Kitson bowed to Featu.

"Nothing for me," She replied. "I do not consume alcohol."

"I see that we all have been properly introduced," Russell said as walked over to the bar and poured himself a strong gin and tonic. He was never a drinker of mixed drinks and never ventured outside of beer until he partnered up with Kitson five years ago in his first mission in Africa, which took place in Liberia. The two of them forged a lasting partnership between the CIA and MI6 in African covert operations, something that the Americans were far behind the Brits. Kitson had served most of his intelligence career both in and out of the military in Africa. The only break came from a two-year assignment in Belfast, Northern Ireland during the final uprising. Kitson was personally marked by the IRA for death and succeeded in avoiding thirteen assassination attempts. There could have been more attempts, but Kitson only documented the ones he knew about that were foiled. Russell learned a great deal from his friend and mentor. The one thing that Russell could not match was Kitson's alcohol consumption. Russell tasted the strong drink and looked at his guests. He walked into the kitchen and poured out the gin and tonic. He replaced the contents of the glass with water and ice. Russell needed his mind clear as he needed to turn Sam toward the life of an operative.

"How many patients did you have at your clinic?" Inquired Kitson as he poured himself another gin and tonic. Russell was not worried about Kitson holding his liquor and counted him at his fourth drink.

"Typically, we had about twenty," Sam replied, and he pointed to Featu. "We ran it for ten months."

"Is this your first time in Africa?" Russell asked.

"Yes," Sam looked back at him quizzically. "If you mean, not on a safari or staying at some five-star resort." Sam looked down at the floor and spoke in a near shameful tone. "We spent three weeks for my high school graduation in Kruger National Forest." Russell did the calculations in his head quickly and estimated that trip for a family would have cost nearly twenty-five thousand dollars – and thought to himself not bad for a high school graduation present. Russell received a used shotgun for his high school present and went out to the backyard of his grandfather's farm and started to blast birds.

"And you formed a good bond with the village elders?" Russell asked. He knew what made a good intelligence operative. Russell inquired further. "Did they trust you?"

"At first," Sam said as he looked at Featu, "they did not trust me. I was the first white man to step foot in the village in over ten years. Little kids ran as they thought I was the heart man."

"Indeed," Kitson added. "Local legend has that the heart men cover themselves in white clay and come to cut out the hearts of young children. It's folklore to keep the children from venturing out of the village at night."

"It worked as I could not get near any of the children for the first three months." Sam thought of his successes and gave a slight smile.

"And you my dear?" Kitson pointed to Featu, "Are you from the villages in the area?"

"No," replied Featu firmly. "I was raised on Tubman Boulevard and educated in Monrovia." Both Kitson and Russell looked at her with surprise. They had very little information on the nurse helping Sam. "I was raised by missionaries after my parents died."

Russell had a full dossier on Samuel Levowitz who was born into a wealthy Gold Coast family. He joined a fraternity but left after several fraternity brothers at Hofstra University were arrested for allegedly fondling underage girls at the annual wild Halloween bonfire. Sam was disgusted that their families paid off the young girls to drop the charges. At Columbia University Medical School, Sam spent weekends going to Harlem to help work in homeless shelters. He was new to medicine and believed he could make a difference. Russell read that the biggest impact to Sam came when he interned at the Center for Disease Control (CDC) in Atlanta under the world-renowned, Doctor Abuja. It was at the CDC that Sam developed a passion for learning everything he could about infectious diseases. Doctor Abuja had observed brilliance in Sam that he had never witnessed in the three hundred and twenty summer interns who had passed through the CDC halls in the eight years Doctor Abuja had been at the CDC. Sam was taken deep into the CDC and educated on the world's most horrific natural predators – contagious diseases. Enclosed vials contained anthrax, Bubonic Plague, Smallpox, and the deadliest of them all – Ebola. These diseases were nature's way of controlling human growth and were studied in depth for potential cures. Sam made it his mission to understand these diseases.

"Dunner raidy," Ike said as he rang a dinner bell chime. The four of them took their seats at the closest end of the table; the other sixteen seats remained empty. Ike brought out the main course of the meal, a goat surrounded by rice and vegetables. The tray was large and heavy, yet something Ike handled easily. Behind Ike came James who smiled broadly. James was used to all of the Minister's weekend guests to this fabled mansion by the beach. James was dressed in a white dinner jacket and held a bowl of soup for the guests to serve themselves from. James was not a normal Liberian child. James was an albino. Juju, witchcraft, and folklore made albinos a threat as they were thought to have the curse of death inside of them. Anyone who touched them would surely die.

"Soup Sir?" James said to Sam in perfect English as he stood close. He moved closer to Featu. "Soup my lady?" James said in a spinoff of a British accent that Kitson had worked with him on for several hours earlier in the day.

"Yes, thank you," Featu said. She looked at James with a sympathetic expression on her face. She was not scared of James like many of the uneducated in the remote villages. "What is your name?"

"My name is James, my lady." He said as he bowed his head slightly. Kitson taught him that as well. Since he was an albino, James would be killed by juju witchdoctors for his bones as ancient native rituals believed that evils spirits would be removed for life by using the bones of albinos.

"Wine for anyone?" Kitson said as he poured a nice red wine from the Tuscan region into his glass. Russell asked for half a glass, but Kitson poured it to the top. Kitson did the same for Sam. Featu covered her hand over her glass to remind everyone that she did not drink alcohol. Russell watched her body movements closely. Perhaps, he could use their relationship as leverage.

At the secure Voctrad safe house in Monrovia, Checkov lifted a stiff drink and looked at the body of the foreign girl that his men had kidnapped. Even at the age of sixty-five, Checkov had no problem holding the girl down and abusing her sexually. He wanted her to fight and looked in the mirror at the scratches on his face. He had a bloody nose and bled on her naked chest as she fought back. He laughed during the entire ordeal. Checkov was evil, a sickened man - plagued by a ruthless power that he was above the law.

The stretch of the former KGB operatives into the ungoverned regions of Africa had made Voctrad one of the most profitable criminal empires on the planet. Human trafficking, weapons smuggling, and illicit diamonds were hard to enforce by the local governments and the UN. Voctrad had many local officials on their payroll to look the other way. Corruption and bribes became a normal way of doing business in post-war-torn nations such as Liberia, Sierra Leone, and the Congo. Voctrad was posed for significant growth as the UN peacekeeping forces were inadequate to stop the illegal activities.

Checkov sat on the bed and looked into the young girl's eyes, which were a vacant stare. He spent a moment and caressed her hair with his free hand. He looked closer at the bullet hole in the middle of her forehead. Drops of blood flowed down the side of her head. The lack of blood surprised him. When he lifted her head, he realized the reason as the back half her of her head was blown out. Shards of skull littered the pillow as well as the plump mass that used to be her active brain.

Checkov pulled on his pants overtop of the scared leg, a brutal reminder of his close encounter with death. When he served in Chechnya, a car bomb destined to kill him detonated early. The explosive force knocked him backward, and shrapnel from the vehicle ripped into his right leg. He used his belt as a tourniquet. Checkov had made a lot of enemies and kept a squad of loyal former Spetsnaz soldiers close to him for protection. He paid them well and demanded loyalty.

"Get rid of this one," Checkov said as he got dress. "Toss her somewhere on Bushrod Island." He paused for a moment as he looked at the dead face. "Make it look like she was taken by a local." Later that evening, several of his thugs tossed the body out of a moving truck on Bushrod Island, the most dangerous areas in Monrovia. Bushrod Island was connected to Monrovia by one bridge that was guarded by UN troops. There was no law enforcement stationed on Bushrod Island as the dense population of squatters and criminals reigned free.

Chapter 6

As he returned from the casino, Anwar sped his sedan past the locals who walked freely in the streets. There were few police officers on the city payroll and none to argue with the locals to stay out of the road. The only time the locals would get out of the way was when the presidential security detail conquered the streets. The Liberian Secret Service used blue SUVs with rolling lights on top and blaring alarms that signaled everyone to get out of the way. There were no street lights or stop signs in Monrovia. The Rule of Law on the street for driving was to go fast and do not stop. Anwar had his car doors locked and windows closed. The vehicle's air conditioner stopped working several weeks ago, and Anwar had to order a part from Germany to be flown in. The lack of tools held up installation. Anwar had to order the tools, and that took more time.

Anwar sweated profusely, yet he knew the windows protected him from being dragged out of the car. Two months ago, a diplomat from Spain was kidnapped at knifepoint when he left a window open. The assailant jumped in the back of the moving car as it sped down the street. Anwar heard these stories, and in Africa, nothing could be discounted. Anwar turned the corner toward the Cape Hotel. His security detail spotted his car and yelled at locals who begged for scraps outside the hotel's gate. The metal gates were twelve feet high and needed to be manually opened by two guards. The guards had fresh gray uniforms with badges that did not represent anything. Anwar chose the badges as more of a symbol to ward off thieves. Since weapons were banned by the UN, the guards had twenty-inch wooden batons on their hips. One of the guards pulled his baton and swung it over his head in a circling motion. The number of locals who remained outside the gates increased substantially, especially in the last two days. Several Germans from Amnesty International handed out money to the locals from their vehicle, and word spread like wildfire. Anwar would have to talk to the foreigners about the impact.

Anwar sped through the open gate and parked in front of the Cape Hotel. He left the car running. He yelled at a bellhop to move the vehicle. Anwar was soaked in sweat. The cool breeze of the air-conditioned lobby shocked his senses. His nervousness alarmed the clerks at the front desk. Anwar closed the door to the security room and began to make immediate preparations. He did not know what form the attack would take, yet he knew it was coming. He pulled out several sets of blueprints. The dates varied based on the additional work completed on the hotel over the years. Anwar never submitted requests to the building inspector as that role did not exist in Monrovia. If the place had four walls and a supported roof, it was considered structurally sound. He called Tareek into the office.

"We need to be ready," Anwar told Tareek. Anwar pulled out a map from his locked desk and spread it open. "Much preparation must be made."

"What's wrong?" Tareek inquired. He had never seen his uncle act like this. Sweat dripped from all over his body. Anwar's shirt was drenched. Anwar was acclimatized to the African heat and rarely ever sweated. He had no need of antiperspirant and never needed to take a shower at the end of the day. However, the agitation of the imminent threat from Hassan made Anwar immensely nervous.

"Hezbollah has plans to take over," Anwar said as a matter of fact.

"A coup?" Tareek inquired. He thought for a brief moment and asked further. "But who will they put in power?"

"The best selection would be the Minister of Defense," Anwar said, "However, he will not be bought by Hezbollah. Minister Urey sees Hassan and his thugs as a threat."

"He will stop them and make sure the coup is toppled."

"Not if he is dead," Anwar said.

"Do you think Hassan would have him killed?" Tareek asked. "That sounds too risky."

"Don't underestimate Hassan." Anwar slammed his drink on the table. "He's a brutal killer." Anwar looked up from the blueprints. "He is cunning and diabolical."

Anwar had seen the brutality first hand when Taylor took power. Charles Taylor was way too smart to have his hands bloodied with the deaths of his enemies and paid Hassan to kill Samuel Doe. Hassan knew a public execution would propel Taylor's legitimacy for control, and Hassan hired a local thug to carry out the task in front of foreign journalists. Doe's face was badly beaten as Hassan worked over the Liberian President to get the information on where Doe buried the money he stole from the National Bank. Hassan found the money hidden beyond rocks on the cliffs below the Presidential Palace and directed Anwar take his speedboat to Casablanca with several suitcases filled with Doe's money. Anwar opened one bag and took several stacks of thousand-dollar bills that helped him renovate the Cape Hotel. Anwar lied about a dead aunt in Beirut who left him the money. If Hassan knew the truth, Anwar would be dead.

"What about the Americans?" Tareek tried to think of other options. "They are invested heavily in Liberia."

"Do remember President Doe? The Americans embraced him after he took power. They did the same with Charles Taylor after Doe was assassinated. The current President is a reformer and not corrupt like Doe and Taylor." Anwar talked fast. He was nervous. "Hezbollah has no bargaining power. They will take the easy road and assassinate." He sat back in his chair and looked at the monitors. Nothing stood out of the norm that would alert him. He did not know when or how the attack would come and that made him very nervous.

"When do you think?" Tareeq asked his uncle.

"Soon," Anwar looked at the maps. "I guarantee they have a plan under development. Something bad is going to happen. We need to prepare for the worse, just like the last civil war." Anwar said as he looked back at the main building diagram. "I can sense it; death is near."

Tareeq looked at the building plans and asked, "If Hassan is going to assassinate the President, why do we need to bolster our security?

"Because he will kill the two of us before his plan is put in motion. We are a threat to him, and he knows it." Anwar said as a matter of fact. "How much money do we have in the safe?"

"About sixty thousand," Tareek said. "We have several past due payments from some current tenants."

"Get the money," Anwar said. "Get everything out of the safe."

"Where are we going?"

"Don't know…anywhere." Anwar pulled out his passport. "Maybe Detroit."

"Uncle, sorry to complain, but isn't Detroit cold?" Tareeq asked. He had never been to America. Anwar had made the trip several times to visit distant relatives.

"Yes," Anwar said. He thought of all of the potential outcomes. He thought of the locals who worked at the Cape Hotel. After a brief moment, he added, "but at least we will be alive."

The newly established Al Qaeda camp in Liberia was located within an old, abandoned military camp less than an hour drive from Monrovia. The Liberian military vacated the camp after the Taylor regime collapsed. The UN did not need the base, and Polish engineers cut trees down across the road entrance. Kamal had his men build a new road out of nothing. In the blazing heat, he watched them toil with primitive tools against the hard dirt. Kamal prayed aloud as he walked past them to a shaded tree. The camp was a perfect solution for the terror that Kamal wanted to inflict. There was a large cement building, three stories high that served as the new barracks. Kamal chose a small bungalow high up the hill, about four hundred yards away as his sanctuary, just in case the virus spread. Kamal had a generator brought in to power his building, not just for the air conditioner, but for the freezer that contained blood supplies – extremely vital for his mission.

Kamal smiled broadly as the three brothers delivered him a present. They opened up the trunk of the car and yanked out an overweight Frenchman who worked with Doctors Without Borders. The man had a hood over his head and hands tied behind his back.

"Good find my sons." Kamal waived his hands in the air high above. "You have done Allah well." Kamal looked into the eyes of the white doctor. "If you do not find the cure to the virus, you will die."

The Frenchmen gagged on the rag stuffed in his mouth and moaned.

"What are you saying?" Kamal demanded. "Take that rag out of his mouth." He ordered. The three brothers never acted until their leader directed them. Once the rag was removed, the Frenchman spat blood.

"You have the wrong man." He replied. "I don't know what you want." His eyes were wide open out of fear. He was about forty years old and had served with Doctors Without Borders on and off since his second divorce. He was fat and out of shape. The man looked at the three brothers and quickly realized he was overmatched. "I am here in peace."

"You are just as bad as those American scum," Kamal said. "France murdered my Algerian brothers." Kamal referred to the long conflict. Bombings became frequent, and unrest over the French occupation brewed heavily. Many French wanted to keep their precious colony at all costs and felt betrayed when Charles De Gaulle agreed to remove French troops from Algeria. The Day of the Jackal was born as an attempted assassination attempt on Charles De Gaulle was foiled. Kamal knew the history of Africa. As an Egyptian, Kamal grew up very well educated on the power of the foreign occupiers on the Dark Continent. He learned in school how many countless times his native land had been invaded. Under the caliphate, Kamal knew his cause would take over the world.

"What do I need to do?" The Frenchman understood his position. He wanted to live. The Al Qaeda videos posted online showed beheadings and torture. He did not want his life to end in that manner.

"You will transfer blood to our patient."

"Where?" He looked around. "Is there a hospital. Is someone injured?" The Frenchman wanted to know what had happened. More importantly, he wanted to live. He knew what was at stake. The white man looked at the local men, and he saw the whites of their eyes get bigger as they viewed him as fresh meat.

"Soon," Kamal said. He wondered if the Frenchman soiled himself in the abduction. Kamal grinned broadly and added, "You are the first piece of the puzzle."

Meanwhile, at the Robertsport's mansion, the dinner party continued in earnest. James hustled back and forth filling the water glasses. He was very pleased with himself. James had spent many hours listening intently to Kitson and worked very hard on annunciating words.

"More water, my lady?" James asked Featu. Seeing an albino up close made Featu curious. She reached out and touched his arm. She could tell that James was African, yet the white pigment changed his complexion. In the bush, James was an abomination, something to fear, something to kill for juju. The jungle witchdoctors cut open the albinos and took their bones that were used in elaborate ceremonies to spread fear among the locals. Fear was rampant and the stories told of the white man who came to their village to kill them harnessed that fear.

"James," Kitson said. "Tell them about our lessons today."

"The Nazis were an evil menace," James said. He looked at his guests and added, "They had to be destroyed."

"And who destroyed them?" Kitson asked.

"The British and American alliance."

"And the Russians," Russell added.

"Yes," James said, "but we don't trust them." Everyone laughed.

"James, can you tell our guests about where you came from?" Kitson knew the story well and thought the guests should hear it firsthand.

"In my village, the elders would not allow me to go to school with the other kids. They thought that I had the juju and it would infect others. They thought that I was evil. My momma never let me play outside as heart men would come take me. One day, a lady in a white dress came to my village and asked for me – James - to go with her to a school for others with my color. We traveled a full day on a bus to Monrovia. We were given school in a church. There were twenty-three of us. The nuns were very nice to us and gave us lots to eat. But they could not protect us when the bad men came for us. I was the only one to escape. I ran and ran. Mister Ike found me in the street alley crying and cold. Mister Ike took care of me and protected me. Mister Russell brought me here to live in this big mansion. One night, a local heart man came and took me, James. Bossman Russell came and rescued me. He beat the heart man real bad, and they never come back looking for James again."

"We saved James that night," Russell said and pointed to Kitson and Ike. "We all saved him."

"Was it juju?" Sam asked. He had rumors of jungle witchcraft but thought it was more ghost stories than anything. The locals called it juju.

"There is still evil, uncontrolled force, in the remote villages." Kitson began. "Juju is the worse form of witchcraft that had been here since the slave trade days. Some of it made its way to the Caribbean islands, and it gave the western world a glimpse into the darkness. The raw form remained unaltered in West Africa and is the vilest form of black magic in the world."

"In my town," Featu said. "The village elder still does not do anything without consulting the witchdoctor." She looked at the others at the table. "Juju is very much alive here in Liberia. I would be fearful of letting James out of the mansion at night. They would come and take him."

"They tried once and felt my fury," Russell said. "If they try again, we will not have mercy." Russell looked over his shoulder at Ike. "Right Ike, we will not let anything bad happen to James."

"Nuh, nuh, notin bad fur James," Ike said in his bush dialect. "James guud. James guud boy."

Russell seized the opportunity to recruit Sam. The CIA needed to validate the antidote for Ebola and needed Russell to get an experienced doctor to handle the mission. Langley's only prerequisite was it had to be an American, someone that Langley could use for future missions. Russell had thought for a long while on how to recruit the young doctor. He had rehearsed what he would say.

"When I was working with providing toys to kids in the cancer ward at Presbyterian Hospital in Manhattan," Russell provided a personal story to build more of relationship with Sam. "One of the guys that I had worked with took his medals off of his uniform, placed on a little girl's bed-gown, and informed her that she was a hero."

"I heard of that," Sam remembered. "I completed my residency at that hospital, and they always talked about it." Russell knew how Sam looked at Featu that he was in love. Russell knew something more powerful – Featu was African. How would that look back on the Gold Coast of Long Island? How would it work for someone who came from poverty to attend a luncheon at the pristine country club that overlooked the Hudson River and Manhattan? Russell handed Sam a piece of paper that had words scratched on it from an anonymous quote about the latest Liberian civil war: 'Doped up soldiers robed in the spoils of war – dresses, wigs, construction helmets, and swimming goggles – fired on civilians and rival factions with equal disdain.' After he read the quote, Sam crumpled up the paper. He witnessed firsthand the aftermath of the savagery.

"Liberia has witnessed a lot of pain," Russell said.

"The effects of the civil war will remain for generations." Sam offered. "These former child soldiers that you see on the streets of Monrovia have no job skills except violence. They cannot be rehabilitated." He paused for a long moment. "They are lost souls."

"I would offer," The elder Kitson stated, "the inability of the UN to offer a fundamental rehabilitation program right after the civil war ruined these men." Kitson pointed at Ike. "Children with weapons murdered his family. They are ruthless killers, and many remained addicted to heroin." It was well known that the RUF used drugs to make the young boys kill without remorse. Silence overtook the table as each contemplated the issue.

The dinner was nearly complete when a knock came to the front door. Russell and Kitson looked back at each other in a surprised look as unannounced visitors in the dark of night were not welcomed in Africa. Neighbors do not walk up to a door at night to knock and ask for a cup of sugar. The darkness of the night holds many threats that Russell and Kitson know all too well. Kitson reached under the table and grabbed the pistol that he had strapped underneath the table as a backup weapon. Russell looked at the closet door on the other side of the table where he had placed a submachine gun. He thought about jumping over the table but did not want to frighten his guests, especially as he needed to show Sam that life as a covert operative was not very dangerous. Ike went to the door and looked out the makeshift peephole and looked back again. He pointed the shotgun thru the door as he opened it and dropped it by his side as he recognized the face. It was changed, but he recognized her.

"Ike," Kitson said. He paused for a moment and shouted in a loud tone, "is everything alright?"

"Ya, bossman," Ike replied. "U hava gest."

"Good evening everyone," Francesca said as she walked into the room. She wore an overcoat that had a concealed spot for a large knife and pistol. Kitson squinted his eyes to make sure he did not see a ghost. Russell immediately recognized his former lover and mother of his son. Francesca moved like a lizard in a fast, seamless motion as she took off the overcoat and laid it over a chair. "Miss me, boys?"

Chapter 7

Across the dining room, Francesca stared intently at their faces. She underestimated that there would be any other guests at the mansion and scanned Sam and Featu several times as she memorized their faces. Francesca would reach back to Tel Aviv to get more information on them. Everyone must be accounted for as a potential threat until proven otherwise.

"What brings you back to Africa?" Kitson asked. He broke the ice after what appeared to be a very awkward long pause. Kitson bounced his gaze back and forth between Russell and Francesca like a rapid-fire world-class ping pong match. An Israeli spy was the last thing that they neither expected nor wanted to see at this moment in time. The stakes were high, and anything that could infuriate Hezbollah was a risky proposition.

"What makes you think that I left Africa?" Francesca shot back quickly. She stood motionless as her hands stuck firmly to her hips. Her right foot was forward and centered on her body. It seemed that she was striking a pose for a photographer. Russell stared on - motionless, expressionless, and wordless. He reached for a glass of water and gulped a portion of the contents.

"You look different," Kitson stated as a matter of fact, and he continued, "Are you planning to remain in Liberia for a while?"

"Let me see how things go," Francesca replied as she walked over to the bar and poured a glass of scotch.

"U hungree?" asked Ike.

"Famished." She replied as she looked back at the guests. "I hope that I am not intruding."

"No of course not," Kitson replied. He looked at Russell and saw a thick red color emerge across his face. "There is plenty, and we were just enjoying a meal with our new friends."

"Oh really." Francesca looked at the guests again. As she walked to the table to offer her hand, she brushed up against Russell's shoulder. As she departed the handshakes and greetings with Sam and Featu, she glided her free hand across Russell's back in a soothing motion. In her other hand, she kept the stiff drink level and protected.

"What are you doing here?" Russell asked Francesca. The tension was thick in the air. He knew that Francesca would not arbitrarily show up in Liberia. It was very unusual for the female Mossad agent to arrive at the Minister of Defense's mansion in the remote, northern part of a fourth world country. Russell knew that there had to be an ulterior motive. Francesca did not do random and would not randomly arrive for dinner. Everything was calculated. Russell confirmed his suspicion that he had been under surveillance for the past several days. At first, he thought it could be Al Qaida as he saw local men with cameras turn their heads when he looked at them. Russell instinctively knew that locals did not walk around with Nikon cameras unless they wanted to get robbed. After he pissed off Francesca's father, Russell knew that the Mossad had kept tabs on him.

"Well...my dear," Francesca replied. "Is that a way to greet the mother of your child?" There was an awkward and uncomfortable silence. Russell fumed and stared at her intently.

"Are you staying in Africa long?" Kitson again broke the silence after a very long moment.

"Just stopping by on my way home," Francesca said. It was a lie, and Russell knew it. She was a seasoned Mossad operative. There was nothing random in her life. Every action and decision was deliberate, except perhaps her pregnancy with Russell's child.

Sam and Featu sat in silence. After a long moment, Sam and Featu excused themselves to go for a walk on the beach. Ike went with them with a flashlight and an AK47 strapped across his back. No one walked on the beach at night, unless they wanted to get robbed.

"How is the food?" Kitson asked.

"Delicious," Francesca replied as she hastily chewed apart the food like a lioness who devoured her prey.

"Just like old times?" Kitson said, more like a statement than a question. Kitson recalled the last time the three of them were together in several past covert operations in Liberia, the Congo, South Sudan, Rwanda, Somalia, and Libya. The three of them were embroiled in numerous deadly matches against some of the world's more notorious terrorists that operated unchecked on the Dark Continent. The alliance of America, Great Britain, and Israel to eliminate terrorist threats was the strongest partnership in over fifty years.

At the newly established Al Qaeda camp within Liberia's borders, the makeshift laboratory took shape. For the past several days, the Frenchman worked all day and night to look at the blood samples under the microscope. The primitive microscope was twenty years old, and he had to take it apart and reassemble the pieces. The cold stone walls were painted white to help with the light from two spotlights hung from the ceiling. The wire ran for three hundred yards toward the single generator at Kamal's safe house. The wire was strung along makeshift poles in the air. The Frenchman had not slept well since being taken off the street a week ago. There was a guard outside the door at all times. The Frenchman took off the helmet. It was a firefighter's helmet stolen from a UN firetruck that had a face shield, which was one of his requests to Kamal. He slowly peeled off the rubber gloves that were for industrial cleaning. The yellow gloves smelled of ammonia cleaner, yet it served as the best and only option to keep the contaminated blood from personal contact. There was a wire from the lights connected to a small refrigerator that hummed loudly as it was on its last stage of life.

The Frenchman looked at the photos provided by Kamal of the deadly virus. The Marburg virus had a very distinctive design. The Frenchman had never worked on viruses. He was a general surgeon out of Paris who did not understand infectious diseases, and he knew time was running short. He kept active and made every attempt he could to mutate the virus by mixing it with other blood samples. He had no idea what he was doing and had heard blood from monkeys may contain a varying strain of the virus. He requested as many samples as possible. The smell from the dead animals was pungent. The Frenchman shined the flashlight on the animal bodies as he entered the dark room. There were five large size chimpanzees hung upside down by their feet from the ceiling. He shined the light toward the faces and the light reflected off their wide-open eyes. The Frenchman disemboweled the primates to inspect the organs and pulled out the hearts from each one. He reached into the body of one and dug out a liver. He brought it back to the makeshift laboratory to slice open some samples and spray painted a number three on the chimpanzee. He matched the primate to the blood samples. The Frenchman had requested the use of the internet to research, but that was not allowed as Kamal knew that somehow, he would call for help. The Frenchman operated blindly and kept busy with hope to find a cure for the world's deadliest disease.

As the night set along the pristine beaches at Robertsport, moonbeams resonated to illuminate the palm trees as they waved in the breeze. Sam and Featu held hands as they walked along the sand. As they walked closer to the water, waves splashed close to them. Featu lifted up her long flowing dress above her hips and walked in the water. The warmth of the water felt refreshing. She reached out to Sam with her left hand. As he grasped her hand, she grabbed hard and pulled him toward the water. They both laughed as a large wave crashed onto the shore and soaked both of them. They toppled over onto the sand and rolled in the wave. Featu landed on top of Sam and leaned in to kiss him strongly. The scene was something out of a south Pacific wartime love movie, all except for Ike who walked a short distance behind them was carrying an AK47.

"I do love you Sam from America," Featu said. She rolled off of Sam and sat up. She looked down at Sam. "What would our life in America be like?" Featu asked. "I have heard many good, but also many bad things."

"You mean about race?"

"Yes," Featu said. "In Liberia, no one would say anything if they see a local woman with a white foreigner. They may say that she is lucky, as you may say in America, she hit the lottery."

"America has come a long way," Sam reassured her.

"Has it?" Featu paused for a moment and inquired further. "Would I be welcomed in your family's home?" Featu asked. She had a rush of insecurity for feeling that way.

"Of course," Sam replied. He lied to her, and she sensed something. What Sam did not say was that he could never bring Featu to the exclusive Gold Coast Country Club.

In the slums of Monrovia, the Voctrad safe house looked much like any other place. The windows were boarded up. The only difference in this house was power. A generator was carried into the back of the house, and power lines hooked up to the house. Lights hung from the plastered ceilings by wire and were spliced into the power lines. A large exhaust pipe was run outside the boarded-up window to keep fumes outside. If the generator was placed outside, it would have been stolen on the first night, even with all of the firepower from Voctrad. Locals would face certain death for a few scraps that could be sold on the black market. In this post-war era, there remained limited commerce. The UN donation supplies had not materialized as many donor nations had defaulted on their promises. The black market was the primary means of trade and thieves operated openly in the red-light district near Bushrod Island.

Checkov studied the maps hung across the walls. There were several safe houses that he set up in and around Monrovia to provide him flexibility and options to get out of a bad situation. Checkov looked at his men who sat around a table and drank straight vodka. Russian vodka was too hard to find in Africa, so they had to make due with an American knockoff. Checkov let them have the liquor. He needed his men to remain happy. Several took a few local girls off the streets the night before and tied them up in a bedroom. Checkov refused to touch the local women. He could not get away from his hatred of anyone not pure, the pure gene that had led the Third Reich to so many victories.

Checkov looked at several safe houses near the smaller airport not far from Bushrod Island, still within Monrovia city limits. Douglas MacArthur Airport was named after famed U.S. general and was seldom used by anyone. When Taylor was in power, it was his private airport and where he routinely greeted his rock star guests. Checkov circled the building close to the runway, which had been unoccupied for over ten years. Checkov studied the flight itinerary of the plane that departed out of a remote Siberian airbase and just landed in Libya. Checkov looked at the men and tossed several stacks of hundreds of U.S. dollars on the table. He informed them that they were headed to the casino. But first, he made them take care of the three local teenagers. Checkov could not allow any chance for their escape. He shouted in Russian at them. Six gunshots rang out in the night as Checkov's thugs double tapped each girl in the chest with two rounds each.

Monrovia's only casino was very active, and Checkov looked at the Hezbollah men as they waived his vehicle to the back of the building. Hassan motioned for his men to open the car door for Checkov.

"This is a better place for us to meet." Hassan motioned to his guard to allow Checkov into his office.

"You trust these men of yours?" Checkov was nervous about what Hassan had planned. Any leak could lead back to him, and he did not want to be on the receiving end of a drone missile from the Americans.

"These men will die for our cause," Hassan said as he slammed his fist on the table.

"What you are buying will change the course of the world." Checkov looked at the Hezbollah leader. Both have killed before. The one difference has been the scale, and now they looked at the chance of an epidemic of biblical proportions. The two men remained late in the night drinking and went to the airport to await the Russian transport aircraft's arrival.

At the Monrovia bus station, there were groups of young women who stayed close to one another. As the morning sunshine pushed out the evil of the night, many Liberians started to come out from their places of refuge. The three brothers slept in the old car and parked down the street. The bus station was the only public means of transportation in the city. Four old school buses were sent in from Philadelphia and donated for the new public transportation system. Every day the buses navigated the beaten up streets and bounced around in the huge potholes. The windows remained open as there was no air conditioning. At night the buses were locked behind the large gate and guarded by locals who were paid by the grant money.

The three brothers needed a victim and wanted to make sure she was special. The oldest brother saw a young woman sitting alone. He thought to himself that she could be somebody who could disappear. He walked over to Fatima and pulled out a gun. Several women who saw him shouted. One man walked toward the brother and shouted at him. The brother shot him dead. No one else moved to help Fatima. The two other brothers ran over and grabbed Fatima as she screamed. The older brother picked up her bag of clothes and followed his kin.

At Roberts International Airport, the air traffic controller watched intently at the blimps on the screen. The weather pattern over the Mediterranean held up the commercial airliner that originated out of Brussels. The arrival time was on schedule as the aircraft departed northern Europe around midnight and arrived in West Africa in the morning. Roberts International Airport had no nighttime runway lights. There was a contract awarded to an Italian company, but delays pushed back the installation by six months. It was a Sunday morning, and the UN soldier from Hungary knew there would be limited staff on duty in the control tower. Just in case there was trouble, the soldier from Hungary held a switchblade knife he purchased from the black market in his lap. He watched intently as the blimps looked very close together. He dialed a new frequency and spoke in Russian.

The Russian military aircraft had arrived in Libya two days ago, and the pilot awaited final instructions to coincide the arrival with the plane out of Brussels. Checkov had bribed Libyan officials to land and keep the Russian cargo plane there until the time was ready. The Hungarian officer quickly switched back to the channel with the international airline. The blips on the screen looked very close together and were separated by less than half a mile in distance and altitude. The approach pattern taken by both aircraft was along the same line.

Checkov waited patiently by the runway at MacArthur Airport. He looked out across the landing strip and saw multiple spots where patches of cement were filled. The white marks were readily visible. Checkov did not know if they would hold under the weight, but there were limited options. Checkov had a half-empty bottle of scotch that he continued to drink from. He passed the bottle to Hassan.

"Is your man a good pilot?" Hassan asked.

"He will land it, regardless of the patches in the runway." Checkov waved his hand in the air. "This airfield is better than what we had in Afghanistan." Checkov reminded his bedfellow of his time around the world fighting wars as part of the Soviet invasion. "At least, he is not being shot at."

"He will need to taxi and get out of here within a few moments, so we are not detected," Hassan said. "Any more time on the ground may put the operation at risk from the satellites." Hassan pointed his finger upward. "The American CIA may be watching." Hassan took a stiff drink from the scotch bottle. The drinking continued from the previous night. Both men needed an extra edge to control their nerves as both knew what was at stake.

The Hungarian corrupt officer watched the screen more intently. The two blimps completely overlapped as the Russian aircraft arrived under the same approach pattern. The Russian pilot had been circling off the coast at thirty thousand feet for over ninety minutes to await the final approach pattern. He switched the frequencies back and forth and communicated the final approach for both planes simultaneously. Checkov looked through his binoculars and saw the smaller jet fly at a lower altitude, less than five hundred feet below and one mile behind the large commercial jet. As the commercial jet passed overhead on final approach, Checkov looked straight above him and saw the landing gear emerge from the bottom of the plane. He rapidly switched his eyes forward and watched the Russian military transport jet descend upon the small runway.

The Russian pilot hit the brakes hard upon the first touch. The aircraft skidded and shifted. The pilot shifted the controls and overcompensated. As the aircraft ran off the side of the runway, the left wing clipped several small trees. The pilot pulled the aircraft controls hard and steered onto the old, narrow landing strip that had not been used in twenty years. The Russian pilot hit the brakes hard. Patches of cement were blasted in the air as the tires ripped them apart. Checkov swore in Russian.

"We need as much gravel as you can find," Checkov yelled in the air as he watched the Russian aircraft come to a complete stop. Time was of the essence, and both Checkov and Hassan knew that they had to get the plane unloaded and out of Liberia in a matter of one hour. Hassan understood what Checkov requested, and he yelled at his men to get out onto the runway. Checkov ran toward the back of the aircraft. He staggered slightly from the alcohol and regained his balance. The cargo door opened. Checkov yelled something in Russian that Hassan did not know.

"Ya ne znayu," The Russian pilot yelled. He jumped from the cargo door before it struck the ground. The pilot ran toward the left wing.

"Was it destroyed?" Hassan shouted over the engines. He shined a flashlight into the back of the cargo plane as Checkov moved forward.

"It's good," Checkov yelled back. "The straps held it in place." Checkov pulled out a large knife from the sheath attached to his hip. He cut through the thick cargo straps after several attempts. Hassan flashed the beam across the weapon. The red-lettered Russian words had faded with age. Hassan did not know the Russian words but assumed that it meant death with the skull and crossbones inscription painted next to the words.

Checkov directed the removal of the wooden crates. Completely assembled, the weapon weighed about eight hundred pounds. For over fifty years, the weapon was stored in four crates in a remote Siberian warehouse. Checkov pulled open the top of the elongated crate. The weapon was made from a combination of Tungsten steel and a Cobalt heavy alloy. The metal was a hard steel gray color and no signs of age. In the Siberian extreme cold, the storage conditions were perfect. The chamber was close to ten feet long and stored the golf-ball-sized glass balls that would be filled with the virus. Checkov opened a smaller crate and inspected the nozzles that would be critical for the weapon's operation. The crate was filled with straw. The nozzles were packed with extreme care over forty years ago. Checkov lifted one of the nozzles that resembled a large boomerang with sharp edges at the ends. He looked closely at the nozzle and ran his fingers over the ejection tube. He passed it to one of Hassan's men. There were twelve nozzles that would deliver the virus. The unloading took over an hour as Checkov delicately handled each nozzle.

The inspection of the left wing revealed no major damage. The one thing that kept the mission in jeopardy was the repair of the landing strip. Hassan screamed out of the window of his car as he drove back and forth. He had over a dozen men who filled in holes with gravel. They moved at a rapid pace. Even with the extra yelling, the departure was delayed by over thirty minutes. Hassan looked upward and prayed aloud to Allah that he hoped the American CIA satellite had not passed overhead.

For the commercial airplane that had just arrived out of Brussels, it was empty except for one international doctor who traveled all the way from America. Doctor Abuja waited patiently in line. The recent violence in Monrovia spiked, and many foreigners were targeted. They paid cash for any airline seats to any location. Most did not care or ask if there was a connection – they just wanted out of Liberia. It was chaos throughout the entire airport terminal. The UN sent Nigerian soldiers who carried loaded weapons. The cold, steel view on their faces frightened many foreigners. Most had heard of the brutality during the Liberian civil war when a battalion of Nigerians parachuted onto the tarmac and opened fire as they viewed everyone as a threat. Over a hundred were killed at just the airport.

Doctor Abuja waited patiently to clear immigration. He stood alone. He had not been in Africa for several years as his work kept him at United Nations headquarters in New York. In his current role, Doctor Abuja had to navigate the politics of the UN to get funding for his African projects. The spread of contagious viruses had always been a threat, yet UN funds were only released to combat the threat if there was a known outbreak. He tried to lobby for more Ebola research funding, yet he was not successful. The Liberian immigration officers questioned Doctor Abuja in detail and closely inspected his baggage. Doctor Abuja was dressed in a suit and felt like he was being interrogated like a criminal. He was a long way from New York. As he stood still, Doctor Abuja caught several glances from foreigners as they passed him to load the last airplane for the day that departed Liberia. The immigration officer looked up several times at Doctor Abuja and reread the letter from the UN Secretary-General that directed his travel to Liberia. A Liberian police officer arrived and after several moments and he called someone on his phone. Very few had come to Liberia. Most had tried to leave, and everyone had to be verified. Doctor Abuja waited patiently to have his passport stamped to allow him access to Liberia for him to fight the world's most horrific virus.

Chapter 8

The morning sun was vibrant, and it illuminated the Robertsport beach. Francesca awoke with the sound of inbound aircraft overhead; however, in her drowsy state, she did not discern that another aircraft had previously passed less than five minutes before. She was exhausted from her travels and needed the fresh air to get her senses back. She ventured out to the beach. The ocean water looked inviting. Within seconds, she stripped off her clothes and jumped in the water. The only identifiable feature on her body was the deep, jagged gash of over eight inches on the left side of her stomach caused during her Mossad indoctrination in Paris. Around her neck, she wore a necklace, a gift from her mother when she was a young girl. Francesca pulled at her necklace. The words inscribed were *'For lack of guidance a nation falls, but many advisors make victory sure.'* It was the only memory of her dead mother that she possessed. Outside of a Tel Aviv market, a car bomb initiated by Hezbollah killed her mother and another dozen Israelis. Francesca dedicated her life to avenge her mother's death.

Francesca walked through the waves fully naked. Her breasts had been enlarged, something that she had artificially corrected after giving birth. She had changed her outward appearance drastically. Her superiors wanted her to complete more seductive missions, whereby she manipulated men. The eight-inch scar across her midsection was the only mark that remained, something that she did not want to give up. The plastic surgeons provided a diagnosis that it would take months of skin grafts and repeated procedures to correct the deep scar caused by grenade shrapnel. She chose to keep the scar and keep her body covered. The cool water refreshed her senses. Francesca kicked at the waves and walked to shore. She thought about her motherhood. Francesca wondered what if she was killed what would happen to her son - Russell's son. If Francesca's father had his way, Russell would have been dead already.

"Har ur cluths," Ike said in his bush dialect. Ike had carried a towel to the beach. Ike held his arms out with the towel and looked in the other direction. He was very nervous about her nakedness.

"Just like old times," Francesca said as she dried off her body. She remained nude. Ike was uncomfortable with a nude woman, especially a white woman in front of him, yet he did not say anything. Ike continued to look at the ocean and away from her nakedness.

"Meeny, meeeny muuns ago," Ike said. Francesca thought about what he had said and quickly deciphered what he meant.

"Indeed, it was five years ago," Francesca replied as a matter of fact. Her mission in Liberia under the cloak of secrecy was to track down a Hezbollah gunrunner named Rajik Nabee. Rajik was injured in a Mossad ambush in Rome and managed to escape to Liberia for surgery and recuperation. Francesca used forged documents and credentials to enter Liberia as a surgeon with Doctors Without Borders. She unsuspectingly met an American named Tom Russell at the Cape Hotel, and an immediate attraction was formed. At that time, Russell had no idea about Francesca's true identity. Russell traveled all over Liberia attempting to uncover evidence that could be used against ousted ruler Charles Taylor in the international criminal court at The Hague. When Russell and Francesca found time to meet up at the Cape Hotel - - passionate sparks flew. Russell only discovered her identity when they found the safe house that she used to interrogate Hezbollah operatives. As he entered the Mossad safe house, Russell held a pistol aimed at her head, and all Francesca said was, "Hello Tom, glad to see you." Francesca wore black rubber gloves that she used to beat the face of a Hezbollah operative whom she had captured. Blood dripped from her gloved hands. Russell checked the captive's pulse, and he was dead. Out in back of the safe house, there were three fresh graves that Francesca filled with other dead Hezbollah operatives.

"U missed us?" Ike asked.

"Indeed," Francesca replied. "Whatever ever happened to Lucy? Your favorite monkey?" Lucy was a baby chimpanzee when Kitson found her on the street offered for sale in the amount of forty U.S. dollars. Kitson was disgusted that the locals sold chimpanzees on the street as pets or worse, the primates were sold for dinner. After he paid for Lucy, Kitson took his boot and crushed the cages that the peddler had. He handed him several British Pounds to compensate and informed him that he would bash his head if he saw him again. Lucy and Ike built a quick relationship, one built mostly out of love and hate. Lucy would sneak into Ike's kitchen to snag plantains, African bananas, several times a day. Ike would become furious, yet overtime he accepted it.

"Lucy, guud chimp." Ike replied, "Ike miss Lucy." Ike had to let Lucy go back to the wild when she was about a year old. Lucy became an adult chimp and weighed close to one hundred and twenty pounds and all muscle. Ike knew that if Lucy got mad, she could tear the face off of a grown man with her strength. Ike brought Lucy to a small island outside of Robertsport that was used by locals during the civil war to hide. Francesca sensed Ike was upset and changed the subject.

"How do you like working for the Minister?" Francesca asked.

"He guud man but Ike nut see him. He live Munrovia." Ike said.

Back in Monrovia, the Minister of Defense had moved into the Barclay Training Center (BTC) compound, which was down the hill from the former Presidential Palace. He had renovated several bungalows and installed steel rods on the outside of the windows for added protection, just in case an assassin climbed over the twelve-foot cement wall that lined the BTC compound. The Minister took up residence in the bungalow that once housed Samuel Doe when he was a Master Sergeant in the Liberian Army.

Before the military coup, Doe was the senior enlisted member at BTC. Doe became President after he walked up the hill one night and murdered President William Tolbert in his sleep. Doe led forty of his men with him that night and seized control of the armory and radio station. Doe informed the general in charge and other officers of the Liberian Army that if they did not follow his orders, he would have them killed. Within days, Doe had reached out to America to approve the installation of a previously disputed radio transmission tower. The tower was used for relaying radio signals from the American submarine fleet as it watched the Soviets transport uranium out of the Congo. Doe cemented his relationship with America to fight the Soviets. The iconic photo was taken of Samuel Doe, and then U.S. President Ronald Reagan assured his legitimacy. From 1980 until 1990, Doe ruled Liberia with an iron fist, and he eliminated dissent. Corruption and greed took hold. Doe needed to go, and the CIA financially backed his opposition out of neighboring Cote d'Ivoire. Charles Taylor led rebel forces into Monrovia and seized power. Doe was tortured in the streets. A young Prince Johnson stood over his body as he plunged a knife into Doe's chest. The photo taken by a London Times reporter was shown around the world, next to the photo of Doe shaking hands with Ronald Reagan. Ike and every other Liberian knew the story of their countries checkered past. The demons of corruption fueled revolutions and death.

Monrovia was a hallowed shell compared to its more vibrant times under Tolbert's rule. Commerce was plentiful in the 1960s and bolstered a plethora of development. Large mansions were built on the hilly part of Monrovia that overlooked Bushrod Island and the ocean. Fine marble was imported from Italy as well as ornate furniture from Barcelona. Liberians lived a very lucrative life by African standards during this period. A middle class flourished, and many Liberians became well educated. Donations from America helped build a world-class university in Monrovia. Many African nations sent their brightest to Liberia to be educated. The mansions were now empty, except for squatters. The wood previously used to board up the windows was used for burning. No furniture or fixtures remained.

Along the Monrovia streets, Russell drove the Land Rover past the row of mansions as Kitson looked out the window. Blank stares from local men were returned to him as they had not seen many white people in this area of town. The once vibrant community was now the most dangerous.

"Stop the vehicle here," Kitson said to Russell. "Back up and go down that street there." Kitson pointed over his shoulder. He had been watching closely. He would have taken Ike with him for added protection, but Kitson needed Ike to keep a close watch on Francesca. If the Hezbollah knew she was back in Liberia, there would be an attempt on her life.

"What do you see?" Russell asked as he slammed the brakes on and shifted the manual transmission into reverse.

"There." Kitson pointed down the narrow street that was bordered by mansion walls. The street could only allow one vehicle to pass and it was packed with locals as they carried away items from a market. Russell slammed on the horn as he slowly navigated the vehicle down the road. "Don't hit anyone." Kitson said, "We do not want to piss off anyone today."

"Well then, we need to walk." Russell hit the brakes and turned off the ignition. "Make sure to lock your door, or we will not have anything to return to."

The market was vibrant, and Kitson saw what he was looking for. He jumped out of the vehicle before it stopped. Kitson hastened his step as he walked into the crowd. Russell was slow getting out of the back door but quickly caught up with his friend and mentor.

"What are you looking for?" Russell inquired of his mentor. They pushed past stalls filled with vibrant tropical colors of all sorts of clothing on sale such as head scarfs, dresses, shirts, etc. Ladies looked at the two white men as they walked past and prodded them to shop with them. Russell and Kitson were the only visible foreigners in this market area that was very far off the beaten path. The U.S. Embassy deemed this area off limits for security reasons. Russell rubbed his hand along the 45-caliber pistol in the holster under his jacket. He wanted to make sure it was secure in the dense crowd. The weapon rested on the small of his back. Russell kept his eyes on the crowd as Kitson moved through the locals. He was polite and replied no thank you each time he was asked to buy something. Kitson's wife was gone, and he did not need to purchase anything special. What he looked for may be sold in the beat-up building at the end.

"Why are we here?" Russell asked Kitson as he continued to watch the crowd. Several men were brave enough to follow them and looked Russell in the eyes. They stayed at a distance but watched closely. Russell put on his sunglasses to look around nonchalantly. Russell looked at his friend and mentor, "Just to inform you, we are pretty far from the vehicle."

"What we're looking for," Kitson paused, "is of the utmost importance." Russell looked at his mentor with doubt. They had been on four previous missions together in Liberia, the Congo, South Sudan, and Libya. And now they are back in Liberia. Kitson looked at Russell, "Do you remember what I told you before?"

"Which time?" Russell asked jokingly. "Yes, I know...Nothing in Africa is what it appears to be."

"What we are looking for," Kitson said, "hopefully we can find in this place." Kitson led them into a dingy, small building. Tribal masks hung on the wall and bones from dead African animals. Kitson spoke to the man who sat on a stool. Russell did not recognize the language, yet he knew that it was a tribal dialect. Kitson mastered many languages in his lifetime and spoke a version of Tegali. The locals understood him. They walked over to the table and looked at a table filled with necklaces of all types. Russell had no idea what Kitson looked for. He watched him carefully as he pushed the decorative items around with a stick. Russell noticed that Kitson was very cautious not to touch the things with his hand.

"What is it?" Russell asked.

"Powerful…very powerful juju magic that we can use," Kitson replied. Russell kept his eye on the crowd that grew behind them. He did not doubt his mentor, yet realized that they needed to get out of there fast.

In the Monrovian clinic that was established years ago with a grant from the United Nations, Doctor Abuja wasted no time in getting to work. He was exhausted from his travels, yet his deep passion for serving the less fortunate drove him. Abuja walked the streets in his white medical coat. None of the locals gave him much interest. Doctor Abuja had a very dark complexion and was short in stature making him look very similar to a Liberian. Outside of the clinic, he saw a line of men. Word had spread that a French company had a new medicine to treat HIV.

"How many have been infected with HIV?" Doctor Abuja asked the old nun who volunteered at the clinic.

"The numbers are low." The clinic's nurse replied. Her hands wobbled as she drew blood from a young man who had unprotected sex and was diagnosed with HIV. She made several strikes and finally found a vein. The man grimaced in pain. "They still are foolish and have sex outside of marriage. Do you hear me?" The man nodded agreement.

"Did you meet the man who brought these drugs here?" Doctor Abuja looked at the packaging. He could not read French.

"They gave me money." She opened the box hidden beyond the cinder block. She looked down at the money and cried.

"Does the drug work?" Doctor Abuja knew bribes were the normal practice, yet he needed to know if the experimental drug worked. "Have you tested it?" There was a sense of concern in his voice.

"There was a girl who came here every day last week. I gave her three doses a day. She did not come back." She paused for a moment and mumbled between sobs. "I think she is dead."

"Until I can do more research on these experimental drugs, we will keep them under lock." Doctor Abuja locked the cabinet door and hid the key under the desk's calendar. "In the meantime, give them a placebo."

"A what?" The clinic nurse inquired.

"Something that will not hurt them." Doctor Abuja gave her a package of about one hundred aspirins. "Just give them this and tell them this is the new HIV drug that arrived." He was smart enough to keep the treatments going as he did not want a riot on his hands.

On the outskirts of Monrovia, the Christian School was modest. There were no windows and no power, yet the single room building was filled with children who wanted to learn. The three nuns who operated the school had several new visitors. Kamal had given the brothers a map and circled the building on Tubman Boulevard. Kamal wanted to make a statement, a strong statement. The three brothers yelled and chased the children out of the school. Kamal looked into the eyes of the three white women. They were not scared by Kamal. They had met violent men before.

"You have insulted Prophet Muhammad," Kamal spoke through his clenched teeth. "Your American orphanage teaches lies."

"Our beliefs are for peace and love," the older nun said. "Our missionary helps educated the children." She had conducted missionary work all over Africa for the past thirty years and as a young lady had cleansed the feet of leprosy victims in Calcutta with Mother Teresa. The other two women who were new to the missionary work were terrified.

"You indoctrinate children in the evil way of America."

"We help those less fortunate live a better life." the older nun replied. "There is so much suffering. These children have a chance at a new life." She looked at the others and pleaded, "Please, please, please."

"You are corrupting their souls." He raised his fist high in the air as if to strike them. He continued. "Mohammed is the only one who can liberate them."

"Is this a trial?" She was bold. She had endured years of threats from thugs, criminals, corrupt officials. The elder nun had seen a lot of pain in her thirty years in Africa, yet she continued to help the very fragile, less fortunate babies through adoptions.

"Yes, this is your trial," Kamal said as he picked up the bright red burning steel rod out of the fire pit. "Your sentence is death." Kamal used all of his strength to push the steel rod into the eye socket of the oldest missionary. She screamed in agony as Kamal forced the rod deeper. Kamal felt the crunch of cartilage as he pushed into the woman's brain. Kamal took his other hand and held the victim's head to better gouge the rod inside the skull. Screams erupted from the other two women as they witnessed the agony of their friend.

"Islam is a religion of compassion." The younger missionary pleaded as she faced certain death.

"Islam is at war," Kamal said. "Our caliphate will rule the world." Kamal pushed the dead body off the end of the metal rod. He placed the rod back into the fire for his next victim. He knew that it would take a few minutes to heat up. In the meantime, he grabbed a chair and sat in front of the two women. "What can you tell me about the American named Russell? He visited your orphanage two days ago."

Kamal continued to ask questions as his goons ransacked the orphanage. His men tore down anything that could resemble Christianity faith. Several older children returned and pleaded for them to stop. His men beat the children. Kamal swung the metal rod in the air and violently pushed it into the older woman. The missionary screamed loud. Kamal smiled broadly as the remaining missionary crawled onto the floor into the youngest woman. He grabbed the back of her head and thrust the metal rod into her chest. Screams erupted from the children. Kamal waived to his men to release the children. At first, the children were skeptical that they would not be hurt. Kamal's goons pushed and kicked them. In a few seconds, the children ran for their lives.

"The American CIA is in Liberia," Kamal spoke into the satellite phone to his contact in Yemen. "Send more followers." The message would be written down and passed in a note to a baghl or a human mule, someone who carried secret coded messages for the terrorist organizations. Within several days, the note would arrive in Somalia. Kamal needed more season terrorists to carry out his plan to recruit and indoctrinate former child soldiers who served in the RUF during Sierra Leone's civil war. Kamal had found the most fertile terrorist recruiting ground in the entire world within Monrovia. Young men released from Sierra Leone's prisons had no future and migrated to Monrovia in search of work, and no one would hire them. The etched letters of RUF on their biceps frightened the masses as most knew firsthand the atrocities committed in the cross-border raids. Hardened memories did not lessen over time.

Chapter 9

Monrovia's only legally allowed casino under the UN mandate that protected the country was packed with a busload of Chinese workers from the remote iron ore camp, about an hour from the Liberia and Guinea border. The Chinese company transported the workers to Monrovia for some relaxation. The workers used of several brothels that Hassan had explicitly established for them. His goons took girls off the city streets in the middle of the night and locked them up in the brothels located near Hassan's secure compound near Marshall. The Chinese paid good money for the local girls. Hassan watched the security cameras that monitored the casino tables. The Chinese workers openly tossed money onto the roulette table. The Peruvian bit boss watched closely. The Chinese worker's hands moved quickly. One had grabbed several casino chips off the table. The pit boss looked at the Hezbollah goon in the corner of the room who had a Kalashnikov submachine gun under his jacket. Several Chinese workers spoke in their native tongues and pointed to the Hezbollah thug. The Chinese worker tossed his handful of chips back at the pit boss. Everyone knew there were no police in Monrovia and crimes were dealt with brute force.

Hassan turned off the casino monitors and focused on the assembly instructions. He had difficulty understanding the Russian as he paged back and forth from a translation book. He was confused. He wanted to know everything about the weapon that would change the course of humankind. Hassan knew the nozzles were the critical component, but what he could not understand was how the mechanism would hold and transfer the weaponized virus. Checkov had promised delivery of the weapon and needed to deliver on his pledge. Hassan voiced his concern to Checkov who sent a request within Voctrad to find scientists who may have worked on the weapon in the remote Siberian camp. Several scientists, close to sixty years old were found and sent to Liberia.

Meanwhile back in Robertsport, Francesca had spent most of the day in the shade under the large oak tree that overlooked the pristine beaches. She had several gin and tonics delivered by James to her makeshift sanctuary. She looked at the monument that the Minister had erected as the final resting place for his father who was murdered by men loyal to Charles Taylor.

Minister Urey had death threats against him after he returned to Liberia from those loyal to Taylor. Many of Taylor's former military officers fled into Sapo National Forest rather than face trial for crimes against humanity. They operated openly in the remote land within Sapo, and there was little anyone could do to bring them to justice. They were heavily armed and had nothing to lose.

"Are we enjoying ourselves?" Russell said in a cynical tone as he walked toward the tree. He drove the two hours back from Monrovia to check up on her. Francesca already had four drinks, and it was early in the afternoon, not uncommon for foreigners in Liberia. However, Russell knew that Francesca was a bad drunk.

"What a beautiful place," Francesca said, "reminds me of the beaches of Cuba." Russell had little knowledge of her background and all of the places that she had traveled around the world. She never provided information. Her life was classified.

"What are you doing here?"

"What do you think?" She replied. "I am here to save the world. Same old story, different mission, different country." Francesca waived for James to bring her another drink.

"How many have you had today?" Russell asked. He already knew the answer as he already asked Ike how many drinks he served Francesca.

"Why do you care?" She shot back.

"Self-protection," Russell replied. "Usually when you get drunk, bad things happen."

"Like falling for you, Mister CIA man." Francesca blurted out.

"That wasn't just my doing," Russell replied. He tried to stay away from Francesca, even forget about her. She had a dangerous quality that drove him toward her, something no American girl could replicate.

"What do you want from me?" Francesca yelled at Russell. She was beyond mad. She was the one who put them in this situation with her father. She was the one who was untruthful with her father regarding her feelings for the American CIA operative. She was the one who broke several critical coded rules that Mossad agents do not compromise the mission for personal matters and most importantly Mossad agents do not have love affairs outside of their kind. Francesca put her status within the Mossad in a tenuous state, and her father had to testify under oath to the Israeli Prime Minister that his only child would never compromise Israeli secrets. Francesca knew that if she did, her father would put a bullet in the back of her head. He loved his daughter, yet respect within the Mossad overruled all family bonds.

"Why did you come here?" Russell threw back at her.

"My nation is in jeopardy, and you know that." Francesca looked at Russell and tried to assess from his facial expressions what he knew. "Ebola is the most dangerous virus in the world."

"And you think it can be weaponized?"

"If a virus is released upon Tel Aviv, it will spread like wildfire." Francesca looked directly at Russel. "Our population is very dense, and the results would be catastrophic." Francesca grew up like many Israeli children who prepared for terrorist attacks. Since the first day of school, children rehearsed how to seek cover from Palestinian rockets or worse a potential invasion. The invasions of 1969 and 1973 were a distant memory for many in Israel, and the new generation had become more complacent to the threat of invasion. The occasional terrorist bombing was the main threat, and their bombs were normally tiny as Hezbollah could not sneak in large weapons. With the new surveillance and missile defense systems, Tel Aviv had not experienced any direct rocket attacks in eight years. Francesca knew fully well what was at stake if a virus penetrated the missile defense bubble protecting Tel Aviv.

"We don't know if the Russian technology even existed," Russell replied. He had copies of the aged photos snuck out of Siberia in the early 1960s. During the Cold War, the use of biological weapons became a horrific reality as both the Soviet Union and America launched a new arms race. Russell wanted to test Francesca to see what she knew.

"The scientist who developed the weapon was not Russian but German." She replied and handed him a photo of three men in three-piece suits. The date on the photo was 1954. "The man to the left disappeared shortly after this photo was taken. Here is another photo taken in Siberia in 1961." She handed Russell another original copy photograph.

"Who is he?"

"Klaus Von Brewer."

"The rocket scientist?" Russell asked. For this mission, he had read the CIA report on any potential former German scientists who could have developed a bomb capable of delivering weaponized Ebola. Russell looked at Francesca and knew that she had something the CIA did not know. "He was killed in a car bomb. The CIA carried out the attack to stop the Russians from developing an intercontinental missile." He paused and looked at the Siberian photo. "Are you saying that he survived?"

"He was not even in Berlin during that time. He was taken by the KGB and sent to the remote rocket facility in Uzbekistan. He became an informant for us. Did you know that his wife's parents were Jewish?" Russell shook his head. "His wife and kids remained in East Berlin after the war and would be sentenced to death if he did not help the Russians. No one knew about his wife's Jewish heritage as she was adopted. She was approached by a concentration camp survivor who informed her that her parents had died in the camps. She was given to a German family. They saved her life."

"And she approached the Mossad?"

"Not at first." She paused for a moment and continued, "It was handled delicately. She was recruited slowly, and soon she recruited her husband."

"How do you know so much?"

"My father was the one who recruited her in the first place." She said. Russell shook his head. He was not surprised. It was not ironic that his former lover had arrived in Liberia to chase a weapon of catastrophic carnage. She continued, "We have a long list of weapons and missile technology that Von Brewer provided Israel. It became one of the primary reasons we were able to…" and she stopped talking.

"Do what?" Russell asked. Francesca was silent. Russell already knew about the atomic weapons that Israel had developed. While he was on a sanctioned CIA mission in the Congo, he helped thwart a plan by two white supremacist brothers bent on the fact that Apartheid was over in South Africa. The brothers discovered the existence of an Israeli made Cobalt atomic bomb that was purchased by the former despot Mobutu in the 1970s. They had planned to drop the atomic weapon on Cape Town that was until Russell had stopped them.

"Does Langley have this intelligence?"

"No," Francesca said. "We usually do not share what we know." Francesca had watched Russell and Kitson work closely together and knew that they did not have any secrets between one another. She knew that the CIA and MI6 regularly worked together, yet both intelligence organizations had very little trust in the Mossad.

"Let me bounce this back to Langley to verify," Russell said. "If you are correct, we may have uncovered one of the biggest intelligence failures of the Cold War."

"After the '73 war, we shared more with America and Britain but kept Von Brewer our secret. He died of pneumonia in 1971 and was buried in an unmarked grave." Francesca replied.

"Does Germany know?" Russell inquired.

"No, they still think that he died in that car bombing." She replied. Russell made a mental note and wondered why the Mossad never informed Germany. Russell had a vested interest now in the security of Tel Aviv. His only child remained locked in a fortress that could withstand an onslaught by terrorist bombs. However, it would be futile against a virus.

"Are any of these men alive?" Russell pointed to the photo.

"Maybe." Francesca had requested the Mossad to track down all Russians involved with the weapons project. "Some of them may be alive."

"So Ebola can be weaponized." Russell looked at the photo. "The world's worst possible fear had been proven in the Cold War and now came out of storage. This is not good." Russell chugged his drink.

The car slowly passed the Robertsport mansion as Doctor Abuja continued to search for his protégé, Sam. Someone at the UN headquarters had heard that there was an American that moved to Robertsport after villagers burned his clinic to the ground. Doctor Abuja requested one of Anwar's drivers from the Cape Hotel to take him across the dangerous roads. It was late in the day when Doctor Abuja found Sam's new clinic.

"You look well my friend," Doctor Abuja said to Sam. Sam looked astonished, and he hugged his mentor who had not seen in several years. They shook hands six months ago at LaGuardia International Airport as they bid farewell. And now they embraced like long-lost brothers. Sam was overcome with emotion.

"How did you find me?" Sam replied.

"News travels fast." Doctor Abuja looked around the one room clinic. "There are not many white men here, and a doctor stands out."

"We were not welcomed at our last clinic," Sam said as he looked downward. "They heard we had Ebola patients and they burned the clinic."

"Fear can do strange things," Doctor Abuja stated as a matter of fact. He knows the African mindset. "There is much fear of the unknown. Tribal law is still prevalent with the locals and can be very deadly."

"In my correspondence, I mentioned Featu," Sam said as he pointed to his nurse. "She has been the one who has helped me greatly." Sam had put a lot of information on Featu in his notes, and his longtime friend and mentor instinctively knew that there was more to the relationship.

"Are you in love with her?" Doctor Abuja inquired outside of Featu's hearing. He sensed something different in his star pupil.

"Perhaps," Sam replied, "she has changed my life."

"Africa can change someone's life forever." Doctor Abuja said. He had served with a lot of foreign doctors and saw firsthand how the Dark Continent changed them forever.

"We are staying at the mansion on top of the hill," Sam said. "It is owned by the Minister of Defense. We were just off to dinner. I can inquire if another guest would be welcome."

"That would be most nice," Doctor Abuja replied. He knew finding a good meal in a war-torn country was difficult, especially outside of the five-star accommodations at the Cape Hotel.

Inside of the mansion's kitchen, the room was full of activity as Ike cooked over the wood stove and James helped clean the plates. With the additional dinner guests, Kitson had hired several young girls from the local church to help him. The three young girls were about sixteen years of age and sang spiritual songs as they cooked dinner. Ike had purchased two dozen lobsters from the local fish market. African lobsters were very different than those found in northern Atlantic waters. African lobsters had no claws to fight back, and their shells were much harder. The lobster meat had the same succulent taste, regardless of the four-thousand-mile distance between Liberia and Maine. Ike pressed the white butler's jacket for James. Ike was pleased to have added guests as the mansion had been so lonely. James and Ike were the only two occupants of the eight-bedroom mansion.

The Minster's father had purchased the land and the decaying mansion. The three hundred acres contained fields of cassava. It was exported all across West Africa. The Urey family became wealthy plantation owners. The parents were very smart to send their money to several banks in Manhattan. The Urey family was spared the massacre after Doe murdered Tolbert and took over the government. The Minister's father served in a Liberian Cabinet position. His father had no choice. Doe would have had the entire Urey family killed if he had refused. The Urey family tried to flee the raging madness as Taylor's forces advanced on Monrovia. Every available boat was packed, some without engines were used to escape. Makeshift paddles were used to flee the invaders. The Urey family became separated, and the young son was able to survive with his mother and two older sisters. The patriarch was found in Robertsport and assassinated with forty others under the large oak tree. When Taylor took over the government from Doe, the banks were the first thing Taylor went after. He looted the banks and safety deposit boxes that contained lifelong savings. The Urey's escaped to America and were supported by a trust established in a Zurich bank. The children were gifted students and attended Harvard University.

"Greetings my friends," the Minister of Defense said as he entered his mansion. Kitson had sent a note to his secretary that there would be a large party honoring several doctors at the mansion tonight. The caravan of six vehicles outside with flashing lights signified the Secret Service had the Minister under guard. "Who do we have here as guests tonight?" The Minister walked around the dining table to greet his guests. At the table were the guests of honor Sam and Doctor Abuja, Kitson, Russell, Featu, and an intoxicated Francesca.

"How is the government responding to the threat of an Ebola outbreak?" Kitson inquired. Out of all of the houseguests, Kitson had developed a very close relationship with the Minister.

"There are a few reports of the virus making trouble," the Minister replied. He did not want to alarm the guests as to the real threat that it posed as the rainy season was just several weeks away. "We have a few reports."

"My clinic was one that reported an outbreak," Sam replied. He had questioned the resolve of the Liberian government before. He felt many levels of the government had failed to react when he alerted that Ebola had arrived across the Guinea border.

"There are many tragedies with this disease, very tragic," The Minister replied. "Were there any survivors?"

"No." Sam drank the rest of his scotch and slammed it on the table. "The village decided to burn my clinic to the ground."

"To be fair," Russell jumped in. "Many in the remote villages fear the disease."

"As they should," Doctor Abuja interjected. He looked across the table at all of the guests and lowered his voice to be very clear. "Make no mistake, if Ebola rages in Africa, it will rage across the world."

"And that is why I am here to make sure nothing happens to my country," Francesca stated in a bold manner. It was no secret to anyone at the table that she was Israeli. Francesca looked at each of them. "If Ebola leaves Liberia, one way or another, many will die."

The tension around the table was pervasive. The Minister took a stiff drink and motioned for James to fetch him another scotch. The dinner was served and was delicious. All of the guests commented on the fantastic cuisine that Ike had developed. Ike was summoned to the dinner table after the main course by the Minister. Ike was embarrassed as he received a standing ovation from the dinner guests. The talk of the lobsters had replaced Ebola.

At the Al Qaeda camp, Fatima coughed up blood into her hand. The deep coughs echoed across the concrete walls. Fatima's cell had limited light from the holes between the bars. The room was part of the former stockade used to hold drunk soldiers but had sat vacant for nearly twenty years. Nothing in the camp was modern. Exposed steel beams were rusted. Part of the ceiling had fallen years prior; however, it was too high for Fatima to reach. When the guards were not looking, she pulled at the rusted metal bars, nothing moved. Her hands were caked with rust fragments. She spat in her hands to clean them, yet she had little fluid in her mouth, and any attempt to clean her hands was useless. She curled up in the corner. Later in the day, her captives had tossed several blankets in through the hole in the door. Bugs littered the floor, yet she did need somewhere to rest. She stomped on as many bugs as she could see with the limited light and nestled her body into a corner.

As night fell, Fatima wiped her nose and could barely see the blood in her hand but knew from the texture that it was blood. Her fever had started yesterday but stopped after the medicine provided by the Frenchman took over. Fatima was awakened every four hours to take pills that were pushed through the rusted bars.

In the morning, Fatima awoke to loud noise - a man yelled in a foreign language. She shivered from the morning chill and had little energy from the lack of food and water. The sound of boots on the aged concrete floor reverberated against the walls. She looked upwards and saw a man stand away from the rusted bars. He had a surgical mask over his face, but Fatima could tell he was not African. Kamal yelled something in Arabic and pointed toward the door. Within a few moments, several of his goons arrived with a bowl of rice and a jug of water. One of them opened the lock while another trained a weapon on her. Fatima had no energy to attempt an escape, yet they would not risk it. More importantly, the goons did not want to get close to an Ebola infected person. Fatima devoured the rice in seconds and coughed hard. Fatima looked at the marks on her arm. She had no idea what was injected into her veins. Kamal needed Fatima to survive. She had the solution to combating Ebola in her veins.

Chapter 10

In the early morning, Russell did not take long to get out of the mansion and head back to Monrovia. He wanted to get far away from Francesca. More importantly, Russell had a good reason to head for the U.S. Embassy. He needed to review recent air manifests for foreigners traveling in and out of Liberia. Russell had a hunch that some nasty people had arrived. Something did not sit right that Hezbollah would be able to pull off building such a destructive weapon. There was no intelligence on the Soviet design of a 1960's era weapon that could carry and spread Ebola over a city. It was a myth that the fundamental technology of pressurizing and maintaining a live virus was ever possible. The only documented spread of Ebola was through human contact. And now, the small nation of Liberia was ground zero for the development of a catastrophic weapon.

At the embassy, Russell reviewed manifests for several hours. He spent another four hours working in the embassy's vault researching top secret information on the classified intranet. He downloaded every bit of data he could find on German doctors who went to work for the Russians. Klaus Von Brewer came front and center in Russell's research. Von Brewer was one of the eight German scientists credited with delivering the first atomic weapon to the Soviets. Von Brewer's design of an anthrax delivery style weapon was documented by the CIA and confirmed in the 1983 recovery of a Russian bomber frozen in the Arctic ice. Anthrax had been used before, and the CIA had known that the Russians could use it. What no one in the intelligence community knew was the Soviets developed a weapon capable of carrying something deadlier than anthrax. Russell waited until lunchtime before departing the vault, just in case he would run into the U.S. Ambassador. He was two days past due giving her an update. He requested casualty data estimates for a virus of mass destruction on a western city, and the request was held up in Langley as they questioned the motives around his request. Russell had no additional information to provide and did not want to go in empty-handed.

Russell departed the U.S. Embassy and walked the short distance to the Cape Hotel. The streets were crowded with locals who washed vehicles for a few dollars. It reminded Russell of when he was in Liberia five years ago. Previously, Russell had hired a teenage boy to wash his vehicle every day. Most of the time the vehicle did not need to be cleaned, but it was Russell's way to give back. Russell looked at the men washing vehicles and wondered if he would recognize the local boy. Russell became fond of the local boy, and on his last day in Liberia, Russell handed the local boy two crisp hundred-dollar bills. Russell won the money at the casino, and he did not want the dirty money. Regardless, he suspected the money was counterfeit. The boy was very nervous about accepting such a gift and after Russell repeatedly pleaded – the boy took it. The teenager who had almost nothing to show for his life shouted joyfully as he ran up the street.

Russell sat with the wall to his back inside the Piano Bar at the Cape Hotel and ordered a gin and tonic. 'Play it again Sam' hammered out some classical music, Mozart or Beethoven – Russell did not know the origin. It sounded very pleasing and soothed his nerves.

"Is everything to your liking?" Tareek asked.

"Except your customers." Russell motioned his head toward the Russians who sat directly at the bar. Russell surmised that they were the advance party for Checkov as he never entered a room without knowing what was there.

"They pay well," Tareek said as a matter of fact as he looked at them. He stared at Russell, and by the expression on his face, Tareek knew that Russell cared little for the Russians. "They are here for the rubber at the Firestone Plantation."

"Just the rubber?" Russell asked.

"What do you think?" Tareek inquired. "Are they here for more?" He spoke softly. "We have heard stories about diamond camps in Sapo." Tareek referred to Sapo National Forest, a primitive area in the middle of Liberia that was inaccessible. There were no roads or large villages. Many of Charles Taylor's soldiers could never return home as they were wanted for war crimes.

"Illegal diamonds are not the only issues," Russell stated.

"Yes, the former child soldiers," Tareeq said as a matter of fact. He looked across the table. "The child soldiers are very dangerous."

"What do you mean?"

"I heard stories about former RUF soldiers from Sierra Leone released from prison," Tareek said. "These child soldiers have now grown up. Killing is part of their mindset. Ten years in prison had not stopped the rage of killing in their minds. Sierra Leone released over two hundred of them as it was too costly to keep them incarcerated."

"Rehabilitation costs a tremendous amount."

"From what I have heard, they were treated far worse in prison than when they fought in the war." Tareek leaned closer. "Brutality is the only means of existence in prison."

"Where do you think they went?" Tareek asked. Russell knew the answer. "They could not go home. No village would welcome back these murderers." Tareek paused to make sure no one could hear him. "These men were prime targets to be recruited."

"By whom?"

"Who do you think is the most hated enemy of the free world?" Tareek said. He moved in closer to speak. "Who took down the towers in New York?" Tareek sat back and looked at the American. "You know perfectly well Al Qaida moved into Africa. It is the perfect recruiting ground. There are many ungoverned areas and no law to bring them to justice. Al Qaida is a vicious virus that has a stranglehold on Africa."

Russell understood all across Africa former child soldiers had nowhere to go. Many were ostracized from their villages for the violence they leveled during the civil war. Forgiveness was very hard for many as lives were shattered. The only group to openly welcome the former child soldiers was Al Qaeda. The recruitment of the next generation of terrorists had already commenced.

"Who's in charge?" Russell understood from prior experience how Al Qaeda operated in Africa. However, he thought that they were segmented. There had been many terrorist groups, over four hundred known that operated in and out of Africa. With many despots and a severe lack of adequate military to control remote regions, terrorist groups have conducted attacks freely for decades.

"A man named Kamal," Tareek stated as a matter of fact.

"Kamal?" Russell leaned closer. "Are you sure?" Russell knew firsthand in his missions in the Congo and South Sudan how deadly Kamal was. In his native Egypt, Kamal had murdered his own father as he was going to marry a non-Muslim woman. He stabbed the woman to death as well. Kamal was with Bin Laden in Afghanistan and Pakistan. He was a trained doctor and knew how to torture like the best. Russell knew this information about Kamal but did not realize that he moved into West Africa. There were rumors that Kamal was killed in a drone strike in Yemen, but there was no means to recover DNA for testing against his father's blood.

"The policeman who drove you here. He had several photos of you and the hotel." Tareek pulled a folded up photograph out of his suit jacket. Russell unfolded it and saw the surveillance photos.

"How did you know that he worked for Al Qaida?" Russell asked.

"He was caught behind the back wall. He had a camera with him." Tareek looked around the room. He already had spent too long talking with the American. Tareek caught several stares from the Voctrad thugs. Tareek continued, "He was in uniform and did not think our private security would question him. He made that mistake."

"Where is he?" Russell asked. "I need to interrogate him."

"We took him out to Monkey Island and got answers from him before the chimpanzees tore him apart," Tareek said as a matter of fact. Monkey Island was a name given to a small clump of land in the Marshall River that became home to a small group of chimpanzees. During the last civil war, a German scientist could not get UN approval to remove the primates that held HIV infectious disease. The scientist left the animals on the island in hopes of returning one day; however, the German was murdered in the street outside of the Cape Hotel along with ten others in an execution-style ritual. The chimpanzees that existed on Monkey Island grew large from the experimental drugs and were very savage.

"What did Kamal's man specifically say?"

"The usual," Tareek responded coldly. "Death to America. Kill any westerner. Allah is great. The caliphate would rule the world for the next thousand years." Russell smirked as it was the same tone again and again.

"And he confirmed Kamal is in Liberia?"

"Not just in Liberia," Tareek replied. "Kamal has built up an Al Qaida camp forty minutes from Monrovia."

Five blocks from the Cape Hotel, Doctor Abuja's hospital gown was covered in blood. Three men came into the Monrovia HIV clinic. They were struck by a Chinese diplomatic vehicle that did not stop. The Chinese were more than likely terrified that they had hit several locals. Even more terrified to stop in a crowded Monrovian street and get mobbed. The accident happened close to Monrovia General Hospital, yet all the locals knew that the Monrovia General Hospital was the place to go and die. The life expectancy there was minimal. The locals knew to leverage any foreign doctors to save them. Doctor Abuja had worked on the fractured legs and several head injuries. Blood covered his gown.

"I came as fast as I could," Sam shouted as he grabbed a gown.

"I can assist as well," Featu said. "Who is hurt the most?" She asked Doctor Abuja. Featu did not wait for a reply and went right to work on replacing blood-soaked bandages. She looked at the wraps Doctor Abuja tied around the legs and tore them off. Featu pulled out bed linen and cut it into long strips. She pulled the material tight against the badly damaged legs. The man screamed, yet she placed her hand firmly against the leg. With all of her weight, she pulled and tied the cloth around a splint.

"She's a good nurse." Doctor Abuja observed.

"One of the best I have seen," Sam said as he smiled slightly at Featu who paid no attention. Featu looked up and caught their glimpses, yet she did not have an expression. She was focused on the task at hand. The next man shook violently from the pain. As she bandaged him, he screamed loud.

"We need to get them to the Jordanian Hospital," Doctor Abuja said.

"Will your credentials help to get them treated?" Sam inquired.

"We shall find out." The UN doctor stated. "We have something that they may want." Doctor Abuja knew he had little credibility with the UN Secretary-General's office. He opened up a locked cabinet. "A pharmaceutical company has tested a new drug to counter the effects of HIV. I met with one of their executives last month in Milan and thought the testing could be beneficial here."

"This can't be legal," Sam interjected. He questioned his mentor. He saw Doctor Abuja in a different light.

"No, it is not approved for testing." Doctor Abuja made sure Featu could not overhear his comments. "Many in the world do not care what happens in Africa. There are broken promises every day. We cannot get the support we used to receive. There is no money for the drugs made in America. They are too expensive for the locals."

"I understand," Sam replied to his mentor, but he also wanted to know the impact. "How do we know it is safe?"

"We don't." Doctor Abuja said. "But we have few options." He looked at the pills. There were sixty bottles of pills, enough to treat twenty patients for three months. He thought about what was at stake in the testing. He had no laboratory to control the testing and make sure the right amounts were dispensed. The patients would leave the clinic every day, and he had no way to monitor them. Doctor Abuja looked at Sam and the disapproval expression on his face. "Let's give them to the Jordanians, and they can use them on their own people." Doctor Abuja had heard the Jordanian soldiers that were part of the UN mission had unprotected sex with local women, many who were prostitutes. The Jordanian soldiers thought it was unholy to use any protection. The impact that was a very high percentage developed HIV. Their deployment was for one year, and there were many cries for help to get rid of the virus before they returned home.

The Jordanian Hospital was built out of the remnants of a hotel on the bluffs that overlooked Bushrod Island. Sam drove Doctor Abuja and the three patients to the hospital. They left Featu to keep the clinic open. As the local men sat in back, they moaned loudly. The doctors did not have any pain medication to give them. Doctor Abuja could only provide aspirin for the pain. Sam made several turns up the steep road and drove past the old, abandoned mansions on Tubman Boulevard. The hospital had a large cement wall erected around the perimeter. It was a four-story building that looked primitive as it had not been painted in nearly thirty years. The windows were replaced with bulletproof ones delivered from Amman, Jordan. For the mission in Liberia, the Jordanian government committed a small contingent of doctors and nurses. The medical staff would treat only UN soldiers that eventually totaled five thousand strong.

Doctor Abuja had to get out of the vehicle and explain the situation to the guards at the gate. One look in the back of the car and they would not allow the vehicle through the gate. The three local men moaned and were definitely not Jordanian citizens or UN soldiers. Doctor Abuja was permitted access to the compound based on his UN credentials. After an hour later, Doctor Abuja returned with a letter and handed it to the guard. They were allowed access for no more than four hours to treat the patients. They had two fractured legs and a severe head injury. Both doctors were pleased to get full access to normal medical equipment.

Down the road at the Cape Hotel, Russell sat in silence and drank a few more gin and tonics. He thought about the Al Qaida threat in Africa and remembered Iraq. He grew up in Manhasset, a small Norman Rockwell type town on Long Island and understood the impact of 9/11 as several neighbors died when the Twin Towers collapsed. The violence in Iraq taught him a hard lesson, something he could not forget. The screams, sounds, and smells from the explosion Russell witnessed firsthand in Iskandariyah, a city thirty miles south of Baghdad, lingered in his thoughts. On February 14, 2004, he had a meeting with the district police administrator in his office. As Russell's armored military vehicle was about to turn the corner toward Iskandariyah police headquarters, a massive bomb ripped apart the entire block. Bodies were strewn everywhere. Smoke filled the sky. Chaos ensued.

Russell ran toward the building and found his contact who stumbled in a daze. The career Iraqi police officer had no time to mourn the dead. He had no time to express any emotion. His country was in despair, and he needed to take action. Russell asked him, "What will you do now?"

"Come back to work tomorrow and the day after that." The police administrator replied in a sharp tone. Russell remained there to help for two days - not sleeping. He returned to one of the metropolis size bases that was built in the remote Iraq desert near the town of Habbinayah to support the massive U.S. military buildup.

Once they had arrived at the base, large spotlights could be seen from a distance. Russell needed food and some rest. He was shocked to see a huge stage built in the middle of an abandoned airfield. It was something out of a Hollywood movie as cheerleaders from an NFL football team took the stage and began a gyrating dance. Russell walked away from the massive crowd toward the large lake. He pulled out the only thing in his pocket. He never carried a wallet or personal items on patrol. The only thing he carried was a rosary from his grandmother. He held it tight as he wondered if a God existed. With a solid motion, he hurled the rosary as far as he could. Russell concluded that any God had overlooked what happened in Iraq. As he walked back toward the bright lights and vivacious music, several inbound rockets from the insurgents put a damper on the party. Soldiers ran in zigzag motions. Over a dozen 107mm Chinese rockets, courtesy of the local Al Qaeda chapter exploded near the massive lights. Russell thought some public affairs officer would get his ass handed to him for coordinating the Iraq Valentine's Day tour with large spotlights.

After Iraq, Russell went to graduate school at Columbia University. He dated someone at the school for several months, and they had moved into a cramped Manhattan apartment together. Everything was fine until Russell's name came onto Mr. Vanderheuse's radar. Russell thought he was in love and thought marriage. When the family found out about Russell, he was invited to the massive Fourth of July party at the exclusive Gold Coast

Country Club. While the poorer parts of Long Island society spent the holiday at the public park at Jones Beach, the uber-rich feasted on quail and duck on the country club's manicured lawns.

"Tom, have you ever experienced a significant loss in the stock market?" Mr. Vanderheuse, his finance's dad, had asked him. Russell did not have a penny to his name at the time. The ten-dollar drink at the Long Island country club was far outside of his budget.

"Sir, your idea of a big loss and mine are from two different worlds." The man with significant wealth did not care for Tom Russell's opinions; he wanted the point known that Russell was not good enough.

"I was scuba diving off Phuket" The uber-wealthy man paused for the sake of his own dramatic effect, "And by the time I got back to the surface I had lost over a million dollars in the stock market crash."

Russell thought about it for a moment and replied, "But those are just paper losses." Russell did not know how to relate to the financial woes of a multi-millionaire. Later in the day, Kristin's sister flatly informed him that they came from old money, back to the revolutionary era. She noted several times that Kristin would be taken out of her parent's will if she married below her society level. Russell did not give a damn for what the Vanderheuse name provided. He did not care about the easy access door to wealth. He had served in Iraq and survived that shithole.

Russell finished his fourth gin and tonic. The Russians had kept their eyes on him. They made sure Russell knew that they watched him. The piano chimed the same song that is played over and over every night. A large local man sang in a deep tone, "The world will release new lovers as time goes by." Russell did not want to face Francesca tonight. He needed to get his head straight. Russell leveraged a wooden chair against the door and placed a pistol on his chest. He tried to keep his eyes open in case the Russians attacked, but he passed out quickly.

Chapter 11

At Cape Hotel outdoor café, Checkov watched several young women as they dove into the hotel pool. Checkov wore long pants to cover his scars from the war in Chechnya. Eight scars zigzagged across his right leg. The injury was caused by a car explosion meant to kill him. He had made his own tourniquet and kept his leg from being amputated. Checkov looked carefully at the crowd that surrounded the Cape Hotel pool. He was patient. He wanted to see the American CIA operative that he had heard so much about. Checkov stirred his drink, but he did not consume anything from the glass. He lived in a world in which he had a lot of enemies that wanted him dead. Nothing was safe for him, not even a glass of water.

Checkov observed his prey closely. There were a half-dozen new American girls who joined a voting rights foundation set up by a former U.S. President. They wore skimpy bathing suits that revealed hard, young bodies. Checkov admired them and wanted to pinpoint one for selection. He liked to pick out someone who could just disappear without a lot of publicity. Checkov usually marked heavier set girls for kidnapping as he preferred them. The new guests in front of him were too skinny. He couldn't risk an abduction at this point in the mission.

Checkov thought about several ways he could beat the American. Foam drooled from his mouth as he contemplated the pain he wanted to inflict. He breathed heavy and was thirsty, yet he did not touch the water. As he saw a man walk toward the pool, he lowered his sunglasses. Checkov watched the American CIA operative as he walked toward a café table. Checkov was surprised to see as the man sat down across from a gorgeous woman. Checkov looked at her long legs under the table. She looked very fit and was very sensuous looking. Checkov would have one of his men trail her and find out the connection to the American.

On the other side of the pool area, the patio table was neatly set with napkins and polished utensils. In the middle of the table were fresh flowers. Everything looked perfect, except for her guest. "What do you want from me?" Francesca asked Russell. She stirred her cocktail with a straw. Francesca wore a disguise that consisted of a long brown hair wig, a large hat, and oversized sunglasses. She looked like a character out of a 1960s Audrey Hepburn movie.

"I should ask the same," Russell lifted his hand and gestured for the waiter to order a drink. He felt several eyes on him and looked toward the pool. He picked the Russians out of the crowd. Russell scanned the man in the lounge chair with his shirt half open. The older man had ghostly white chest hair flowing out of the open shirt. He wore slacks, something very out of the ordinary for the pool. Russell focused his attention back to Francesca and asked. "Why you. Why did they send you?"

Russell knew the answer. Anytime the Mossad could get an advantage over the CIA by bringing in a former lover; they would. In the embassy vault, Russell researched the CIA archives for operatives who went rogue to help Israel. Story after story involved an extremely sexy Israeli woman who ended up working for the Mossad. In the eight cases Russell read from the 1990s, the poor bastards had no idea what hit them. Several tried to defect to Israel and chase the loves of their lives. One former CIA operative made it to Tel Aviv at his own expense and discovered the Mossad agent whom he fell in love with was married and had three young children. His body was found dumped in the Gaza Strip. An Israeli newspaper reported that the American was on holiday, got drunk, lost, and was shot in the back of the head for being an American.

"The best always goes first," Francesca replied boldly. She was arrogant, yet Francesca knew that she was one of the best killers in the world. "Isn't that why the Langley boys sent you?" Russell looked to make sure no one heard her comment. His presence had already raised alarms.

"That's not what I meant." He leaned close. "What about our son?"

"You care about him now?" Francesca replied. "He had a birthday last month and asked about you. You are not part of his life."

"I know." Russell looked down. "Yeah, I know. There is a lot in life that I have regrets for."

"Is your son a regret?" she inquired.

"Absolutely not." Russell shot back and continued. "You know the reason why. If your father and the Mossad were not in the picture, we would have the picture-perfect family life."

"That would be nice. A house with a white picket fence and a dog." Francesca said as she smiled widely. She had dreamed of it.

"It would have to be a Rottweiler as we would have constant visitors that wanted us both dead," Russell said. They both laughed slightly at that. They both knew what difficult life-altering choices they had made and the dedication and sacrifice of their own respective intelligence organization.

"We have eyes on us," Francesca said. "Don't get up. Let them follow me. I could use someone to work out my aggressions on." Francesca stood up from the table and gave Russell a deep kiss on the lips, something to get the Russians attention. She walked off the patio and did not look back as she knew that at least one of the Russian thugs would follow her.

Russell remained at the table and waited a few more moments for the sunset. He ordered another drink and a freshly caught grouper with Liberian hot pepper sauce. He had not tasted the infamous Liberian hot pepper sauce in five years, and the shock of one bite rang through his body. The locals loved the spice while the brave foreigners who attempted the taste grimaced in pain. Russell drank his water and waved the waiter for a refill. The local man hurried over. Russell looked out over the ocean. He remembered the mission to get Charles Taylor. Russell led a small team into

Cameroon, and they waited at a border crossing as a very tired Charles Taylor attempted to cross from Nigeria, where corrupt leaders protected him. The CIA had a jet ready to bring Taylor back to Liberia where he was immediately arrested at Roberts International Airport for crimes against humanity. Taylor was confused as he exited the airplane and Russell made sure that he gave Taylor something to remember. As Taylor began to exit the aircraft, Russell leaned in close to the former dictator and said, "We got you, you son of a bitch." Russell did not anticipate the backlash from Taylor's bastard son Chucky who snuck into Liberia to rescue his father. Unbeknownst to Chucky, the UN moved Charles Taylor to the Netherlands for trial at The Hague. Chucky went crazy and attempted to overthrow the government. Russell's team captured Chucky alive and arranged for him to fly to the Bahamas handcuffed and drugged. By the time the drugs wore off, Chucky was on his way to a Federal Court in Miami. Chucky did not realize that Americans could be charged for crimes against humanity committed outside of the United States. Chucky was sentenced to ninety-nine years in an American federal prison.

Russell laughed aloud as he watched the Russians attempt to talk to the young American girls at the Cape Hotel pool. The girls did not understand and dove back into the pool. Russell headed back to the Piano Bar for another drink. As he walked up the back staircase, he paid more attention behind him in case he was followed. He did not see the cane fly from around the corner. The cane struck him across the front of his head, and he fell backward down the staircase. Checkov moved deliberately down the stairs and watched closely for movement. He did not underestimate this American CIA officer and had his cane ready to strike. Checkov pulled the phone out of Russell's pocket and dialed the last number.

"Are you coming to see me tonight?" Francesca asked. A heavy breath was on the other end of the phone. Checkov was out of breath from his onslaught. Francesca knew instinctively that Russell was in trouble. "Who are you?"

"My dear, you are both in a perilous country and may disappear very easily," Checkov spoke into the phone. He had no idea the identity of the woman on the phone.

"Please don't hurt my lover." Francesca gave a fake weep. She was the master of manipulation.

"For you, I will only inflict some pain." Checkov laughed and hung up. In the next few moments, Checkov beat Russell with his cane. Blood erupted from the side of Russell's head.

On the other side of Monrovia, near the new Liberian government buildings, the buildup of UN forces continued. Several container ships recently arrived with tons of building material. Under the UN Mission to Liberia, donor nations to include Russia, China, Italy, France, Great Britain, and of course their big brother the United States provided over sixty million dollars in outright contributions. The tower of supplies was just the first installment with the second more expensive part as the four thousand more troops that UN forces promised.

In Africa, nations that donated forces received stipends to pay their troop's salaries. Due to the conditions in many struggling African nations, the soldiers received supplemental funds for hazardous duty pay and as well as extra money to purchase groceries. In Monrovia, there were two economies – the black market in the red-light district and the exclusive market shop with security guards who lined the perimeter. Kitson observed the long lines for scant resources in the red-light district. As locals struggled for existence, the wealthy foreigners had plenty of gourmet choices from fresh fish, meat, and dairy products. Routine flights delivered fresh goods, and the local fishermen received ten times what they would if they sold fish in the red-light district. The price for a fresh fish was more than a typical Liberian earned in a month, yet the foreigners lined up with bulging wallets of cash to procure food. Cash was the only instrument of trade. There were no credit card machines. Smart device payments on mobile phones were something out of a science fiction movie. Kitson lived in Monrovia for a period of ten months, and he was amazed at how the condition had not changed. There was very little development. Roads were still severely damaged by the war. Buildings remained hollowed shells.

Kitson turned into the UN compound. He wore his British military uniform. The Pakistani soldiers at the gate were mystified as to what country he was from as they did not have any British soldiers who served under the UN Mission to Liberia (UNMIL). Brigadier General Abbas looked out from his suite atop of the UN compound that was once a large hotel in Monrovia. He had arrived two weeks ago to assume duties as the Deputy Commander of Operations. He had previously served in Uganda.

Abbas was Nigerian and pleased to take a follow-on UN job as the spoils of war were good to him. He felt betrayed by his own Nigerian government as the oil men made billions of dollars and the high-level military staff made peanuts. Abbas watched with disdain as the Nigerian oil executives gained more and more wealth. The global energy crisis and the surprise increase in oil prices made them extremely wealthy, beyond every Nigerian's expectations. Abbas wanted his cut, and he squirreled away small canisters of rough, untraceable diamonds.

After the recent Liberian and Sierra Leone civil wars, there were tighter restrictions on the flow of illicit, blood diamonds. The Kimberly Accord signed in Kimberly South Africa helped limit the flow of blood diamonds to international brokers, yet only a portion of the world's governments signed onto the document. However, many of the former Soviet Union states, China, and Iran had not signed the Kimberly Accord. More significantly, Al Qaeda and the three thousand other global terrorist groups would never abide by the Kimberly rules to track rough cut diamonds. The movement of illegal diamonds became a significant windfall for Abbas, and he made sure every position he attained helped fill his coffers. The safety deposit box in a Zurich bank account was only known to him, not even his wife or children knew.

"Greetings my old friend," Kitson said. "I should call you Sir now."

"No, no my friend," Abbas replied. In their last mission in Liberia together, five years prior, both men wore the same rank. Kitson had since retired and moved into full-time work for MI6 while Abbas kept plugging away a meaningless existence in some of the worse shit holes across Africa. "What can I do for you?"

"Ebola," Kitson said. "We think that something is coming."

"An outbreak?" Abbas inquired. "Here in Liberia?"

"Not an outbreak," Kitson replied. "We suspect that there are criminal enterprises developing a weapon capable of delivering Ebola."

"Interesting," Abbas replied. "In my life, I have never heard of such a thing. I have been in the military for thirty-one years and have not seen such a thing."

"It was tested a long time ago," Kitson said. "Something that came out of the Cold War."

"The Russians?" Abbas asked. "You think the Russians are here building a bomb?"

"Perhaps. But they have no need for a bomb," Kitson said. "We might want to look at Hezbollah." Kitson paused for a moment. "It may be the man who runs the casino."

"Hassan?" Abbas replied. "No, you must be mistaken." Abbas waved his hand in the air and smiled largely across his face. "The Lebanese here are not harmful. They are hardworking people and have greatly helped

Liberia's commerce. There was not much here after the war, and the Lebanese have built businesses."

"But at an expense," Kitson retorted. "The Lebanese control most of the commerce in and out of Liberia. They control the five hotels in Monrovia. Hassan bribed his way to open the casino here."

"Accusations. All accusations." Abbas waived his hand in the air. "You see my old friend this is Africa, and the British or American rules have no bearing here."

"What about Nigeria's rules?"

"We like to keep a very close watch on our local brothers and sisters in West Africa," Abbas replied. "Too many wars, too many dictators." He looked at the map on the wall and pointed to the thirteen countries that encompassed West Africa. Over the next forty-five minutes, Abbas recited how Nigeria had helped each one. Kitson thought that he had just tuned into an infomercial. He concluded with Liberia. Abbas turned to Kitson and said in a more political voice, "And our neighbors in Liberia had witnessed far too much strife. We are here to make sure no more wars."

"Does that include Sapo?" Kitson referred to Sapo National Forest, a region in the interior of Liberia that was impenetrable. After the civil war, many of Charles Taylor's loyal troops fled to Sapo to hide and regroup. Taylor promised that he would return. Many of his men remembered Taylor standing on the steps of the Presidential Palace the day the rebels seized control of Bushrod Island. Taylor wore a military uniform and the rank of a general with a circle comprised of five stars. He screamed at the top of his lungs that he would return, but for his protection, he was going to Nigeria to wait out the rebels. He promised his men that he would return and bring victory. Several reporters in the crowd snapped Taylor's photo and equated it to Douglas McArthur who wore five stars leaving the Philippines as the Japanese advanced. Kitson watched Abbas to gauge what was the truth.

"No, no, these men here in Sapo are not a threat," Abbas said. "We have looked at these men, and they are very soft now. Many have taken bush wives and live a good existence panning for gold every day."

"Do they have a new leader?" Kitson inquired. The previous leader was a man named Colonel 'zigzag' Marzah. He got his nickname for running back and forth between machinegun bursts during the prior civil war against Samuel Doe. Marzah was a wanted war criminal for the brutal practices his men perpetrated on the Liberian populace. During Charles Taylor's civil war, Marzah was assigned to put together a Special Forces team that mimicked the U.S. Army Rangers. A camp was established on the outskirts of the Firestone Rubber plantation, and Marzah indoctrinated his recruits into deadly tactics.

The Black Berets were formed and upon first missions proved very deadly to clear out rebel strongholds. Taylor leveraged the success of the Black Berets to make them his own death squad. Taylor provided Marzah with lists of his enemies, some were political and had not taken up arms against Taylor. Regardless, Marzah led his men in the middle of the night into deadly assaults that murdered countless men, women, and children. After the UN's arrival, Marzah fled with over two hundred of his loyal followers into Sapo National Forest to hide from prosecution. Many of his men had warrants issued for their arrests and were deemed outlaws. They operated on the fringe of Liberian society and started criminal enterprises to forge an existence. Bush wives were kidnapped from remote villages, never to be seen again. Taylor's men could never return to society as a responsible element as they only knew violence as a means to an end.

"We have no information on any new rebel leaders," Abbas said as he pulled out a large envelope of pictures. He placed a dozen photos on the table. "These were taken by someone we paid handsomely to smuggle these pictures out." Abbas pointed a pen at several of the photos. "As you can see, these men have made an existence in the jungle. They have bars, restaurants, and families now."

"Sounds like utopia," Kitson remarked cynically. "What about the young girls that they have kidnapped? What is the UN doing to get them back?" Kitson paused and added, "British Intelligence believes that young girls from Liberia are victims of human trafficking out of Liberia destined for Asia. They are just not keeping them as bush wives. They are selling these girls in exchange for weapons on the world black market."

"Many difficult decisions." Abbas sounded like a politician again. Kitson knew his format all too well, any difficult discussion became a political sidestep. "These men would be shooting in the streets of Monrovia if they did not have such a nice existence in Sapo. As you can see by these photos, they are very happy." Kitson looked down at the photos quickly. A long-range camera took the photos on a warm sunny day. Many of Marzah's men still wore their old uniforms. They were visibly drunk and enjoyed watching young girls dance on a stage. One former soldier held a gun to a girl's head. Kitson thought of the horror this young girl had endured, ripped from her family, and enslaved by brutal men – war criminals.

"Are you not going to rescue the girls?" Kitson asked pointedly.

"These are very difficult decisions." Abbas pointed to the map on the wall. "We have such limited resources and many, many miles to cover."

"But you know where they are." Kitson pointed out. "You know where Marzah's men are. We told you where to find them five years ago when we went in and got him." Kitson referred to the snatch and grab operation that he and Russell completed in the remote Sapo jungle. With the assistance of two brand new Liberian officers who were trained in America, a small team ventured deep into Sapo to capture Marzah. As Russell walked into his bedroom, Marzah surprised him from behind, and they wrestled for the knife in Russell's hand. As Russell flipped Marzah into the air, he plunged the eight-inch knife into Marzah's chest. Under the flood boards, Russell discovered a treasure trove of information that was used in Taylor's war crimes trial to help convict him.

"These men pose no risk to us now." Abbas looked out the window. "I am very worried about the rain." Everyone knew that the rainy season was days away. Liberia had the dubious honor of being the second wettest place on the planet with twenty-two feet of rain that arrived within a three-month period.

"What about the Ebola threat?" Kitson wanted more information and needed to know the UN response efforts. "We have reports that an outbreak could erupt."

"These things you hear they are such fascinating things." Abbas smiled broadly, something that pissed Kitson off, yet the professional British officer held his tongue. "We have heard these reports before, and nothing has come of it. Every week some UN doctor claims some outbreak will decimate Liberia, yet nothing has happened."

"Are there UN plans to prepare for an outbreak?" Kitson wanted to ask more probing questions as to really what would happen in Liberia. "We have so much building to do." Abbas pointed to a schematic drawing on the wall. "You can see we have four thousand more troops coming and that will need many more buildings."

"Why are you bringing more UN forces? What is the threat? You said Marzah's men are nothing."

"There is much to do to help our Liberian neighbors," Abbas said. "Many more troops are needed to help stabilize everything."

"Do we have to wait for more troops?" Kitson had operated in Africa for over twenty-eight years and had been very successful with minimal troops. The UN took the storybook page out of the American force buildup in Iraq with large bases and huge amounts of infrastructure that equated to a lot of eaters and shitters. Kitson was used to going in light and living with the locals. The UN forces kept themselves within their compounds, except to drive straight to the exclusive fresh market in Monrovia.

"These things are very far above us. We are just humble men." Abbas smiled broadly and waved both his arms outward. Kitson knew the answer as he requested MI6 to investigate the construction in Liberia and discovered many senior officers received bribes and kickbacks from contractors, much worse than what was discovered in Iraq and Afghanistan.

Kitson was disgusted as he walked out of the UN offices. He spat openly in the direction of the large amounts of construction supplies. Kitson knew time was of the essence and was furious at how corrupt Abbas became. He had heard the same issue of Nigerian military officers who were reluctant to pursue the Boko Haram terrorist group in their own country. Kitson looked up at the sky. He was very nervous over the upcoming rainy season. West Africa had the second most amount of rainfall on the planet and what made it more challenging was the fact that a majority of the rain arrived within a two-month period.

Kitson observed firsthand the horrific living conditions during the rainy season. Liberians took shelter anywhere and crowd together to get out of the rain. There were very few options as many of the buildings were heavily impacted by shelling during the civil war. Many buildings looked like Swiss cheese with multiple bullet holes from fifty caliber machineguns. The rainy season brought not only misery but despair as the locals endured a steady pelt of rain that lasted days, upon days. Kitson knew instinctively that if Ebola was unleashed during the rainy season a large number of people would die.

Francesca sped back toward the Cape Hotel. The vehicle's horn blared warnings as she dashed around locals who walked in the street. At times, she jumped the vehicle onto the sidewalk to avoid several innocent older women who pushed their goods in an old wheelbarrow down the street. Francesca knew the short cuts and fastest way. Within several minutes, she sped into the Cape Hotel compound. Inside the lobby, she saw Russell was moved to a couch, and Tareeq knelt near him with a white towel that was soaked with blood. Tareeq had explained to the inquiry guests that the man had fallen drunk down the steep back staircase that led from the Piano Bar. Tareek did not want to alert any of his high paying guests to the fear of the Russian's retaliation.

"Get his feet," Francesca ordered Tareeq. She reached under his shoulders and lifted him off the couch.

"Where are we going?" Tareeq asked.

"Jordanian Hospital. We can't take him to the American Embassy as they will ask too many questions." As a doctor, Francesca knew there was precious time to get him examined to ensure there was no internal brain swelling. She added, "With this head injury, it is not good."

"And he would die at Monrovia General." Tareeq offered.

"Yes," Francesca stated as a matter of fact. "More than likely, he would die there." She grabbed his arms and lifted his heavy body with all of her strength. "We need to go." Francesca looked at Tareeq who was very hesitant. "Now!" She shouted.

Chapter 12

Thick waves of rain and severe flooding were horrific events that attacked Liberia at the start of every rain season. Out of nowhere, the rain punished everything with brutal force. And what came next was something close to biblical destruction as swarms of mosquitos attacked. The small, white colored mosquitos were indigenous only to the West Africa region and brutally hungry. The most compelling concern in the rainy season was the spread of malaria. The Jordanian Hospital was a mile up the road from Bushrod Island that was ground zero of the mosquito onslaught. The Jordanians were prepared at the hospital and placed duct tape around the windows and mosquito nets over the patient's beds. The netting was hung from the ceiling and covered the patients, top to bottom. Kitson walked into the open bay ward and thought it looked like something out of a science fiction movie with the beds resembling cocoons. Kitson had looked at the half-dozen dead white mosquitos killed by the chemicals on the netting, and he brushed them to the floor. The temperature in the room was dropped by several more degrees. Kitson felt the chill. He shivered for a moment and pressed his arms rapidly against his chest a few times to get the blood flowing faster. Russell had several tubes coming out of his body.

"How are you doing?" Kitson was concerned and shock Russell's arm to wake him. He added, "Are you alright?"

"What happened?" Russell mumbled out of the corner of his mouth.

"Checkov does not like you much," Kitson stated in a blunt manner.

"The feeling is mutual," Russell said as he wet his lips with some water to moisten them so he could speak. "I bet he looks worse than me." He tried to laugh a little, but it hurt. He pressed his right arm over the top of his ribcage. Everything hurt. "How long have I been out?"

"Two days," Kitson replied. "Do you remember anything?"

"Not much." Russell tried to sit up some and could not. He looked at the tubes coming out of his arm and abdomen. He found a control to move the bed up and pushed it. Slowly, the bed lifted his battered body upward.

"Take it easy," Kitson replied quick, "we need you to get healthy."

"I'm good," Russell said in a soft tone. He hated people watching over him, let alone his mentor. "Two more days and I'll be out of here."

"Hold on there," Kitson said, "your private doctor said that you need more time to heal." Kitson waived his arm at the door as Francesca walked in wearing a white doctor's jacket and a stethoscope around her neck. She looked the part. Kitson pondered if the Jordanians knew that she was a Mossad undercover agent. If the Jordanians knew about her, Kitson doubted that Francesca would have received the same VIP treatment Francesca displayed her French identity and spoke the language fluently. Kitson had vouched for her and even had the British Ambassador to Jordan send a letter of gratitude to the Jordan King. Word of the British thanking Jordan, a nation that has not been much of an ally on the war on terror, became big news at the far distant hospital. Francesca did not need to show any professional documentation or accreditation. She had full access to the laboratory and all medical supplies she needed.

"How is my patient?" Francesca asked sarcastically as she smiled with those sparkling teeth. Her smile was brilliant and hypnotic, yet Russell looked farther up into her eyes to see if he could read her expression.

"Fine." Russell retorted shortly. He hated anyone taking care of him. "Tomorrow, I'll be ready to go tomorrow." He stated in a demanding tone.

"Hold off there…Marine," Francesca replied. "I am your physician, and I will tell you when YOU are allowed to leave."

"Seriously, I don't need a mother here," Russell replied.

"Is that what you are thinking about me, that I am mothering you?" Francesca said. She waited a moment for a reply, but Russell was silent. "You may not recall, but I was the one who zipped out of a helicopter and snagged you before a witch doctor could put a knife into your heart." Francesca referred back to the last Liberia mission five years ago. Russell went after the witch doctor who kidnapped James. Francesca continued, "It was the Colonel who found you." She pointed to Kitson. "And he fought to get you into this hospital so you would not get an infection or something else at the Liberian hospital. It was me who stitched your beaten body back together. So, stop feeling so damn proud and let us help you." With that, Francesca got up and walked away. Both Kitson and Russell looked at her when she walked away. Russell looked even closer at her hips as they swayed back and forth underneath the doctor's jacket. He could tell that she still maintained a very hard body, even after giving birth to their son.

"Damn," Kitson said. "You must have really struck a nerve."

"I need to see the Ambassador." Russell looked angry.

"Then let's get you dressed," Kitson said as he knew the mission had top priority. There was little time to waste, and he needed to update Russell on what had transpired over the past two days. MI6 sent Kitson satellite imagery that revealed a large buildup at the Marshall compound Hezbollah used. A dozen more docks were rapidly installed since the last imagery two weeks ago. Each dock had a fast boat moored. Inside of the Marshall compound over twenty large canopy tents were erected. Kitson felt something was brewing large for Hezbollah operations in West Africa and now he had confirmation. Over the next three hours, he went into intricate detail to update Russell on what he had discovered.

Tom Russell, CIA operative, walked into the security office at the U.S. Embassy and asked to see the Ambassador. The Marine guards looked surprised to see him. News quickly spread about the CIA agent who was previously persona non-grata in Liberia was allowed to remain against the

U.S. Ambassador's objections. Russell looked up at the security camera and did not smile. He went to the vault and downloaded the classified brief that Langley developed based on his reports and assessments. Russell looked the information over several times and highlighted several important facts. He locked the presentation into a satchel bag. Even the U.S. Embassy personnel had access to highly sensitive and classified information; this presentation was for the U.S. Ambassador's eyes only.

The U.S. Ambassador read the intelligence estimate for the fifth time and placed it back down on the desk. "Let me understand this Mr. Russell." She lowered her glasses to look him in the eyes. Russell sat across the large oak desk. He looked at the craftsmanship and assumed the desk was old. He saw several holes in the wood that resembled bullet holes. Russell recalled from his training that the U.S. Embassy in Liberia was the most evacuated in history at a dramatic eight full-scale evacuations, which equated to eight instances whereby conditions were so unstable that the U.S. Ambassador had to depart the country. She continued, "You believe that Al Qaeda operatives have partnered with Hezbollah to bring terror to the world and launch that mission out of Liberia?"

"Yes, ma'am," Russell replied, "but there was more if you read the second page."

"I did." She replied with a stern tone. "Your assumptions that a former KGB operation is operating in Africa and delivered weapons of mass destruction to Liberia."

"It is a weapon to deliver a contagion," Russell replied, and he added. "A weapon of mass destruction."

"You mean a virus." She paused, "Right?"

"Yes, ma'am," Russell stated in a polite manner, not to upset her. He knew that he was on thin ice with the seasoned diplomat.

"And you assume that this weapon would deliver Ebola." The U.S. Ambassador stated. She continued to look at the intelligence report.

"Possibly could be utilized to weaponize a virus such as Ebola," Russell stated calmly.

"And fly it around the world." She said as she looked up for a brief moment. "And deliver an attack."

"We don't know where the target would be." Russell provided the comment as he knew that might be the next question.

"But you have assumptions. That is what this is all about right – assumptions?

"We believe the first strike is against Tel Aviv," Russell stated firmly as he stared at the seasoned diplomat.

"We believe?" She paused for a brief moment and asked, "or is it you Mister Russell who believes?" The U.S. Ambassador inquired. "I have from reliable sources that your former lover is an Israeli Mossad agent." She paused for a moment and asked, "No?" Russell did not respond. His face was blank as he rehearsed in his mind again and again over the past five years what would happen if someone asked him about Francesca. The Ambassador thought that she would have struck a nerve but did not. She pulled a photo out from the desk and tossed it in front of Russell. The picture was of a young boy playing with a soccer ball. There were joy and laughter on the boy's face. Russell had not seen his son in eighteen months. He had grown. Russell looked up at the U.S. Ambassador. "Are our priorities straight Mister Russell?"

"There are no issues here." Tom Russell of the CIA, a proven combat veteran, and upholder of democracy, said as he looked at the seasoned diplomat. Russell wanted to say that many body bags would be needed by the end of his mission. Russell picked up the photo and placed it in his jacket. He hated getting called to the carpet of the U.S. Ambassador. Langley requested Russell's presence after a lot of prodding from the State Department. Russell heard from the desk officer at Langley that his assumptions made it into the Director's briefing book and the Director planned to brief the President personally in the next twenty-four hours.

"I will review your concerns, Mister Russell." She pulled off her glasses and looked straight at him. Her eyes were cold steel. She ended the meeting as she stated firmly. "You are dismissed."

After he left the Ambassador's office, Russell walked alongside the high embassy walls. He recalled aged photos in his mind of the bodies that were piled up along the walls during the civil war. Liberians screamed for big brother America to step in and cease the fighting; however, that would have given Taylor enough time to regroup his forces and strengthen his position around Monrovia. Liberians carried their dead to the U.S. Embassy gate and piled them up in protest. At one time, over sixty dead bodies were stacked upon one another. The horrific smell of rotting corpses permeated the air and Russell assumed it must have been ghastly. The only nation to intervene was Nigeria. Over eight hundred Nigerian troops landed at Roberts International Airport and began to fire indiscriminately at anyone who carried a weapon, regardless of what side they were on. Within a day, the Nigerians secured the perimeter surrounding Monrovia and began to clear house by house. Anyone caught with a pistol, rifle, or machete were imprisoned. By month's end, the jails were filled, and peace had arrived in Monrovia. A nighttime curfew remained in place for six months until more UN forces arrived. No locals ventured out at night as they knew the Nigerians would shoot.

At the Cape Hotel, the afternoon party scene was in full swing. Since the guests completed their meetings for the day, they headed toward the beach. Anwar had his concierge men in full white jackets and white slacks. Their dark, African complexions stood out against the uniform. The support staff hustled back and forth to deliver food and cocktails to foreigners. Several of the young girls who worked for the charity formed by a former U.S. President giggled as they saw Russell walk by them. Russell had on tan slacks, a crisp white shirt, and a suit jacket - out of place for the party scene. Russell did not have time to guess what humored the girls. He walked right toward Kitson. Russell found his old friend sitting on the patio. Kitson had a gin and tonic in his hand and an empty glass that housed his second gin and tonic rested on the table.

"How did the meeting go?" Kitson asked. He looked up from his lounge chair. Kitson waved to the waiter with two fingers in the air.

"Not good," Russell replied. He tossed the photo on his lap.

"Your son?" Kitson replied. Russell nodded as he sat down. Russell pulled off his suit jacket and dress shoes. He hated wearing the outfit, and the new shoes hurt his feet. When the waiter returned, Russell handed the man his shoes and suit jacket and informed him that he could have them. Russell and Kitson sat in silence for a few moments and watched the waves topple over and over again. They were men of few words.

"Let's get drunk," Russell said. The sun started to settle on the beach. Kitson and Russell had more drinks, about eight each. One of Anwar's private security detail drove them to Wave Tops.

Within Monrovia city limits, Wave Tops bar was a very unusual and hard place to find. The building rested along the Marshall River and overlooked Bushrod Island, the most congested place in Monrovia. Wave Tops bar was located atop a makeshift terrace on the fifth floor. The foreigners felt comfortable on this side of the river as they could overlook the dense shacks from a safe distance. The bridge from Bushrod Island into Monrovia was the only means to cross, and that was guarded by UN personnel twenty-four hours a day. There were over eighty thousand people that lived inside of Bushrod Island's eight square mile area. This area was the highest crime area in the city, and dead bodies were found every morning along the beach. There was no police element on Bushrod Island as they would be overrun. UN personnel would never enter the island unless in armored vehicles and only to pass through.

"Not a bad crowd tonight," Kitson said. He eyed the room from the corner table. It was an ingrained, natural habit for intelligence operatives to scan the room. Kitson looked at Russell who had his face deep into a pile of fries after downing a hamburger. Russell did not look up. He had no care at the moment except food. "Are you able to stay focused on the mission?"

"We need to eliminate the threat," Russell said between mouthfuls.

"And whoever is behind it," Kitson added.

"No prisoners," Russell stated as a matter of fact.

"No prisoners." Kitson returned. It was a declaration between the two intelligence operatives from MI6 and CIA that they would rather put a bullet in someone's head rather than have them sent to a remote jail cell to be interrogated for years. It was a faster justice.

The bar was full of foreigners who sought the refuge from the daily turmoil that they dealt with in the post-civil war nation. Each of them drank heavily and laughed even louder as they discussed their African exploits. The Russians stood out as they had no expression on their faces. Kitson watched the former KGB General move across the room. Checkov looked behind him and made sure his protection was with him.

"My friends," Checkov said as he waved his arms in the air. "How is the British and American alliance?" He slammed an empty beer on the table. "You look better my American friend. I heard about your skirmish." He paused for a moment. "Liberia is a dangerous place these days."

"Checkov," Kitson said with a flat tone. "Are you still looking for young girls?" Kitson replied. MI6 had close surveillance on Voctrad's safe house from the constant satellite feed. Kitson requested the slug from the dead foreign aid worker and the Chief of Police in Monrovia obliged. After input into the global forensic database linked to the western intelligence organizations, the slug matched several unsolved murders from Cairo to Lagos to Accra and Cape Town. The young foreign women found were sexually assaulted and murdered with a single gunshot to the forehead with a 9.27-millimeter cartridge. MI6 believed the weapon used in the murders was the Makarov pistol, a weapon of choice by the KGB.

"You British have a way with words." Checkov looked at Kitson with his cold steel eyes. "We have no issues with our British friends." Checkov smiled broadly, "but look at your American." Checkov laughed at Russell. "Typical American…can't handle the booze."

With a knee-jerk reaction, Russell flipped the table in the air. He stumbled as he stood. Kitson was slow to react as he was caught off guard by Russell's overt action. Russell dove toward Checkov with his fist in the air and connected on Checkov's jaw. He knocked out two of his teeth and blood spurted. Russell swung back to hit the bodyguards but found himself on the front end of a boot against his chest. The ex KGB and former Spetsnaz soldier kicked Russell hard enough to knock him against the wall that was nearly three feet away. The other bodyguard pounded Kitson with several punches. Russell staggered and fell to the floor. He looked up at the large Russian who was about to step on his head. Russell closed his eyes and put a hand over his head to protect him from the blow, but it never came. Russell opened his eyes and observed a swirl of movement as tables and chairs were tossed aside. The Russians were attacked and beaten badly in a flurry of kicks and punches. Russell saw someone dressed in all black. At first, he thought that it was a man, but then he saw the long hair as it emerged from under the hat and realized it was Francesca.

At the Al Qaeda camp, the three brothers sat close to one another and away from the other recruits. They did not mingle or pray with the other followers. They kept to themselves and remained quiet. The former child soldiers had fought during the Sierra Leone civil war in the early 1990s. The letters RUF were etched by razor blades into their arms. The small little arms of young boys grew into strong men while they were held in prison for ten years. The three brothers entered prison with the oldest just turned twelve years old, and they returned in their thirties. They had no skills, no education, and no hope. Kamal believed they would become superb terrorists.

The Frenchman took more blood samples from Fatima. He watched the guard rotations and did not understand what they said as they spoke to one another. He surmised that they spoke in Tegali. They would not allow him access to the internet as they feared he would contact for help or worse a CIA drone would drop a bomb on the camp. He looked over the pages upon pages of the Marburg virus. The first known case of a human contracting the virus occurred over two hundred and fifty years ago. The story was passed down from storyteller to storyteller in the tribe until the English priests arrived in Africa to teach Christianity in the remote villages. The priests were the first to document and publish the reports in the 1880s to the western world. Tribal elders knew from their fathers how ferocious a disease passed by monkeys could be. The name Ebola was attached to the Marburg virus. Ebola outbreaks were recorded very regularly in the remote regions of the Central African Republic and the Congo region. There were very few registered outbreaks in West Africa.

The Frenchman looked at the photos of the virus and the blood samples under the microscope. There was a match. Fatima had the virus. The blood that Kamal gave him had been tainted with the world's deadliest virus. This was no game, and he had to get out of there. He watched for a chance, anything to get out.

"We should not be meeting," Hassan said. He looked around at the Africans as he got out of his car. His youngest nephew drove him, and he sat in the back of the sedan just in case anyone watched.

"You need to see what we have," Kamal said. "This may be something of interest to you." He led the leader of the Hezbollah terrorist organization in West Africa toward the former army barracks. There were no visible lights in the building. Hassan and Kamal followed one of the Africans who carried a lantern.

"She has been infected," Kamal said. There was one light that hung from the ceiling that barely illuminated the room. Fatima was wrapped in a wool blanket and shivered from the initial effects of the virus.

"We already have the virus," Hassan said. Hezbollah operatives traveled all over the remote areas in search of Ebola. They found victims close to the Guinea border, not far from where Sam had his clinic.

"But do you have the cure?" Kamal inquired.

"There is no cure for Ebola."

"There may be a cure," Kamal said. "There are blood samples that we have from survivors. We will inject that into her as she gets sicker. The virus has mutated in the past and can form an antidote."

"Bring her to me," Hassan said. "We can use her blood."

"You will need a laboratory to develop the antiserum," Hassan said as he pointed to his makeshift laboratory.

"Don't worry, the Russians have delivered on their promise." Hassan looked at the primitive setup. "New equipment was smuggled in by boats last night. We have a state-of-the-art facility now."

The Frenchman looked up from his microscope as they passed the open door. Hassan looked at the white man closely. He did not need any loose ends. After they had walked past, Hassan looked at Kamal and asked. "The white man in there," Hassan pointed to the building, "Who is he?"

"A Frenchman." Kamal responded, "Someone who we needed to administer the blood."

"Where did you find him?" Hassan inquired.

"Outside a UN clinic," Kamal said.

"The foreigner saw my face," Hassan said.

"He's expendable," Kamal stated with no remorse. Kamal had no more use for the Frenchman and craved the execution that would come. Kamal had the video of him chopping off the foreigner's head smuggled out of Liberia. It was too dangerous to send on the internet with the Americans watching. Kamal had several faithful messengers that would take a long journey by sea around the African continent to Somalia. Kamal was pleased that he would kill the Frenchman.

Chapter 13

The heavy amount of alcohol had decimated Russell's senses. In the late morning, he awoke with a very bad headache, something that would not go away immediately. His head pounded. He sat up in the bed and found himself intertwined in a mosquito net. Russell was confused, very confused about his location. The mosquito net had lined the bed. He knocked off a few dead white mosquitos, the kind that spread malaria. The small mosquitos could not penetrate the protective netting and were killed by the chemical treatment of permethrin. Russell heard the air conditioning unit that hummed. There were two-bedroom windows, and both were protected by steel bars. Russell swung his legs onto the marble floor. The coldness helped alleviate some of the pain in his body. He shivered. The air conditioning unit was set on the coldest possible setting, and it hummed loudly. The coolness of the room helped ward off the white mosquitos. He opened the bedroom door and walked into a meeting.

"Good morning Mister CIA man." The Liberian Minister of Defense said, and he added, "You are looking very tired." After he observed the expression on Russell's face, Minister Urey released a short laugh. The Minister sat across from Kitson and another Liberian officer. Russell immediately recognized Major Forleh whom he worked with in the past. That was five years ago. Forleh was a Second Lieutenant then, and now he wore the rank of Major.

"Did someone get the license plate of that truck that ran me over?" Russell said as he sat down at the table. He quickly surmised that he was in one of the back bungalows on the BTC compound and proximity to the Minister of Defense office.

"Truck?" The Major Forleh questioned. "We heard it was a bar fight." Major Forleh did not get Russell's joke, even though the Liberian officer had spent six months training at the Marine Corps Basic Officers Course in Quantico, Virginia. Although Forleh had spent time in America, he still had a long way toward understanding American phrases.

"I think the Russians know you are here now," Kitson said as a matter of fact. He was not pleased that Russell lost his temper and started the fight. Even worse Kitson knew Francesca's cover was compromised as she came in to clean house on the Russians.

"Voctrad had been tracking my movements since the Congo." Russell shot back. "Voctrad is a bunch of criminal thugs. What really concerns me is a Hezbollah and Al Qaida alliance. Nothing good can come of that." Russell paused for a moment to look at the men at the table. He felt the hangover in the front of his head pound his skull like a jackhammer. "Can I get a cup of coffee?"

"Ike, can you get Mister Russell some coffee?" Kitson asked.

"Ya bossman." Ike delivered the coffee and a fresh muffin that he had baked. Ike smiled at Russell. Several of Ike's front teeth were missing, but Ike did not care about his appearance. He wanted to please his boss.

"We have rebels entrenched in Sapo." Minister Urey pointed at the location on the map. "But they are disorganized. We will have to take care of them later." He paused and looked at Kitson and said. "We have more immediate threats." Minister Urey placed several photos on the table. "These photos are of the Marshall compound along the river. Many Lebanese have moved there."

"Most likely Hezbollah." Kitson pointed out. "How many fighters do they have?"

"Hard to say." Minister Urey said. "They do not come through the airport, so we have no customs information on them."

"Boats?" Russell asked.

"Speedboats that meet ocean liners offshore." The Minister said. "It is difficult to prevent. We have no Navy."

"They have been doing that for years." Kitson proclaimed. "It is hard to know how many Hezbollah are there and what weapons they have."

"Does the Minister know about it?" Russell asked.

"Know what?" Minister Urey asked. He raised his voice. "This is my country, and there should be no secrets held from me." He looked at the two foreigners and toward Forleh. "Major Forleh is your direct liaison to me. He has been cleared at the highest levels of our closest secrets."

"What I am about to tell you cannot leave this room." Russell looked at both men. "It will create utter panic." Over the next thirty minutes, he explained in exhaustive detail on his analysis that Hezbollah and Al Qaida have linked up to create the mother of all bombs that would be unleashed on Tel Aviv. The Liberians listened patiently as Russell provided extensive details. Russell concluded and provided a closing statement. "With this information, your lives are now at risk."

"I should have died long ago," Forleh responded. "RUF soldiers attacked my village. A few of us boys ran and hid in the weeds. We had bugs and snakes crawl over us before we tried to run again. They shot one of my brothers as he ran across the field. I have seen much death. It does not scare me anymore." For a moment there was silence as the words of a man who witnessed horrific death lingered.

"We are committed to freedom." Minister Urey stated firmly. "We will die for our nation."

Kitson and Russell looked at one another and nodded. They knew that they had to get Liberian support. There were too many variables that could make things go drastically wrong in an instant.

"We know the Russians are involved," Kitson said. "They have a weapon from the Cold War."

"Voctrad is the name of their criminal organization," Russell added. "After the fall of the Soviet Union, KGB officers needed a new source of money and began to smuggle weapons out of Russia and sell on the black market. Their criminal empire is extensive, and they have tremendous resources."

Kitson watched the Minister's body movements closely. The Minister listened intently, and Kitson knew that he could be trusted. Kitson added, "There is information that made us believe a weapon was developed in the early 1960s in a remote Siberian military base. This weapon is similar in design to the anthrax weapon discovered in a Soviet bomber that crashed in the northern Arctic. However, this weapon had something different, very peculiar. It had to contain a virus. No weapon known to the western world had been able to control and release a virus. For the time, this was very advanced technology and has not been replicated even today. The knowledge had been lost in the archives of the Soviet collapse."

"The Russians?" Minister Urey replied. "This could make sense."

"What makes sense?" Kitson inquired.

"Several weeks ago, there were three Russians who entered Liberia," Minister Urey said. He opened up the binder in front of him and shuffled through pages. "Here... these men." He pointed. Next, he added, "They arrived from a flight out of Kyrgyzstan."

"I pulled all the entry visa forms. I did not see anyone coming from any former Soviet state, especially Kyrgyzstan," Russell said. He looked at the photos. The men were in their late sixties. "How did they enter undocumented?"

"The plane was a private jet," Minister Urey said. He placed another photo on the table. "It was a very expensive airplane. There was someone who met the plane. Here is his photo. I have never seen him before, but evidently, he paid off a UN air traffic controller. General Abbas gave me this information from the undercover investigation on the UN officer. Here is his photo, a Captain from the Romanian army."

Kitson picked up one of the photos and pointed. "That man is Checkov." He looked at Russell and saw the stern look on his face. "He is the one we ran into last night at the bar. He is a member of Voctrad and extremely deadly."

"I see." Minister Urey looked at the photos. "These old men do not look deadly."

"The weapons that they create would be very deadly," Russell replied. "If they worked on the Cold War project, they could be the missing link that Hezbollah needed."

"Colonel Kitson, you mentioned earlier that Al Qaida is here." Minister Urey looked at his notes from the discussion prior to Russell rolling out of bed. "These terrorists, what are they doing in Liberia?"

"We speculate that they have formed an alliance with Hezbollah for the mutual destruction of Israel." Kitson held his hands together and looked the Liberian in the eye. "Make no mistake, these are dire circumstances. Al Qaeda has been trying to get ahold of a weapon of mass destruction for many years. Even after Bin Laden's death, this terrorist organization is still powerful and very prevalent in Africa. While the world watched what happened in Pakistan, Al Qaeda recruited a small army of loyal followers from the former child soldiers held in prison. These men were perfect recruits after the civil war in Sierra Leone. They have mastered killing and are not welcome back to their villages. They have no home. They have no future." Kitson showed the report on the massive Sierra Leone prison break the prior month. Over a hundred for child soldiers had disappeared, and only a few were recaptured.

"I have heard this man Kamal is deadly." The Minister stated.

"Indeed. We tracked him in the Congo." Russell said. "He eluded our capture." He paused for a moment. "We will not make the same mistake." Russell thought back to the Congo. He had Kamal dead in his weapon's scope but lost him as a crowd swarmed around Kamal after he crashed his motorcycle. Kamal had escaped and not be heard of by western intelligence sources - until now.

"You said that he is here…near Monrovia…right down the road." The Minister said loudly as he pointed to the map. "Let's go kill him now."

"It's not that easy." Russell jumped in. "Kamal has unlimited resources and can vanish instantly. Kamal is at the top of the CIA kill list, and once they have a lock on his position, a drone will take him out."

"But how reliable are these drones?" Minister Urey said. "Let's get in my car right now and drive there. I have several AK47s in my trunk. We go there today and put a bullet in his head."

"I understand your eagerness, but we must have a positive ID." Russell continued. "We only have second-hand reports that Kamal is here."

"Then why do you waste my time with speculation. If he is there, we shoot him. If he is not there, we shoot anyone who moved into the old army compound." Minister Urey became irate. "Any terrorists in my country must die. I make a proclamation now that I will hunt any terrorists down and kill them myself." Kitson watched as the Minister wiped some drool from the side of his mouth as his lips foamed from the dryness. "We must kill every Al Qaeda."

"We need to make sure Kamal does not know we are onto him." Kitson tried to ease the eagerness. "We have heard that there may be a link between Al Qaeda and Hezbollah. If they are working together, this would be something we have not seen anywhere and could prove very deadly, especially for Israel."

"Is that is why your girlfriend is back?" Minister Urey looked directly at Russell.

"She's not my girlfriend," Russell responded.

"But she was sent by her government." The Minister fired back.

Kitson saw the redness come back to Russell's face. Kitson surmised that Russell had replayed in his mind the conversation with the U.S. Ambassador. Kitson jumped in before Russell put a foot in his mouth. "She's a valuable intelligence asset. We would have not known about the Russian connection without her."

"If she is on our side, I am ok." The Minister looked at the maps and paused for a long moment. "What do we need to do?" Over the next hour, they formulated a plan of attack.

After the meeting concluded, Russell walked to the rear of the BTC compound. He needed to clear his head. The BTC compound's exterior walls were all white washed. He put his fingers in the bullet holes where Doe executed twenty-two government officials. Doe lined up the relatives of former President Tolbert and shot them dead. The Presidential Palace remained remote and isolated. It was a dark cavern of lost souls. Doe had walked the short distance up the hill from BTC and murdered President Tolbert in his sleep. When Doe celebrated one year after the hostile coup on April 12, 1981, he pushed open the large metal green doors onto the crystal white sands of the beach. Doe had invited many dignitaries from all of the nations that returned their diplomats to Liberia. As he opened the large metal doors, the guests observed dozens of tables spread across the beach, filled with food and drinks. Into the night, they celebrated the murder of the Tolbert regime and Doe's subsequent rise to power. Russell stood and observed the thick rust spots that engulfed the steel doors, which had not moved in the fifteen years since President Doe was murdered.

Russell walked along the BTC compound walls. He saw a small pond and kept close to the outskirts of the tall sawgrass reeds. A small movement caught his eye. It was a snake, not any snake, but a deadly black mamba that stretched over eight feet. The black mamba had a gray mouth and fangs exposed as it raised its body. Russell stepped aside as the snake was about to strike. Before he had a chance to move, the fast-acting Major Forleh swung his machete toward the snake's head and sliced it in the air.

"Wow," Russell said. "Thank you. I was lost in thought." Russell looked at the dead snake and kicked the body that still withered without its head. "Damn thing came out of nowhere."

"You're welcome Sir," Forleh replied. "Shall I stay with you to keep you safe?"

"Sure," Russell said. He could use the company. For a few moments, they walked before Russell spoke again. "Tell me about your wife and sons. Last time we were together was almost five years ago."

"We live a good life on the military base, not far from Monrovia. It was an old firing range, and the government built housing for the officers and senior enlisted to live there. There is a school."

"Sounds a lot better than living in the city."

"Much different, a new way of life." Forleh thought about his comments. "Liberia is still very dangerous to live in the city. There are few police, very few to protect the citizens."

"Didn't the UN budget pay for a thousand new policemen?"

"Few have passed the background test. It is the same issue that we had with getting the Liberian Army stood up. There were not enough who can pass the background examination." Forleh reminded Russell of the difficulty and costs encountered when Russell worked in Liberia five years ago. Based upon the history in Liberia, there is much distrust of the military and rightfully justified after Samuel Doe's military coup. Every single recruit had their photo plastered over their villages to see if any were involved in the last civil war. The UN attempted the same process with the police. They discovered that many applicants who were previous upholders of the law were indeed the worst offenders during the brutal civil war. Russell looked at his friend and said, "You have done well in your military career so far." Russell added. "Liberia is lucky to have you."

"We have seen so much violence. Now is the time for peace. From the war, there are very few jobs. The military is one of the few steady jobs." Forleh thought about this county's situation and felt embarrassed. "America will always be Liberia's big brother, and we need you more than ever." Russell pledged that he would do all possible to help. They walked the entire perimeter. Russell did not just want to clear his head, but he also wanted to examine the ten-foot-high walls and security as he would remain there for the next several days.

At the new Al Qaeda camp, Kamal watched as the three brothers loaded Fatima into the back compartment of the enclosed truck. Fatima rested on a stretcher made out of wood and old clothes. She did not move. Blood trickled from her ears. The three brothers were careful not to get close to her. The Frenchman injected Fatima with the blood of an Ebola survivor, which Kamal had transported from the Central African Republic. After Fatima was infected with Ebola, she became a test subject. Kamal believed the blood from an Ebola survivor could cure someone infected. However, in this case, it did not work as Fatima was near death. Hassan wanted the test subject before she died to continue the experiment. Kamal watched as the three brothers loaded Fatima in the back of the truck. She was expendable. The large diesel truck lumbered out of the camp.

The Frenchman watched from the window of his cage as the vehicle departed. He knew what was next. Everyone in the camp knew what was next. The new terrorist recruits came out in droves from the old barracks. Kamal sharpened the long butcher's knife with a sharpening stone for almost an hour. At times, Kamal looked up and smiled at the Frenchman. A crowd had formed around Kamal. His men yearned to see the infamous Kamal kill the foreigner. A video camera was set up. Several followers pulled the Frenchman out of his cell. He was repeatedly beaten with punches and kicks. Kamal yelled at the infidel, "Death will come to all who do not obey Mohammed." The Frenchman whimpered in horror as he observed the scene that unfolded in front of him. Kamal waved a sword back and forth over his head. Forty devoted followers chanted. "Death, death, death." Kamal looked at them and shouted, "Sharia law will rule the world." Kamal wanted the Frenchman to suffer more. Kamal walked a hundred yards up the hill toward his bungalow.

A sound, similar to a large gust of wind caught Kamal's attention. As he turned, a missile from a CIA drone struck the barracks and exploded. The fireball plume ignited the building. The explosive force ripped apart the barrack's foundation. Kamal watched as the entire front wall collapse. He did not hear anything. The force of the concussion waves deafened him. Kamal held his hands over his ears as he ran toward the bushes. He did not wait to see the second missile that struck the area where several survivors stood up. The third missile struck his bungalow and obliterated it.

Down the road, the three brothers drove without knowledge of the attack on their camp. The jungle was thick, and they did not see the fireball or smoke. They continued toward Monrovia. The roads were filled with motorcycles and locals who walked in the middle of the road. Motorcycles veered in and out of traffic. The oldest brother honked the horn repeatedly, yet it had little impact. The rainy season would arrive at any moment, and the locals knew that this was probably the last chance to obtain any supplies or fresh food. The afternoon clouds remained and started to form more clear signs of rainclouds. The first drops came slowly. Within a moment, a torrential rain ensued. The wiper blades on the large diesel truck partially worked. Motorcycles sped faster as riders attempted to get out of the storm's path. The headlights on the truck were ineffective in the heavy rain.

The three brothers cursed at the rain and leaned forward to look out the window. They wiped away the interior fog on the windshield. The brother in the middle shouted, yet it was too late as they hit a man on a motorcycle. They kept going. The road ahead was packed with locals as they moved to get out of the tumultuous rainfall. Traffic became a complete standstill. The crowd was thick as the locals rushed for cover. The brothers heard something bang against the rear of the truck. Bang. Again, another bang. By the time the brothers got to the back of the truck, several robbers were already inside. The looters illuminated the back of the truck and were surprised to see nothing of value inside the locked truck. The three brothers fought their way through the crowd to the back of the truck. The commotion caused a lot of interest and more would be robbers descended upon the open truck. Fatima jumped out and pushed through the crowd toward Bushrod Island. In the dense rain, blood flowed openly from her nose and ears. Fatima struggled to stand, yet she rushed quickly into the crowd and vanished. The dense rain washed away the blood from her face; however, just for the moment.

Chapter 14

The annual presidential gala was the highlight of the Liberian social calendar; however, it was postponed twice as the President had to undergo minor surgery in Paris. Many wondered if the President would even return as the newspapers had photographs plastered across the front page that showed a pile of luggage being loaded onto a private jet. Many speculated that the President took out large amounts of cash from the national treasury. Mistrust of government officials was commonplace in Liberia, especially as Liberia had a long history of governmental corruption and hostile military coups. Based upon all of the negative press and scrutiny, the President made a point that they would host the annual presidential gala no matter what – regardless of the rain.

The thick rain came in waves during the past forty-eight hours. Liberians prepared as best they could as they braced for the impact of the rainy season. Scrap pieces of wood and metal were used wherever possible to seal up holes. Most of the government buildings leaked. There were no computers to worry about, just papers. And the government workers put cardboard above their desks to keep things dry. Monrovia residents had a much harder time as many of the cement buildings had no roofs at all. Artillery bombs and resulting fires from the civil war destroyed many buildings that subsequently were never rebuilt. Water poured into the hollowed buildings and flooded the staircases. In the streets, children played in the massive mud puddles, against the will of their parents. From the downspouts poured water and naked children took showers while adults watched them in plain view.

Russell looked out from his bungalow at the BTC compound and debated if he should wait for Kitson or make a sprint for it. He was much faster than Kitson and leaped into the rain. They both moved as fast as possible to dodge the onslaught. They hurried into the vehicle.

"Wow," Russell said, "I forgot how much it rained here."

"Second wettest place on the planet," Kitson said as a matter of fact. Hawaii had the lead spot for rainfall, and West Africa was second.

"I didn't know you had a uniform to wear," Russell said. Colonel Frank Kitson Jr. wore his British Army dress uniform. On the sleeve of his jacket, there were embroidered crests of the British Crown. On his shoulders were the rank insignia designations of a Colonel. Russell thought how the American military equivalent rank was an eagle, an American symbol of pride. The British version resembled the British Crown.

"It was flown in on a routine military transport out of Heathrow." Kitson referred to London's international airport. Russell thought that most of Kitson's items must have been placed in storage after his wife passed. He entrusted lifelong friends to care for his personal items.

"Is that the Queen's Medal?" Russell asked. "The one you told me about?" Kitson nodded and did not say anything.

Contrary to the award process for the American military, the British did not give out many medals. A decorated British soldier may only possess four to six medals that they earned over a twenty-year career. Colonel Frank Kitson wore six medals on his chest below a master parachute badge that he earned while a liaison with America's Delta Force in the late 1990s. Russell looked at the first medal in order and noticed the symbol of the British Crown above a medallion that had light blue and white fabric. Kitson received the Queen's Medal as a Second Lieutenant in Northern Rhodesia. There were only six of these medals ever issued, and Kitson was the only living recipient. Russell knew the story well as a young British officer walked out into the blazing sun to negotiate the surrender of rebel factions.

During the brutal civil war, many of the farms owned by the white Rhodesian were raided. They received retribution for decades of abuse. Many were butchered and hung upside down to bleed out. Wild animals chewed on the bodies. A cease-fire was declared and the magistrate, Ian Smith, declared Rhodesia would be divided into two nations: Zimbabwe and Zambia. The young Kitson was entrusted with a platoon of twenty-eight men. There were over four hundred rebels in the area. Kitson believed that they would be slaughtered. He needed to do something. Kitson walked out in the open, over five hundred meters as his men watched with their weapons ready to fire. Kitson sat and waited in the blazing sun for hours. Sweat dripped from his body, yet he remained still and waited. As the sun set close to the horizon, a gleam of light blinded him and his men. Hundreds of rebels who were heavily armed surrounded him. As the leader dismounted a horse, Kitson offered him some of Britain's finest tea. As Kitson poured the tea, a reporter with the London Times snapped the iconic photo. One front-page caption back home read, '*Young British Officer Captures Rebels with her Majesty's Finest Tea.*' Kitson thought about his award over the years. It seemed like a lifetime ago, yet he knew one thing that he saved his men from slaughter.

Kitson pulled out a flask of alcohol and drank two large sips. He passed it toward the back seat. The rain pounded the vehicle's metal roof, and Russell thought the sound resembled heavy machinegun fire. It was miserable weather, yet they had to make an appearance. Kitson had persuaded Russell that they must attend the gala to keep up the hope that everything would be alright in this post-apocalyptic nation.

"For God and Queen," Kitson said as he raised a glass to toast.

"For America," Russell replied. It sounded awkward, yet the only thing he could think of to rival the famous British quote.

At the same time in the Monrovia clinic, Doctor Abuja kept the surgical mask tight against his skin as he operated. From his years of training at the CDC, he instinctively knew never to touch his face with blood-soaked hands. He was extremely thirsty and completely exhausted. His stomach growled from lack of food, yet he pushed himself. The locals preferred foreign doctors, and they lined up for service.

"Next patient?" Doctor Abuja asked. There were four tables crammed into a room that was supposed only to have one. Blood pooled haphazardly on the floor. Blood splattered against the wall resembled something out of a horror movie.

"Another gunshot," Featu shouted as she pulled the body off the rusted steel gurney. She kept the blood-soaked rag tight against the patient's body with the assistance of two strips of duct tape. Blood contaminated with HIV was a threat, and no one knew who was infected and who was not. Featu knew how to effectively treat gunshots.

"Chest wound!" Doctor Abuja shouted to Sam. He worked at the table behind him on a patient who had been shot in the leg. The man had hobbled over a mile to the clinic. The man had waived toward taxis, yet no one stopped for someone who was openly bleeding. Sam looked over his shoulder at the patient.

"Do we attempt to save him?" Sam asked. It was the solemn oath that all doctors undertook to save lives regardless of the circumstances. Sam watched the blood gush upward as he tore away the duct tape.

"Need a surgical tube." Doctor Abuja snapped. "Got a bleeder." Sam dropped the bandage that he had started to wrap around the man's leg. The patient grabbed firmly onto Sam's lower arm. There was no medicine to put patients out completely. Few morphine ampules remained. The patient with the leg wound was not worthy enough of the painkillers. The man with the chest wound had received one morphine ampule. Sam pushed the man's hand away and moved quickly toward the other surgical table. With his hands, Sam promptly plunged a surgical tube into the man's chest and his right lung.

"Under control," Sam replied as he completed the procedure. The patient breathed heavily into the surgical tube.

Sam looked at Doctor Abuja and observed his eyes. They were both exhausted. For the past fourteen hours, they have attempted to save lives. They have not had any food or water since they walked into the room. Both brought an extra change of clothes as they knew the threat of contaminated blood made cleaning impossible. Everything would be burned. Sam and Doctor Abuja worked on the chest wound for another ninety minutes.

"Doctor are you alright?" Sam asked his mentor. "I can finish the procedure."

"No....no," Doctor Abuja replied. "I can stay longer." He paused for a moment and looked upward from the chest wound. His eyes rolled backward, and he staggered slightly.

"Doctor?" Sam spoke loudly. He did not get a reply. He repeated himself, even more loudly. "Doctor?" And now he shouted. "Doctor Abuja, are you alright?" There was no response from Doctor Abuja as his body crumpled under its weight toward the floor. Sam released the surgical tube and quickly grasped the instrument that kept the vein closed. He focused on the patient as Doctor Abuja crashed toward the floor. Sam quickly moved his hands as he stitched the pierced vein. Featu lifted Doctor Abuja out of the operating room as Sam finished closing the chest wound. He bandaged the wound and rechecked the vital signs. He had no time to guess if the man would survive. Sam went back to the man who had been shot in the leg. The patient looked up into Sam's eyes. Death was all around him, and the man nodded gratitude. Sam had no medicine to provide the man. As Sam tightened the bandage, the patient grimaced in pain. Sam nodded to Featu, and she removed the patient. Two more bodies replaced the previous ones.

Across Monrovia, violence had gripped many who lived in the poorest areas of the city. The wealthy lived in secluded compounds with hired guards for protection. The most impoverished citizens lived day to day for survival. They scrounged an existence out of whatever was available. Former children soldiers had no place to go and formed motorcycle gangs. They evoked fear. During the day, they slept. But at night, they terrorized their fellow countrymen. Guns were illegal in the post-civil war, yet plentiful on the black market. Some had dug up buried weapons hidden from the UN inspectors. Others used machetes as their weapon of choice. Across the city, violence had spiked.

As Ike drove the vehicle down the deserted streets, the heavy rain pelted the windshield. Kitson tried to look out the front but to no avail. He motioned for Ike to slow down more as visibility was near zero. The road to the Liberian Cabinet passed the hollowed shell of the former Presidential Palace that Tolbert, Doe, and Taylor lived in. Russell looked out the car's window at the building. The heavy rain and darkness made the Presidential Palace seemed like a horrific haunted mansion. The former Presidential Palace was over three football fields long and four stories high. In its day, the entire Liberian government worked there. Under the Doe regime, horrific events occurred. Tortures, molestations, and executions were conducted in the basement. Enemies of Samuel Doe disappeared in the middle of the night - never to be seen again. Sometimes bodies were tossed from the cliff behind the mansion into the ocean for the tides to take away. Rumors circulated that Doe built a large furnace in the basement to burn the bodies as a way to hide the evidence. There were many rumors to the brutality conducted in the official government building, and most stories were factual.

The line of vehicles extended down the street as many dignitaries remained inside their vehicle as a means to avoid getting soaked. Ike informed Kitson and Russell that he would drive them right to the building. There were no protests as the rain became thicker and thicker. The first deluge of the rainy season was always the worst as the moisture had been held for a long time in the atmosphere over the northern African coast.

Kitson and Russell jumped out of the vehicle before Ike could attempt to open the doors for his guests. Ike jumped back into the vehicle and drove down the street to wait.

"I am Mister Russell," He said to the Liberian police officer who checked the invitation list for his name. "I am on the British guest list." Russell knew the Ambassador would not have approved his invitation from the embassy personal list. There were very few Liberian police and Russell mused that it seemed most were at the presidential gala. Russell held back both his CIA and U.S. military credentials and provided forged invitations. The local guards looked at them with suspicion as it stated on special permission of the President of Liberia with the country's coat of arms. They allowed him to pass through the metal detector.

As Kitson walked through the metal detector, the alarm buzzed loudly. "Sorry, must be my commendation awards," Kitson said as he walked through the metal detector in his full-dress British Army uniform. The other item that contained metal was secretly hidden. Under his uniform, he kept a snub-nosed pistol that held two forty caliber cartridges. It was the size of his hand and was concealed very easily. Kitson did not trust Liberian security and speculated that there may be an assassination attempt on the Liberian President and wanted to be ready. Kitson knew the Liberian police would not question him.

Russell hated the idea of wearing a tuxedo and black tie, especially in Africa. As millions starved, he watched a handful of cooks who moved back and forth catering the buffet line. He pulled at his collar to loosen it up. Many of the dignitaries sent items to support the party, especially since resources were very limited. The French sent pastries; the Russians sent alcohol; the Portuguese sent fish; the Chinese sent several ice sculptures; the Americans sent a giant slab of beef from Texas.

Russell had hoped enough dignitaries would be present to conceal his entry. Russell assumed he was persona non-grata for the event by the

U.S. Ambassador and hoped he would not run into her. He had little care for what she could do to his CIA career. Several dignitaries watched as Russell walked the receiving line to greet the Liberian President. Most of the U.S. Embassy staff knew that the Ambassador had tried to have Russell kicked out of the country and Langley told her to go to hell, which made the Ambassador even more determined to get Russell out of Liberia.

The ballroom was made by removing the cabinet member's desks. The marble floor was cleaned from decades of grime and revealed an ornate design with superb craftsmanship. Russell eyed the floor. As he moved his gaze across the ballroom, he caught a glimpse of a dancing couple. To his surprise, Russell watched his former lover and mother of his child dance close with the Frenchman. Russell admired how her tight fitted black dress silhouetted her perfect figure. Within a few moments, jealously raged.

"May I dance with the lady?" Russell asked the Frenchman who was surprised at the request. The French Ambassador was aroused by the beauty of this woman and was not pleased with the interruption. Russell did a formal bow to Francesca and took his hand. He moved in close. "What are you doing here?"

"Keeping my options open," Francesca replied sarcastically.

"With him?" Russell snapped back. "The French? Really?"

"Frenchmen are great lovers."

"To hell they are," Russell shot back.

"And you would have experience?" Francesca inquired. She knew how to push Russell's buttons. He pulled her close to him and squeezed hard against her lower back. He wanted to inflict pain, yet did not want to cause a scene. She breathed out a lot of air and pushed him away. She contemplated using a palm thrust to break his nose. They were indeed a dysfunctional couple.

"I want to see you tonight," Russell whispered into her ear. The sight of her with another man drove him mad with rage.

"Perhaps," Francesca pulled back and looked into his eyes. "But I must do something first."

Francesca walked toward the French Ambassador and pulled her body close to him. She spoke in French and moved in even closer. The French Ambassador, a sixty-year-old man, was beyond arousal. He did not notice that she pulled the badge out from the inside right breast pocket of his suit jacket. Russell observed the interaction and made the assumption that Francesca had just requested a romantic interlude. Russell found Kitson seated at the bar.

"Is everything alright?" Kitson asked.

"Same issue," Russell said sarcastically. "Another shithole … another shitty situation."

"Are you guys ever going to get back together?"

"Let me think about it," Russell paused while he drank a straight shot of the Russian vodka. "Hell no… we are never getting back together."

"Dysfunctional?" Kitson inquired.

"To say the least," Russell replied. "If she could kill me, she would." Russell waved for the bartender and motioned for another shot. "I must be too valuable alive for her not to put a bullet in the back of my head."

"She hates you that much?"

"Let me put it this way," Russell said coldly. "A highly trained Mossad operative gets impregnated by a CIA agent. What do you think they have to say in Tel Aviv?"

"Langley as well?" Kitson inquired. He ordered another drink to keep pace. He would never allow an American to drink more than him. It was a matter of British pride.

"They cleared me. I had to take a polygraph to show my allegiance to the red, white, and blue." Russell said. He thought for a moment and added. "I'm really surprised she had not killed me." The two of them began to drink heavily. The free Russian vodka tasted very good.

Francesca eyed the room one last time as she moved backward toward the terrace. When no one watched, she jumped over the side and landed fifteen feet below in the grass. Rain pelted her, yet she moved fast. She held the high heels in her hands as she ran barefoot. After five a minute drive, she was at the French Embassy. The wall surrounding the compound was tall, about eight feet in height. Francesca stripped down and donned dark pants. Gone were the fancy dress and high heels. Francesca was over the wall in a flash and entered the Ambassador's office from the rear door of the building. She found the safe under the carper behind his desk and cracked the safe after she drilled a hole and injected an explosive charge. Within the safe were many personal documents, several stacks of American cash, and a sealed envelope. She ripped it open and confirmed that she had the location for the safe house used to hold kidnapped girls destined to serve in Europe's underground sex trade.

Several hours later, Francesca looked across the street at the tall cement wall that protected the BTC compound. She mused to herself that this climb would be more difficult. The walls were over ten feet high and much more difficult to scale. She tossed a rope tied to a small grappling hook over the wall. She was inside the BTC compound undetected within a few seconds. Sounds from the church adjacent to the military camp echoed throughout the night as locals praised their savior. Slowly, she unlocked the bungalow's front door, and Francesca slithered into Russell's bedroom. She stripped naked as she walked toward the bed. She climbed under the mosquito netting and jumped on top of the inebriated CIA operative. Russell was surprised at first, yet he did not complain.

"Do you love your son?" Francesca looked into Russell's eyes. She was not one for small talk, yet she had some questions that had floated around in her for the past eighteen months. She called Russell once after her father attempted to kill him. It was a short, brief conversation – her trademark. Conversations with Francesca were short. She was not wired to sit down for hours with her girlfriends to chat about life's tragedies. She lived a tragedy every day. While she waited for Russell's response, Francesca mused that it would be interesting to attend a tea party with some ladies at a plush country club. They would talk about how their husbands have wandering eyes for someone much younger or complain about their maids. When they would ask Francesca how her day went, she would have an arcane reply that she just killed a terrorist with a kitchen knife. Her eyes sparkled while she looked at Russell.

"Until my death," Russell replied. "He will always be part of me."

"Is that soon?"

"Is what soon?" He shot back.

"Your death?" Francesca paused for a moment. "Do you plan to die soon?"

"Not if I can help it. There is still a lot more that I would like to do in life."

"Like kill more terrorists?"

"If that's what it takes to keep America safe," He said as a matter of fact. Russell looked at Francesca and held his reply for a moment. He wanted to be calculated and direct in his response to her. "Are you happy?" He stopped for a moment. "Are you content being an assassin?"

"If that is what you call it." She replied. "You have a strong desire to protect your country just as I do." Francesca thought for a moment. "Your CIA has no moral compass and has killed many more times than we ever have." Francesca was calculated and waited for the right moment to start implanting thoughts into Russell. "Your country is not on the verge of being wiped from the face of existence. Without the Soviet Union as the big bad boogieman, you have no direct threat to destroy your country."

"Al Qaida remains a threat."

"Three airplanes did not destroy your America," Francesca replied. "If anything, it woke your country up to what we experience every day."

"And what about it?"

"In Tel Aviv, there are evil people who will do anything to kill you," Francesca replied sharply. "Not just you, but your family, your children, anyone that shared your bloodline." She sat up and wrapped her chest in a sheet. She wanted Russell to focus on the conversation and not how her new breast implants looked. "Israel has fought for existence from the beginning. Many have forgotten the horrific atrocities in Nazi death camps. In my lifetime, my nation was invaded twice. We have been bombed. My mother was killed by a terrorist's bomb."

"I know," Russell responded in a soft voice. They never talked about Francesca's mother. "You were young."

"From the day of my birth, I was recruited and groomed to be Mossad." She stopped. "This is what I am, take it or leave it."

"How will this be for our son?" Russell wanted to know. He had worried every time intelligence reports had revealed another attack on Tel Aviv. He had an aerial map of the location his son stayed and looked at every morning when he woke up. The photo of his son, taken eighteen months ago, rested on his desk.

"What do you mean?"

"Should he come live with me in America?"

"Just him?" Francesca inquired. "What about me?"

"Do you think the Mossad will ever let you go?"

"There is only one way out of the Mossad, and that is a bullet in the back of the head."

"I could protect you," Russell said. "Langley could protect you." Russell thought for a long moment as he knew the stories of Americans who committed treason spying for Israel, and he wondered what if he could recruit the mother of his child to spy for America. As he held her close, Russell spoke softly, "If you came over to our side, we can protect you."

"Perhaps," Francesca replied. Now she had him. Francesca was highly manipulative and knew Russell could be easily recruited into the Mossad, especially as his son was in play. Francesca turned her head toward him, kissed Russell on the lips, and added, "I love you Tom Russell of the American CIA."

Chapter 15

The heavy, cold steel rain hammered Monrovia, and the temperature dropped nearly twenty degrees. A cold chill hung over the city. Coupled with the driving rain, it made a miserable existence. Faces peered from dilapidated buildings into the abysmal weather. There was no let-up. The rain was relentless. In the BTC bungalow, the heat between their bodies kept Russell and Francesca warm. From the night's activities, the mosquito net was torn from where it hung off the ceiling. Francesca crept quietly from the bed and slid onto the floor. Russell was dead sleep and snored loudly. She shivered in her nakedness and tossed on clothes she had found in Russell's drawer. Francesca looked around the room for any information for the mission and did not see anything. There was a notepad that had several scribblings on it with circles and lines drawn between the circles. Names were etched into the loops. She snapped a photo of the document. It could be useful. She moved like a panther around the room without a sound. She took one last look at the man whom she believed she loved. It was complicated, to say the least. Her father wanted Russell dead. Her son does not know his father. Her Mossad leaders wanted her to keep a close relationship with Russell and recruit him to spy for Israel – the whys she did not know yet. Francesca did not want to relive the previous evening and slid out of the bed as Russell slept hard.

"Well good morning," Kitson said as he looked up from his newspaper and coffee. "How did you get in here?"

"The usual way," She pulled out the key she had made from a set she stole from Russell. She waved the key in the air.

"You're off early," Kitson said. "Want some food, coffee?"

"Just coffee," She said. Kitson poured the thick, black contents into a mug. Steam rose in the coldness. They sat quietly for a few moments.

"Does Russell know?"

"Know what?" Francesca asked.

"That you love him," Kitson replied as he sipped the hot tea.

"Just protecting my interests." She replied with a slight smile.

"And your interest happens to always be when Russell is in a tenuous situation."

"Once this mission is over, I am leaving Africa."

"Are you certain?" Kitson pressed her as he knew that there was more to the story. Moreover, there was more to Francesca than any intelligence agency would ever obtain. Kitson read detailed MI6 reports on one of the world's most deadly operatives. Death and destruction followed her missions.

"There is more to life." Francesca blurted out. It was something Kitson did not expect.

"Now that you have a son," Kitson said as a matter of fact.

"Something like that," She paused for a moment and in a more confident tone repeated herself, "I am leaving Africa."

"To where?" Kitson inquired.

"Destination unknown," Francesca replied and added after a long moment. "Thanks for the coffee." The large sweatshirt loosely covered on her slim frame, but kept her warm in the morning rain as she hastily walked toward the front entrance. Her vehicle rested untouched on the outside perimeter.

On the other side of Monrovia, Fatima staggered between the buildings on Bushrod Island. She found little shelter as the throngs of people in the area were packed tight under the shelters. Anything that could be made into a roof was used as a means of housing. Sheets of cardboard were linked together, yet served as no protection. Rusted metal roofs had massive holes and the shelling during the civil war. Water rapidly entered the buildings. Plastic was a commodity and something that was quickly stolen if left unattended. There were Liberian police; however, there was no law on Bushrod Island. On Bushrod Island, it was survival of the fittest and the most violent prevailed.

Fatima shivered and kept the burlap sack she found wrapped tightly around her body. The rain penetrated her clothes, and the coldness sent a shiver up her spine. Several men drank in the corner of the room. They passed a bottle filled with palm wine back and forth. Several empty bottles of liquor were on the ground. With the rain, there was no work and little means to make a living. For many, there was nothing to do but drink. Local women knew better not to travel out alone, even during the daylight – not on Bushrod Island. Fatima caught the men looking at her, and she left the makeshift structure quickly. She stepped out into the drenching rain and walked into several massive mud puddles. Mud covered her legs. She placed her free hand against her nose and felt something warm. The blood dripped freely from her nose, and she held her hand against it to stop the bleeding. The rain washed away the blood that dripped from her ears.

Fatima saw shelter fifty feet in front of her that was packed with locals. She had nowhere else to go and staggered toward the open building that had a rusty tin roof overhead. In the former days, prior to the civil war, the building was a warehouse storing fresh fruit that waited for sea transportation to the European market. Fatima did not hear the four men approach from behind as they ran after her. The men splashed through the puddles with heavy feet as they descended upon their victim. Eyes peered out from inside the old warehouse as many watched in horror. Seconds ticked as if in slow motion as one of the men raised a stick and hit Fatima on the back of her head as he ran past. She tumbled over into a large mud puddle. She attempted to get up to her feet and was kicked in the face. More blood poured out. The men took her by the arms and dragged Fatima to an abandoned car. Fatima was at death's door and screamed at her attackers. Several of the men stared at the locals who peered out from the warehouse. No one did anything. Stares were traded back and forth. The older local women remembered the atrocities committed during the civil war.

A United Nations report estimated that more than eighty percent of Liberian women were assaulted sexually at one point or another during the fourteen-year civil war. The older women stared down the attackers. Blood erupted from Fatima's face and covered the men. They did not realize that they were just infected with the world's deadliest virus. Fatima's nightmare lasted over an hour as the men cycled in and out of the back of the abandoned car. The faces of the elderly women still peered out from the makeshift shelter at the violators of peace. No one said anything. There were no screams from the vehicle. When the men left, no one ventured out in the rain to investigate. Everyone cared more about their own survival. Fatima breathed her last breath. Contaminated blood continued to flow from every orifice. The attackers found shelter down the road and drank heavily into the night. Blood hung off of their clothes and rubbed against those in the way as they crowded close to get out of the rain. The Ebola virus was already in their system.

In the remote countryside, less than an hour from Monrovia, a convoy of vehicles drove in the thick rain. Kamal looked over his shoulder at the line of three cars and six trucks that lumbered down the beaten-up backroad. Kamal needed to avoid detection as he moved his new operation to the former Black Beret camp. He knew the CIA watched carefully, but he had to pass through the Firestone Rubber plantation. The plantation was over an hour from Monrovia and was something out of a socialist propaganda film.

The neatly lined streets with small brick houses made it look like something out of an old Soviet documentary. Everything was provided for the workers at the legendary rubber plantation that had been in existence since 1929. The Firestone Company had signed a ninety-nine-year lease with the Liberian government.

During the civil war, the remoteness of the plantation helped it avoid the onslaught of the violence. The buildings had not been changed in forty years and looked the same. The workers prided themselves on collecting rubber sap from the trees. The local market was built out of necessity and flourished. A school with actual running water was erected. There was no need for anyone ever to leave the plantation. The company hired its own doctor and nurse from Ghana and airdropped medical supplies every two months. Bartering back and forth was the primary means of how the plantation workers survived. There was a general store, but it was set up with accounts. There was no exchange of money. Workers built up money in their accounts and could receive a lump sum when they retired. Most left the money in their accounts; it was safer.

Kamal looked out the backseat window of the sedan. One of the brothers drove the vehicle. Kamal was furious that they had lost Fatima while delivering her to Hassan. The clothes hide the fresh wounds on the brother's back after Kamal thrashed each of them with a chain. The brothers did not scream as Kamal unleashed his fury. The brothers prayed to Allah for forgiveness as they were flogged. Kamal looked down at the bag that contained four syringes with what he believed would be a cure for Ebola. He did not want to dwindle his supply as he had more significant use for the antidote as the world's population became infected with the horrific virus. Kamal heard about a survivor, a woman who worked in a clinic at the northern beach. She would have to be captured and brought to Hassan. Her blood would be needed for the solution to the Ebola.

Kamal stood on the porch at the Black Beret camp and yelled at the new recruits. Several bomb makers had arrived from Somalia under fake passports and visas that showed them as Kenyan businessmen. They were adept at explosives and had participated in the building the car bombs that destroyed the U.S. Embassy in Nairobi. The bomb makers studied the plans that Kamal developed and worked on the remote trigger device. They smuggled several electronic components in gutted out laptops. Liberia customs was not robust enough to electronically examine the laptops to see that there was nothing inside but electronic components to trigger a bomb.

Kamal sat on the porch that was the same building previously occupied by the British and American spies, Kitson and Russell, five years ago. The jungle had taken over most of the camp in the past five years. There was much work to happen, and Kamal whipped the backs of the new recruits with a long stick. As darkness arrived, Kamal laid out an ornate prayer rug and began to chant loudly. Afterwards, he walked toward the fire. Kamal was worshiped like a god by the men who sat around the fire. Word spread quickly among the villages that Kamal had arrived in the area. Legends were told about his fight against the Americans in the Tora Bora mountain region in Afghanistan and how Kamal had moved into Pakistan with the rest of their Taliban brothers.

"The American is getting to close to the truth," Kamal said. "If the American CIA finds out about what we have planned, it will surely end our mission here." His new recruits listened intently to every word out his mouth. Kamal provided guidance to his men and said. "We can never use radios or phones and must always travel at night." He pointed his finger upwards, "Because the CIA satellites are watching."

"One bullet to the head, just give me the order and I will finish the American." One of the new recruits proclaimed.

"Patience." Kamal paused and drank some tea. The rich taste reminded him of a flavor in his native Cairo. When Kamal was at Cairo University, he studied late into the night, and the thick coffee helped him pass his medical board exams. Kamal missed many things from his native land. Kamal had a trial in absentia and was convicted of his parent's murder. He would never return to Egypt. Kamal looked at the brother and said. "The American will meet his fate soon enough. To get him, we must get to his Mossad girlfriend." He handed several photos. "These were taken two days ago. Wherever she goes, we will find the American CIA enemy. Now is our time to inflict damage and kill the Israeli spy."

The rain stopped temporarily and the morning sunshine broke across the horizon. It was a temporary reprieve from the rainy season onslaught, such was a common occurrence as one day of horrific weather would be followed by beautiful sunshine on Africa's West Coast. Russell walked out of the U.S. Embassy after his call with Langley. He stopped at the Cape Hotel for coffee. A private security guard stood outside of the hotel gate and opened the gate for him. Anwar had added another four men to his security detail, making a total of twelve. Anwar had informed his foreign travelers and dignitaries that the Cape Hotel would provide twenty-four-hour protection. New room charges were added to the hotel bills. Everything was paid in cash, and the safe was full. Weather planners predicated the rainy season would continue tomorrow, yet for one day Liberians rejoiced to have sunshine again. The mental fatigue of day after day of rain wore on the populace. Children raced across the beach. Russell watched from the balcony as locals enjoyed the sunshine.

Francesca slammed the horn and waived for Russell. As he approached the vehicle, he sensed something was not right. He looked in the back and saw several boxes covered with blankets.

"Where you going?" Russell asked.

"Two hours north," Francesca said and added. "I need your help." Russell knew that it was rare to hear Francesca ask for anything. Against his better judgment, Russell climbed into the front seat. He watched

Francesca's as she shifted the clutch and launched the vehicle into drive. She smiled and shifted the vehicle into full throttle as she navigated out of the gate. Pedestrians who walked haphazardly across the busy road jumped out of the way. Francesca weaved the vehicle through oncoming traffic. A truck lumbered in their direction. She saw the vehicle coming and sensed that the driver would not slow down. Francesca jumped the curb to avoid a collision.

Two months ago, a Canadian doctor stopped his vehicle after he collided with a motorcycle. He and the three nurses that were in the vehicle attempted to assist. The motorcycle driver screamed in agony and yelled that it was the foreigner's fault. A curious crowd grew within seconds. Many men in the crowd started to shout that they should take the victim to the Jordanian Hospital since the white man had struck him. The familiar slogan in Liberia was the foreigners get taken care of at their own hospital while the locals go to Monrovia General Hospital to die. The crowd became more enraged as the doctor said they would take the injured driver to the local hospital. Men pulled the driver out of the vehicle. Several enraged men beat the doctor. A few others attacked and pulled the nurses out of the vehicle. The vehicle windows were shattered. The three Canadian nurses were assaulted in the street. The injured motorcycle driver screamed in agony as no one had helped him. Such was the existence in post-war torn Liberia with limited few police officers.

Russell held his hand to the passenger side door very tightly as Francesca zigzagged around traffic. She shifted fast on the clutch pedal and gear shift. The vehicle jerked and launched forward as she navigated the busiest stretch of roads in Monrovia. "Are you going to tell me where we are going?" Russell asked.

"Out of town," She paused and added, "toward Sapo."

"What's there?

"Young girls were kidnapped and will end up in a brothel in some European city if we don't act now."

"How did you hear about this? Russell looked at her. From the directness in her voice, Russell sensed Francesca was pissed.

"My last mission in Nigeria was to expose a human trafficking ring that stole girls for the Boko Haram. What I discovered was a robust smuggling operation that operated freely in post-war-torn African nations that sent young girls to live as sex slaves in Europe right under everybody's nose. These girls are tortured and forced to work as sex slaves or be killed."

"I bet Voctrad is behind it," Russell added. "These former KGB bastards have a far-reaching influence on organized crime." Russell pulled out his phone to call Kitson to get his thoughts, but there was no reception. "How did you hear about this ring?"

"There was chatter last night about a big shipment of prized young girls from a West African country that had no protection against speed boats moving in and out. It did not take much to put two and two together and realize Liberia had now entered the market as one of the top producers of girls for global human trafficking. It used to be former Soviet states, and now it is Liberia."

"How much further?"

"About two hours should put us close."

"And how will we know."

"Easy, just wait for the bullets to start flying and watch for holes in the windshield."

The next ninety minutes were quiet. Neither of them wanted to talk about the previous night's romantic encounter. The ride was surreal. The break in the weather from the previous night's monsoon rainfall was a welcome relief. There was still a lot of tension between them. Russell looked over at Francesca several times and observed her tone arms exposed from the tank top shirt. She smiled back at Russell. There was no continued conversation from the morning when they awoke together. The drive was eerily quiet. Villages were very sparse. There were no signs that informed them of what community or tribal area they encountered. They did not slow down or stop. Children would peer out from behind their mothers at the two white folks who drove deeper into the country. Most were surprised to see a woman drive. Deeper into Liberia they pushed. Russell wondered if Francesca misjudged the time as they had driven for nearly two hours.

As they passed the last town before Sapo National Forest, Russell heard the distinctive sound of metal on metal contact. Another sound caught his attention as the round ricocheted off of the vehicle. The next two bullets landed in the windshield. Russell quickly surmised that Francesca was correct when they would arrive.

"Where's the shooter?" Francesca shouted as she slammed on the brakes. She shifted her head back and forth as she scanned the area.

"Should be straight ahead," Russell replied. He grabbed the submachine gun from the box in the back of the vehicle. Russell jammed a magazine clip into the weapon and shot several times toward the building. He used the sound of the weapon firing to create some noise and confusion as he ran toward a fallen tree. Out of the corner of his eye, he saw Francesca climb into the back of the vehicle. Russell fired the entire magazine of thirty rounds in the general direction of where the shots came from. As he dropped down behind the fallen tree to reload, more shots were fired at his direction. He estimated another three shooters had joined.

Russell took cover and looked at the vehicle. He was astonished to see the back door of the Land Rover launch open as Francesca's kicked the door. On her shoulder was a missile launcher. Her eye was on the lens, and she aimed the launcher toward the building. With the squeeze of the trigger, the missile burst out of the tube and exploded against the corner of the building. Smoke consumed the vehicle from the back blast of the missile launch. Russell popped his head over the log and observed a significant portion of the structure had collapsed. He wasted no time and ran toward the half-destroyed building. Smoke and dust filled the air. He heard cries inside, female shouts. On the ground, he saw two men as they rolled around in agony. Both appeared to have abdominal wounds. Blood soaked their shirts. He looked at them and thought for a moment how he could help them. The moment evaded him as Francesca walked up and squeezed the trigger of her Desert Eagle fifty caliber pistol. She leveled the cannon of a pistol on the other man. He looked up and grimaced as she blew his head apart.

"No prisoners?" Russell inquired. He assessed the situation rather quickly as he saw several women run out of the smoke. They screamed irrationally and waved their hands in the air. Over forty girls ran out of the building through the gigantic hole caused by the missile. Russell observed that the front doors were sealed on the outside by several chains and locks. Even the men who guarded the girls were not allowed to leave. Russell followed Francesca into the haze. She stepped on a dead body. Russell was startled as Francesca put a bullet in the dead man's head. Parts of his skull flew in the air. Francesca kicked open the office door.

"Here." She paused and shouted. "Help me!" Francesca grabbed a pile of papers out of the box.

"What are these?"

"Orders," Francesca said coldly. "Orders for girls across Africa."

"These documents are in French," Russell had no idea what the document meant.

"I know." Francesca pulled out the envelope that she stole from the French Ambassador's safe. "Human trafficking is one of the most overlooked criminal offenses in the world." She handed the document to Russell. He opened it and observed locations on maps, yet he did not understand French. He shrugged his shoulders and handed it back. Francesca interpreted it for him as she said. "It basically says that Liberian girls are kidnapped from these tribal areas, brought into Sapo where they are marked for international sale, and smuggled out of the country."

"And that was why you danced with the French Ambassador?" Russell asked. He felt stupid for his previous jealous rage.

"To get his access card and break into his safe."

"Are you going to kill him?"

"In this case, no." She read the documents. "From what I got out of his safe, there's enough here to publicly humiliate him." Russell was amazed that she had not put a bullet in the back of his head. Francesca sensed that Russell was not convinced she would not kill the French Ambassador. She added. "When I lived in Paris, the one thing that I realized that would hurt a Frenchman more than death was public humiliation. The French are brutal in the tabloids." Her experiences in Nigeria opened her eyes to human trafficking, and she was committed to doing everything to end the savagery.

"We would prosecute him just as fairly as the international court." Russell defended his country.

"Yes, but you have human smuggling all over America and what had been done with it." She replied. Russell knew that she had a valid point and looked down at the documents.

"So, what about these scumbags who placed the order." Russell looked at several names on the document and addresses.

"These men," Francesca pointed at the papers, and she replied in a very harsh tone. "We can hunt them down where they live in Europe."

Chapter 16

Inside of the newly refurbished hangar at MacArthur Airfield, Checkov watched the scientists smuggled into Liberia as they welded a large piece of metal onto the cylinder tube that was over ten feet long. They used Cold War era instruments to check for leaks and found several caused by age along the joints. The weapon was made form Tungsten steel with a Cobalt alloy was still the same color as it was from 1962 when it was forged. The elongated chamber remained open, and the motor was pulled apart. The shafts and gears were intricately removed, labeled for the exact position, and dropped into a fifty-five-gallon drum of lubricant. The bitter dry cold of Siberia had preserved the metal, yet the gears would seize if operated. The motor was not functional and required a complete replacement. There was nothing in Africa or in most of the modern world that would serve as a suitable replacement. The motor had to pressurize up to three pounds per square inch, something the Soviets has used in the Vostok space capsule.

After full assembly, the weapon's support arms would attach underneath a Syrian military jet and needed new welds to support the speed of the attack aircraft. The Soviet design had focused on much slower aircraft of the 1960s. Hassan's masterful plan focused on the use of a low flying aircraft at breakneck speed to avoid Israeli early warning systems. The Russian scientists needed more time to complete the weapon.

"When can the weapon be ready?" Hassan looked at his watch. He became more impatient as more problems were identified.

"A new motor is critical for operation." Checkov pointed to the parts all over the table that his scientists had ripped apart.

"These delays put the plan at risk." Hassan became more adamant that the timetable must be adhered with. They were far behind schedule and every extra day placed the operation at risk of being discovered. "The Americans are getting too close to finding the truth." Hassan had moved the families of many of his Hezbollah operatives out of Monrovia and into the Marshall compound. A tanker ship had anchored four miles offshore. Liberia had no Navy to check on the vessel, and many believed that the boat had a mechanical failure. Hassan planned to transport over two hundred and fifty Lebanese via speedboats to the tanker ship. From there, they would seek refuge in Libya.

"Several more days," Checkov said. "We need several titanium parts that are only available from the Siberia base. Voctrad has sent a courier to fly with the critical parts."

"When we purchased this weapon, it was on condition that it would work," Hassan said as he tested the Russian. Hassan had paid over two million dollars in rough cut, untraceable diamonds.

"You will receive the weapon when it is ready," Checkov stated boldly. "I will deal with the American CIA man."

On the other side of Monrovia, Doctor Abuja looked around the room for a clean dressing and could not find one. The patient had a knife wound in his back as he ran away from a fight. He informed Doctor Abuja that it was a robbery attempt. Doctor Abuja did not judge. He served all of his patients without question. The man pleaded his story was true as he thought that would help his cause. He did not want to go to Monrovia General Hospital. With his open wound and blood freely flowing, he might have been mistaken for an Ebola patient and stuck with all of the dying.

News of an Ebola outbreak on Bushrod Island launched fears all across Monrovia, mainly since many previous Ebola outbreaks occurred in the remote countryside. Newspapers had quotes from the Liberian President that the situation was under control. No one believed the Liberian government or UN officials for that matter. In the newspapers, photos of men wearing what looked like space suits were taken. Several local men brought to Monrovia General had escaped when they heard that they were infected. Doctor Abuja's worse fears had come true as he folded up the newspapers. He neatly added paper to the stack that he would bring to the UN headquarters in order to lobby for more Ebola research funding. Newspaper images of patients with bruises and blood covered faces struck fear in many. Fear was rampant. No one could be trusted.

At the clinic, the local man informed Doctor Abuja that he was clean of the Ebola, and he would have taken care of the wound himself; however, it was in his back, and no one from his own family would touch him. Doctor Abuja nodded as he fully understood the rapid change in conditions on the ground. Anyone seen with blood flowing in an open wound could not be trusted. Anyone seen with the signs of severe illness would not be trusted. Anyone seen with drips of blood from their nose or ears could not be trusted. Everyone was deemed infected. Within a little less than a week, the horrific fear of Ebola had arrived; every Liberian feared for their lives.

Russell walked into the clinic with a box of medical supplies. Russell looked at the primitive conditions. The windows were boarded up. Wires hung several light bulbs. There was no fan to circulate air in the room. Stale air and the smell of sweat permeated. The blood-soaked rags littered the ground, or at least Russell thought that they were bloodstained. Doctor Abuja had on a mask and motioned for Russell to put one on his face.

"Is he infected?" Russell inquired with a sense of worry. He watched the doctor inspect the patient. He was very thorough.

"Hard to say." Doctor Abuja looked the man in the eye as he continued to stitch up the wound. Doctor Abuja had a surgical face mask and rubber gloves as his only protective means. "He has lost a lot of blood?" Doctor Abuja sensed the worry from Russell, and they stepped outside.

"Your clinic is at risk," Russell stated. "If an Ebola patient comes here, it will be disastrous."

"There are so many plagues running rampant around Africa." Doctor Abuja pontificated for a moment. "From the cradle of civilization, it can create enough death to wipe out all mankind."

"Is there a cure?" Russell needed to know. On a dingy Monrovian street, in a war-torn country, Russell looked at the most knowledgeable man in the world on combating Ebola. Russell watched his body movement and continued. "You don't think there is a cure?"

"Several years ago, we worked on finding a cure. It was a long project that took eight months. We were taken to the Nevada desert, far away from Las Vegas, at some old military base. There were four scientists including me. I was the only one from the CDC. The other scientists were from research universities. Every day, we worked on a hybrid gene that could be used as an antidote for a virus."

"Such as Ebola?" Russell asked.

"Yes, for Ebola, for the Hantavirus, Small Pox, and other of the world's deadliest diseases. We were dedicated and thought we were making a difference." Doctor Abuja said.

"What happened?"

"We were close to a solution. Claudia Marks from Harvard Medical School found what we thought was a solution by attacking the membrane that enclosed the virus." Doctor Abuja was silent for a moment. Russell sensed that the man attempted to recall every facet. "The solution seemed plausible."

"Is there a solution to destroy the virus?"

"Not just a solution, but a means to generate antibodies to eradicate the virus. We tested it against other deadly viruses. We were careful, so very careful." Doctor Abuja listed his clean shirt sleeve to wipe several tears from his eyes. "We made all necessary precautions."

"What happened?" Russell pressed him for more information.

"Because we dealt with such deadly plagues, we each were moved into quarantined zones. We could see each other through the large glass walls. We had curtains to change and shower. We could hear one another. Everything was recorded. In our fourth day of testing the antidote, Claudia became sick, and several large scabs appeared on the side of her face."

"Smallpox?"

"Yes." Doctor Abuja looked down at the ground. More tears flowed. "To this day, I do not know how she could have contracted the virus."

"Did you try the antidote on her?"

"It was one of the first things we did, and she got worse." Doctor Abuja sat on the ground next to the cold concrete wall on the dingy street.

"Did you finish the research?" Russell sensed something was not right. He looked down at one of the most brilliant men in the world.

"We were all despondent. It was so hard to watch a colleague die from Smallpox in front of you. We worked hard to modify the antidote." Doctor Abuja looked down at the floor as he continued. "We did not sleep for days. I started to hallucinate from lack of sleep. Eventually, the project was shut down."

"And the other scientists?" Russell inquired. "Did you ever keep in contact to try to resolve the antidote?"

"Yes, but several months after, Nicholas was killed in a car crash with his family and the other scientist Katrina took her own life with sleeping pills. I am the only one left."

"You're the only one alive?" Russell asked. Doctor Abuja nodded and sunk his head between his legs to cry. The sharp cries of pain echoed down the alley. As Russell walked away from the dingy alley, he pulled out his satellite phone to call Langley.

The Cape Hotel seemed desolate and had fewer visitors than usual. As Russell walked into the hotel compound, he saw Tareeq help load luggage into vans to transport foreigners to the airport. Additional flights were added to carry frightened foreigners out of Liberia. The planes arrived empty and departed packed full. At the U.S. Embassy, the line of Liberians who attempted to gain an exit visa to travel to America increased substantially. They wanted out too. Russell heard that the new scheme that was perpetrated involved locals who visited relatives and then sought asylum due to the Ebola threat.

Russell pulled up a bar stool and watched 'Play it again Sam' jam out some classical music on his piano. The sounds were different, more patient, more linked to the current situation. Gone were the happy sounds that he played. Any sounds of happiness would be a frail attempt at keeping everyone calm. 'Play it again Sam' played several famous pieces from Nina Simone, the legendary African American singer.

"Are you staying?" Tareeq asked Russell. "Many foreigners are leaving Liberia." He sensed something and looked Russell in the eye. "I assume you have more to do here?"

"Do you know where Checkov is?" Russell said as he twisted the glass full of scotch around.

"He has gone deep undercover," Tareeq replied. He looked around the room quickly to see if any of the Russian goons were present. He had not seen any of them in several days. "We have contacts all around the city, and no one has seen him. The Russians have many safe houses."

"Damn," Russell shout aloud. He wanted to say more, yet remained silent. Few could be trusted, and Russell needed to be careful. "Do you have any guests missing?"

"We have missing guests all the time," Tareeq said calmly. "Most are never found once they go missing. Sometimes their bodies are found on Bushrod Island." He looked at his glass. "If they go to Robertsport without our security team, they usually get kidnapped on the remote roads."

"This country has a lot of issues," Russell replied.

"There are a lot of bad people running around freely in this country." Tareeq poured himself a glass of scotch and slid the bottle toward Russell. They drank in silence for a moment.

"This must have been a beautiful country."

"Utopia," Tareeq said.

"Beg your pardon?"

"Utopia." Tareeq repeated himself, "Utopia in Africa. The only place where democracy and freedom flourished outside of evil dictators." Tareeq looked out the windows toward the rolling ocean waves. Locals crisscrossed the former pristine beach in front of the hotel. The beautiful resting spots of chairs, umbrellas, and tables were all stolen. The hotel compound was on lockdown. No locals were allowed inside. "This was a beautiful country."

"That was until Doe and Taylor took over." Russell sounded very cynical. "Back to back bastards who killed more Liberians than malaria."

"There is no future for us in Liberia." Tareeq thought for a moment and continued, "With no foreign workers coming, we have no business."

"Are you planning to leave Liberia as well?"

"There is nothing for us here," Tareeq said. "Maybe we go to America." He paused for a moment and thought about what Uncle Anwar told him about Hezbollah's plan. Everyone was trying to get out of Liberia – foreigner aid workers, locals, and now the Lebanese. Tareeq stared out the window for a long moment. Tareeq excused himself to tend to his few remaining guests.

Russell grabbed a table close to the piano and listened to the music. He poured a stiff drink from the bottle and looked at the alcohol in the glass. Russell did not want to think about the Ebola outbreak. He did not want to think about Francesca. However, he did want to think about his son. He had not seen his Dominic in a long time. The pain had been great. Russell was isolated from his son by the boy's grandfather and most definitely isolated by his CIA position. Russell drank in isolation. He stayed at the Piano Bar until close to midnight. One of Anwar's armed guards drove him the short five blocks to the BTC compound. Walking the short distance was not an option. Russell knew that he would have been an easy mark for robbery or even murder, especially after heavy drinking. Not to mention, Ebola fears were rampant, and no one was trusted, not even a foreigner.

In the morning, Russell found Kitson sitting at the table eating a plentiful breakfast that Ike had prepared. Ike enjoyed serving Kitson again, and he moved quickly around the room. Russell heard him humming a tune.

"Hungree?" Ike asked Russell.

"Thanks, Ike," Russell said as he sat down. "Any news on the Ebola outbreak?" Russell asked Kitson who was reading the Monrovia Gazette.

"Twenty more dead from the virus yesterday," Kitson said. "Paper says Monrovia General is overloaded, yet there are no local patients at the Jordanian Hospital. There is a quote from an anonymous UN official that Jordan will not allow its doctors to work on Ebola patients."

"I thought Jordan pulled out their medical teams three days ago?"

"They did, and they are all in a sixty-day quarantine in Cyprus before being allowed to go home," Kitson said. They both knew the local paper was full of incorrect information that has fueled protests and more unrest. "The situation has turned grave. At this rate, we could see four hundred dead a week. It still has only received sparse attention in the international news. But I know what's coming."

"Langley advised our State Department to freeze all flights leaving Monrovia until there is better testing on the ground at the airport."

"How are they going to do that?"

"Defense Department will have to set up a team at Roberts International Airport," Russell said. He looked at Kitson, and both men knew that it would not happen overnight and many would die. "The orders were given last night, and they are mobilizing."

"On the streets here, panic has set in," Kitson said as he drank his cup of coffee. "We need to make sure we stay Ebola free."

"That's ok. I should have died a long time ago in Iraq." Russell replied in a sarcastic manner.

"I'm not worried about dying," Kitson said pointedly. "I'm worried about killing these bastards before we succumb to being too sick to fight."

"There may be a solution," Russell replied. "An antidote." Russell spent several minutes detailing his conversation with Doctor Abuja and provided his thoughts on what happened with the three other scientists. Kitson listened patiently with his hands wrapped around the coffee mug.

"Do you think Doctor Abuja may have developed the solution?" Kitson asked. "An antidote?"

"If he did, it's locked away somewhere," Russell replied. "We've been at this game too long to have coincidental deaths in the same year and expect that no one had targeted assassination."

"Why not Abuja?" Kitson asked. "Why is he still alive?"

"There must be something else," Russell replied. "The UN has not made an effort eradicating infectious diseases in Africa. Billions of dollars have been spent, yet there is no trail for the money and very few results."

"Like the mosquito nets?"

"What about them?"

"There was a large shipment sent to Sierra Leone to help ward off mosquitos, and they were stolen. Within a day, the nets were being sold on the black market to locals and foreigners. Mostly foreigners purchased them. The locals can't afford to eat, let alone purchase something that they deem as a luxury on the black market."

"Was it an inside job?"

"Of course," Kitson shook his head. "UN shipments are well known and lucrative targets," Kitson replied. "Nothing comes into Africa without criminals knowing about it. For large shipments like this, Voctrad was behind it. They have a feeder system of local criminals selling stolen items, and they get the cash. If the locals steal from Voctrad, they end up dead."

"It's amazing how the Russians moved into Africa," Russell said.

"Voctrad has their dirty hands in every business in Africa," Kitson said as he drank his coffee. "From uranium, weapons, diamonds, gold, and sex slaves, they are plugged in."

"More than Al Qaeda?" Russell asked his mentor.

"Definitely," Kitson stated as a matter of fact. "Voctrad has been here since the fall of the Soviet Union and probably even before then. Russian operatives sought uranium in the Congo during the early 1960s."

"Yeah, I remember the Congo," Russell replied. The two of them had completed a mission there a year prior. Information on Voctrad started to appear as they unraveled a sinister plan that involved destroying the South African diamond district with the release of an old atomic weapon.

"What about Kamal?" Kitson asked. "Do you think he is dead from your CIA drone strike?"

"Don't know. When Ike and I looked around the camp, everything was pretty much destroyed, and bodies were beyond recognition. I took DNA samples from the bodies there and sent them off to Langley." Russell said, and he paused for a brief moment. "From what we provided, there were no matches for Kamal." Both of them wanted Kamal's head.

"Kamal's elusive." Kitson thought for a moment as he looked at an Africa map on the wall. "He could be in Libya or Algiers by now."

"I don't think so," Russell replied. He tugged at a large wooden crate and motioned for Ike to help him drag it out from the spare bedroom. The metal nails that held the wood together made a screeching sound against the tiled floor. "He's going to want this back." Russell lifted open the box lid and revealed shining gold bars. "There are three more boxes like this."

"Where did you get it?" Kitson inquired. He picked up a bar and was briefly mesmerized by the brilliance of color.

"At the abandoned army compound that Kamal took over, Langley did satellite imagery after the strike, and something did not add up. The missile destroyed the bungalow that Kamal stayed in, yet there was something untouched that must have been buried. It was easy to find these and damn hard to get them out of the hole."

"Must weigh about four hundred pounds." Kitson estimated.

"Probably. I just know Ike, and I nearly broke our backs lifting these out of the holes."

"Dunta ferget the truk," Ike said.

"Right," Russell continued. "And we almost broke the axle on the truck we borrowed from Anwar."

"Must be about twenty million dollars here." Kitson did a quick estimate in his head."

"Maybe." Russell thought for a moment. "I didn't tell Langley."

"Really?" Kitson replied with keen interest. "I know you don't like following the rules, but keeping twenty million in untraceable gold bars laying around, don't you think that perhaps dangerous?"

"There is too much at stake." Russell quickly replied. He knew the answer. He rehearsed the answer if Langley did find out. "We may need a bargaining chip."

"The Russians?" Kitson inquired.

"Precisely," Russell informed his mentor. "Voctrad plays by their own rules and when it comes to money."

"Or gold." Kitson tossed in.

"Right, gold," Russell continued, "They can be bought. If we can't find Checkov, perhaps we can bribe one of his co-workers."

"Let me get on that," Kitson replied as he pulled out his phone. He dialed an international number. "I have a contact in the Ukraine who may know of a Voctrad arms dealer."

Russell and Kitson agreed that the best means to safeguard the gold would be to bury it. They both concurred that there was only one location in Liberia that no one would think of looking. Russell and Ike drove back toward Robertsport. They drove down paths that appeared to be roads at one time in history. When they arrived at their destination, Russell looked across the water and thought for a brief moment how beautiful Liberia was. Thick clouds moved fast across the mountains in the distance. Sunshine beat down between the clouds. The rain would arrive later, and he knew that they had a brief repose from the torrential onslaught. Russell bent over and put his hand in the water to feel the coolness. He lowered his African bush hat into the water to soak it. He placed it back on his head. The wetness felt comforting. Ike pushed Anwar's boat into the water.

Ike motored the small boat close to the tall grass along the shoreline. There was still danger in the area as former child soldiers under the Taylor regime looted the area. Ike knew that there were attacks on fishing boats in the area. They used motorized boats that made it out to the open ocean, and they used the channel to travel deeper inland. Ike cut the motor and guided the boat into the tall grass.

"What is it?" Russell asked. "Rebels?" Ike put a finger to his lips and cut the engine. The boat guided to a stop against a fallen branch from a large tree that fell into the water. The hum of engines sounded louder and louder. Between the grass, Russell watched the two boats as they passed. There were four young men in each boat. AK47s were lifted in the air. Russell did not want a fight with the child soldiers. They had a mission to bury the gold. More importantly, their boat limbered very slowly with the added weight; at an extreme disadvantage. After ten minutes, Ike started the engine and thrust the boat in reverse to pull out of the tall grass.

Water flowed over the edge of the boat as Ike steered it out into the channel. The island was straight ahead. It could have been on the other side of the world as it took four times as long with the added weight. Ike opened the engine to full throttle, and the sound echoed across the water. Russell looked around with a set of binoculars to see if any rebels were nearby and there was no movement. He did not know how many rebels were in the area. Even with all of the CIA resources, no one could tell him how many boats or rebels were in the area. Ike had been his best resource. Ike estimated about sixty former child soldiers moved into the area after being released from prison in neighboring Sierra Leone, which was only a two-day walk. Ike released the throttle and the boat slowly guided to the island.

The weight of the boxes forced a significant amount of momentum. Ike had misjudged the distance to slow down and quickly thrust the engine into reverse. The engine screamed as the boat jumped into reverse. The boat struck hard against the shoreline. The large jolt knocked Russell out of the boat, and he landed in the shallow water. He quickly jumped up and moved to the island. Russell raised his sub-machinegun just in case there were any rebel inhabitants. After Ike cut the engine, the sound of birds erupted as the boat must have scared them. Russell waved for Ike to follow him.

Previously, the island had been a sanctuary for locals who hid during the civil war. Minister Urey hid here with his mother and sister while his father, a cabinet member in the Tolbert government, was executed and buried in a mass grave with many others. The island was too remote for Taylor's men to find the last remnants of Urey family. Others sought refuge from the brutality as well. Word passed among the locals of the secluded island, and the population increased rapidly. At the highest point, the island had over two hundred residents. The Urey's escaped from the island and made their way to Sierra Leone on foot and eventually found their way to freedom in America. Ultimately, all of the island's residents had escaped Liberia. The only resident of the island for the past three years was Lucy.

"Ike mus Lucy," Ike said as he looked down the path. Ike looked in the trees for his chimpanzee.

"Someone has been here," Russell said as he picked up a cut vine and waived it in the air for Ike to see. "Slow," Russell said. He trained the weapon on the trail.

A pungent order filled the air – the smell of death. Russell looked out as he lowered the weapon. The clearing had an open fire pit formed by several large rocks. He touched wood in the fire pit, and it was cold to the touch. To the left were several makeshift buildings formed by large branches tied together. Scraps of plywood and rusted tin dotted the exteriors and roofs. The humming sound of flies and the smell helped guide Russell to the dead bodies. Inside of the room, two men had their faces ripped off. Deep, penetrating scratch marks were noticeable. Their eyes held the horror of death.

"Wuz it Lucy?" Ike asked.

"Most likely," Russell replied. Russell looked out into the jungle for the five-year-old chimpanzee. Kitson had saved Lucy from the cookpot when the primate was just two months old. Kitson had paid forty U.S. dollars on the streets of Monrovia, and Ike kept Lucy with him until she got too big. Everyone knew that the chimpanzee would have grown to one hundred and forty pounds and more importantly had the strength of three grown men.

Russell kept his weapon leveled at the tree line. In the thick canopy, he saw a slight movement and debated to open fire. A large animal jumped down ten feet out of the tree and emitted a growl as it landed.

"No shuut," Ike said. "Lucy guud chimp." Ike stepped in front of Russell and walked toward the chimpanzee. He had tossed out a batch of plantains and stood still. The large chimp walked closer and gobbled up the fruit as she rested on her hind legs. Over the past three years since Ike moved Lucy to the secluded island, the chimp had grown more and became very territorial, hence the two dead bodies in the makeshift buildings. Ike had not visited the island in over six months, yet Lucy still remembered Ike. Ike turned to Russell and repeated himself. "Lucy guud chimp."

"Ok," Russell replied. "Let's get the box."

"Whut bout daad?" Ike asked as he pointed at the dead bodies. Russell turned back to look at Lucy. She did not look like a murderer. She was calm. She knew Ike. Russell knew better not to get close as she probably had forgotten him a long time ago.

"If any other rebels show up, they will be scared to hell and back." Russell walked to the small scrappy building and pulled one of the bodies out by his legs. The corpses would be entirely rotted in another month, and the skeleton bones would ward anyone off. Russell grabbed a shovel, counted one hundred steps north of the fire pit, and started to dig. Ike helped. Behind them, the grass rustled and they watched Lucy move behind them. Lucy sat behind several shrubs and watched the men dig a large hole. Russell and Ike carried the heavy boxes from the boat and rested them in the hole. Within several moments, the gold was buried. Gold that Al Qaida would never get.

Chapter 17

Kamal watched intently as his new recruits ran through the obstacle course that Charles Taylor's Black Berets trained on. This elite team ultimately became Taylor's personal death squads. The area had not been used for some time. Kamal heard the British resurrected the camp five years prior right after Taylor's departure. Some of the buildings were destroyed by the explosion that targeted the British Colonel, who happened to be Frank Kitson. Kamal looked at the hand-written note from Hassan and crumpled it up. The three brothers had let him down. Kamal thought about killing the three brothers, yet he needed them. Kamal had lost nearly thirty men in the missile strike, and the two-dozen new, fresh recruits would not be reliable enough for the next mission. He needed the three brothers.

"We need a survivor of the virus," Kamal said to the oldest brother who looked down at the ground. The oldest brother was ashamed of their failure. "There is word about a nurse who served in a clinic in the northern territory near Sierra Leone border." Kamal pointed to the map of Monrovia. "She is here." Kamal pointed to the clinic's location in Robertsport. "Here is a photo of her." Kamal handed a picture of Featu. "She is with this white man." Kamal pointed to the picture of Sam taken by the reporter from the Monrovia Gazette for his work opening a new clinic in Robertsport. The three brothers moved quickly out of the building. They needed to redeem themselves in the eyes of their ultimate master. Kamal watched them depart. He walked over to the tarp that covered a large pile. Kamal lifted the tarp and looked at the stack of artillery shells. There were over two hundred stacked in neat rows. The shells possessed enough explosive force to take down a large building. He had paid the rebels in untraceable, rough diamonds for the load.

Later in the evening, Russell and Ike arrived back at the BTC compound after they buried the gold. Russell was exhausted and slept in his clothes. In the morning, Kitson came into Russell's room and kicked his boots to wake him up. They needed to move as they had actionable intelligence. Kitson got information from his Ukrainian contact of the location for a Voctrad safe house. From the BTC compound, Ike drove the Land Rover away from Monrovia. The destination was over two hours away. Ike drove as Kitson and Russell sat in the back seats. In the passenger front seat, Ike kept a jacket that covered a machete, just in case. At times, Ike looked back at Kitson and Russell as they snacked on some of the food Ike had packed. Ike stopped the vehicle several times to ask questions from the locals. At each stop, Kitson gave the locals several Liberian fifty-dollar bills, about two dollars in U.S. currency, yet it could buy a day's worth of food. After three hours of driving and asking questions, they navigated toward the town of Buaccahan along the ocean in the southern part of Liberia. Ike heard from the locals about Russians moving into the area.

The locals were knowledgeable about the foreigners and provided a detailed location for the safe house. There were no roads into the area, just several footpaths. The locals said many white men moved in and out of the trails and were seen waiting beside the road for a van with no windows to pick them up. It did not take much calculation to put the puzzle together.

Russell and Kitson moved through the brush very quickly. Kitson asked Ike to remain with the vehicle as they needed the means to escape just in case. Russell watched the small house a short distance from his hiding spot. The safe house was concealed by overhung tree branches to shield the place from satellite imagery. Kitson knew the Russians were there. What Kitson did not realize was how many and how much firepower was present.

"We will have to wait," Russell said as he watched the path closely. After about forty minutes, he saw something. "We have movement. Thirty meters to the right of the house."

"Don't see anything," Kitson spoke softly.

"You will in three seconds," Russell whispered.

"Got 'em, Kitson replied. "Looks like they're dragging someone."

"Can't tell who it is with the hood on," Russell said. He peered through the binoculars. "Doesn't look like a dinner party there," Kitson replied. "The Russians are after something."

"Let's not give them an opportunity," Russell said.

"What do you think about prisoners?" Kitson said. He checked the magazine that was inserted correctly inside the AK47. He had a lot of experience with the AK47 and knew that he could toss it in the dirt and it would still fire. Regardless, Kitson was a professional soldier and always checked his weapons. "I am thinking none, what are your thoughts?"

"Let's at least find out what they are after first." Russell looked through his scope. A direct assault was the best means. He asked his friend and mentor, "Ready?"

"For God and Queen," Kitson said in the headset as he ran as fast as his body could take him. He looked half his age as he sprinted. For a sixty-year-old man, he was dominant. He lifted his leg and kicked the door hard. At the same time, he saw from the corner of his left eye Russell jump in the air straight toward the window. Russell smashed into the glass and entered the room as Kitson's foot slammed against the middle of the door. The three Russians were surprised, yet they still had the sense enough to start firing. Bullets bounced off the wall near where Russell landed. Kitson caught them off guard from behind and shot one in the back of the head. The other two spun around. Russell fired as he laid on the floor and sprayed the Russians in the back with the automatic fire. Kitson jumped out of the doorway back outside as several bullets came close to his head. He rolled onto the dirt outside and pulled his body against the wall.

"You ok?" Kitson yelled inside.

"All clear," Russell replied. "Two KIA and one with several holes in his chest."

"Well, let's help him meet his maker," Kitson said as he stood up and brushed the dirt off of his clothes. Even in civilian clothes, Kitson tried to remain impeccable.

"Kak vas zabute?" Russell asked the Russian his name.

"Yuri," He replied. "I speak English." He coughed up blood as he rolled onto his side.

"Good," Kitson said. "We have many ways to make you speak. You are dying." Kitson looked at him. "Do you wish to tell us anything?"

"Nyet," The Russian said, which meant no. Kitson looked at the Russian's wounds. He had a few moments of life remaining. He looked at Russell who shook his head. Kitson pulled out an eight-inch knife from its sheath and thrust it into the Russian's chest.

"We were not about to get anything from him," Kitson said.

"Who do we have here?" Russell asked as he pulled the hood off of the Liberian. Both men were shocked to see their Liberian liaison officer, Major Forleh, badly bruised about the face and unconscious. They searched the rest of the rooms in the house. There was nothing worthy of any intelligence. Russell dragged the bodies into the far room while Kitson tossed some water in a bucket. They spent the next thirty minutes cleaning up the mess. Russell knocked out the rest of the glass in the corner of the window and put a full window that he found in the kitchen in its place. To keep it together, he took some lard out of a can and plastered it on the edges to hold it in place. It was the best option. Russell carried Forleh out of the house over his right shoulder. The Liberian soldier weighed one hundred and forty pounds, yet he had no ounce of fat on him and was pure muscle.

Kitson checked the tension in the thin wire that ran ankle high across the interior door. They did not have many explosives and needed to make a dramatic impact with what they had. Kitson looked at the two grenades in the empty sauce can and made sure that they were packed tight before he pulled the pins. The plungers that would initiate the explosion did not move. Slowly, Kitson walked backward with his eyes on the booby trap. He had a lot of experience in Northern Ireland on these types of devices. Kitson mended the front door to conceal any damage.

"Whur to?" Ike asked. Ike had the vehicle started and helped load the battered officer in the back. Ike knew better than to ask any questions.

"We need to get him to a hospital," Russell said, "But I would not bring him to a Liberian hospital. The best option would be Sam. He and Featu are helping Doctor Abuja at the Monrovia clinic."

"It's a long ride," Kitson said. "Hopefully he can make it."

"No time to waste," Russell replied. "We need to get moving." Russell remained in the back of the vehicle with Forleh. There were several deep bruises on the side of his head on the right side. Over his left eye was a severe cut that bled wildly when Russell lifted the towel off his head and quickly returned the pressure to the wound as the bleeding resumed. Russell kept his hands pressed firmly against the injury. He would not check again as he knew from the quick look that the gash could not heal without sutures. The distance from Buaccahan to Monrovia was about eighty kilometers. However, the road conditions prevented any speed above forty miles per hour. Ike pressed the gas harder several times and had to lessen the speed as the Land Rover bounced around on the unimproved road. Their best bet was Sam who had extensive emergency room experience.

The clinic was on a street that was littered with trash as sanitation services were halted due to the Ebola outbreak. Russell looked out the front windshield and observed a white man run past the piles of garbage. Russell `tapped his free hand on Kitson's shoulder who nodded as he already observed the commotion. The white man ran toward them.

"They took Featu," Sam screamed. He did not wait for the vehicle to stop and shouted again. "They took her." Sam was out of breath. He held his arms and hands behind his head as he tried to catch his breath.

"What?" Kitson yelled. "Who, where?"

"They came into the clinic." Sam was out of breath. "Three men stood in the road with weapons."

"What did they look like?"

"Locals," Sam said. He was despondent and continued, "Africans."

"Are you sure?" Kitson asked. "It was not the Russians?"

"No, they were African men." Sam looked despondent. "They were medium build and strong."

"What did they say?" Kitson asked. "Do you remember anything that they said?"

"No." Sam cried out. "They just pushed me down."

"It doesn't make sense." Kitson tried to explain out loud. "There was no threat against her. If anything, they would have come after you." Kitson looked down the street in each direction. "How long ago?"

"Thirty minutes… maybe an hour" Sam said. "They knocked me out." He put his hand on his head as he recalled being struck. "They took Featu." Tears flowed down his face.

"What color was their vehicle?" Russell asked.

"I don't know. I heard an engine before the door was busted open." Sam was in shock. His hands shook. Raged filled him.

"We need to get a trace started." Kitson picked up his satellite phone and dialed a number. "I am ready to go secure." Kitson pressed the actuator button on the phone signified with a red button. On the other end of the line at a secure facility in the heart of downtown London, the agent on duty responded, "You are now secure." Kitson began. "I need immediate satellite imagery for twenty-two degrees sixty minutes for any vehicle traffic. Trace all vehicles to final destinations and send one by two thousand-pixel photos for any safe houses." Kitson was very specific. In his line of work, any misstep could result in death. The MI6 agent on the other end of the line confirmed the request. Kitson turned to Sam and said, "We will do everything possible to find Featu."

Russell got Major Forleh out of the vehicle with Ike's help. They brought him into the clinic and put him on the cleanest sheet that they could find. Russell watched his mentor carefully as he tried to soothe Sam's angst. They needed Sam at his best. After ten minutes, Sam came over to Forleh and started to administer to his patient. Russell pointed to Kitson, and they both walked outside.

"Who do you think it was?" Russell looked at Kitson.

"Hard to say." Kitson poured two scotches from the bottle that was in the back of the Land Rover. After the prior mission, he had wanted a stiff drink and thought Russell would appreciate the same. "The Russians could have outsourced some local thugs."

"But what would they want Featu for?" Russell paused. "Leverage?"

"No, there's nothing Sam would have that they needed," Kitson replied. "It doesn't make sense."

"Abuja would be more of a target." Russell thought aloud. "With his work on developing virus antidotes that could be worth money."

"Possibly. But Hassan would need an advanced lab and like you mentioned the CDC took all of Doctor Abuja's notes," Kitson said as he sipped the scotch. "He would have to start from scratch, and that would take too long. I believe Checkov is working on a compressed timeline. Something big is going to happen; and more than likely soon."

"Too soon I am afraid to think," Russell stated. "I asked for more support and Langley has coordinated a Special Ops team that is on the way from Germany."

"How long?" Kitson asked.

"Two days, maybe three at the latest."

"We have a short window for action."

Over the next forty minutes, Sam administered to Major Forleh's head injury as best he could with the primitive equipment at his disposal. Sam had an insufficient supply to work with. Doctor Abuja had purchased some supplies on the black market. Kitson and Russell waited patiently for Sam to provide his assessment.

"This man needs more than I can provide here," Sam stated. "He is stabilized now, but he really needs more."

"What does he need?" Russell inquired.

"I cannot tell how much damage was to his head." Sam pointed to several bandaged areas. "There is no seepage from his ears."

"That's a good sign," Kitson said. From his many days in the African bush, sometimes primitive, medicine was the only means. The ear check was a first measure to see if a severe concussion was present.

"We need to get him a head scan."

"Let's go." Kitson directed them and added. "Let me make a call to the UN on the way."

Sam sat on the ground and did not budge as the others loaded Major Forleh into the vehicle. Sam had a very impatient look on his face and did not conceal his angst. He held his hands against his face. He needed his nurse. He needed the woman that he had fallen in love. "What about Featu?" Sam paused for a moment and looked Kitson in the eyes. "Where is she?"

"London confirmed that there was a vehicle at the time we stated in this area. More than likely it is the same vehicle as there is not much traffic in this area." He paused for a moment. "The satellite traced the vehicle to a house in Monrovia. A quick analysis revealed that it is owned indirectly by a shell company and most likely a front for Voctrad." Sam gave an inquisitive and Kitson elaborated. "Voctrad is a global criminal enterprise operated by the Russians."

"The Russians?" Sam asked. "Why would the Russians take Featu?"

"They may be after something more," Russell said. He looked at the computer display. "There are voice transcripts from a call between the cell phone we tracked on Kamal to someone with a heavy Russian accent, probably Checkov. Voice recognition is underway. Kamal stated that he had a replacement for the survivor. Langley speculates that the survivor was someone exposed to Ebola."

"And they think Featu has the antibody?" Sam asked. "We were exposed to Ebola, but never contracted it. I checked our blood every day, and I still test it. We were fortunate. There were no signs of any Ebola in our veins. What the hell are they thinking?" Sam was livid.

"We don't know what goes on in Kamal's head." Kitson tried to calm Sam but added. "He is deadly, very deadly and unpredictable."

"And he took Featu." Sam snapped back.

"We have a location." Russell looked at Sam. "Don't worry." Russell pulled out a submachine gun from the bag in the back of the vehicle. He handed Kitson a pistol and Ike a shotgun. "We will get her back."

After Sam got into the vehicle with Major Forleh, Kitson pulled Russell to the side and asked, "Why did you lie to him?"

"Even jeopardizing the mission?" Kitson grabbed his arm firmly. "We have to stay focused and finish the mission."

"I understand, but we need to at least give him hope we can return Featu, he is going to crawl up in a corner. We need him focused on treating Major Forleh."

"Agreed, just don't give him false hope," Kitson added. "Checkov may have gotten the blood samples he needed. I would not put it passed him to get rid of her and put a bullet in the back of her head."

"Then we better move fast," Russell said as he jumped into the back of the vehicle. He checked the magazine inserted in his pistol and reinserted it into the weapon.

Chapter 18

While the nation faced one of the most severe Ebola outbreaks in decades, the Jordanian Hospital - the most modern hospital in all West Africa - was off limits. UN soldiers from India diligently guarded the outer gate. As the vehicle drove up, Kitson waived his UN credentials to gain access. The Jordanian Hospital was state of the art compared with the dismal Liberian medical standards. The old hotel was gutted and transformed after a four-million-dollar investment by Jordan. Three massive generators powered the complex. Kitson talked with one of the Indian soldiers. He returned to the vehicle, and the expression on his face caused concern.

"The last of the Jordanian doctors are gone," Kitson stated coldly.

"What?" Russell said. "I thought that they would leave several doctors behind."

"Evidently, the conditions on the ground here for the Ebola outbreak are too severe for Jordan's King to worry about," Kitson said in a somewhat disgusted tone. "He pulled them all out."

"What are all of the UN soldiers supposed to do?" Russell said. He thought for a quick moment and added. "Heck, what are we supposed to do if we get infected?" No one answered him.

The Jordanian Hospital was eerily quiet. The air conditioner hummed as it pushed cool air through vents. Sam and Doctor Abuja placed their patient on a gurney. The elevator worked, and they went to the operating room that was on the fifth floor. Sam fumbled with the equipment to get a scan of Major Forleh's head. Kitson checked the remaining rooms. Food was left in the kitchen on the table as it appeared the Jordanian medical team left at a rapid pace once the King of Jordan ordered their removal. It was a tragedy on all levels. Kitson tossed the food in the trash.

After the doctors were established to treat Major Forleh, Russell and Kitson departed the hospital to look for Featu. They drove around Monrovia looking for any vehicles that matched what they saw from the satellite shots. They drove around for several more hours. Each turn revealed nothing. There were very few vehicles in the city, and more importantly, no vehicles had matched the description.

"Should we go back to the hospital?" Kitson asked as he drove through the deserted Monrovia streets. The rain slapped against the windshield at a violent rate of speed. Visibility was near zero, yet Kitson sped fast. The sporadic downpours in the rainy season were iconic. One moment, the clouds would separate to allow sunshine. And the next moment, the horrific rain resembled a biblical event. Kitson wiped a rag against the interior windshield as it fogged up.

"Not without Featu," Russell replied. "We need to keep Sam focused on helping Major Forleh. We can't afford any distractions."

"Look at them." Kitson pointed out the window at the locals. "They're huddled underneath anything that can stop the rain."

"And with the Ebola," Russell conjectured, "That's probably not too smart." He looked out the window at the faces that peered back along the sidewalk. Bodies were pressed firmly against the walls and packed into entrances to get out of the rain. "I would rather stand in the rain and get soaked than getting Ebola."

"They don't think that way," Kitson said. "You need to remember this is Africa." Kitson shifted the gears into a lower speed as the Land Rover bounced into a large pothole. Deep waves of brownish water splashed high into the air. "They're in survival mode … immediate survival mode. You can say what you want, but they will only think about what is right in front of them. Thinking at a higher, more complex level is a challenge as the entire education system was destroyed. There is an entire generation in this post-war nation that will remain uneducated for life."

"They should be able to change their destiny." Russell looked out the window. Everything was soaked, and he was surprised to see men work in the rain. He repeated himself, "They can make a change."

"Not here." Kitson rebutted. "Not in Liberia. Perhaps in America or London if they got their gold ticket out of here." Kitson referred to the all who sought after visa application approval to get out of Liberia. The lines at both the U.S. and British Embassies were typically long, now with the Ebola threat, the lines increased fivefold. Thousands wanted to get out of Liberia.

"No one is leaving here soon," Russell replied. "I just heard from my embassy that the airport has been shut down."

"News will travel fast." Kitson looked around. "We need to get off these streets." Both of them knew that violent unrest would ensue once word spread on the airport closure. Once the rains stopped, the locals would flood into the streets, and an unimaginable angry uproar would grip Monrovia. Liberians felt slighted by any small change. They have been abused and tormented for over a decade by a horrific civil war. Every fiber of existence was torn and shredded. Families were separated, and many never found the truth about their lost members. Minor changes in Liberian society caused significant unrest.

"BTC is five blocks away," Russell said. "We can go there."

Back at the bungalow, Kitson and Russell got out of their soaked clothes and dried off. Both changed into what clothes they could find. The bungalow had been their oasis from the city as it was protected by the ten-foot-high stone walls and guard towers. The steel bars on the bungalow windows and solid doors made the small bungalow somewhat secure. Nonetheless, Russell checked his weapon to make sure the rain did not hinder any of its functionality. Once he was convinced it was ready to fire, he placed it on the table.

"How about one?" Kitson said as he placed a bottle of twenty-year-old scotch on the table.

"Definitely," Russell replied. "I need something to get the chill out of me from that horrific rain."

"You would never imagine in a million years how the African rain could be so penetrating. In my first year in the bush in Kenya as a teenager, I remember my father saying the dried creek beds would be massive rivers in another two months. I did not believe him that was until the rains came. From England, I had seen dreary rainy days, but nothing prepared me for the rains in Africa. The onslaught is something that you miss over time."

"I don't think that I will miss the rain."

"Trust me." Kitson's voice inflection sounded like a teacher. "It may be today or tomorrow. But someday in the future, you will recall the African rains and how beautiful everything looked afterward. It really shows how minuscule we humans are in the cradle of life."

"Philosophical tonight?" Russell inquired as he finished the three fingers of scotch in one deep gulp. Kitson sipped his drink and patiently enjoyed the taste. Russell filled another glass for himself and topped off his mentor's glass.

"After every near-death experience, it is always good to take a moment to reflect." Kitson looked at his drink. "We live in a dangerous time and have many enemies."

"Hassan and Checkov are currently top of my list," Russell said.

"The conditions are pretty dire." Kitson lifted the glass of scotch to his lips. His hand moved slowly, deliberately as his eyes watched the liquor swash around in the glass. "Ebola will rip this country apart." Kitson kept his eyes pointed downward. "Family, friends, and neighbors will not forsake their loved ones for survival, and they will be infected. The disease will spread at epidemic rates like the world has never seen. Liberians do not know better. They are a very friendly society." He paused for a moment. "It is this handicap that will crush them." Kitson looked at the steel bars on the bungalow's windows. "Many foreigners don't understand what has happened. Small steps were made after the civil war to integrate the child soldiers. There is an entire lost generation. Some have gotten jobs and started families in an attempt to quash the nightmares."

"Any type of war is horrific" Russell added. "Especially for kids."

"It is worse for them. At that young age being told to murder or be killed?" Kitson let the question linger for a moment as he conjectured further. "How can they ever become a fabric of society again?"

"A lost generation," Russell stated coldly. "The stakes are against them and now with this Ebola…true fear and terror will resonate again."

"The reports out of the government are not accurate," Kitson said as he handed Russell an MI6 report on death estimates.

"How many dead today?" Russell asked. "Ebola deaths?"

"Too many," Kitson stated bluntly. He rose from the table and walked over to the cabinet to retrieve a full bottle of scotch. Kitson stumbled and placed his hand on the table to regain his balance. He tossed the empty liquor bottle toward the trash can and missed. Kitson poured a stiff drink and continued. "A team from your CDC finally arrived here yesterday to get an idea of the death count. They're already overwhelmed. Bodies are being burned in the back of Monrovia General. I saw the flames. Bodies are just tossed on top of the flames. There's no service - no prayer - no humanity. It is horror, utter horror." Kitson wiped a tear from his eye. "I have not smelled that disgusting smell since I was a boy." He paused. "That smell haunted me for decades."

"Burning bodies?" Russell inquired. He sensed his friend was not in a good place.

"Yes," Kitson paused for a long moment, "the bodies." Kitson downed the glass of scotch and poured another. "When I lived in Kenya with my father, the rebels under Joseph Kenyatta rounded up a village that was loyal to the government – men, women, elders…. and worse of all, the children. They butchered them with machetes and burned the bodies in a large pile. That horrific smell resonated. For weeks, I smelled death. The winds carried the smell for miles. My father plugged all of the holes in the house, yet it still resonated."

"To make sure the Ebola does not spread more, they have to burn the bodies." Russell did not know what to say. "It is the only way."

"I understand. It's death. Death comes rapidly in Africa." Kitson lifted the glass of scotch to his lips. "Killing comes easy. The disposal of bodies," He paused again. "Now, that is the hard part."

"It's going to get worse," Russell said. "There are almost three hundred dead in the past week and another thousand infected."

"And we cannot locate Featu," Kitson said as he pulled the drink to his lips. "We are not doing well at our jobs." He looked toward the wall. Maps covered the entire stretch of the wall. There were circles and arrows of suspected Voctrad, Hezbollah, and Al Qaeda known locations and suspected safe houses. Kitson pulled out recent satellite imagery from London and looked over the photos with a magnifying glass. There were more than twenty-five marks on the large map. "Where are you Featu?"

Inside of the old, dilapidated building, Featu shivered. She looked at the chains around her ankles. She rubbed the skin around the metal and attempted with earnest to get her fingers underneath the metal. She pushed hard, yet could not get her thin fingers inside. The metal wrapped her ankles with an anaconda-like grip. Rain filtered indiscriminately through the spotted holes in the roof. Featu leaned her body close to the wall and looked through the crack. It was extremely dark outside. She heard voices – foreign voices, unrecognizable. A cigarette burn ignited the darkness as the foreign man puffed hard on it. She recognized that it was a man as he pulled hard on the cigarette and brightened his face in the pitch darkness. Featu listened closely as the voices stopped abruptly. She looked out the crack in the wall and saw what the foreigners had watched.

On final approach, a commercial jet had the external lights pointed toward the runway. Featu was confused at first as the lights were high in the sky, yet they approached fast. The commercial jet landed and screeched its tires as the pilot braked. The sound was deafening as the jet passed the building Featu was in. She covered her ears. The numbing body sound of the jet engines in full reversal mode ignited the night like a volcanic eruption. The pilot was informed ahead that the runway was four hundred feet short and he would have to send the engines into a full reversal mode. The building Featu was in shook violently as the backward thrust from the engines ripped into it. The noise ripped her senses apart. Featu pressed her hands tightly against her ears. Seconds felt like hours. And in a moment, the sound was gone. Featu heard the foreign men yell. She saw one of them, the man with the cigarette in his mouth get off of the ground. What she did not see was the other two Russian scientists were knocked to the ground as well from the engine's power. The older men had difficulty getting off of the concrete and slowly placed their legs underneath. They pushed hard to get back up. They spoke loudly, and Featu speculated that they swore.

Inside of the old hangar, spotlights gleamed on the large sheets of solid plastic that formed an isolation room. Inside of the sealed room, rested a weapon – something from the past that would be resurrected again to inspire the most horrific cruelty known to man since the bubonic plague. The Russian scientists had assembled the shaft and gears into the weapon, yet they kept the elongated chamber open for the pressurized motor replacement. The boomerang type nozzles were locked into position. At full assembly, the weapon resembled something that would be seen on the bottom of the ocean – a bottom feeder that crawled across the ocean's floor.

Along the wall of the isolated plastic room, the scientists had erected several tables and intricately assembled an array of vials, glass tubes, beakers, and burners. To Hassan, it looked like something out of a science fiction movie. To the Russian scientists, it was something that they knew. The Ebola virus had to be controlled and kept alive. The Russians used a gel-like substance made from pig's blood that kept the virus active for a short period of eight days – the clock was ticking. Glass balls would be used to keep the substance concealed and able to withstand a high level of pressurization. The Russians had calculated the pressure required that was slightly over twenty-eight pounds per square inch. The pressurization took into account the aircraft speed and rate of decent. Hassan watched the Russians test the loading of the glass balls with the substance. He was only ten feet and the protection of a plastic isolated room from the world's most deadly virus. He felt uncomfortable so close and went to find Checkov.

"Is this everything you need?" Hassan asked as he looked out the window for the commercial jet come to a complete stop. The roar of the engines was loud, a deafening sound. Hassan was forced to repeat himself, "Everything? Is this everything that you need?" He looked at Checkov who had an open palm near his ear to listen more intently.

"We have everything now," Checkov shouted over the noise of the aircraft.

"And the woman?" Hassan asked.

"We need to examine her blood," Checkov said. "With this equipment," He pointed to the airplane as it came to a complete stop in front of the hangar. "We can test her blood and develop our own antidotes."

"My families need the antidote," Hassan said.

"Is anyone infected?" Checkov asked.

"No," Hassan replied quickly. "We moved everyone out to the Marshall compound."

"Good," Checkov said as he looked at the aged Russian scientists. "They will have the antidote completed."

"Are you leaving Liberia?" Hassan asked. "They cannot contain the Ebola in the streets."

"You will be surprised," Checkov said. "The Americans will come to Liberia in force to save them. They have done it before and will do it again." He thought for a moment and added. "It will be their downfall."

"Just as long we are long gone by then," Hassan said.

"Unlike you," Checkov replied. "My men and I have no place to go. Many countries will gladly take you back after Israel is destroyed. For us, there is no place for us in the new Russian. The KGB are long gone. The new Russian government is weak. We live on the edge, in the shadows."

"After Tel Aviv is destroyed," Hassan paused for a brief moment as he looked at the weapon. "They will be after you."

"I am not concerned about the American CIA," Checkov said. At the same moment, his cell phone rang. Checkov spoke in native Russian and screamed into the phone. He hung up the phone and pulled a pistol out of his belt. With the rapid update, he changed his mind on the CIA. "That bastard Russell just hit my safe house."

"He needs to die," Hassan said. "Let me get Kamal after him." Hassan watched Checkov and needed him to focus on the weapon. "Kamal will cause chaos. It is what he does best."

At her Mossad safe house, Francesca looked at her encrypted computer. The screen showed a map of Tel Aviv and projected impact if Ebola was released over the city in an airburst fashion. She had seen previous predictions for an atomic bomb detonation in the Israeli capital. She had never seen any predictions for what an epidemic of biblical proportions would do to her homeland. She looked closely at her neighborhood and zoomed into the street and then the building that housed her son. The computer model simulated that the neighborhood would be decimated within four days with over eighty-five percent dead. The hospitals would be overwhelmed within one hour and would be ground zero for the infectious rampage. Israeli first responders were equipped to deal with an atomic detonation, yet not equipped to deal with an infectious disease of Ebola's rampant nature. Infection would be widespread. She looked at the West Bank and the population density. She wondered why Hezbollah would destroy their own people as certainly they must have concluded the outbreak would reach Lebanon. Israel was viewed as the occupying force. From her interaction with Hezbollah, death was common. Sacrificing one's life to kill Israelis was commonplace. Families were rewarded with money and food if their son became a suicide bomber. Releasing Ebola onto a city was one of the most horrific, catastrophic events that could even happen.

Francesca knew firsthand the horror of terrorism as her own mother was blown apart from a suicide bomber. Her mother's body was beyond recognition. There was nothing to recognize, and it was a time before DNA was collected, and video surveillance was widespread. What Francesca remembered was watching from the inside of her mother's car as flames ignited the deli. Francesca never saw her mother again. She looked at the home that protected her Dominic. Her son would be killed. Many Israelis would certainly die. And those few who survived would more than likely be invaded within a year. The situation was not good, and Francesca held the necklace in her hand. Everything she had worked for, everything she had fought for would be crumbled into obliteration. She pressed the phone against her ear. The number on the satellite phone was already loaded. The rings penetrated her mind – three, four, five… no answer. She waited patiently as she knew that her father would look hard at the number. On the tenth ring, her father answered.

"You should not be calling." Her father stated coldly.

"It is not too late. Dominic should be reading now before bedtime." Francesca stated.

"That is not the point." Her father was career military in the Israeli Defense Force, otherwise known as the IDF. For half of his military career, he served in the Mossad. After his official military retirement that made all of the newspapers in Tel Aviv, it was stated that he would move to the countryside to fish in his old age; far from the truth. He went on to lead the most clandestine part of the Mossad known only to a few as the Lion Hearts, after the famed English King who led a crusade to free Jerusalem. Mossad operatives in the field do not call home.

"Just this once," Francesca pleaded. "I need it."

"You are on a mission and know the rules of no contact." Her father lectured. Francesca knew the rules, lived the rules. Mossad agents were required to cease all contacts with family on missions. Nothing was allowed to limit their focus on achieving success. More importantly, it would put all of their families at risk if communications were intercepted. Even with satellite phones that scramble communications, the ability to tap into the conversation existed.

"This time is different." She fired back at her father. "Our homeland may be destroyed."

"There have been other times." He provided as a reason. "Many other times that we were near extinction and the rules of no contact followed." He paused for a moment. "Is it the American?"

"What?"

"The American Russell," Her father said. "Is he putting thoughts in your head?"

"No," She had already started to cry aloud. "He has not infiltrated my mind. It is the other way. It has always been the other way. I control him." Francesca knew what to say, "He is controllable."

"Are you certain?" Her father had a long dossier on Tom Russell of the American Central Intelligence Agency. He did not like him at all. He knew that Francesca did not appreciate the gravity of the situation both of them were put in when Russell fathered the son of an Israeli Mossad assassin. "I should have killed."

"And tell Dominic what?" She shouted back. "That her father fell off a balcony while visiting us and accidently had a bullet in the back of his head." She paused for a moment. "He would learn the truth, maybe not the next day, or year, but sometime in his life he would know."

"Perhaps," Her father replied.

"Promise me, you will not kill Dominic's father."

"He is an American CIA operative." He father scolded her. "You may think America is our ally, but let's remember that we are at war with everyone. Israeli has no friends."

"Tom Russell can be turned toward our side," Francesca advised her father. "He will want me once again, and then we will have him."

"You are not cleared for this type of mission. You have too much emotional baggage. It will not work out."

"It will work," She paused for a moment. "If you just have faith in me and my abilities. I can control Russell."

"It is late now. We have talked too long. Even with the scrambler, they may have recorded our conversation. If you are listening my Langley friends, tell your man Russell that I will kill him next time that I see him."

"You are too paranoid father."

"What do you want me to tell your son?"

"Just tell Dominic that mommy loves him," Francesca said. The line disconnected and Francesca cried into her pillow. Motherhood surprised her as she was ruthless in her daily job. The repeated missions kept her away, and she realized how much she loved her son.

Chapter 19

The beaches out in front of the Cape Hotel were littered with trash. The once pristine beaches were ransacked in a matter of days. Locals had stolen the lounge chairs and umbrellas. Garbage was openly tossed. Human feces littered the sand. Without the constant protection of the beach, it became an immediate eyesore. To keep his guests safe, Anwar had moved all of his security to cover the interior perimeter of the hotel compound. Everything on the outside the main gates disappeared overnight.

Inside of the hotel's office, Anwar sat behind the security monitors and watched the chaos unfold as many locals outside of the gate chanted for the foreigners to save them from the Ebola. Rumors circulated that many foreign doctors sought refuge within the Camp Hotel. Anwar heard the shouts from his window as the crowd grew louder. He looked back to his desk and counted the money again. Anwar counted ninety-five thousand dollars. It would have to be enough. Once he pulled out of the Cape Hotel, he knew immediately that everything would be stolen. From the beds to the utensils to the linen and even to the toilet seats, everything would be stolen. Anwar thought about his decision to leave, and he was certain that it was the right one. Once he departed Liberia, there would be no coming back. Anwar put the money back into the safe and closed the hidden panel that concealed it. Anwar had invested a lot of money in a good safe just in case of another military coup.

The Piano Bar was empty, and Anwar walked behind the bar to get a drink. The sunlight pierced the windows and heated the room. It was a welcome break from the massive rain that had chilled the air. He sat at a table close to the balcony. Anwar enjoyed the sunlight as it beamed on his face. The stiff scotch combined with the sunshine felt euphoric. Anwar was deep in thought and did not hear the steps behind him. Immediately, he was knocked to the floor. Anwar lost his senses and looked up toward his attackers. He recognized them right away.

"What did you tell the Americans?" Hassan asked.

"Nothing," Anwar replied as he looked up. He studied the faces of the two other men with Hassan. He recognized both as being Hezbollah. They were two of Hassan's henchmen who worked at the casino. "I didn't say anything to the Americans."

"And this man Russell?" Hassan asked. "He's your friend."

"I am friends with all." Anwar pleaded. "I'm a businessman. We must be friends with all." He paused for a moment and added. "You know this from the casino. We are in the hospitality business."

"I could give a damn about your guests," Hassan said in a stern tone.

"I have not said anything to anyone." Anwar assessed that he was in a bad situation that was going to get worse. "The Americans are close to the Liberians, maybe they told him." He paused for a moment and added. "I don't know." He pleaded. "I did not say anything."

"We shall see," Hassan said. He nodded to his men who unleashed thunderous kicks on Anwar. They kicked him in the head and belly. Anwar was smart enough to curl up into a ball and cover his head with his arms. He held his body firm and took the shots. Growing up as a Christian, he was regularly beaten by Palestinian youths. Anwar grunted in pain.

"Stop!" Came the shout across the room as Tareeq ran into the room. He shouted again. "Stop!" Tareeq picked up a chair and flung it at one of the thugs. He attempted to punch the other one but was caught by the man's fist. Anwar attempted to stand. As he moved toward his feet, Hassan stuck a butcher's knife that he took from the bar into Anwar's back. Anwar flailed as he tried to reach behind him to get it out. Hassan pulled the blade out and stabbed Anwar two more times. The loud noises had alerted the security and

Hassan heard shouts outside. He motioned for his men to depart. Before he left the Piano Bar, Hassan kicked Anwar in the middle of his back. Anwar fell onto the floor.

At the BTC compound, Kitson awoke with a blistering hangover after he passed out from alcohol consumption. He tossed some water on his face and went right to work on his computer. He drank several cups of coffee and focused in on the newly generated reports. The intelligence update that MI6 provided had an exact location of Voctrad's safe house in Monrovia. Kitson looked at the map on the wall and circled streets that seemed passable. He spent several moments looking at the satellite image of Monrovia and matching to what he saw on the ground. Kitson used different color lines for threat levels to get in and out of certain neighborhoods. As a white man, he knew that everything was impassible once the sun went down as local gangs comprised of former child soldiers controlled the streets.

"We got them," Kitson stated. "I have an exact location of Voctrad's safe house." Kitson looked out the window. "Weather looks like shit, and that's exactly what we need."

Heavy dark clouds emerged along the horizon over the ocean. Kitson looked in the direction of the sea and was surprised to see how fast the clouds traveled and estimated the speed was over thirty knots. During the rainy season, the storms traveled from both the land and the ocean. The storms that originated from the ocean were more severe as clouds picked up more moisture.

"How many men?" Russell asked as he picked up a submachine gun.

"Hard to say," Kitson said as he grabbed his automatic weapon. "Looks like the rain is coming back." Kitson continued. "And it could be to our advantage."

"Possibly." Russell thought for a moment. "As many locals will be under cover and not in the streets."

"Precisely," Kitson said as he jumped into the driver's seat. They sped out of the BTC compound and served around locals who scurried for supplies before the next avalanche of rain.

Within moments, the clouds unloaded and a deluge of water cascaded down the streets. Kitson drove in the middle of the street. There was no other traffic. Water passed them at a faster speed than they had traveled. Voctrad's safe house was located in the center of the Monrovia slums. Kitson parked the Land Rover several blocks away and let Russell out. He waited patiently as he saw the young Russell sprint down the city street. The deluge of rain was severe, and Kitson lost sight of Russell in between the windshield wipers as they swiped the rain, back and forth. Russell grew tired quickly as he ran into the face of the torrential rain. He stopped and placed his hands on his hips. Faces peered out from behind the rusted sheets of twisted metal sheets. Some of the metal sheets were used as protective barriers during the last civil war and the large quarter size holes from the direct fire of anti-aircraft guns were pervasive. In the streets of Monrovia, the Liberian troops turned the heavy guns toward the ground instead of the sky. From the high bluff where the Presidential Palace loomed largely, the troops loyal to Charles Taylor's troops fired into the city. Anything that moved was considered the enemy. There was no mercy. There was no place to hide from the heavy artillery barrage. Buildings were destroyed. Nearly every structure had bullet holes as a testament for history as to how severe the carnage was.

From behind the metal sheets, Russell saw several boys peer outward into the deluge of rain. Their little fingers were pressed firmly into the holes made from war to hold the protective barrier tight against the concrete as the wind whirled. Russell stood motionless. The boys looked closely at the white man who carried a large weapon, something they had seen before. The boys knew what an AK-47 looked like. Their father was a rebel and kept it wrapped in bags under his bed, just in case another uprising occurred. The boys snuck into his room when he went to work and touched the weapon. They taught themselves how to load it and pretended how to fire the weapon. Strange words were etched on the side of the weapon, in a language from a foreign nation far away – Czechoslovakia. Notches were gouged into the wooden stock of the weapon - fourteen total - from the soldiers their father killed. The father never told the boys about the war, but their grandmother did. She told the boys when they were babies how their mother was killed by the government soldiers and how their father took up arms against the corrupt Taylor regime. Many men fought against Taylor and not just child soldiers. The aging lady told the young boys that their father was a hero of Liberia. The boys were thirteen and eleven years old, a prime age to be recruited into war. Their father saw the ravages of war. The grandmother knew the horrors of war as she was raped by Taylor's troops.

"Whatca ya luuk at buyz?" The grandmother shouted from within. She peered out at Russell drenched from the onslaught. "Cum har white man. Har." She shouted at Russell. "Ya cumm."

"Thank you." Russell looked at the boys as they pushed the metal sheets back in place to cover the doorway. The boys tied a rope through the aged bullet holes and pulled the rope tightly. Russell smiled at the boys.

"U soldier?" The grandmother asked, and Russell nodded. "U far from America."

"Yes," Russell replied. "American Marine."

"Ahhh," she paused for a moment and replied, "Marine?" Russell nodded back. "U protect embassy of big bruttar."

"Not really," Russell said, and he added. "I protect Liberia."

"America big bruttar no stop Taylor death." She looked down.

"Charles Taylor was one of the evilest tyrants in history, just as bad as Hitler and Stalin," Russell replied. "And we brought him to justice."

"U wait long. Taylor soldiers kill. Murder me only girl." Tears dripped from the aged face, a lady who saw more horror and unimaginable violence. "Why big bruttar not stop Taylor?"

"We made many wrongs in Liberia," Russell said as he looked at the boys. He sensed that they knew their charred history just as well as he did. He looked into their eyes. There were innocent stares as these young boys witnessed the ravages of war as infants. And now they were of fighting age.

Russell looked at the boys and thought that they needed to know. He stopped his mission for a moment and took time to explain. "America made a big mistake with Samuel Doe after he murdered Tolbert in his sleep. We needed someone in West Africa to rely upon so we can put up large antennae to talk with our submarines. We were more worried about the Soviets than what was really happening in Africa." Russell looked at the locals and knew that they did not understand. Russell knew the real reason around what transpired. America did nothing when Taylor overran the country and had Doe killed. America allowed Taylor to smuggle millions and millions of dollars of 'blood' diamonds out of Sierra Leone. America looked the other way when children were stolen from villages and recruited into the RUF to become soldiers. Taylor brutalized his own country.

"America big bruttar needs to do more."

"Yes, America is Liberia's big brother, but we turned our eye when you most needed us. We should have taken Taylor out years ago."

"But u got em now," The grandmother said in her broken dialect. She lifted up the newspapers that she kept. The pages were carefully wrapped with plastic. She meticulously protected her prize possession showing the arrest of former Liberian President Charles Taylor at Robert's

International Airport for crimes against humanity. She held the papers upward to show Russell.

"That was a good day for justice," Russell replied. He never saw the Monrovia Gazette front-page article for Taylor's arrest. In the photo, he could see Taylor being pushed from the airplane by a large African American man who was named Captain Stone and one of Russell's right-hand men. And Russell saw the arms of UN troops pulling Taylor off the airplane steps. What the grandmother did not see was a white man who held a pistol at the back of Taylor's head just in case there were any forces loyal to Taylor who tried to retrieve their disgraced leader. Russell recalled how he held his pistol firm and really hoped for a situation to erupt so he could blast Taylor's brains all over the tarmac and in front of the world's photographers to capture. Russell recalled the moment again in his thoughts. It was one of his proudest moments going into Cameron to capture an escaping Taylor from Nigeria. Russell remembered the last words he said to Taylor vividly, "We got you, you son of a bitch."

"U see, Taylor go to resort jail." The grandmother said. "Ya shulda hang hum."

"He will get his justice." Russell looked outside, and the forcible rain slowed down. "I must go now."

"Ya hunt bad men?"

"Yes, very bad men. Men who do not want peace in Liberia."

"En u kill em?" The grandmother grabbed his right arm that held his weapon. She grit her teeth tightly and looked up at Russell. Her eyes were large as she opened them wide. "U kill em," she paused, "all ov em."

Russell nodded as he pulled the makeshift door open. There was still no movement in the street as the storm continued its onslaught. He looked back at the boys as they fastened the door shut. Their little eyes peered out through large holes in the walls. Russell waved farewell as he ran up the street. He made a mental note of the location of the building and the street so he could return with some food.

Russell ran fast up the steep hill and toward the center of the Monrovia business district. There was still no one in the street. Torrents of water washed down the sides of buildings and formed fast moving streams in the middle of the street. The water rushed over Russell's boots as he ran. He was still a marked man and knew Checkov would not wait for the weather to stop. Russell pulled out the map. It was soaked and crumpled. He made several notes on it, yet the rain made it practically unreadable. Russell would have to go off his memory. He would have to look closely for Checkov's building to stand out. Back and forth, Russell zigzagged between the streets in one of the most condensed areas of Monrovia.

Russell knew he had a short period of time to take action. Any vehicles moving in this weather would be a sure sign of a pending attack. Harder he ran up the steep hill as water raged toward him. His boots were covered with water when he pressed them against the pavement. It slowed down his pace, yet he trudged onward. Locals watched curiously as a white man moved in an area that he should not belong. If the rain was not present, many of the locals would be in the street, and more than likely someone would have the idea to mug the white man. Russell kept the AK47 close to his side and under his jacket. Russell converted the weapon to a short stock by sawing off part of the wooden stock, and he made a makeshift pistol grip. The weapon would be harder to control in full-automatic fire, yet he needed something he could conceal, not only from view but also from the soaking rain. The last thing Russell needed was a malfunctioning weapon when he arrived to pay his respects to Checkov.

Russell moved fast. Two more streets and he turned right. His breathe heaved in the air. In a flash, he moved from the center of the road and implanted his body against a stone wall. He made sure there were no windows close to him in case someone had the great idea of reaching outside to attempt a mugging. Russell caught his breath for a moment. Across the street, in the second-floor window, several local men pointed at Russell. One of them returned with a machete and waived it in the air. They smiled at Russell and motioned for him to come to their side of the street. Russell thought about showing his weapon to scare them off, but wondered if perhaps these men may be a lookout for Checkov. No one could be trusted. Russell thought of the next best thing and raised his middle finger on his non-shooting hand as the international sign of screw you.

One more block Russell thought as he pushed up the street. The rain started to pick up again. The wind blew the rain sideways, and it stung Russell's face. The temperature had dropped a few degrees and was nearly fifty degrees now. For any country in the northern hemisphere, fifty degrees would not be all that bad for the winter period, but in West Africa, it was downright cold for the locals. Russell was used to the extreme cold from his hiking days in the Pacific Northwest and did not let the weather phase him. It was always a test for him – more of a contest of man versus nature. Russell was glad the heavy rain was present to mask his assault.

Within thirty feet, he saw the end of the block. In one motion, he pulled the AK47 out from under his jacket and chambered the first round. He held the modified pistol grip tightly with his right hand. He had test fired the weapon, yet he never fired while running. Red door to the left – it was a mark for the gate to the outside generators. The intelligence he received was correct. He looked for the second point of reference that was an open window on the third floor for a look out. Russell moved down the opposite wall slowly as he watched. He kept the weapon aimed at the window. Russell carefully crossed his steps, one over the other. His motion was steady. There was a slight movement by the open window. Russell saw a puff of smoke from a cigarette. He did not wait for the sniper to check the area. Russell opened fire as he ran across the street. He could see several rounds hit against the brick and send puffs of dirt into the air. He saw several rounds hit the sniper in the chest and blood spirt outwards. It was less than eight seconds from first firing his weapon until Russell kicked open the outer door. He knew that the door would be locked tightly, so he unloaded the rest of the magazine as he aimed toward the hinges on the other side of the door. Russell knew it was a common mistake for many to fortify a door at the lock side when the exposed hinges were the most vulnerable. Russell fired about twenty rounds into the rusty metal hinges that ripped them to shreds. Russell's kicked the outer door sent it spiraling inward. As he entered the building, he inserted another thirty-round magazine.

There was warm food that simmered in bowls on the kitchen table. Russell counted three as he slithered past. He held his fire as not to give away his position. He saw the stairwell and leaped to the second floor. A bullet bounced at the wall behind him from below. He fired several rounds behind him and heard a moan. He quickly pulled the weapon back in front of him and shot along the wall to his right. Russell took the chance to clear the room to his right with gunfire, and it worked out well as he heard a body fall. Russell leaped the short distance to the other door and tossed a flashbang device into the room. A thunderous sound echoed throughout the building. Smoke filled the room. Russell peered within, and he saw the Russian put his arm over his eyes to clear the smoke. Russell shot him in the head with one bullet. Russell entered the room and immediately closed the door behind just in case of any more Russians stormed up the stairs.

"Clear," Russell said softly into the microphone to Kitson.

"Five seconds out," Kitson replied as drove toward the building.

"Second-floor room, top of stairs." Russell gave his location.

"On my way," Kitson replied as he slammed on the brakes.

"How far out?"

"Seconds." Kitson slammed on the brakes, and the vehicle skidded.

"Holding my position."

"Coming up stairs," Kitson spoke into the headset.

"Coming out," Russell said. He motioned his hand to the room on the right that he buzzed with a clip of automatic fire. They both moved across from the door, not next to the wall in case someone fired at them. Bullets would have easily penetrated the wall. Russell raised his right hand and motioned a 3-2-1 countdown with the fingers of his right hand. Kitson nodded in agreement. As his first rolled up, Russell kicked open the door and somersaulted into the room. Kitson already followed behind him and shot the body on the floor in the head. The Russian was already motionless from three other bullets in the chest, yet Kitson wanted to make sure the Russian was not a threat, and Kitson shot the Russian in the head. Blood splattered on the wall, and skull fragments bounced off the floor as half of his head exploded.

"No prisoners. Right?" Kitson asked as a matter of confirmation.

"Right," Russell replied. Neither of them ever suspected a member of Voctrad would ever talk. These villains were former KGB and Russian military Special Forces, Spetsnaz.

"Looks like they had someone tied up," Kitson said as he picked up some ropes off the floor. "Probably Featu."

"We got maps on the wall," Russell said as Kitson streamed live video to London. Russell grabbed several papers that were in Russian. Russell went outside to get a can full of diesel fuel from the generator and poured fuel all over the room. Kitson nodded to Russell. They ran before the grenade exploded. Within seconds, the entire building was engulfed.

Chapter 20

From the brutal attack on Fatima, the virus spread. Ebola raged in the populated and dense area of Bushrod Island, on the outskirts of Monrovia. The rapid spread of the virus was like nothing any Doctor Abuja had ever witnessed. No one had heard from the UN clinic on Bushrod Island. Several UN doctors volunteered to investigate. They crossed the bridge that connected Bushrod Island and ran back moments later. The UN doctors asked the Nigerian guards to let them through; however, the Nigerian soldiers had direct orders to shoot anyone who left Bushrod Island. The UN doctors fell to the ground and prayed to let them pass. The Nigerian soldiers did not budge.

The Nigerian soldiers were disciplined. More importantly, the Nigerians knew that what happened in Liberia could happen in their home county, two hundred miles to the south. One doctor looked at the Marshall River and estimated that it was a twenty-foot drop. He made the quick calculation in his mind and took action. Before the Nigerian grabbed him, the UN doctor flew in the air and did a makeshift dive, more of a plunge into the water. He surfaced to the top of the water, and observed bullets hit the water around him. He looked up and saw the Nigerians aim at him. He waved for them to stop. His next memory was of pain as a bullet penetrated his eye socket. The other UN doctors looked at the floating corpse, and for several moments they talked among themselves. After ten minutes, they stood up and walked back toward Bushrod Island to treat the Ebola victims. There was no pleading with the Nigerians.

Farther up the hill from the bridge to Bushrod Island, Doctor Abuja had several maps stretched across the table at the Jordanian Hospital. He looked out the window at Bushrod Island and the masses of people that lived in the condensed area. He drew lines around Bushrod Island and labeled it "ground zero." He wondered if the numbers of those contaminated by the

Ebola virus in other parts of Liberia were correct. He called UN headquarters in New York and pleaded for more support. The British, Americans and French would send supplies, and the Germans would send more doctors. The transportation requests had already been submitted, yet it was still days away before the first aircraft would land.

A colleague sent him an article that was on page ten of the New York Times. The paper reported a small outbreak of Ebola in the remote region of West Africa had started. Doctor Abuja shook his head in disbelief as everyone underestimated the impact of the Ebola outbreak in Liberia. The density of Bushrod Island would magnify the intensity of the outbreak. The UN Secretary-General personally called him earlier in the day to express his disbelief at Doctor Abuja's assessment. Doctor Abuja was respectful, yet he informed the supreme UN leader that he was out of touch with reality. Doctor Abuja knew that this outbreak would devastate Liberia, especially since the nation was still recovering from fourteen years of civil war. He did an inventory of the medical supplies left by the Jordanian doctors as they hastily departed. He had plenty of means to treat normal patients, yet nothing could stop the Ebola virus. Doctor Abuja knew he could not do much and went back to treat Major Forleh.

At the BTC bungalow, maps were spread across the table, and Russell attempted to translate the Russian words with the assistance of an online CIA application. Russell knew some Russian, yet he took photos of the words and loaded the phrases into a CIA language software program. Russell was exhausted, yet he pushed his mind to study the maps intently.

"Checkov is coming after us with everything he has," Russell said, as he heard Kitson enter the kitchen. Russell did not look up as he continued to read intelligence updates on his computer.

"Don't forget about Hassan too," Kitson said as he poured a hot cup of coffee. Steam lifted into the air. The morning temperature was cold for West African standards, near forty degrees. Kitson drank some hot liquid and looked at the newspaper. "See," he pointed out, "we even made the local news." Kitson looked at the Monrovia Gazette that had a picture of the secret Checkov safe house on fire. "It said that there were three bodies in the fire that were not identified."

"Lucky for us, Liberia does not have any forensic laboratory to exam the bodies' post-mortem." Russell paused for a moment as he looked at the photo. "They would have realized very quickly that bullets caused the death and not the fire." Russell thought of Checkov. "He will be after us."

"Checkov will not avenge these men. You have to understand men like Checkov. He is old-school Russian KGB. He is ruthless. He has no family and only cares about his own existence. " Kitson paused and continued. "Checkov would be more concerned about what information we may have collected. In this brutal game, it is about what you know."

"Once we take out Checkov, we can remove Hassan," Russell said as he looked at the maps in more detail.

"Did Langley give any updates on Kamal?"

"Nothing." Russell looked up from the computer. "Here is a satellite image of a suspected Al Qaeda camp." He twisted the screen toward Kitson.

"That is the old Black Beret camp near the Firestone Plantation," Kitson remarked. He knew the area well as he had first resurrected the camp there five years ago when he first met Russell in Liberia.

"Here are several time elapsed photos." Russell showed. "There was activity there two days ago and today." He paused for a moment as he clicked the updated screen to show Kitson. "There is nothing."

"We need to get that bastard as well," Kitson said as a matter of fact. He was very pointed when he added. "It would be a privilege to put a bullet in Kamal's head."

"More than likely, we can only take them on one at a time," Russell said as he suggested how best to deal with three fanatical killers who ravaged Liberia.

"Agree, one at a time," Kitson confirmed. "We can only fight one enemy at a time with our limited resources." Kitson hovered over him to look at the map of the primitive airfield that was built during World War II. He continued. "And Francesca? Do you trust the mother of your child?"

"Israel has a great deal to lose." Russell looked up. "They could easily experience a million casualties."

"That didn't answer my question."

"I understand what you want to know." Russell paused and contemplated the situation. "We have to trust her." He paused for a moment and continued, "We have no other choice."

There was another dignitary event in the evening, and Kitson thought their presence would be required. Russell shook his head as it seemed the Liberian government officials gave the impression to the foreign diplomats and potential investors that everything was alright in their small, quaint West African nation. They both took hot showers and got dressed. This time Kitson wore a suit to blend in more with the diplomatic crowd. Russell looked in the mirror at his appearance in a cleaned three-piece suit. The white shirt was crisp and pressed well. Ike had done a great job on cleaning the suit Russell had left in Africa five years before. In the darkness, Ike drove Kitson and Russell in the Land Rover. The rain had stopped for the moment, and the streets were filled with locals. Merchants opened their shops for the quick sale before the rain returned.

They drove past the deserted former Presidential Palace toward the Liberian Cabinet where the function would be held. The entrance to the compound was a severe choke point. Liberian police stopped each car to physically check for any explosives. Kitson smirked as he knew that they did not know better. Most of the dignitaries and foreign investors were exposed in their halted vehicles as they waited screening to enter the compound. There were no barriers, and someone could have easily driven a bomb-laden truck across the grass.

"Let's remember that we're exposed," Kitson said as he opened the vehicle's door. "Don't shoot at anyone tonight." He turned toward his protégé. "Will you do promise me, mate?"

"Sure," Russell responded.

Kitson hid a small revolver in his breast pocket. "There will be metal detectors I suppose." Kitson fixed his bow tie. "Well, we should not leave them guessing." Kitson put an engraved flint lighter in his breast pocket on top of the pocket size revolver. Kitson's operational experience taught him always to be prepared, even with the smallest of options.

"Do we know if the Minister of Defense will be here?" Russell asked as they walked across the wet grass toward the Liberian Cabinet.

"He'll be here. As well as we can expect your friend, the American Ambassador."

"Great," Russell replied. "I have been dodging her for the entire week. Langley has kept her off my back, yet it has not been easy."

"She still doesn't believe the situation on the ground is critical?" Kitson inquired.

"No." Russell thought for a moment and continued. "She has a hard time understanding that an international crime syndicate has moved in."

"And Hezbollah's planned attack on Israel?"

"Same," Russell replied. "The Ambassador supported the Liberian government when they stated that there is no Ebola threat."

"My friend…you don't know politicians well," Kitson said as he poured himself a three-finger scotch. "In Africa, it is all about appearances. The President of Liberia has made statements that there is no Ebola outbreak and nothing to worry about."

"They are lying to her," Russell said. "I talked to the Defense Minister, and he would not listen to the truth. There will be a war in the streets. A war that no one has seen here in almost eighty years. That was the last time a plague of biblical proportions wiped out half the population in West Africa."

"I know," Kitson replied. His father taught him the impact of 1932 epidemic in Africa. While the world dealt with the economic collapse associated with the Great Depression, parts of Africa dealt with human annihilation as disease raged.

"We need to change their minds," Russell thought for a moment and added. "Or many more will die."

With the use of spotlights, the Liberian Cabinet building illuminated brightly. Generators were set up in front of the building and on the rooftop. The Liberian Cabinet celebrated the March tenth date when Harriet Tubman died, the founder of the American Underground Railroad movement to free American slaves. The date's celebration was significant in history. Additionally, the Liberian Cabinet wanted to send the message that their country was still open for business regardless of what the news had projected on the Ebola outbreak. The dignitary line was long, and Russell became impatient.

Kitson stood still and smiled as the Belgium diplomat in front of him who talked mindlessly about going to the bush to search for the near-extinct West African elephant. Kitson listened intently on how the diplomat described recent sightings of the abnormally small elephant compared to its larger cousins. The West African elephant was a dwarf and sightings were very rare, especially after the civil war when any creature was used for food. Kitson mused to himself how these diplomats had no basic survival training and would take on an adventure to go into the bush. Russell shook his head as he suspected they would be carjacked and killed. The line moved slowly. The humming sound from the generators at the end of the building sputtered. The spotlights dimmed and then grew faint. The generators ceased, and the Liberian Cabinet building went pitch black. Within a split-second, darkness took over.

"Looks like the party is over before it started," Russell said sarcastically. "Probably out of fuel."

"Quite right," Kitson said in a formal tone. "More than likely the Defense Minister will head to Robertsport." He paused for a moment. "We need to get him on board with our plans."

"I agree," Russell replied.

"Ready to move?" Kitson asked.

"Shucks and I thought that I would get a dance with the Ambassador." Russell quipped.

"Let's get out of here before panic sets in," Kitson interjected.

At the Robertsport mansion, Francesca had already drunk a bottle of wine by herself. The red wine smelled obscene. It was not a good vintage, yet she did not care. She thought about the man she loved. From her father's perspective, Russell was taboo, and maybe that was why he became so irresistible to her. She ran her fingers over the necklace charm. It meant so much to her. It was her past. It was her family. It was her pain. The small photo was the last one taken as a family before a Hamas bomber killed her mother. The inscription read, '*For lack of guidance a nation falls, but many advisors make victory sure.*' It meant a lot to her. It was the only thing that she knew from her youth.

Francesca finished the bottle of wine by herself and went back to sleep. She was exhausted, yet her mind raced with thoughts of her future or her son. In the middle of the night, Francesca awoke in a deep sweat. The nightmare was the same, a continuous haunt that attacked her deep, inner conscious. She watched the little boy wave one hand in the air. In the other hand, he held an ice cream cone. It was a white ice cream cone, probably vanilla, yet it dripped a reddish color. The blood-like color fell from the cone and pooled by his feet. The pool became larger and larger and spilled onto the street. A man walked behind the boy into the ice cream shop and then departed. Within a moment, a horrific explosion ripped apart the building. And her dream went blank. There was no aftermath of the destruction to determine if the boy survived. It was the same horrific dream every night for the past month.

Francesca grabbed a blanket and wrapped her semi-nude body. Her clothes were spread across the floor from where she tossed them, and she left them there. She covered her body as much as possible. There was a chill in the air. The fire in the massive wood burning stove had gone extinct. Francesca found her way to the dining room and looked for something stronger to knock her out.

"Can't sleep?" Kitson asked. His voice startled Francesca.

"When did you arrive?" She asked.

"Not long ago, maybe an hour," Kitson said. "Just enjoying a nightcap." Kitson paused for a moment as he noticed something was not right with her. "Something wrong?"

"There is too much on my mind." She pulled the blanket tight around the body as not to show any skin.

"Mister Russell?"

"And my son," Francesca replied. "With the potential fate of my country hanging in the balance, there is cause for concern."

"We will get through this and destroy whatever Hassan and Checkov have planned," Kitson said with confidence. He could sense that Francesca was concerned with something more. "Is everything alright?"

"I have dreams." Francesca drank half of the glass that contained scotch and continued. "There is a boy and an explosion."

"Is the boy close to the age of your son?"

"Hard to say, but probably," Francesca replied. "He's eating ice cream - Dominic does love ice cream." She paused for a moment. "Ah, what am I doing here?"

"What do you mean?"

"I came back to the Mossad on the condition that the assignments would be short duration. I have been gone for almost two months now. He's young and will not understand."

"Isn't your father watching him?"

"Sometimes," Francesca replied. "Truth be told there is a camp for orphan children that the Mossad runs." She stopped for a moment. She had revealed a secret, something that could cost her life, yet she did not care anymore. "The children are trained at an early age to speak all types of languages and learn a lot of cultural information."

"That seems nice,"

"Until they turn age ten and they start learning how to become a trained killer." Francesca looked at Kitson. "Once they are in, they are in for life."

"Is that how you started?"

"No, my mother would not allow my father to have the Mossad indoctrinate me. I chose the path of medical school and wanted to help others. After my mother died, everything changed. My life changed. My father changed. Everything changed for the worse." Francesca held back a sob. Kitson picked up on the emotion, something he never saw from this highly trained killer.

"I was recruited into MI6 after Belfast."

"Another shit hole,"

"Indeed," Kitson replied. He elaborated more. "Did you know that I am the reason an entire family was murdered?" Kitson drank the rest of his glass and poured another three fingers of scotch. "It was my first tour of duty in uniform, right out of Sandhurst. We had intelligence that a hardware store was building pipe bombs and the family's four sons were in the IRA. We had surveillance on them. One night, a man ran into the back of the place. I was on watch across the street in a vacant building. I radioed the main office, and they asked me to investigate further. I found the man inside. He was trying to steal from the store, and he clobbered me with a stick. He beat the hell out of me. I tried to chase him and fell unconscious outside. When I awoke in a London hospital four days later, they pointed to the pictures of the four brothers and wanted me to identify my attackers. I did not know what to say. I was scared to say it was not one of them. I was scared to say that it was, but I pointed to one of them." He finished the drink. "A week later, I reported for duty and was informed that my position was compromised. I did not know what that meant. I dug into the news clippings and found a story that alarmed me. An apartment in Belfast exploded in the middle of the night. It was reported bombs were being made there. The entire family was killed." He looked down and said. "Was it retaliation … maybe it was." He paused for a moment and said. "I never asked. Actually, I never had a chance as they sent me to the farthest place on the globe."

"Rhodesia?" Francesca asked. "That's when they sent you to Northern Rhodesia."

"Indeed," Kitson replied. "A place on the brink of chaos." He looked at the bottom of his empty glass. "White settlers thought it was their God-given right to shoot the locals." Kitson paused for a moment and said. "Bastards."

"They gave you the Queen's Medal." Francesca knew the story - everyone close to Kitson knew the story. A young Frank Kitson walked out of his camp unarmed and negotiated the surrender of over four hundred heavily armed rebels.

"Did you know that I was damn scared to wait there?" Kitson replied. "I was even more scared to go back to my men and say we had to hunt down the rebels."

"But you survived."

"Right." He thought for a moment. "I always survived." He added after a moment, "Luck."

"No." She paused. "Skill." She knew Kitson. Every intelligence operative in Africa, regardless of nationality or affiliation, knew about Frank Kitson, Jr.

"I'm getting too old for these operations," Kitson said as a matter of fact. "I should be home fishing and cooking something nice with my--" He stopped. He remembered that his wife of thirty-five years was deceased. After a moment, he continued, "well maybe in another lifetime." He looked at Francesca and asked. "And you, my dear?"

"Yes?"

"What are your plans afterward?"

"Take my son far away. Far away from my father." Francesca boldly said. "I will not allow Dominic to fall victim to the Mossad."

"And what of Mister Russell?" Kitson inquired. "Will he be part of the boy's life?"

"Perhaps." She smiled for a brief moment and continued. "Perhaps, if he starts another line of work."

"Ha." Kitson blurted.

"Maybe Tom will become an insurance salesman." She laughed.

"Or a truck driver," Kitson added. "Imagine him behind the wheel." They both laughed aloud abruptly at that thought.

"The roads would not be safe." She laughed.

"Our line of work is inherently dangerous." The elder intelligence operative offered. "There are many things in life I regret."

"We all have our skeletons in the closet."

"I could not agree more." Kitson offered.

Francesca stood up. She turned back to Kitson. "But I do feel safe with you boys around." She winked at the elder Kitson and went off to bed.

Kitson sat at the table and poured another glass of scotch. There was a storm brewing, and he sensed the danger. The worse possible trifecta of former KGB agents, Hezbollah operatives, and Al Qaida terrorists working together sickened Kitson. He felt something in his gut, perhaps a premonition that something very evil would come. Kitson thought about Liberia and the pain that this nation had endured. The sheer carnage from the fourteen-year civil war and the threat the nation posed. Kitson looked at the empty glass and jiggled the ice cubes against the glass. He was deep in thought and slowly dazed off into sleep at the dining table.

Chapter 21

Francesca awoke again and once again in a deep sweat. The nightmare raged in her head again, and she dared not to go back to sleep. It was close to morning, and the Robertsport mansion was eerily quiet. The sun started to rise, and sprinkles of light penetrated the window. She put a robe on. The late-night drenching rain chilled the air. The temperature dropped fifteen degrees with the new cold front associated with the monsoon rains. She snuck down the hallway on her tiptoes. Even with a severe headache and a blistering hangover, she had stealth tactics. Francesca walked down the hallway and opened the bedroom door slowly. She peered within the room. She looked at Russell. He did not move. She thought for a brief moment about all of their troubles – her pregnancy - the birth of their son - her father's rage. Russell had put her in a precarious position. Mossad agents were strictly forbidden from romantic relationships outside of assigned order. Female Mossad agents were trained in seduction to lure men into the bedroom in order to divulge secrets or blackmail. Francesca had crossed the lines with the American CIA officer. She had no plans for marriage, yet Francesca used backchannel resources to keep close monitors on Russell. For Francesca, her tracking Russell became her passion - no - her obsession.

Francesca closed the door. She could not sleep anymore and needed fresh air. Despite the cold air, she tossed the bathrobe back onto the bed. She needed to clear her head, and the chilled air pierced her senses. Her overbearing father wanted Russell dead. Francesca pulled open a picture of Dominic. He had Russell's eyes. She closed the door and left the mansion. The rock lined path led down the hill toward the beach. Nothing moved in the morning mist, not even animals. There were no dogs that lived anymore as they were butchered for food during the latest civil war. The animal population was decimated, any meat sufficed. Today, no locals possessed animals as the expense to feed another mouth was too large. Those with money knew that any pets would be stolen and served up as a meal. The morning fog held firm to the ground and blanketed Robertsport. Waves crashed, and the force of the spray pushed back the dense fog.

As she walked across the beach, the sun's beams broke through the thick cloudbank and illuminated the beach. The waves crashed across the shoreline as high tide lingered in the morning sunshine. Elements of bright sunshine rose from across the ocean. Trickles of sunshine splattered into the air from the waves. The scene was beautiful, and Francesca was partially immobilized by the scenic view until she caught a glimpse of movement about two hundred yards away. Francesca was deep in thought, yet she realized that she was not alone. She did not see anything, yet she had sensed something of a threat.

On the front side of the Robertsport mansion, Kamal pointed toward the white woman as she exited the mansion. The oldest of the three brothers acknowledged and grabbed three machetes. With the binoculars, Kamal watched the brothers as they raced toward the beach. He looked out across the fog and watched the bodies disappear into the pea soup like conditions. Kamal looked over his shoulder to see the dozen new recruits who waited patiently for his instructions. Kamal did not have long to train them, yet he did not care about sacrificing them for the caliphate. Kamal looked toward the beach to see if they overtook her. The fog remained thick.

Hassan had specific instructions for Kamal that he wanted the American dead, but he would be very happy to see a dead Israeli spy as well. Kamal thought of the photos he would publicly post of Francesca's mutilated body. Kamal was eager to sacrifice everything to kill both of them. He watched the mansion though the binoculars. He gave the brothers ten minutes to attack the Mossad agent first. After they killed her, Kamal instructed the brothers to attack the mansion from the rear. Kamal wanted no one to escape the inferno that would ensue.

Francesca's senses were keen, and she rapidly analyzed an emerging threat from the rear. As the three brothers ran toward the beach, they made noise. One of them clumsily bumped into a lounge chair. The fog was thick across the sand. Francesca estimated the threat at less than two hundred yards. The three brothers pressed forward into the fog's thickness and raised the machetes over their head. What they woefully underestimated was a trained assassin, a seasoned Mossad operative, a woman who had killed men with her bare hands. The three brothers ran at a brisk pace toward their target. Kamal provided them details on the woman and made them think the target would be easy. The brothers ran fast down the beach.

Francesca heard fast approaching sounds from a distance of fewer than fifty yards. Up ahead along the sand was a branch that washed ashore. It was small, about two feet long, but it would serve a purpose. In one hand, she picked up the branch and twisted it around in a complete circle. She kept the branch concealed along her body as she walked forward. Francesca wanted to bring them closer. Francesca kept walking. She needed the element of surprise and saw a cabana erected on the beach less than twenty feet away. She took off in a dead sprint as the three brothers emerged out of the fog. The brothers were surprised as she started to run and they increased their speed. Up ahead, she saw something that would work as a makeshift kill zone. Francesca dove behind the cabana and rested on the sand. In her free hand, she filled it with sand. The brothers arrived at the same time and ran past the cabana as they looked for her. In the open beach, they did not see her movement. From behind, Francesca attacked the closest brother and thrust the branch into his back. The brother moved awkwardly as he attempted to remove the branch. She needed one of them to drop their weapon.

Francesca tossed sand toward the face of the closest brother. It had little impact, yet served as a good distraction. With all of her leg force, she leaped in the air and somersaulted on the sand. As she completed the maneuver and from her knees, she slid the machete across the abdomen of the brother. He grimaced in pain as he fell. He was not close to death; however, he was injured enough to be slowed down for a final kill. Francesca focused on the last brother as he swung the machete with both hands in an overhead motion. She swung her machete in an upward motion to break the movement. The blades bounced off one another with a loud metallic sound. Rapidly, she moved her feet and positioned herself behind him. Francesca swung the machete with all of her might and severed the man's head off. Pain erupted in her shoulder. She panted heavily as she walked over to the injured brother who attempted to push his intestines back into his body. She struck him in the chest. He fell over and looked at her with open eyes as he died. The final brother still slivered on the beach as he attempted to free himself from the branch. She was more patient with him.

"Who sent you?" Francesca asked.

"Allah sends me," The brother responded. Francesca kicked him in the chest, and he fell over onto the branch. The force of the fall pushed the branch all the way through his body.

"Who sent you?" She shouted back. She slapped him across the face with her backhand.

"I will die before anything is said."

"I can help with that." Francesca pushed the machete into his chest. She pushed her hand off of the machete as she stood up. She knew that the next attack would be on the mansion. How many attackers, she did not know. She hobbled up the hill toward the mansion as fast as she could. Her right leg was hurt, yet she pushed herself. Sunlight was just breaking. As she rapidly moved into the kitchen, Ike looked at her with surprise.

"Watt happun?" Ike yelled.

"We got company," Francesca said. "Where's the Minister?"

"Hem thar." Ike pointed up the spiral staircase to the main bedroom.

"Rorke's Drift…. Rorke's Drift… Rorke's Drift" Francesca yelled. It was an agreed upon code word that Kitson provided them at the start of the mission just in case an imminent threat arrived. Very few would know of the British stand against a massive invasion of Zulu warriors. It was a solid code word for emergencies.

"What?" Kitson stumbled out of the dining room chair. Francesca was already down the hallway toward the library to get a weapon. Kitson yelled. "Where?"

"On the beach," Francesca yelled upwards. "Three attackers." She panted heavily and continued, "Locals…machetes."

"What the heck is going on?" Russell shouted from upstairs.

"There's an attack," Kitson shouted from over his shoulder as he vaulted down the stairs to the library. Russell did not wait to run down the stairs. He let gravity do its job as he vaulted over the railing and landed on the floor twenty feet below. From a dead sleep, his adrenaline had spiked. Russell had taken control over his senses. He landed on his feet, somersaulted his body to lessen the impact of the fall, and was in full sprint mode toward the library.

Outside of the mansion, the missile launcher was aimed at the second-floor window. The plume of fiery air from the missile launch was loud and surprised Kamal. He had shot an RPG rocket before in Pakistan, yet this was an old anti-tank missile that he now fired at the Robertsport mansion. Kamal kept his legs firm as he ignited the rocket with one light touch of the red button. His eyes were glued to the large corner of the mansion. Within several seconds the rocket traveled the three hundred yards to the mansion's second floor and blasted the side of the mansion apart. The massive explosion shook the building.

"Get down," Russell shouted as debris filled the air, and the mansion shook violently from the explosion.

"What the bugger was that?" Kitson shouted. He looked around and up at the ceiling and stated the obvious. "We've been hit."

"It was a missile strike," Russell shouted. Their eardrums were punctured by the noise. "We need to get out of here." He looked upwards, and a ball of flame had already engulfed the ceiling above them.

"Where's Francesca?" Kitson asked. "She was ahead of us."

"There," Russell shouted. "By the armory door," Russell shouted. "Help me." He jumped over a fallen beam and started to lift it.

"Bossman," Ike yelled. "Bossman." He yelled more as he ran toward them from the kitchen. Ike looked above his heads and saw flames ignite the building's interior. "Bossman, u ok?" Ike saw Kitson on his feet and grabbed hold of him to help him walk. Francesca was knocked unconscious.

"Ike," Kitson ordered. "Go help Francesca."

"Yahh bossman," Ike responded, and he jumped into the room to help Russell. Kitson looked up the staircase and the wall of fire. He instinctively knew the Minister of Defense did not survive. His bedroom was the point of a direct hit.

"Grab her," Russell shouted at Ike as he pushed his shoulder against the burning beam to provide a small space for Ike to slide Francesca out from underneath. "Get the door open," Russell ordered next as he saw Francesca was freed.

"Go!" Kitson yelled. "As he stumbled over the burning beams as they fell to the floor. "Get in the tunnel," Kitson shouted.

"The Minister?" Russell asked. He knew the answer, yet he needed confirmation. Kitson shook his head back and forth. Ike had picked up Francesca and put her over his shoulder. Ike was strong and very fit for his age. Russell kicked the back panel of the closet open that revealed the tunnel. He grabbed lights that were neatly placed on the stand and a pistol.

"I got more weapons," Kitson yelled as he grabbed a bag. "Go…Go!!!"

Kamal held the scope close to his eyes. He watched for movement and did not see any. Flames ignited the morning Robertsport skyline, and smoke billowed in the air. He motioned for his new recruits to fire on the mansion. The newly indoctrinated terrorists walked in a straight line toward the mansion. Hundreds of shots filled the air as a dozen of his new recruits fired indiscriminately at the mansion. They reloaded magazine after magazine and must have fired over a thousand rounds into the windows and walls. Kamal smiled. He was pleased the American was dead. The death of the Liberian Minister of Defense would make a great propaganda video.

Inside the secret passageway under the mansion, Russell was shocked by the assault and quickly tried to wrap his mind around the assault. He quickly assessed the weapons in the bag next to him. Within a quick moment, he grabbed a pistol and loaded a magazine.

"How many do you think?" Russell asked.

"Hard to say," Kitson responded. "We need to be safe for now and plan our revenge later."

"We'll get these scumbags," Russell was pissed, "you can count on that." He slammed his hand against the wall.

"Is she ok?" Kitson asked as he looked back at Russell. He kept a pistol and flashlight trained on the tunnel. There was no movement, yet he did not know if Al Qaeda obtained the building plans for the mansion. If anything moved, Kitson was ready to fire.

"Looks like a small crack on the head. Blood has stopped." Russell paused for a moment. "She's tough as nails." He had to say it more for himself than anyone else. From the time, he had met Francesca, nearly five years prior to Monrovia, she had been the invincible one. She was a highly trained killer. Nothing had stopped Francesca previously. She was tough.

"Heck of a way to wake up," Russell said aloud as he looked at Francesca. She was out cold. Her warm, cozy pajamas were ripped. Russell looked at her firm breast that stood like small mountains. The cosmetic operation had changed her outward appearance. A female operative with dazzling looks could open more doors and gather more information at a faster rate. He wished that the game was over. And a family would be the next step, yet that was something to dream about. When he arrived the previous night, Russell had checked on her when they arrived the night prior, and she was stone drunk and passed out in her bed. He did not bother to wake her. He looked down at her face that was nestled on his lap. He propped her head up on his leg and put a cloth against the wound on the left side of her forehead. "We need to get these bastards." Russell slammed his hand against the bricked wall. He shook it. "Damn," he shouted aloud. "James...We forgot about James."

"No, James moved out of the mansion," Kitson replied. "The Minister sent him upcountry two days ago to go live with a group of nuns. It is a very safe area."

"What about the juju and killing of the albinos?" Russell replied questioning the decision.

"The medicine doctor who had hunted the albino children for spiritual rituals was killed," Kitson stated coldly. Russell did not ask by whom. He watched Kitson look at Ike and quickly deduced that Ike may have had something to do with the medicine doctor's untimely death. Witchcraft remained paramount in West African society today, and fanatics worshiped the occult. Voodoo was very much alive and actively practiced in the remote regions. The only way to protect the albino children was to make a public statement by cutting the head off the snake or in this case the elimination of a tribal elder who secretly served as the local witch doctor.

"We need to think retribution," Kitson responded with a thick British accent. Russell knew that the accent was more prevalent when Kitson was pissed.

"Checkov was behind this," Russell responded in the darkness. "And I want to be the first to put a bullet in his head."

"Get in line," Kitson responded.

"Where...where are they?" Francesca asked as she slowly opened her eyes. Her body jolted, and Russell held her tight as she regained consciousness.

"You're safe," Russell said. "We're safe." He tried to reassure her. "They're somewhere out there," Russell said as he pushed some hair out of her face. She lifted her left hand to her forehead.

"How bad is it?" She inquired. She quickly gazed into the tunnel.

"The wound or our situation?" Kitson asked.

"Both," Francesca said as she looked around the tunnel to better assess the situation.

"Well, we are more than likely surrounded. There is still gunfire outside. Someone is still shooting at the mansion that they just blew up." Kitson started. "The Minister is more than likely dead. Checkov is making a weapon of mass destruction for Hassan who will unleash it on Tel Aviv. And don't forget Kamal and his Al Qaeda recruits who happen to be former child soldiers from the civil war are running rampant all over Liberia."

"So basically, the situation looks grim," Francesca replied.

"I can think of some more crafty words to express our situation," Kitson replied, "however we are in the presence of a lady." It made everyone chuckle for a moment at their situation.

At the MacArthur Airfield, Checkov looked over the plans and yelled in Russian at one of the scientists. Checkov pointed to the nozzles and picked up the bottle of half-drunk vodka and tossed it on the floor. The glass shattered. He shouted at his scientists loudly. Checkov looked at the plans again. His scientists had inverted the nozzles. The flow and release of the virus would not work based upon the air pressure. The weaponization of the Ebola called for a pressurized released of the virus in glass capsules that would bombard a city. The capsules were pressurized as well for the altitude of up to six thousand feet, and the virus had to remain active. Any higher distance could not be stabilized. At the higher altitudes, the capsules would internally explode from the air pressure difference. Checkov read the plans in detail and was pissed at his scientists. He paid these men well to come to West Africa out of Siberia, and he was not pleased. The scientists had been drinking every day and for the most part, were drunk the entire time. Checkov pulled out his pistol and smacked one of the Russians on the head. Blood gushed out from the fresh wound. He yelled in Russian that he was going to blow his head off if they screwed up again. Checkov ordered several of his Voctrad thugs to watch the scientists more closely.

Outside the hangar, the trained Hezbollah thugs maintained a tight security perimeter around the hangar. The men walked back and forth and communicated by headsets. Their voices could be heard. Featu listened intently, yet she did not understand the language. As the men moved past, she attempted to free herself again. Featu could barely move as her legs were shackled to a cement block. She pulled hard against the chains, yet she could not free herself. Blood dripped out of Featu's arm. The area of her arm was lacerated where they took multiple blood samples. The Russians did not care. The older one groped her breasts and laughed in a sinister tone. To them, Featu was an end to a means. After a brief moment, they departed. With all of her might, Featu tugged at the chain, yet to no avail. She listened to the voices outside in the foreign tongues. No one spoke English. Featu curled up into a tight ball. From both her eyes, tears flowed openly. She kept the sobs under control. She held her breathe several times to avoid crying out in anguish. She held her belly tight. Her monthly cycle did not arrive as predicted for the second month in a row. From a woman's instinct, Featu knew that she was pregnant. Featu sobbed deeply and wondered if she ever see the love of her life again. She wondered if she would be allowed to live.

Checkov checked his watch and wondered if Kamal had completed his attack on the mansion in Robertsport. He had used Al Qaida operatives before and knew their men would die for their cause, or whatever they were told to do. Voctrad had developed a closer relationship with the fanatical Islamic fundamentalists who operated much like they did on the fringe of society. Checkov knew the more instability brought to the world, the more money he would make. He never thought of retirement. Checkov thought of revenge upon America after the Soviet Union collapsed. He remembered the feeling of betrayal as most of his KGB unit was dismantled. In the post-Soviet era, there was no future for him in modern Russia.

Later that same day, Checkov wore the uniform of a Hungarian General and told the UN troops from Sri Lanka who stood at the gates of the Jordanian Hospital that they were relieved by the Russians. His men wore military uniforms and looked the part of a security detail. The UN troops were more than pleased to depart. Rumors swirled among all of the UN troops stationed in the three large compounds inside of Monrovia. Ebola raged in the streets, and the UN troops knew it was just a matter of time before someone they knew got infected.

No local workers who cleaned up after the UN were allowed into the compounds anymore. The garbage piled up, and the bathrooms became disgusting. Many troops pleaded with their leadership back home to get them out, yet few leaders trusted that they were not infected. Outside of Jordan, no nation wanted their troops back immediately as the threat from Ebola in their native lands was realistic. Few nations had effective Ebola testing procedures and apparatuses in place to treat the hemorrhagic fever.

Morale among the UN troops was dismal. Their futures were linked to Liberia's survival of the Ebola outbreak and looked bleak. Ebola raged across Monrovia, and dead bodies were left to rot in the street. UN troops observed the carnage from the top floors of the old hotel – protected by the ten-foot wall and heavily armed gate.

Checkov's men drove three large trucks into the compound. Several of his men had been infected with the Ebola virus and were segregated to the last vehicle away from everyone else. Checkov did not trust his aging Russian scientists to develop the antidote, and he wanted to find the one man in Africa who could – Doctor Abuja.

Chapter 22

The flames from the Robertsport mansion rose over a hundred feet into the morning sky. The tunnel was well protected from the heat and flames that raged above. The Minister had designed the escape tunnel to serve as a safe room for up to a week with adequate supplies. When he built the mansion, the Minister thought more about the past hostile military coups and rebel factions. Violence was common in Liberia, and he wanted to be prepared. The ventilation unit was fully operational and pumped fresh air into the underground tunnel. Sounds from outside could be heard as Kitson moved toward the exit.

"Is everyone ready?" Kitson said. They had no idea what to expect outside when they opened the concealed door. "Once we open up, it is go time." Kitson chambered a round in his pistol and placed the weapon into the holster on his chest. He picked up a submachine gun and inserted a magazine. He locked and loaded the weapon. The others completed a weapons check and nodded that they were ready.

"Let's go," Russell said. Ike helped Kitson push open the concealed door. The rusty hinges ground and squeaked as they thrust it open. "Move," Russell shouted. Within several seconds, they emerged with weapons raised and pushed out from the embankment below the mansion. A group of locals who watched the horrific fire screamed as they saw the weapons pointed at them. Once they realized that there was no threat, they lowered their weapons. Ike quickly calmed the locals.

"Bossman, gut yar truk har." Ike pointed to a truck that he has used for taking garbage from the mansion. The back of the truck had several bags of trash inside, and Russel tossed them on the ground. As they hid in the bed of the truck, they gazed upon the massive plume of smoke that blanketed Robertsport. Several locals screamed as they believed war had returned. Within a few moments, the team was on their way out of Robertsport and headed toward Monrovia. They had no time to mourn the loss of their friend, the Minister. Francesca, Russell, and Kitson laid in the back bed of the truck as Ike sped down the road. They did not know who was behind the attack and if the attackers remained in the area. Each of them kept their weapons ready. They bounced up and down as Ike did not slow down over the bumps in the road. Kitson felt his back hurt, yet he would not complain. After fifteen minutes, they were on the desolate road, and the three of them sat up in the back. They looked out at the casaba plantation fields. Massive fields crossed the landscape. It mesmerized them. Each of them was deep in thought as each came to grips with the attack on the mansion and the death of the Minister. Nothing in Liberia would be the same. Unbeknownst to them, Kamal had another catastrophic event planned and already in motion. Kamal escaped Robertsport in a speedboat and headed down the coast. He sent his recruits back to Monrovia to prepare for the next phase of his plan.

As they approached Monrovia city limits, there were very few people in the streets. Parts of the city seemed abandoned. Russell looked surprised as he saw more locals in the streets just a few days prior. He surmised quickly that the Ebola threat drove many to flee the city. Russell looked upwards into the sky. As fast as the storms arrived during the epic rainy season, the lull in the storms was sometimes far worse. The air across Monrovia was stale – no ocean breezes arrived. Even worse, there was no active sewer system, and human waste provided a vile smell. The novelty of flushing toilets did not exist in the war-torn country. The heavy rain soaked the city and washed away the foul orders. However, after an entire day of no rain and blistering heat. A pungent smell filled the air. With no ocean breeze to lift and untangle the disgusting web, the odor was horrific. Kitson, Ike, Francesca, and Russell arrived back at the BTC bungalows. In the back of the truck, the smell of the city was a far cry from the fresh air that they had breathed in Robertsport that was until Kamal blew up the mansion.

"We need to get satellite imagery of the Robertsport attack," Kitson said as he dialed the line to MI6 headquarters. "We need to know which one of them was behind it."

"I don't think it matters much anymore," Russell said. "Between Kamal, Checkov, and Hassan, they all are scumbags."

"Agreed," Francesca said. "We need to take them out now."

"Let me make sure we know who it was," Kitson said as he walked out of his bungalow. Russell looked at Francesca.

"While you sit around here looking at your reports, I am going to save my country," Francesca said as she slammed to door to the bedroom. Russell could hear through the door the distinct sound of metal on metal contact as Francesca chambered rounds in her weapons. He did not have time to worry about her and looked at the maps on the table.

"What have you heard from Sam and Doctor Abuja?" Kitson asked.

"They're safe. They are still at the Jordanian Hospital watching over Major Forleh." Russell said. "Forleh is stable now."

"But not stable enough to go to Monrovia General?" Kitson inquired. He knew the answer, yet he asked the question anyway.

"No," Russell responded. "Absolutely not - he would most likely die there. And things have gotten worse as more Ebola patients were brought in from Bushrod Island." Russell looked at the Monrovia city map on the table and pointed to several areas on Bushrod Island. "These parts are the worse." Russell pointed to all of the areas with close proximity to Bushrod Island. "The virus has exploded."

"The best that can be done at this time is to contain the population," Kitson stated. "Block off all these roads." He pointed to the map.

"But that is not as easy as you think," Russell replied. "There are reports of outbreaks all over the city." He pointed to red circles on the map. "And in these other villages."

"We need to finish our mission and get the heck out of here," Kitson said as he looked at the red circles. Russell looked at the bedroom door that was half opened. Francesca was changing, and Russell caught a glimpse of her skin, and he watched her. She turned to see him after she pulled down her clean shirt. For a brief moment, their eyes connected. Russell did not know what to think as he stared at the mother of his child. His instincts told him to protect her, yet Russell knew that Francesca was her own warrior. He held the stare for a long moment and wondered if this would indeed be the last time, he saw her. Francesca pushed past Russell as she exited the bungalow, no more words were spoken.

It was near midday as Kitson walked out of the bungalow. He had talked with the senior African analyst at MI6 headquarters in London. All of a sudden, Kitson heard a commotion outside of the main gate. The guard reluctantly opened the large steel door and quickly shut it. The look of absolute fear covered his face. Kitson caught a glimpse of bodies that ran past. Kitson heard loud shouts from men as they ran past. Kitson did not wait for a second glimpse, he ran toward the tower. Ike was on the porch sipping tea and dropped his cup when he saw Kitson run. Ike sprinted as fast as he could across the parade field.

"What has happened?" Kitson yelled at the guard. The guard had no reply and looked frightened. Kitson heard a lot of voices as the crowd passed outside the BTC compound. Kitson climbed the tower as fast as his body would allow him.

"Bossman," Ike shouted upwards, "wuut tis it?" A sound of fear resonated in his voice. Ike had witnessed firsthand the brutality of civil war.

"Bossman?" Ike shouted. The nervousness of his voice was prevalent. Kitson looked down at his longtime assistant and friend. He had never asked Ike about what side he fought on during the bloody civil war. The only thing Kitson knew was that his entire village was slaughtered by the RUF child soldiers out of Sierra Leone.

Kitson climbed the rusted tower at a heightened pace. He pulled his sixty-two-year-old body up the precarious ladder. He heard bolts pop from his weight and he wondered when the last time someone had climbed the thirty-foot tower. For his age, Kitson was very agile. After his wife passed away, he committed himself to defend the Crown. To do so, he needed to prove to his MI6 superiors that he was just as capable as men half his age. Kitson grabbed another metal bar and pulled his body upward. He stepped his right foot on the next bar, and it bent downward, breaking. Kitson dangled for a brief moment, at about twenty feet in the air.

"Bossman," Ike screamed. "Ike cum halp."

"No, stay there," Kitson ordered. He knew that Ike would do anything to protect him. "Too dangerous…I have it." Kitson placed his foot higher and placed it gently. Ike walked to the wall and looked through holes in the brick at the mass of locals who walked and ran past. Kitson pulled his body to the top of the tower.

From the BTC tower, Kitson watched the throngs of people crowd around the Presidential Palace gates. Many started to climb over the metal fence posts. The police blared sirens on their vehicles, but it did not stop the crowds. The thought of a hidden trove of money in the Presidential Palace, any money, spurred their curiosity. In a nation where the unemployment rate was near eighty percent, most Liberians had nothing. A few were lucky to get a few U.S. dollars from working to support the foreigners. Most had to scrounge for food on a daily basis. Kitson was shocked by the number of people who stood outside the gate and estimated the crowd at about a thousand strong. The mass of bodies pushed close to one another.

Far below the former Presidential Palace and away from the violence, Kamal watched from a speedboat far below the cliff where the former Presidential Palace stood. From this vantage point, he saw throngs of people who ran along the beach to climb the rocks. His plan had worked. He picked up the local newspaper and reread the headline. '*Millions of dollars found – Taylor hid money in the walls of Presidential Palace.*' Kamal had a loyal follower who worked in the newspaper's printing room. He got access to the next day's release and changed the headline. He entered a fake photo of a local man holding thick packets of U.S. dollars. Kamal fully understood that Liberians were gullible enough to believe what was published in the news. The story went into many specific details on how Taylor took truckloads of money out of the state-owned banks in the final days of his presidency. As Charles Taylor looked to seek refuge in Nigeria, he stole millions from his countrymen. As the rebels advanced on Monrovia, the story stated that the money was too heavy to carry on the Gulfstream jet, and Taylor was forced to hide the money in the walls of the Presidential Palace. The story seemed plausible and had many westerners scratching their head when they picked up the morning edition of the Monrovian Gazette.

For the past two weeks, the three brothers snuck a pile of old artillery shells into the former presidential residence. The brothers carried the bombs up the steep hill from the beach. The front of the mansion was blocked by metal gates, and regular police patrols kept out looters. The Presidential Palace remained untouched since Taylor was deposed. The building's interior was looted and would cost an exuberant amount to recondition. Many Liberians believed that the Presidential Palace was haunted by the souls who were tortured in the basement.

Kamal waited patiently as hundreds poured into the mansion. The new Al Qaeda recruits were directed to rush the gates of the old Presidential Palace and kill the police guards. They quickly gutted them with makeshift knives. From his vantage point in the speedboat, Kamal could not see the crowds of men and women who climbed through the broken windows of the Presidential Palace. Kamal just imagined the walls inside the old mansion being ripped apart. Kamal started the boat's engine. He did not know how far he needed to be away from the cliff. The line of wire that led up the cliff moved gently in the water. To make sure there was more of a dramatic effect, Kamal had the brothers carry jugs of gasoline and placed them on top of the artillery shells. The bedroom of the former presidents overlooked the cliffs and Kamal had a perfect vantage point. The artillery shells were neatly stacked, and the remote explosive trigger was ready.

The Presidential Palace had a horrific history. Charles Taylor was the last occupant. Before him, Samuel Doe led a brutal regime and murdered President Tolbert in the same bedroom where Doe ended up sleeping. Eventually, Doe was murdered by Prince Johnson in the Monrovian streets. Prince Johnson was not smart enough to know the impact of world sentiment and had his picture plastered across the globe as a murderer as he stood over top of Doe's body with a knife. Prince Johnson's political career did not last long. Taylor was more cunning and used that as an opportunity to get the backing of the American President to take over. He would be the second Liberian President in a row who took power through assassination.

Inside the Presidential Palace, about twenty locals had climbed the staircase toward the third floor and ran toward the closed door. The door was boarded and nailed closed. They used primitive tools to tear apart the door. As they entered, the locals were surprised to see a pile of bombs. They could not escape as hordes of more locals filled the hallway.

Kamal patiently waited as he kept his hand on the boat's throttle. He estimated the explosion would be large, yet he still had nothing to compare it with. He checked links to Al Qaida websites and saw how other terrorists built and detonated large fuel bombs. What he did find was a bomb combined with old artillery shells and explosive fuel. Kamal estimated that the time was right and pushed the detonator. Within a few seconds, a massive explosion ripped through the former Presidential Palace. A huge fireball erupted and engulfed the mansion. The Somalia bomb makers had proved worthy.

Kitson watched in horror as he saw the explosive power of eighty-five artillery shells wrapped together with detonation cord and C4. The top of the mansion was blown off. Shards of metal rained down on the crowd and screams erupted. There was mass panic as the throngs of people immediately departed the kill zone. Bodies were crushed as peopled pushed hard to flee. Kitson watched as death in Monrovia spiraled out of control once again.

Kamal pressed hard on the boat's throttle and screamed at the boat to move faster. Large pieces of wood flew around him and landed in the ocean. Several pieces of burning wood landed in the back of the boat. He had no time to toss them overboard as he needed to escape the explosive area. Kamal prayed out loud to Allah to get him out of danger. Kamal raced the speedboat out of Liberia and headed north toward his next destination, somewhere near Libya.

At the Jordanian Hospital, the concussion from the explosion over three miles away rattled the windows. Checkov looked at his watch. Kamal was about thirty minutes ahead of schedule. The change in the timeline did not worry Checkov. He had more important things on his mind as his men were contaminated with Ebola virus and most significantly, Checkov himself worried that he would succumb to a violent death. The vibrations of the explosion rattled the entire city.

From the force of the explosive blast, Doctor Abuja dropped a glass beaker of contaminated blood onto the floor. The blood splattered and Sam quickly tossed a towel over the glass to contain the blood. Even with their contamination space suits on, the risk of exposure remained great. In the active state, the Ebola virus was extremely contagious. Doctor Abuja looked out the window to see what had transpired. A thick cloud of smoke moved over Monrovia. Visibility was limited, yet he surmised that it was massive. He looked at Sam and went back to work.

"Do you remember the process?" Sam asked quietly as he looked into the microscope. The hood over his head was cumbersome to move and hard to hear, yet Sam did not want Checkov to hear.

"It has been too long," Doctor Abuja replied. "The formula was complex. It involved stripping out particles from the blood of a survivor. The vaccine needs to replicate the Ebola and protect the immune system instead of breaking it down. The only way to kill the virus is to penetrate the membrane around it. Without the blood from a survivor, we are helpless. We need those blood cells."

"The Russians are impatient, and they will kill us if we do not succeed," Sam pleaded with his mentor and friend. "I cannot die here." Sam leaned in closer and said, "I must find Featu."

"I know," Doctor Abuja paused and added. "I can tell that you love her dearly." He thought for a moment as he looked at the armed guards and asked. "How are we going to get you out of here?" Sam was about to mention his thoughts on a rescue plan but was interrupted by the banging of the bottom of a pistol against the glass.

Upon hearing the explosion, Checkov ran to the windows. He fumbled with his phone and checked the message from Kamal. Checkov smiled broadly as his diversion plan was in full motion. Checkov looked through the glass contamination door that isolated the laboratory and watched the doctors inspect the blood samples under the microscope. On the wall outside of the laboratory, Checkov looked at the giant model of the Ebola virus that Doctor Abuja had drawn. There were strange markings and arrows that Checkov had no idea what they meant, yet he knew it was significant. Checkov needed the antidote as he was concerned with his own safety. After a few more minutes, Checkov pointed to the doctors to exit the laboratory. After completing the necessary decontamination in the separate room, the water flushed all of the toxins off the self-contained medical suits that kept the doctors safe. The light in the room turned from red to green, a sign that no Ebola was present.

"Can you cure the virus?" Checkov asked as Doctor Abuja and Sam exited the laboratory.

"The blood you have provided does not show the properties for the antidote," Doctor Abuja stated coldly. He did not know that the blood he looked at under the microscope belonged to Featu. He unwittingly did not know that he just signed her death sentence. "We were successful by utilizing the genetic properties of the antidote. A simple blood transfusion will not work. The blood is too contaminated with the virus."

"You worked with the American CDC to develop an antidote," Checkov said as he walked past the doctor and around him. "You have dedicated your life to finding a cure. We know much about you, and now you will complete your work."

"There is no cure," Doctor Abuja pleaded. "There is just death."

"Death," Checkov laughed abruptly and continued. "Let me inform you that I know a lot about death." Checkov lifted his pistol up and pointed it. "Let me ask you. Do you fear death?" Checkov inquired as he massaged the barrel of the pistol with his free hand.

"Everyone fears death."

"Death has been my life's work," Checkov replied. He looked out the window at the smoke plume that blanketed over Monrovia from the explosion at the Presidential Palace. "My men have killed more people that the Ebola." He paused for a moment and turned to the two doctors. "Do you understand me?"

"We cannot make the antidote," Doctor Abuja pleaded more.

"If you do not assist," Checkov raised a pistol against Sam's head and continued. "Death will find you very quickly."

"It has been a long time," Doctor Abuja said. "My memory is not as good." He paused for a moment. "It was a long time ago."

"Come, doctor… time is precious. Your study on Ebola is well known." Checkov raised the pistol.

"But it was not proven." Doctor Abuja replied. "It was just a study. We had no funding to actually test it." He pointed back to the operating room that they had tested Featu's blood. "We need the blood from an Ebola survivor to see what the properties are. And we do not have that."

"We have a survivor." Checkov smiled broadly at them. He knew that the woman that they had captured was intimately involved with the American doctor. "If you want to see her alive, you will cooperate."

"Featu?" Sam asked. "She's safe?"

"For now," Checkov responded. "It all depends up to you now."

"Don't you dare hurt her," Sam yelled. Within a flash of a second, one of the Voctrad goons smashed Sam in the face. The force knocked Sam on the floor. Another goon kicked Sam in the stomach with his boot.

"Stop." Doctor Abuja shouted. "Stop!"

"So, you are going to help us now," Checkov asked. "Yes?"

"We cannot just generate an antidote." Doctor Abuja pleaded more.

"Really," Checkov looked out the window. "Tell me, good doctor," Checkov paused for a moment and continued, "How did the American CIA get their hands on your report and develop an antiserum?"

"I know nothing of that." Doctor Abuja stated.

"Are you not working with the CIA?" Checkov pointed the pistol away from Sam's head and placed it in the middle of Doctor Abuja's forehead. Doctor Abuja thought about his research. He spent a long time locked away in the secure U.S. government laboratory to work on the world's most volatile viruses. Out of the four scientists who worked on the project, he was sole remaining survivor out of the five original doctors. Each of the doctors were hand selected by the CDC. Each were experts in hemorrhagic fever and infectious diseases. Each knew the hazards, yet they volunteered for the four-month assignment at remote Air Force base in the Nevada desert.

Doctor Abuja remained silent. Checkov's goons picked up Sam and tossed him outside out the door into the hallway. Sam pretended to be unconscious. One of Checkov's goons kicked him in the gut, yet Sam did not move. Sam slid the cell phone out of the wrap around his ankle. He kept his cell phone under his pants leg as a means from theft in case he was mugged. Sam texted a message to Russell with just three digits - 911. For any American, regardless of what country you were in, the use of the number meant something bad had happened.

Chapter 23

From the Presidential Palace, the massive explosive force of the artillery shells shattered Monrovia's morning tranquility. The thunderous explosion rattled nerves across the city. Rapidly, rumors circulated. The Liberian President and many cabinet members who were in a meeting were taken to a protective bunker. In the streets, old women fell to the ground and yelled aloud. Their screams pierced the air. Smoke billowed. The chaotic scene made many believe war had returned to Monrovia.

"It's horrific," Kitson shouted down from his position atop of the tower. Russell staggered out of the bungalow after the explosive sound ripped through the air.

"What's going on out there?" Russell screamed as he ran across the military parade field toward Kitson.

"They blew up the Presidential Palace," Kitson shouted down.

"Is the President dead?"

"No, it is the old Presidential Palace," Kitson shouted.

"Why would they blow that up?" Russell shouted upwards.

"Wait one," Kitson said. He looked out over the water. "There is a speedboat." Kitson paused for a moment. He wished that he had a scope to see it. "There is a boat moving at a fast clip away." Kitson paused for a moment. "Hard to tell how many onboard but it is surely involved with the explosion." Kitson looked down at Russell. "Can you get some satellite coverage on that boat to trace them?"

"You got it," Russell said. He pulled out his cell phone and saw the 911 text message from Sam. Russell shouted upward. "The doctors are in trouble." He turned and yelled. "Gotta go to the hospital." Russell raced across the field toward the bungalow. Russell shouted an obscenity into the air as he ran to the bungalow. It seemed everything in Liberia went to hell in the past twenty-four hours.

"Don't wait for me," Kitson shouted as he looked down at the forty-foot drop. He quickly surmised that it would take him several minutes to climb down and every moment counted. Ike remained at the bottom of the ladder, and he had a frightened look on his face as Kitson started to climb slowly down the ladder. Russell observed Francesca load equipment into one of the vehicles. He had no time to find out what her plans were. She was on a totally different page than them.

Inside of the bungalow, Russell grabbed several bags filled with equipment and raced out. He jumped into the Land Rover and accelerated out of the military compound. Russell spotted several elderly women who knelt in the middle of the street and cried. They waved their arms in the direction of the explosion. Russell pressed the brakes hard and down-shifted the gear. He spun the wheel as he maneuvered around them. He had to be very careful as many locals stood like zombies as they watched the Presidential Palace burn. Russell took his eye off the road for a moment and shifted his eyes toward the rear-view mirror. He observed a giant plume of dark smoke from the cliff, and he could see flames reach skyward. Russell sped the vehicle up the back streets. He hit the brakes and spun the wheel at each turn. The area was dense with old, dilapidated buildings. Russell accelerated the vehicle. He made fast, split-second decisions. Every second mattered. Russell's senses were keen.

Russell did not know what happened to the doctors. He quickly surmised it dealt with Checkov as he saw several Russians at the hospital gate. Russell slammed on the brakes and shifted the vehicle into reverse. He looked over his right shoulder toward the back window to see where he was going. He shifted the wheel back and forth while he pushed the gas paddle to the floor. The engine screamed. Russell shifted the wheel hard and jumped a curb. The vehicle came to rest with the back wheels stuck in the air spinning. Russell turned off the ignition and sprinted up a side street. He ducked into a dilapidated building. Half of a wall was blown away by the civil war. He deduced that more than likely it was a large bomb that destroyed it. There was a stairwell, and he vaulted the staircase at a rapid speed. As he turned the corner, a frightened mother grabbed her child and nestled the young girl into her chest. There was utter fear on her face. Russell did not have time to express any empathy to her. He pushed on and noticed the same effect by the occupants on the third, fourth, and five floors.

Like many of the burned-out buildings in post-war Monrovia, squatters had moved in and taken refuge. For over a decade since the truce talks, no one had laid claim to the buildings. Some were owned by foreign companies who would never do business in Liberia again. However, most were owned by Liberians who fled to America and dreamed of returning one day to the cool breezes off the West African ocean and magnificent sunrises over the crystal white sand beaches a few hundred feet below.

Russell pushed his legs hard. His boots pounded against the cement staircase. The echo fueled a deep level of nervousness for the building's inhabitants. The top of the roof was empty, except for piles of human waste spread unevenly across the roof. Russell deduced that this was the designated bathroom spot. He covered his mouth and nose with his forearm. The smell was horrible. He remembered many bulletin boards and signs posted around Monrovia declaring that locals should use buckets for human waste and dump it into designated drains throughout the city. Since the sewage treatment plant was destroyed during the war, the locals were left to fend for themselves, and they found the easy way to go to the bathroom. Infections and diseases were prevalent from the raw sewage as heavy rains rushed down the staircase.

Out of one bag, Russell pulled out a grappling gun and two hundred feet of rope. He looked at the backside of the Jordanian Hospital and did not see any Russians there. He shot the grappling hook over the top of the Jordanian Hospital wall and through a window. He pulled the rope tight and secured the end with a double figure eight knot around a cement column. Russell hooked his harness and jumped from the ten-story-tall building into the air. He zoomed toward the hospital at breakneck speed. In his right hand, he held the submachine gun and pointed it forward just in case one of Checkov's thugs appeared. As he came closer to the end of the rope, he disconnected the quick link and fell toward the ground. Russell completed a somersault as he landed and crouched low with his weapon pointed forward. He regained his senses and moved toward the building.

Russell crept up the staircase. There was a handmade sign in Russian that he did not know what meant, but the skull and crossed bones sketch was a sign he was in the right place. Russell looked through the crack in the door and saw Sam on the floor. Sam was battered, and he held a bloodied rag against his forehead. Russell pushed the door slightly open. He locked eyes with Sam who motioned his head toward the operating room. Russell peered down the hallway and saw four heavily armed thugs standing. He pushed the muzzle of the pistol into the gap. Within a split-second, he weighed the options. Should he assault the Russians? How many more were inside? Where were Doctor Abuja and Major Forleh? There were too many unknowns. His decision was quick and deliberate. Russell grabbed Sam by the collar and pulled as hard as he could. One of the Russians shouted and fired toward the doorway.

"We need to move now," Russell screamed. He pulled Sam to his feet and helped him down the stairs to the next floor. More than a dozen bullets rang out. "Here." Russell pulled Sam into a room. "Grab the sheets," Russell ordered. "Wrap them like this." Russell intertwined the sheets into figure eight knots and looped the knot back through for a double figure eight knot. "This will hold us."

Russell took a chair and tossed it into the window, nothing happened. The exterior glass of the building was protected glass as the hospital was prone to receive random gunfire. Russell looked around, and the only object in the room was the bed and cleaning supplies in the closet. He took several containers and mixed them together into the bucket. A viral smell erupted. Russell saw one container was pure bleach, yet the others were not labeled. The door pushed open, and Russell flung the contents of the bucket in the air. The Russian shot toward Russell and hit the closet door. The bullet penetrated the thin wood and scraped Russell's right bicep. The Russian screamed as a torrid mix of chemicals burned his face. Russell ran and jumped kicked the Russian in the chest. As he flew back into the hallway, he was caught in a maze of automatic fire. The other two Russians stopped firing after they realized that they just killed their companion. Russell seized the opportunity and slid out on the floor and fired the captured sub-machinegun. Russians dove for cover.

"Take the stairwell," Russell shouted at Sam.

"I got the linens," Sam shouted from behind. They vaulted to the top. Russell assessed Sam's abilities under stress from a brief moment and was impressed that he could coherently respond and act under pressure when his life was on the line.

"Tie the sheets to that post," Russell ordered. "I'll hold them off." Sam tied the sheets and did not hesitate to climb over the side of the four-story building. Sam descended the building and jumped the remaining fifteen feet after there were no more sheets tied together. Russell was immediately behind him. Shouts echoed across the compound from the Russians. "What about Doctor Abuja?" Sam asked as they sprinted down the street. He was out of breath.

"We will get him out." Russell replied, and he added, "Keep running." He panted heavily.

"When?" Sam asked. There was no reply. They passed several locals sitting on the side of the road. The locals both looked at one another and back at the two white men who appeared to be running for their lives. Very few white people came this way. Russell heard the locals shout something, but they had already turned onto another street.

"We need to get to the safe house. It is up here." Russell pointed toward the next street. He had driven these streets dozens of time as he moved supplies in and out of his safe house at the Masonic Temple. It was abandoned nearly three decades ago and served as the perfect safe location.

Russell went to the one place he knew neither Voctrad, nor Al Qaida, nor Hezbollah would find them. They ran onto Tubman Boulevard. Everything was eerily quiet. Russell quickly deducted that the massive explosion must have scared everyone that war had returned. Russell directed Sam up a concrete staircase. Russell knew this route as he saw an old World War II cannon that was a gift to Liberia by General Eisenhower for allowing the Allied Forces to fight the Nazis from Liberian soil.

"Here's the path," Russell said as he made sure Sam was still right behind him. They moved very carefully down the steep embankment. Russell pushed through a thick row of thorn bushes. The building in front of them rose up high into the night. Sam could not make out the wording but realized from the design and stone that it was very old. Russell pushed open the door and lowered his weapon when he saw Kitson had already moved to the designated safe house.

"Are you alright?" Kitson asked as Russell and Sam entered into the main ballroom.

"Voctrad took over the Jordanian Hospital," Russell said as he panted heavily.

"Doctor Abuja is still there," Sam said as he tried to catch his breath.

"Checkov is becoming more reckless," Kitson replied. "We need to take him out." He paused for a moment. "We are more secure here. After you left, we took several incoming artillery shells."

"Was it Kamal?" Russell asked.

"Hard to say," Kitson said as he unrolled several maps across the table that Ike had just set up. "They did not have a return address on them." Kitson was not happy at the moment and had a mean look on his face. Russell knew better not to push him right now.

Several blocks away, the security team at the Cape Hotel was focused toward the front gate. Over the past week, many foreigners had remained within their rooms and waited patiently for flights to resume out of Liberia. The World Health Organization had shut down the airport for all outbound air traffic. The inbound flights were closely scrutinized to make sure no stowaways got on board the departing flights. The foreigners who remained at the Cape Hotel looked out of the window panes at the crowds. They feared the outside. They feared the hotel staff. Food was left at the doorstep. Cleaning ladies were not allowed to enter any of the rooms. The rooms smelled. The bed sheets were soiled. And the water supply was sporadic as it all depended on the five-thousand-gallon water truck that delivered potable water to the four large water tanks behind the Cape Hotel. Within a few short days, the diplomats who thought about going to the bush to get a glimpse of the fabled West African elephant shuttered themselves in their rooms out of fear.

The one thing that did bring the foreigners out of their hiding places was the massive explosion. The Cape Hotel was further away from Presidential Palace than the BTC compound, yet the explosive force was just as tumultuous as the windows rattled. Several foreigners dared to come out of their protective rooms to witness the horrific event first hand. Many had entered the Piano Bar to gain access to the balcony. Some looked at their friends with suspicion to see if they had Ebola signs. No one shook hands or hugged. Even in this direst situation, they kept their distances. From the balcony, they could see the large plume of smoke.

A few guests had touched the grand piano as they walked back to their rooms. One of the guests sat behind the piano and played with the keys. Several notes lingered in the air from a melody that he knew a long time ago. He missed a few keys and smiled to several of his old friends as he tried to remember the song "As Time Goes By" from the famed Casablanca movie. Their circumstance that each of them waited for permission to leave Liberia was eerily similar to the fate of those who waited for passage to America in order to escape the Nazis. 'Play it again Sam' could play the song like a master, and the guests were heartbroken to hear that he had died from the Ebola. A few of them singing the song and others hummed the tune as they looked at each other with utter fear. Liberia was a war zone. There was no escape.

In his top floor apartment, the explosion had knocked Tareeq out of his bed. He looked out the window and knew he needed to calm his remaining guests. He looked in the mirror and cursed as he turned on the faucet. The water dribbled. For the drops that he touched, Tareeq cherished them and lapped them toward his face. The thickness of his facial hair halted the movement toward his skin. He pooled more water and lifted it toward his eyes. Crusts of dirt filtered away from his eyes, and he rubbed them. Tareeq looked upwards into the mirror and into his reflection. He was disgusted at what he saw. In the corner of the room was his closet that contained several crisp white suits protected in plastic. For a man who wore a suit every day regardless of the heat, Tareeq was in utter dismay. As he sat on the bed, he lifted a photo of his Uncle Anwar who always knew what to do. Uncle Anwar was his rock. Tareeq was shocked by the brutality inflicted on his uncle.

Tareeq mustered all of the inner strength that he could and got dressed. The foreigners were pleased to see Tareeq as he entered the Piano Bar. Tareeq stopped his pity and smiled broadly for his guests. The guests asked about Uncle Anwar's rehabilitation. Anwar was fortunate to be airlifted out of Monrovia for surgery in Accra, Ghana prior to the suspension of flights. After Anwar was stabilized, he booked a flight to Detroit. Tareeq informed everyone that he had hired men who used to serve with the French Foreign Legion to protect them. After he calmed the guests, he asked them to return to their rooms for their safety. Tareeq walked behind the bar and opened a bottle of scotch. He poured three fingers of the alcohol into a glass. He raised it to his lips for a moment and then thought of Uncle Anwar. He thought of his guests. He thought of what the Cape Hotel meant to the locals who worked there.

On the other side of Monrovia, Francesca drove in and out of traffic. She avoided the many locals who stood in the middle of the street and pointed at the smoke in the distance. She did not inform anyone where she was going. She had her own safe house, and she raced out of the congested area of Monrovia. The safe house was past the new Chinese Embassy, toward the more commercially developed area of Monrovia. The existence of a satellite antenna on a rooftop would not garner that much attention in this area. The words on the outside of the building were written in Chinese to make locals believe the building was part of the Chinese development in Liberia. For the Chinese, the sign said, 'Not your property,' which had many of them questioning why someone would have a sign stating that. She checked to make sure no one saw her enter the garage. Francesca went back deep undercover. She had new orders from Tel Aviv to find the Ebola weapon at all costs and don't trust the British or Americans. Israeli leaders wanted photos and schematics to dissect the weapon design and create their own.

Chapter 24

Inside the Masonic Temple, it was dark, and Sam took a candle to find the bathroom. He walked across the marble tiles and could tell that the stone had intricate designs. The sounds of his footsteps echoed across the room. The Masonic Temple was built in the early 1950s out of solid stone. In the heyday of Liberian social life and before the multiple civil wars, the Freemasons were heavily involved in the government. Liberians kept close ties with their American brothers and mirrored the same Masonite rituals in Africa. The temple was permanently closed by Samuel Doe, who despised the upper crust wealthy Liberians. Doe was poor and hated those from wealthy families. He made his enlisted friend's members of his inner circle. Doe purged the Freemasons from the government, and the Masonic Temple had been shuttered for nearly twenty years.

"Have your American satellites any information on Kamal?" Kitson asked. He believed the CIA had a dedicated lower orbit satellite positioned over West Africa.

"Nothing," Russell replied. "I suspect that he is gone…long gone."

"And his gold is buried," Kitson confirmed.

"We hid it on Lucy's island." He paused for a moment as Kitson looked perplexed at the decision. "Safest place that could find in the area."

"And Lucy?" Kitson inquired. "You said that you saw her?"

"She is bigger than I thought she would be." Russell showed Kitson several photos that he took with the digital camera. "Must be from the plantains on the island." The African style bananas were a favorite for Lucy.

"What about anyone snooping around?" Kitson asked as he looked up from the camera. He looked back at the chimp. She was large. Larger than he ever thought she would be by this age.

"Lucy is territorial. She will watch the island closely," Russell said. "I also sent the coordinates to Langley to make sure we get alerts from satellite imagery if any boats land on the island."

"It's a lot of gold," Kitson offered.

"Kamal is not going to find it," Russell replied. He paused for a moment and asked. "Do you think Kamal has the virus?"

"I would not doubt it. There is a global manhunt on for his head," Kitson said. "We will get him." Each knew Kamal was deadly. Kamal had a group of dedicated, fanatical followers, bent on the destruction of the free world. Kamal believed firmly in the caliphate and the words of his former master Osama Bin Laden.

Russell hovered over the maps that were spread across the table. Kitson completed more detailed research on the latest attack and had new satellite imagery photos. They passed the photos back and forth. They looked at them in chronological order. The first photos were time stamped the morning before and showed a picture-perfect afternoon. So much had changed in one days' time after the coordinated attacks.

"Kamal was definitely behind the attacks." Kitson laid the photo on the table. "At the mansion and the Presidential Palace."

"For what purpose?" Russell asked as he thought for a moment. "What if Kamal was the ruse?"

"Really?" Kitson inquired, "To throw us off base?"

"Not just to throw us off base, but to divert our attention elsewhere." Russell looked the maps. "We know that the Russians have someone under payroll in the control tower. What if they snuck an airplane into Liberia?"

"But where?" Kitson remarked. "The UN controls the airport."

"Here," Russell said as he pointed toward MacArthur Airfield. "There is a runway here. Do you remember last week, we saw some imagery of the area. It looked like someone had cleaned up the area and there was a heat source recognized in the thermal pane analysis of the hangar."

"Checkov?" Kitson asked.

"More than likely," Russell said. The puzzle was coming together in his mind. "Look." Russell pulled out some photos. "This would make sense. These Russian scientists were reported to have departed out of Siberia. Here is an overhead satellite shot taken of the Marshall compound last week. See the bare white heads in the photo." Russell pointed to the three men. They were seated in chairs on one of the docks. "These men are definitely not Lebanese." None of the men had dark complexion.

"I see your point," Kitson said. "Francesca was adamant that the Russians had developed an Ebola weapon in Siberia and perhaps Checkov brought these scientists into Liberia to put it together." Kitson paused for a moment. "Look at these trees." Kitson picked up a magnifying glass and examined the photo. "It looks as if something had cut them off midway up their trunks."

"Like a chainsaw," Russell commented.

"Perhaps." Kitson thought for a moment. "What if a plane had landed at the airfield and smashed into those trees." He looked at the photo. "If anyone had cut down the trees, they would have taken the wood. Look at how these were all plowed over, and it is the same pattern on both sides of the airfield."

"Like a giant plane had landed that was too big for the airfield," Russell speculated.

"Most definitely," Kitson said. "This is our strike zone." Kitson took a big red marker and drew a circle around the hangar.

Kitson shifted the frequency of the shortwave radio to the UN channel and requested to speak with General Adbbas. Kitson spent thirty minutes updating the Nigerian general on what he had observed firsthand on the ground. As much as Kitson had expected, the UN base was on complete lockdown. UN personnel were not permitted to leave Liberia regardless of the empathetic requests by nations who had contributed troops for the effort. Kitson attempted to explain the deadly sequence of efforts between Al Qaida, Hezbollah, and the former KGB agents in Voctrad, but his request went on deaf ears. Kitson surmised that the UN scrambled to find out what had gone wrong. Kitson was not pleased with the conversation with the Nigerian general. The UN was in charge of keeping the peace in Liberia, and no action was taking place. Russell did not want to call the U.S. Ambassador as she did not trust what Russell was doing in Liberia.

"The CDC sent a team to Buchannan five days ago," Russell reported. Buchannan was a small town along the ocean. It was in close proximity to Sapo and the Russians. "They have not been heard from."

"What do you think happened?" Kitson asked.

"Hard to say," Russell said. "It could have been criminals. Locals may have seen them as a threat." Russell looked at the map. "Or someone needed protective equipment."

"I would surmise that they are probably dea," Kitson stated as a matter of opinion.

Sam had found a bedroom in the back of the Masonic Temple. He was despondent, beyond reproach. Anyone in the United States would look at Sam's qualifications, his education, his family's name, his trust fund, and say that he was a worthy catch. Sam had received a continuous barrage of letters from female admirers from the elite country club. Many thought it was romantic and noble for Sam to go help in a fourth world country, yet none of them signed up to stand beside him in the horrors of the remote African world, far away from Manhattan's landscape. At his farewell party at the country club, many shared experiences of their youth traveling the Serengeti plains in well-protected vehicles with personal guards. They shared stories of how they were treated to five-star accommodations after a day in the bush, which was realistically a luxury ride in an open jeep. They asked Sam to take photos. After Sam posted photos of orphaned children, many country club women distanced themselves. Some commented on his posts that they thought he went native. A few women who dreamed of marrying Sam for his wealth remained in touch and believed that they would be the ones who would turn Sam around once he returned back to the Gold Coast. The suiters imagined a fairy tale summer evening wedding with warm breezes that flowed gingerly over the massive country club lawn.

Sam had a written letter to his parents with hopes that they would better understand why he came to Africa. Sam pulled out the unfinished letter and reread it. The contents resembled something out of a tragic play. Sam wrote in the letter why he decided to help in Africa. He attempted to explain what he needed to do especially as his parents wanted him to join a lucrative position at a local hospital. Sam tried to convoy why he needed something more powerful than a country club membership, a nice house, and picture-perfect family to fill his soul.

Sam remembered the first day in Liberia when he started the letter. He just drove past blown apart buildings, relics from the fourteen-year civil war and eyed the locals who lived in utter despair, beyond any poverty he ever witnessed in his life. Sam was shocked at what he observed.

With both hands, Sam pressed the letter onto the table to iron out the wrinkles. He cried as he wrote about his Featu. He finished the letter with a remark of 'your forever loving son' and neatly folded it. Ten months in Liberia had been a long time by any standards.

Sam did not know if he could ever go back. He pulled out a photo of Featu, a glimpse of their blossoming relationship. They were at a waterfall by the Sierra Leone border, high in the mountains. Featu stood under the chilled water as it tumbled down from a cliff. Her soaked shirt revealed the firmness of her body. Sam held the photo above his head as he laid back. He studied the intricate lines of her silhouette and yearned to hold her. Sam was beyond destitute.

On the other side of Monrovia, Francesca had taken action to get answers. Mossad agents were trained to deliver three interrogations tactics. The first usually involved immediate damage with multiple bullet holes in the subject. The second involved a considerable amount of physical abuse and pain. While the third involved experimental hypnotic drugs that regularly resulted in death. Francesca had followed a vehicle from the casino in the middle of the night and watched the men depart into a house. While they fell asleep in their drunkenness, she slipped into the building. She tied them up. To awake them, Francesca squirted the bleach into their faces. The bleach awoke them from their drunken slumber, and they screamed. Each wiggled and swung their bodies in the air as they tried to move away from the danger. Francesca kept shot more bleach into their faces. The shouts were halted as she stuffed rags into their mouths.

"What do you know about an Ebola weapon?" She asked. Their eyes burned, and they could not see who their attacker was. They surmised from her accent that she was Israeli. The rumor of a deadly Mossad agent who operated in Liberia had filtered throughout the local Lebanese community.

Over the next hour, Francesca slowly and methodically tortured the men. She shot each of them in the right leg, above the knee. She used a piece of wood to smack him in the wounded area. The screams kept her energized. She used the screams of agony as a means of motivation. After the hour of direct torture, she removed the rags out of their mouths and asked them again if they knew anything about the Ebola weapon. The first one to speak up directed his friends not to provide any information. Francesca thrust a knife into the front of his neck, and his friends could hear blood gurgle from his throat for a few seconds before he died.

Francesca looked at the window and noticed daylight was coming soon. She injected an experimental truth serum into the next victim's veins. The heavier man jolted back and forth as he went into cardiac arrest. He was obese, and the experimental drug rapidly accelerated his heart. He died in a few moments. Francesca went back to the remaining prisoner and plunged the remainder of the syringe into his veins. The man's eyes rolled in the back of their sockets. The truth serum kicked in within several minutes, and he talked openly about a mysterious hangar that had a glass room. Francesca squirted another syringe into his arms. The man was dead within moments without providing any information.

On the Monrovian streets, it was not a surprise to hear a motorcycle; however, it was surprising to see a white woman drive one. Francesca shifted the weight of the motorcycle back and forth. She zigzagged around the traffic. Even in the early hours, the traffic was heavy as many businesses attempted to get their supplies before later in the day when the bandits would come out.

Francesca down-shifted the motorcycle and braked slightly as to avoid skidding. She pulled at the throttle and accelerated faster into the traffic. A slick spot of the road covered with oil shown bright as the morning sunlight reflected against it. Francesca knew that she entered a dangerous zone and lifted off the throttle gently. Seconds passed, and it seemed like an eternity. Francesca approached the oil slick road and felt the motorcycle tires slide underneath her. She lost her balance and slid across the pavement. A few locals looked at the white woman. No one came to her assistance.

Francesca picked up the motorcycle and started it again. Within seconds, she was on the move again. Pain ruptured throughout her body.

At the MacArthur Airfield, Hassan walked into the hangar and held his hand close to his face. He did not know what to expect. He looked at the chamber that was constructed. The thick sheets of plastic were ten feet high and linked together with steel pipes. The door was made of glass and had a vacuum seal. The laboratory equipment was in active use.

"Is she infected?" Hassan asked. He looked at Featu who was strapped to a surgical table.

"She has the elements of the virus," Checkov said. He looked at the medical charts that were in Russian. "She was infected by the Ebola and is healthy." The men looked at the surgical table and watched as the scientists monitored Featu's vital signs. "The equipment your men have obtained has worked well." Checkov pointed to the suits and the high-tech digital meters that were formerly the property of the American CDC.

"Can your men develop the antidote?" Hassan looked at the equipment set up in the laboratory. The Russian scientists drew on the plastic sheets in different colored markers. The life size picture of the Ebola virus had emerged with many arrows to different elements of the strain.

Hassan looked at the thick plastic sheets that were sealed together with adhesive compounds. The laboratory's ventilation was checked and rechecked. The only way to inflict the Ebola virus was in direct contact, yet Hassan's men were paranoid. They suspected that the girl was deadly and would kill them instantly. None of his men approached Featu. The Russian scientists had carried her into the makeshift laboratory and restrained her onto the surgical table. Her limp arms hung off the side of the table.

"Now that we have the blood," Checkov pointed to the patient, "We will be able to manufacture the antivirus."

"And the weapon?" Hassan asked impatiently, "when will the weapon be ready."

"We can only do so much." Checkov spat on the ground as he tugged on his cigar. "What do you want first – kill Israelis or save your people" Checkov paused for a moment. "We can't do both.

"The timelines were not adhered to" Hassan objected. "There was a detailed plan that was agreed upon. The plan is in motion."

Checkov became irate and replied. "This is Africa and not a damn thing goes to schedule."

Checkov thought about his own personal situation. Several of his men had been infected by the Ebola. The one man in the world whom he knew that could do develop the antidote happened to be in Liberia. Checkov continued, "From what we have from the UN doctor, my men will complete the antidote and the Ebola weapon." Checkov yelled at his men in Russian. He picked up his phone and dialed the number to his senior operative at the Jordanian Hospital. He yelled in Russian as he learned that one of the doctors had been rescued. He lost his bargaining chip with Doctor Abuja and tossed an empty bottle of vodka against the wall. Glass shattered. Checkov swore and directed his driver to take him back to the Jordanian Hospital.

Chapter 25

The gate to the Cape Hotel was closed tight – no one was allowed in or out. From the inside, Tareeq had the gate barricaded with an old truck. The hotel was in complete lockdown. The former French Foreign Legion soldiers had AK47s that Tareeq purchased on the black market. They took up positions on the roof just in case someone tried to climb the wall. Kitson estimated the distance to the building at about a four-minute walk from the Masonic Temple. Kitson and Russell moved quick along the streets down the hill toward the Cape Hotel. Kitson knew of the secret back entrance that led from the outside into the compound. Uncle Anwar had shown Kitson the tunnel that was built after the first civil war when Doe seized power. With the proximity of the U.S. Embassy, the Americans had paid for the construction just in case any of their diplomats were caught outside of the embassy compound. The small building was secured strongly by a metal front door, and there were no windows for anyone to break into the building. The key was encased in a brick on the right corner of the building that bore the symbol of the bald eagle. Once Kitson stuck his knife into the fake plaster, the brick jettisoned from the wall.

Tareeq had opened the Piano Bar to guests as the only means of joy. Tareeq had finally come out of the darkness that encapsulated him after Uncle Anwar was injured. Tareeq had doubted his abilities. After the Presidential Palace was destroyed, the foreigners rallied around his strength. They needed a leader, someone to say everything was going to be alright. It did not matter if Tareeq lied to them. He just needed to say it with enough confidence to quell the fears. Tareeq was clean and wore his crisp white suit as he served guests drinks. Several Norwegian lawyers who worked with the World Court at The Hague had remained. They assigned to research crimes against humanity committed by Charles Taylor

Tareeq was busy behind the bard when he observed Kitson and Russell stroll into the Piano Bar. He waved to them with a bottle of vintage, thirty-year-old scotch. Kitson and Russell looked at themselves and their appearance in the bar's mirror. Tareeq carried a pistol in a shoulder holster that was slightly concealed by his white jacket. Kitson and Russell took a table in the corner. Tareeq brought over a bottle of scotch and placed it on the table. Music filled the room as one of the Norwegians rattled the piano keys as he attempted to remember a song. The piano had been deadly silent since the former piano player, 'Play it again Sam' had succumbed to the Ebola and died. News of his death arrived a week later as the names of the dead were posted in the local paper. The list grew long. Prior to the outbreak, the Piano Bar became one of the most vibrant scenes in Monrovia. After the outbreak, it was desolate, yet another sign of Ebola's impact.

"How many men does Hassan have at Marshall?" Kitson asked.

"Forty, maybe fifty," replied Tareek. He thought for a moment and added. "They are heavily armed,"

"What about the casino?"

"Closed," Tareeq said. "Hassan shut it down and walked away." He handed them copies of passport photos. "Several of my guests have disappeared."

"Were any of them doctors?"

"Yes," Tareeq said. "But they were not doctors to help sick people. They were more like scientists."

"From America?" Russell inquired.

"They were from Atlanta," Tareeq replied. "Here are copies of their travel documents." Russell looked at the documents.

"CDC," Russell stated. "Looks like they were tracking the CDC."

"Probably for their equipment," Kitson confirmed as he looked at satellite photos of Marshall River.

"What does this one show?" Kitson handed the photo to Tareeq.

"The Marshall dock was expanded by at least four times the previous size." Tareeq pointed to the pier. "Before, they only had spots for several boats, but now it looks like a dozen boats could fit there."

"For a massive escape." Russell conjectured. "Maybe they are planning a major exodus out to a larger ocean liner or freighter to whisk them out of Africa."

"That makes sense," Tareeq offered.

"What makes sense?" Kitson asked.

"There are rumors about a cargo ship taking many of the Lebanese out of Africa."

"So, if Hassan was indeed pulling out of Africa," Kitson thought for a moment, "he would attempt to liquidate as much as possible."

"He will need every penny as he will have a bullseye on him," Russell snapped.

"Do they have money in the local banks?" Kitson asked.

"Doubtful," Tareeq offered. "Banks can be easily confiscated by the government. More than likely, the money has already departed the country."

"What are you going to do?" Russell asked.

"My uncle will be back," Tareeq said with confidence. He looked around the Piano Bar. "He expects me to run the operation and keep our guests safe." Tareeq walked over to the bar. "There is one thing you can do for me before you depart." Tareeq used his key to open a sealed glass cabinet door behind the bar. Inside, there was a bottle of thirty-year-old scotch that still had its seal intact. "How about having a drink with me?" Tareeq asked. He needed a friend.

"Could not think of a better time to have one," Russell said.

"Until we meet again," Kitson said as he raised a toast to Russell and Tareeq. After they drank the scotch, Tareeq filled the glasses again.

Kitson walked over to the double balcony doors and pushed them open. The ocean breeze lifted briskly into the Piano Bar. Kitson saw a few young children who played with an old soccer ball. He thought about how poverty did not restrict the children from joyous fun. The five kids played nicely together and shared the ball that was held together with duct tape. Even in the midst of extreme poverty and outright survival, children played.

Kitson stood at near attention as he spoke into the phone. "Yes, Mister Prime Minister." Kitson used his British upper lip accent, a tone that was perfected at Sandhurst Royal Military Academy where he taught Prince William and Harry. Kitson was a lifelong member of the Royal army. His father excelled in the British military culture and wore the rank of a three-star general. From an early age, Kitson was exposed to the highest reaches of the British hierarchy, yet he was well grounded from following his father across the globe. Most of the assignments were in remote African regions. Kitson watched his father battle the politicians as much as enemies of the state. In the early 1960s, his father helped suppress a bloody rebellion in Kenya. Kitson saw the horrors from the insurgents as many of the white British farmers in the rural Kenya landscape were slaughtered. Images of death ransacked his brain and haunted him in his dreams. Russell thought how unusual Kitson looked; however, he surmised that he would probably do the same thing if he had talked with the President of the United States.

"Yes, Mister Prime Minister. However, I would offer that the only way to get a solution is by direct means, sir." Russell overheard Kitson as he concluded the call.

"Did you get confirmation?" Russell inquired.

"More of the same discussion. We need to get more facts on the ground," Kitson said. Kitson was deep in thought as he watched the children as they continued to play. The innocence of the local children who had witnessed horrific events surprised him. Their clothes were torn, no shoes, and more than likely underfed. However, the children played with joy. Russell sensed his friend needed something more spiritual and he had an idea. They had passed a church earlier. Songs erupted in the air.

As they walked back toward the Masonic Temple, they arrived at the makeshift church. The building was small, less than the size of the Piano Bar, and it was fabricated with sheets of tin and discarded cement blocks. Russell walked into the open doorway and directed his gaze toward the priest. Russell thought that perhaps they needed some spiritual help. The situation looked grave and got worse by the hour.

"God will give you salvation," The local priest shouted in the air. There was no microphone or electricity. "God is watching you. If you believe, you will be protected from the Ebola." Russell felt the vibrations of singing as the voices echoed against the granite inside the windowless building. The old building was converted into a church after the civil war as most of the churches in Monrovia were burned to the ground. "Trust your faith. Evil is here, and Evil will prevail if you allow it."

"Amen." Chanted the followers.

"Ebola will not kill you. What will kill you is your lack of faith." The priest said. His eyes were wide, and he annunciated his words clearly. "Death has come for the non-believers."

"Amen." They chanted again and again.

"Go and find someone with Ebola." The priest demanded. "Feed them, pray with them." He paused a moment and continued. "Hug them as you are blessed by the Lord Almighty and protected." The priest jumped off of the old wooden crate. He dipped reeds into a bucket of water and waved them in the air. Drops of water flew over the crowd. The followers lined up behind one another and patiently stood still as the priest hugged each one. They walked out of the abandoned building and down the hill toward Bushrod Island. They would cross the river at night in makeshift boats. Some would drown. All would more than likely get infected with the virus.

"Why would you send them out?" Russell asked the priest. He was young, younger than Russell.

"Our God will not forsake us. Our God will lift us up," The priest said. Russell sensed something was not right about him as he would not look Russell in the eye. The man was afraid of Russell.

"You are sending them to their certain deaths. There are proper medical procedures in place."

"You foreigners speak of that." The local man's eyes opened wider. "Foreigners have killed more Africans than the Ebola." The man talked fast, and hatred filled his voice. "You people have never protected us and never will. You Americans think you are Liberia's big brother, yet you have done nothing for us."

"You are sending them to their certain death," Russell pleaded.

"No," The priest demanded. "They're are doing the Lord's work. I am sending them to salvation."

"Bloody hell," Kitson interrupted, "If you want to help, we have a need at the hospital up the road."

"The foreigners?" He asked. "No, we will not help those who victimize Liberia. We will help our own."

"They do not have any protective equipment. If they come work at the hospital, there are suits that will keep them safe," Russell pleaded.

"The Lord shrouds them in protection." The priest pointed to the pieces of wood tied together, which resembled a cross. "He will protect us." The priest rushed out of the building toward the river. He would lead his followers into the river and across the water like a biblical Moses event.

Back at her safe house, Francesca pulled the bandage from her right hip and tossed it on the floor. It was soaked with blood from the scrape on the pavement. She looked at the morphine injector, and she plunged into her thigh. Her eyes had rolled into the back of her head. She was in pain. She needed to alleviate the pain and the best option, realistically the only option, she knew was to call Tel Aviv.

"Can I talk to him?" Francesca said as she held the satellite phone.

"You know better not to call." The man's voice on the other end of the line stated. "Are dying?"

"No. I was injured. I did it for Israel," Francesca said. "I did it for my son. And now I want to speak with him." Francesca demanded.

"Wait." The gruff voice on the other end of the phone in Tel Aviv spoke. The time was well past midnight.

As she waited, Francesca reflected back to Paris. It was a lifetime ago, she thought. Her father had wanted her to be Mossad. He rose to the rank of Brigadier General in the Israeli Defense Force and retired from there to work at the Mossad full-time. In her last year of medical school, her father gave Francesca the ultimatum to join the Mossad or leave the family.

Francesca did not hesitate to swear allegiance to the Mossad and hunt down her mother's killers.

Francesca rubbed her hand across the scar. The eight-inch indentured mark into her side was a reminder of her commitment. In Paris, she was given orders to pick up and treat a known terrorist from the infamous terrorist group, the Italian Red Brigade. She was undercover in Barcelona completing her medical residency when she made overtures that she did not believe in government control. Francesca joined a Spanish separatist movement known as the Basques, and she made herself readily available for assignments across Europe. In Paris, she was needed to provide medical treatment to a Red Brigade commander who had several abdominal gun shots. The Red Brigade commander was quickly under her mesmerizing spell, and he gave her valuable information in his last moments of life. What Francesca did not see was the hand grenade that he placed under his back. As he breathed his last breath, Francesca rolled him to his side to check for a wallet. The grenade rolled, and the pin popped out. Francesca tried to move out of the way, but it was a quick release detonator of a half second – a trick used by the Red Brigade in case they are ever wounded. Francesca caught a large piece of superhot metal in her left side that caused a gash. She quickly poured the remaining sulfur into the wound and passed out from the pain. When she awoke later that night, the dead body of the Red Brigade commander was gone. Whoever came for him, left her to fend for herself.

Francesca's existence was predetermined. From the earliest age, Francesca was taught survival tactics. At the remote family farm, Francesca was trained in multiple weapons, while other girls her age played with dolls. The farm overlooked the Golan Heights, and the shooting range backed up to the settlement zone. Francesca became a disciplined shooter early on as her father scolded her for missing a target. Her father not only set life size targets, but he also put photos of known terrorists where the face would be. Francesca was driven to learn her enemy.

Her first kill was when she was thirteen years old. There was an uprising at the Golan Heights, and many of the Palestinian settlers fled the violence. Her father waited in the top window of the barn and shot several of the settlers who attempted to cross the farm and sneak into the Gaza Strip. One of the settlers survived the gunshot, and her father tied him to a chair. When Francesca awoke, she was summoned to the barn. She observed a man with a blood-soaked bandage wrapped to his chest. His arms were tied behind his back. Francesca was handed a serrated knife and was directed to kill. Francesca was young, innocent, and reluctant to kill. Her father berated and shouted at Francesca to kill. She was terrified. Francesca pushed with both arms, but she still could not get the knife to penetrate the skin. Her father wrapped his hand around hers and pushed strongly. Blood erupted from the man's chest. In the aftermath, Francesca could not sleep for days; nightmares lingered. Francesca wanted her son to live a normal life, yet she knew that they would have to leave Israel. She needed an exit strategy.

"Momma?" the five-year-old asked.

"Yes, my dear Dominic. Your mother is here."

"I miss you, momma."

"How was your day?" She asked. Her son, Russell's son, reminisce about his day as he played ball with several boys in his neighborhood. He did not mention the bodyguards who watched over him, dark shadows who protected his existence. The boy was too young to know about those things. Francesca listened closely as she sprawled across the bed that was until she dropped the phone. The morphine took over and sent her into a deep sleep.

Chapter 26

The highest area of Monrovia was off Tubman Boulevard. On the far side of the boulevard were the jagged cliffs that provided a defensive means for the city and served as a protection from any possible invasion. The remnants of large cannons from the late 1800s were nestled alongside more powerful guns installed by the Americans during World War II. Down the street was the Masonic Temple. The building towered like a giant compared to the other buildings in the area. Humungous stone pillars rose over forty feet tall in the front of the structure. The building had been abandoned, yet it survived the Liberian civil war and was relatively unscathed. Artillery rounds pummeled most of the structures by the fourteen-year civil war. The Masonic Temple held firm and was not penetrated. The main reason was that the walls were nearly three-foot-thick marble. The artillery rounds bounced off the solid stone.

The Masonic Temple was Kitson's and Russell's last safe haven. Russell needed to decompress and spent several moments to admire the architecture. The craftsmanship was superior to anything Russell had seen. Candles flickered in the darkness and shadows hovered along the walls. Russell slid his right hand over the sculptures that were embedded into the stone walls.

The scenes depicted free slaves who arrived back to the shores of Africa. The returning freed slaves were dressed in their finest clothes as their ship arrived at a rustic port of call. The local tribesmen who greeted them were nearly naked and carried spears. From the pictorial, Russell surmised the underlining theme was that the returning former slaves were of superior intellect. From his knowledge of history Liberian, Russell remembered that it took months for the white Abolitionist men to purchase swamp land for the reintroduction of now freed people back to Africa. The educated elite became the foundation for the Freemasons in Liberia's earliest days. The Freemasons had slowly taken over more control of Liberian society and became the most affluent. Former Liberian President, Tolbert was the last Grand Master of the Liberian Grande Masonic Lodge. After Tolbert was murdered in his sleep by former Master Sergeant Samuel Doe, the Masonic Temple was locked shut. Doe arrested any known Freemason and tortured them in the basement of the Presidential Palace. Life in Monrovia had changed under President Doe. Fabrics of Liberian society were untangled as Doe purged the upper crust. There was a tremendous brain drain as many educated Liberians departed and sought political asylum in America.

Russell moved his hands in and out of the mosaic pictures. Additional scenes showed the legacy of Liberia up until the 1960s with the rise of the Freemasons. What it did not show was their ultimate demise of two civil wars in the span of fourteen years with over three hundred thousand dead and over one million displaced from the violence. The structure of the building was the size of five football fields. Vines grew up the side of the building. There were no exterior windows for criminals to break into. The mosaic glass on top of the building was the only means for natural light. Russell had to use the candle to see more of the intricate design. Russell thought how this craftsmanship should be displayed at a world-renown museum.

When the Soviet Union had a massive reach across the globe, the communist government mingled in African affairs. Doe made public statements that he would not allow Liberia to become another Congo whereby the Soviets set up a puppet regime. Russell knew from reading his history that Doe had no political view except for self-existence. Doe routinely butchered his enemies in the Presidential Palace, sometimes even when he had guests present. There was a story that Doe beat a man to death because he wanted his wife for his own. Doe got blood on his shirt. When his dinner guests asked him about it, Doe commented it was from the goat that he just helped butcher for their meal.

Russell knew the story of Doe's brutality when he took over Liberia. On the backside wall of the BTC compound, Doe lined up the entire Tolbert family and shot them dead. Russell remembered how he touched the bullet holes. Russell thought how eerily similar the bullet holes felt compared to the grooves on the intricate design. For one nation, Russell thought that Liberians had experienced so much hope yet so much despair. The Liberian coat of arms depicting a seventh-century schooner sailing into a harbor with a palm tree in the background was carved into a solid stone block. The nation's motto, '*The Love of Liberty brought us here*' hung over the top of the national coat of arms. Russell contemplated that it must have taken years to complete this massive engraved depiction of national pride.

Russell found the bathroom and attempted to clean himself up. Russell had not shaved in almost a week and felt the scruffy beard with his hand. The Masonic Temple was the best place for them to hide and prepare for the final phase of the operation. Neither of them would be welcomed at the U.S. Embassy. The British did not have a diplomatic delegation in Liberia. Russell had tossed his embassy issued cell phone out of the vehicle so they could not track him. He was skeptical of providing the Ambassador any details on the looming attack. Russell fought his urge to help fight the Ebola epidemic on Bushrod Island. He instinctively knew any contact would not only weaken him but potentially kill him. They had to stay safe and more importantly, they had to stay healthy. Russell came out into the main ballroom and found Kitson cleaning the weapons again for the third time. Kitson was very meticulous.

Russell did not feel much cleaner. The old razor was very dull. There were about a half-dozen nicks. Blood drooled down his neck. He attempted to clean as much as possible, yet he failed. Blotches of blood dotted his face.

"Did you get into a fight in the bathroom?" Kitson laughed.

"No, just a bad razor," Russell replied as he ran his hand over the cuts and wiped up the blood.

"You could have Ike give you shave with a straight blade," Kitson said. "He helps keep me clean."

"No thanks," Russell replied. He thought of Ike and recalled how Ike had killed fifteen RUF soldiers who had attacked his village. His only weapon was a knife. The child soldiers were horrible shots, and Ike quickly maneuvered behind grass huts. Ike pounced on them and slashed the attackers. Ike cut them apart with his knife.

"Suit yourself." Kitson looked at Russell and pointed his finger at him. "Just don't go out with running blood on your face as it will scare the hell out of the locals. I know that you are not infected, but they sure do not."

"It's an easy way to get taken." Russell referred to the new process instituted by the Liberian police that if anyone is seen on the street showing signs of Ebola that they would be quarantined immediately. White vans were loaned by the UN. The Liberian police traversed the city all day. Men in protective space suits jumped out and grabbed suspected Ebola victims. Many of the locals did not go willingly as word spread about the bodies that were burned in large pits in the back of Monrovia General Hospital. Prisoners convicted of petty crimes were released to make room for those with Ebola who did not go willingly. An entire wing of the prison was devoted to suspected Ebola patients. Four to six were locked into a single cell. If they did not have Ebola beforehand, they more than likely contracted it now. Word spread like wildfire about the prison. If the locals were not frightened by the Ebola outbreak, they were horrified now.

"Did you hear today's body count?" Kitson asked. He opened his computer that was logged into UN headquarters. He turned the screen to Russell. On the graph, the black line signified deaths and the red line was used for projected infections. The black line had spiked over four hundred percent in a month as eighty-four died from Ebola yesterday. The red line was more daunting as it projected within a month that six thousand would die every day.

"The situation is not good," Russell said as he poured himself a stiff drink. It was ten in the morning, and he needed something stronger than coffee. "There are pharmaceutical companies working on an immune booster that would help prolong life, but it is not tested." Russell paused for a moment and added, "It's not going to help the dead."

"Or those severely infected now," Kitson remarked. "From what MI6 found out if the Ebola incubates more than forty-eight hours, the immune booster will have no impact."

"I heard the same from Langley," Russell said. "But we can save a heck of a lot of people." From his battlefield time, Russell knew that tough decisions were required. Triage would be required to determine who would receive the antidote. "We cannot trust any of the locals to administer. We need Doctor Abuja to come up with the antidote."

"That may not be easy," Kitson said. "Checkov will not just give him back." Kitson thought for a moment. "Voctrad needs the antidote just as much as us. Their sinister plans are on a global stage."

"That is why I have a few presents for him that I need to pick up at the airport," Russell smirked. "Langley sent me some supplies to help out."

"Does the Ambassador know?"

"Of course not," Russell continued, "And I am not telling the UN as we still have an arms embargo here."

"So much for controlling the weapons flow into a war-torn country," Kitson stated as he continued to wipe a cloth along the sniper rifle. The UN had imposed a weapon's ban in Liberia after the civil war, and it seemed more illegal weapons flowed from the Russians, Al Qaeda, and Hezbollah.

"Let me take Sam to the airport," Russell said. "The U.S. military arrived, and they are setting up a hospital there."

"Where is he?" Kitson asked.

"Still in the backroom." Russell motioned toward the back of the building. "He is really upset over Featu's disappearance. It would be good to put his skills to use." Russell added. "And I promised him that we would break Doctor Abuja out of the Checkov's deadly grip."

"How do you plan on doing that?" Kitson asked.

"Still working on that one," Russell said. He knew Kitson wanted to have detailed plans as he was more of a stricter rule follower than Russell. Russell saw the concern on Kitson's face and replied. "We got some experimental missiles coming in from Langley and some other fun toys for Checkov and his Voctrad thugs."

Ike drove Russell and Sam to Roberts International Airport. There was little talk as they looked out the windows. The once thriving outdoor market in the red-light district was empty. Few dared to get close to one another, let alone stand in a dense crowd. Russell checked his voicemail messages and confirmed that the box of equipment and weapons sent by Langley on a private jet had arrived. As they approached the flight line, Russell saw a massive C5 Galaxy military cargo plane being unloaded. The giant aircraft was near twice the size of the commercial airline jets parked on the runway. There was a dozen U.S. Air Force personnel to unload the C5 military cargo plane. Forklifts moved back and forth at breakneck speed. On the flight line, there were bulletproof military vehicles with large machine guns mounted on top of the vehicle. Marines were positioned behind machineguns just in case there was a breach in the perimeter. Several gigantic U.S. military aircraft were on the taxiway awaiting to have gear unloaded. Hundreds of pallets were neatly stacked close to the terminal building. The weather had cleared finally, and Russell looked upward in the sky. He observed four additional cargo planes that circled above as the pilots awaited landing instructions. The break in the weather had to be optimized, and everyone knew that. Known as the second wettest place on Earth, Liberia and the rest of West African nations lived up to the reputation with massive amounts of rainfall and the rain season was only in the third week with another five weeks remaining.

Russell smirked at the massive amount of relief efforts stacked neatly in rows. He did not mention to anyone that he came from Monrovia as they would suspect that he may be infected with the virus. Russell had to show several identities to gain access, and they would not allow Ike or any local into the compound. Sam was fortunate to show his medical credentials, and the guards quickly assessed that someone with knowledge of the Ebola virus would be an asset. Ike waited outside while Russell drove the vehicle into the compound.

"Are we ever going to find Featu?" Sam asked. He had not said much at all in the past day since he was rescued from Checkov's clutch.

"We will." Russell looked at him and said it again. "We will."

"Do you think she is alive?" Sam said softly as he looked out the vehicle's window as they entered the compound.

"I know she is," Russell replied. "Something inside me says she is alive." Russell wanted to reassure him.

"I feel the same," Sam repeated. "I feel the same." Sam was quiet again. He had a long stare in his eyes, something Russell saw with his men in the aftermath of a brutal firefight. Sam was horrified for what may have happened to Featu, and there was not much that anyone said that would help. Russell had no words to comfort him. There were no intelligence updates on anyone meeting her description at the morgue or in the hospital. Langley had heard nothing from Kamal after he parted Liberia. Kamal had the answers to Featu's fate.

After he found his shipment of weapons, Russell connected Sam with the senior U.S. Navy doctor in charge who was very pleased to add Sam to the team who would treat Ebola survivors. Russell handed the Sam a box of experimental antidotes to combat the Ebola that Langley had sent in. Russell pocketed several ampules just in case he got infected. Russell asked several Marines to help load the boxes in the truck. They looked with suspicion at the missiles and knew that whatever this man was up that it was not going to be good.

Russell walked toward the new surgical hospital under construction by the Seabees. Russell needed some lumber to brace the box carrying the missiles. Several of the Seabees looked at Russell. His clothes were very dirty and needed a shower. On his back, Russell had a submachine gun. He carried a nine-millimeter Berretta pistol, standard issue U.S. military across his chest in a holster. On his right hip, he carried a long machete. Russell looked like he had been through hell.

"Can I help you?" The Chief Petty Officer in charge of the Navy Seabee detachment inquired. "Are you looking for something?" He paused, "Or someone?"

"Nope," Russell replied. "Just looking."

"You've been out there?" The Chief Petty Officer pointed toward Monrovia. "Is it as bad as they say?"

"You ever do time in Iraq?" Russell eyed the man and surmised from his expression that he was more inquisitive of the threat than scared.

"Yeah," The career sailor pointed to his team. "We all did time in that shithole. Most of our time was in Fallujah during the first offensive when they pulled all of the Marines back because they worried about civilian deaths." He looked at Russell and did not know what to make of him. Was he Special Ops, Navy SEAL, Ranger, or Delta Force? "Another vacation spot." The Chief Petty Officer wore a clean uniform and looked at the man in front of him. His clothes were torn and dirty. "Were you army?"

"Marines," Russell boasted proudly.

"Really?" The Chief replied. "Looks like you had a fight with a razor. Never knew Marines, even former Marines, to go without a shave."

Russell grabbed his half-cleaned face with the nicks and rubbed it, "Guess I could use a better razor. Been too damn busy to go shopping."

"Take some supplies," The Chief said as he handed Russell a box. "You headed back out there?" The Chief asked. The Navy man who just arrived from Virginia had sensed Russell had something on his mind. Russell had that thousand-yard stare right after long combat operations.

"Have to," Russell replied, "there's a lot of bad men that I still need to kill." Russell shook his hand. The newly arrived sailor forgot the first rule mentioned in the safety brief – absolutely no physical contact with anyone, especially someone who has been in close contact with any Ebola patients.

Russell drove out of the perimeter of the newly constructed gate. Ike distanced himself from the other locals. As Russell stopped, several men approached the vehicle and asked for food; however, Ike said something to them. Russell did not understand what Ike said in his bush dialect, yet assessed that it was effective. Russell rechecked the ropes. Once he was confident that the load was properly secured, he jumped in the passenger seat. On his lap, Russell opened a box of CS gas canisters and inspected them. He put together the new gas masks and showed Ike who was confused at the contraption on Russell's head. Russell spoke with the gas mask on his head, and that made Ike laugh. The ride back into Monrovia was bumpy, and they stopped several times to check the rope. The missiles were still in the testing phase. Russell had asked for the experimental missiles just in case. At the time he requested them two weeks ago, he did not know what he needed them for. Now, he had a plan to utilize the experimental missiles.

Chapter 27

The abandoned hotel that now housed the Jordanian Hospital had large walls erected on the exterior perimeter. The stone block walls were over eight feet high and had rusted steel spikes on the top edges. The Russians pulled back from the main gate and moved their security posture into the building. The doors appeared barricaded, and there seemed no direct means of entering the building. Russell and Kitson had decided the best course of action was to draw them out. They would both simultaneously fire missile shots at the building's foundation to rattle the Russians. The commotion would most certainly anger the Russian former Spetsnaz soldiers. From Kitson's experience with the Russians, they always wanted a fight.

Down the street from the Jordanian Hospital, Wave Tops bar was deserted and in shambles. Russell assessed that it appeared locals had looted the place. Empty bottles of liquor littered the floor. Wood was stripped from the walls to burn in a makeshift fire pit in the middle of the floor. Russell kicked at the charred remains. Dust filled the air, and Russell realized the place had been looted a long time ago. The surfer from California's Manhattan Beach who had opened Wave Tops had long been gone. The owner worked at an international teacher's organization that helped bring school supplies to Africa. Many foreigners exited Liberia at a record pace, before the cessation of air travel out of Roberts International Airport. Wave Tops was just one example of a foreign-operated business that had shuttered in the Ebola outbreak. Massive amounts of foreigners and their money had flowed out of Liberia.

The front of the Jordanian Hospital was locked tight. The old entrance had wood haphazardly nailed together to close off any entry. The Russians used the smaller entrance in the rear of the building. The right side of the building looked like the best option to fire at. Russell made Ike stand next to him as he lined up the Javelin missile at the bottom floor of the building. The instructions seemed pretty simple to Russell, and he explained to Ike to remain away from the exhaust end of the missile.

"How are you doing on your end?" Kitson asked in the headset. He set up the operation in the same building that Russell had used to rescue Sam. Kitson lined up the missile shot for the rear corner of the Jordanian Hospital.

"All set here," Russell replied.

"Let's shake things up, mate,"

"Countdown," Russell said. "Five, four, three, two, one." At the same time, they fired the experimental missiles toward the building. Kitson's weapon malfunctioned. He pushed the trigger again. The weapon did not fire. He watched out of the window at the smoke trail from the top of the five-story building that housed Wave Tops on the top floor. The smoke trail was visible against the pristine blue sky. Kitson played with the device again and attempted to fire with no luck.

"Missile failed!" Kitson shouted. "I had a failure."

"Malfunction?" Russell asked. He waved his hand as the smoke filled the room. Russell observed the impact the missile had on the side of the building. Within several seconds, he heard automatic weapons fire, yet he did not dare to look back at the building. He pulled Ike close to the floor out of the window. "Damn," Russell shouted into the headset. "Plan B, then," Russell said.

"There was no plan B," Kitson said sternly. He was never impressed by how his American intelligence counterpart wanted to wing things more than often than have a deliberate plan.

Russell popped his head over the window's ledge quickly and saw about a dozen of Checkov's goons outside the building. They had weapons raised and fired at Wave Tops. It was easy for the Russians to trace the smoke plume from the missile. "We'll draw their fire," Russell informed Ike. There were few options. Ike understood what they needed to do and he popped his head over the wall. After the Russians fired at him, Ike ducked down low. "If we draw them out," Russell spoke into the headset, but he was cut off by Kitson.

"Then I can enter the backside of the building and rescue Doctor Abuja." Kitson completed the sentence.

Russell looked down at the box of gas canisters and placed eight on the bar. He picked up one after another and tossed them. Russell estimated about three seconds of flight before the contents ignited. Russell watched the Russians as they moved closer. Checkov's pointed toward the stairwell. Russell popped up and threw several more gas canisters. Bullets flew past.

"Ike, where's the pistol I gave you?" Russell asked.

"Ike uz tis," Ike said as he waved the shovel in the air. He knew Ike hated violence from his experiences during the civil war. Russell heard heavy coughing from the CS gas impact. The Russians were blinded, yet they ran into the building. They heard the boots on the staircase. Ike stepped forward and swung the shovel as hard as he could at the first body that emerged from the top of the stairs. Several bullets vaulted into the air toward the opposite wall.

"Ike," Russell shouted. "Are you ok?"

"Yay bossman," Ike shouted. "Got un."

Russell saw a grenade fly through the window and shouted. "Grenade." He did not know if Ike had heard him. The grenade bounced off the wall and exploded behind the bar and launched debris into the air.

"Bossman," Ike whimpered as he was injured with a small piece of shrapnel. Ike placed his hand against his scalp as blood vaulted out the wound and flowed down his face.

"Stay still," Russell yelled as he grabbed a rag to place on the wound. Russell assessed the situation and knew that they were in trouble. "We need to move."

"Yay bossman," Ike replied. Russell helped lift him.

"Move!" Russell shouted. He haphazardly dragged Ike across the room. Russell looked back toward the windows and saw something in the air. "Grenade" Russell shouted again and tossed Ike on the floor with brute force. Russell landed on top of him. The grenade failed to explode as it rolled across the floor. Russell watched it roll past them and over the edge of the outdoor patio. In a few seconds, it splashed in the river. Russell looked into Ike's eyes, and both of them realized how lucky they just were.

"Move," Russell ordered as he hauled Ike off of the floor. "We're going over the side," Russell shouted as he pushed Ike toward the edge of the outdoor deck. He sensed the hesitation as Ike looked toward the openness. Russell believed Ike did not know how to swim, yet he was not waiting for a conversation on his swimming ability. "Go!" Russell yelled.

"Aggghhh!" Ike shouted into the air. His arms flailed in the air as he fell over forty feet to the water. From above, Russell watched Ike as he hit the water.

"Damn!" Russell shouted as he looked behind and saw multiple grenades fly through the air. He stepped back and launched his body into the air. He heard a thunderous explosion from above. He did not have time to worry about the explosion as he trained his eye on the river. Below him, he saw arms splash on top of the water as Ike attempted to swim. Russell crossed his legs and arms before he plunged into the brownish water. He pushed his arms into the murky water rapidly as he swam toward where he thought Ike would be. He swam the breast stroke at a very fast pace until he struck Ike's torso. He slid his body up behind Ike and pulled him backward.

"I got you," Russell shouted into the air. "I got you Ike," Russell repeated himself as he pulled Ike's chin flat against the water's surface. Ike flailed his arms in the air. "Kick," Russell yelled between breaths. "Kick your feet." Russell looked toward the river's edge about twenty feet away. The current was fast and pushed them downstream. Russell looked toward Bushrod Island where the current was taking them. He rapidly assessed that as a bad decision to land there. There would be no extraction point there. The UN had orders to shoot anyone trying to get out of Bushrod Island. Russell kicked his legs as hard as he could and pulled into the water with his free arm. "Kick harder," Russell yelled between breaths. "Kick!" Russell felt Ike's legs push into the water with rapid kicks and quickly assessed that they made progress against the current. "Kick harder," Russell shouted. He looked at the faces which peered out from the building. Several old women looked at the bodies that splashed into the water. The women were stuck on the Ebola contaminated side of the river. No one swam in the river. Anyone in the river meant something had gone dangerously wrong.

At the same exact time, Kitson moved along the back wall of the Jordanian Hospital. The rifle fire caught the attention of many locals, and they peered out from their dark corners. Several locals waved at Kitson as they observed the rather tall, slender man in a British Army uniform move along the back wall. Kitson spied several remote electronic sensors that would trigger his presence. He moved cautiously toward the part of the wall that was repaired after looters attempted to gain entry to the compound after they saw the Jordanian troops depart. Kitson kicked at the newly installed cement blocks. He stepped back and kicked harder. He moved back further and got a running start. In his third attempt, Kitson kicked hard and successfully gained entry into the hospital compound. He quickly gained access inside the rear door and vaulted the back staircase. Kitson found the surgical ward isolated and eerily quiet.

"Here," Kitson spoke quietly from the side of the door. Doctor Abuja kept his eyes focused on the microscope. He did not dare to look at the fighting that raged outside. Kitson spoke a little louder, "Here." Checkov gave Doctor Abuja explicit instructions to review the work done by the Siberian scientists to make sure the antidote worked. Checkov did not care about his men infected by the Ebola and directed Doctor Abuja to test the antidote along with a fake placebo on his men to track their progress combating the Ebola virus.

"Over here," Kitson said again softly.

"Where did you come from?" Doctor Abuja was stunned as he saw Kitson in full tactical combat gear in his British Army uniform.

"Don't worry about that," Kitson said. "Follow me." Kitson looked around. "We need to get you out of here."

"Wait," Doctor Abuja said. He picked up several documents that he had wrote all over and stepped back to look at the vials that contained the antidote. "This may replicate the cure that we discovered before."

"We don't have time," Kitson said impatiently. He looked inside the intensive care unit. Several of the Russians were close to death. Kitson saw the massive hemorrhagic blisters that formed on their arms, torso, and necks. They had giant bruises from the disease. Several lifted their bodies up from the bloodstained sheets to look in the direction of the door. One of them had mustered all of his strength and began to walk toward the door. Blood dripped steadily from the sides of his mouth and resembled a small stream down the side of his face. The Russian moved haphazardly as the massive hemorrhagic blisters limited his movement. Kitson thought that the man's movements resembled something out of a zombie movie.

"One moment." Doctor Abuja looked at the papers sprawled across the table and grabbed several documents.

"Is this door secure?" Kitson asked.

"For contamination?" Doctor Abuja looked at the Russian who moved toward the door. "Yes, there is a testing system; however, the patients could walk out." Doctor Abuja continued to rifle through his documents. Kitson wasted no time and donned a chemical mask, opened the door to the intensive care unit, and shot the zombie-like Russian. He fell dead about ten paces away from the door.

"We need to secure these doors," Kitson said as he grabbed several chains and crisscrossed them into the door handles. Kitson locked the chains together. "Are you ready?" Kitson asked. He looked out the window at the firefight Russell, and Ike had started with the Voctrad goons...

"Almost ready," Doctor Abuja stated. "I have many documents here for my research." Doctor Abuja sounded rattled from the interruption and rescue attempt.

Several large diagrams of the Ebola virus covered the laboratory wall. The pretzel-like shape of the well documented Marburg virus that became commonly known as Ebola stretched across the entire wall. Various colors depicted the cell structure elements. Doctor Abuja walked to the wall and scribbled more notes on the diagram. "I think that I may have solved the problem with the Ebola membrane. The antidote the Russians are working on is not complete and would only appear to cure the patient." Doctor Abuja picked up his notes and pointed to several drawings of chromosome cells he drew. "You see it is here." Doctor Abuja pointed toward his drawing. He had used the hospital wall to draw a five-foot replica of the Ebola virus that resembled a contorted pretzel with a snake-like tail.

"I don't understand," Kitson said as he looked out the window, "and we need to get out of here."

"The lipid membrane can be penetrated with a ubiquity protein that can gain access to the internal nucleocapsid." Doctor Abuja pointed to the detailed drawing on the wall of the visually dissected spiral structure.

"Ebola is a complex protein molecule that has this spiral structure. Within is this gene here." He pointed to the photo from the electron microscope. "This polymerase complex protein is the solution if it can be destroyed by sending a barrage against the lipid membrane." Kitson watched as several more Russians struggled to stand and zombie walk toward the door.

"Doctor Abuja," Kitson said sternly. "You need to get your stuff or whatever you want to carry and follow me NOW!"

After Checkov heard the rocket strike against the building, he had raced out of the Jordanian Hospital. At first, Checkov looked up into the sky and wondered if it were a CIA drone strike. He quickly surmised that it was a local attack when he observed the smoke trail as it dissipated in the air. Checkov ordered his men to attack the building. He grabbed a sealed, hardened rubber box that had a skull and crossed bones on the outside. Checkov took several samples of the blood that contained the Ebola virus. He knew it was just a matter of time before the CIA would have a massive strike on the hospital.

Checkov and several of his goons ran the five blocks toward the bridge that linked Bushrod Island. The bridge remained guarded by the Nigerian troops. There was an abandoned house along the water. Checkov took possession of the structure illegally, and his men built a boat ramp inside and sealed it up with chains. They were prepared for a rapid escape if needed. With the back of his AK47, his second in charge broke the lock off. The back door of the building was sealed with plywood. Along the perimeter of the frame were explosive charges. After he boarded the boat that rested on a ramp, Checkov pushed a button that exploded the back door off of the building. Wood flew in the air. The Nigerians pointed their weapons in the direction of the explosion and prepared to fire. Checkov heard screams. The ramp had a slick surface, and the boat quickly descended into the river. Checkov smiled as his escape plan had worked.

Checkov looked toward the rear of the boat as water sprayed in the air from the boat's engines. He looked over his shoulder at the Nigerians. They did not fire at him. Checkov laughed aloud. He swung the speedboat into the river. Checkov watched the water that sprayed into the air as the motorboat sped down the river past the Monrovia slums. Dark faces peered out from the shacks strewn together with rope and heavily rusted corrugated steel sheets. The loud noise of the boat's engines pumped an unfamiliar sound into the air. Checkov's boat moved at a fast clip.

In the water, Russell heard the noise from the boat's engines and checked his pistol. He had four rounds left. He quickly thought about what to do and pulled out his cell phone. It was still soaked. He hit against his leg several times. He hit redial on it to the Langley desk officer he talked to earlier about the weapons he had requested. Russell asked for a drone strike or an airstrike to blow Checkov out of the water. He watched as the noise got louder. He pointed the pistol at the boat and fired the last four shots he had. With the movement of the boat, he missed hitting the target at all. Russell asked for a direct satellite feed to track Checkov as he escaped. The desk officer asked him question after question about the mission. He questioned whether Russell had sanctioned approval to kill a former Russian KGB Colonel? After ten minutes of having to debate the situation, Russell hung up the phone. A few moments later, Kitson arrived with Doctor Abuja and picked Russell and Ike up on the side of the road. Doctor Abuja checked Ike's wound and placed several sutures in his scalp. After Ike was treated, they took Doctor Abuja to Roberts Airport where he could do some good.

Back at the Masonic Temple, Kitson looked at the map of the area around MacArthur Airport. Several small trails were visible from an overhead satellite photo. The area was far from anything. There were local villages near and few roads. It was the perfect location to set up a secret base.

"We need to take out Hassan," Kitson said as he pointed at the map. He paused for a moment and added, "Here is where he met Checkov."

"Are you certain?" Russell asked. "We don't have time to chase ghosts. We need actionable intelligence."

"I understand your frustration." Kitson attempted to calm Russell so they could both focus more. "We will get them."

"Let's just blow up anything that moves."

"We must remain calm," Kitson replied. "We got this."

"Doesn't look like we have shit right now." Russell blurted out.

"MI6 had information on a SIM chip that Hassan used in one of his international cell phones," Kitson said, as a matter of fact, to show that the British Intelligence technology was superior to the Americans. "When he activated the phone, the SIM chip was traced to this abandoned airport."

"Great, let's call in a strike."

"Not so fast, my leaders are skeptical that the bomb ever existed. The Ambassador and your President would not be too kind if the British bombed their little brother Liberia." Kitson added. "And for that matter, do you really think the U.S. Navy will launch a strike off an aircraft carrier for tiny Liberia." Kitson looked at the reports. "No one believes us, we are on our own."

"Point well taken," Russell replied.

"We need to stop Hassan and Checkov."

"More than likely he is going to attempt to fly the weapon out of Liberia," Russell said as he looked at the map. "It's a relatively small airport. Doesn't look like much on the map, maybe a four-thousand-foot runway."

"If even that," Kitson replied. "Any pilot would have difficulty landing on that runway."

"We need to get satellite imagery for the last forty-eight hours," Russell said as he looked at the coordinates on the map and wrote them on a piece of paper for Kitson.

"We need to take the head off the snake." Kitson dialed MI6 headquarters on his secure phone and requested immediate assistance on satellite imagery of MacArthur Airfield.

Chapter 28

Hassan hid in the back seat of the vehicle. He was paranoid that the Americans tracked him with satellites. He would not risk exposure. Hassan kept underneath the blanket and hid from view. He was paranoid that any reflection would be seen and captured by the American satellites. Hassan smelled the thick, musty wool blanket and nearly vomited. He swallowed hard and kept his food down. The vehicle stopped on a random road. Hassan heard his men shout. He heard a car rush past and the brakes squealed it to a stop. The door to the back of the car opened and several of Hassan's men pulled him from the backseat and stuffed him into the trunk of another car.

All throughout the movement, Hassan kept the nasty wool blanket over his head. Hassan hurt his back as he landed in the trunk and pushed some tools out of the way. There were multiple holes punched into the trunk for ventilation. Hassan would not move. Space was cramped, yet he did not care. He was driven by the mission. Hassan knew that millions of people, those with the same desire to destroy Israel, depended upon him. He focused the pain inward as the vehicle bounced along back roads. After an hour, the vehicle stopped. Ten minutes later, there were two knocks on the back of the trunk. A moment later, it opened. Sunlight cascaded through several palm tree branches. Hassan was pleased that his men followed his instructions to park directly under the large tree. He wasted no time in the open and ran toward the hangar. Hassan went directly to inspect the weapon. He looked at the enclosed chamber that housed the weapon. One of the most catastrophic weapons in the history of humanity was assembled entirely and rested a few feet away.

The Russian scientists had completed the Ebola weapon. It stretched outward with the addition of the boomerang looking pressurized nozzles. One each side of the weapon, six pressurized nozzles protruded. At the end of each nozzle outlet, there was a release tube for the glass projectiles, which were slightly larger than golf balls. The weapon had aerodynamic features to help stabilize it from turbulence during the final attack phase. The original design was based upon the speed of a Russian 1960s era jet that traveled no more than four hundred miles per hour. Hassan's plan required the weapon to be stabilized for turbulence for a military jet flying up to six hundred miles per hour, a significant increase in airspeed. New joints and brackets were welded on top that would assemble the weapon to the exterior fuselage of the Syrian MIG 28.

Hassan watched two of the Russian scientists as they opened the massive pressurized device. The incubator was the new piece of equipment that kept the virus alive. The Russians tested the gel-like substance and were pleased the virus remained alive. From their experimentation to replicate the deadly VX nerve agent developed by the Americans, the Soviets had mastered the development of chemical reactions to stabilize and keep viruses alive. Hassan watched the control panel as multiple lights indicated the virus was adequately contained and active. Sealed tubes were linked to the four-foot-high centrifuge that isolated the virus. From the centrifuge, the Russian scientists carefully lifted out the one-foot vials and delicately poured the gel into the pressurized device that injected the glass balls.

Hassan looked at the front page of the Monrovia Chronical newspaper. The photos from Monrovia General Hospital caught his attention. He was confident in his decision to close the casino two weeks ago and move all of his men to the Marshall compound. His men had loose morals and enjoyed the local prostitutes. Hassan could not risk exposure to his compound, and more importantly, Syria would not allow them access if they were infected. The risk was too great. The front-page photos were grotesque. The impact of Ebola on the human body was horrific, something that resembled biblical connotations as cells exploded, massive internal bleeding, almost every organ damaged, and extreme bruising. The story provided more information on the carnage. Bushrod Island had over a thousand deaths in the past week and was completely enclosed by UN forces. Liberian soldiers wore face shield helmets to protect them from the blood that splattered as they beat anyone who attempted to cross the bridge. Nigerian soldiers fired along the river to prevent the escape in makeshift boats. Reports of gunfire were heard throughout the city. Hassan smiled as he knew that the chaos that raged in Monrovia was the perfect diversion to cover his escape.

"Where's Checkov?" Hassan shouted at one of the Russian scientists as the man emerged from the isolated laboratory. The Russian pulled the lever for the shower that dosed him with salt water. He saw Hassan speak, yet he was unable to hear anything with the hood on his head. The Russian removed the locked seal that kept the helmet in place. Hassan thought that the equipment resembled more like a deep diver's gear than scientists. Hassan kept his distance and yelled to the Russian. "Where is Checkov?" The Russian put up his arms as to now knowing, either he did not know what Hassan had said, or he had no idea where his boss was. Hassan shouted as he turned, "He has not returned any of my calls." Hassan had turned back to the laboratory and looked at Featu on the surgical table. Hassan wondered if he should kill her now.

Throughout the day, Hassan had become even more paranoid. He looked at his phone and thought for a moment that he heard it ring. He put it to his ear and did not hear anything. The phone had an international SIM chip loaded within, something that was not cheap. Hassan navigated the call history and got suspicious. For a moment, he thought that the American CIA might have hacked his phone. He looked at it one more time and tossed it on the concrete floor with all of his might. He jumped on the pieces with his boot. He bent over and retrieved the SIM card that he could use in another phone at a later time. Hassan needed to be a ghost until the aircraft arrived to carry the Ebola weapon out of Africa.

Hassan looked closer at the weapon. After the last of the twelve nozzles were installed, the chamber was pressurized to check for any leaks. The scientists delicately loaded the glass balls that carried the Ebola. The weapon would be attached underneath the aircraft by the large braces that were welded. The weapon's design helped with the aerodynamics, yet it would still be challenging to fly. The pressurized nozzles would keep the glass balls from prematurely exploding based upon the change in atmospheric pressure. The weapon was updated to account for the aircraft's altitude variation as the attack would start at eight thousand feet and end at five hundred feet over Tel Aviv. The pressurized nozzles would shoot the glass balls by forced air through the chamber. As the plane descended rapidly, Ebola would be spread across the city. With the twelve pressurized nozzles, Hassan estimated that they could fire four thousand glass balls.

Hassan drank straight out of a vodka bottle that rested on the table. He took another cell phone out of his pocket and inserted the SIM chip. He attempted to contact Checkov again. The weapon must be completed as the aircraft landed the next day. The weapon would be flown to Damascus. Afterward, the weapon would be outfitted underneath a fast jet aircraft for the final assault. When Checkov did not answer, Hassan pulled out the SIM chip and smashed the phone.

In the Masonic Temple, maps were posted on the walls with large printouts of selected targets were updated. Aerial photos of various active parts of the country were plastered all over the walls. Photos of several UN soldiers were posted, and several were circled as potential conspirators with Voctrad. MI6 completed dossiers on several officers from Hungary who were on their watch list. A British spy plane had passed overhead at forty-five thousand feet and snapped photos clear enough to see a man's eye color. The printer worked for over an hour from the download to provide clear pictures of the targets. Kitson took the photos and drew lines between them differentiating the targets from Hezbollah and the Russian scientists. He placed target numbers on each one and identified who would make the shot on each one and at what time. Kitson spent several hours working through the puzzle to choreograph the assault at the airport.

"How much time from start to finish?" Russell inquired.

"Three minutes," Kitson stated as a matter of fact. He had completed the calculations in utmost detail for how many direct shots needed to be fired and even estimated a ten percent error factor for not eliminating the targets within one shot.

"Langley has debated a surgical missile strike," Russell replied as he continued to insert rounds into a magazine, "perhaps something off of Navy submarine." After he finished filling the thirty-round clip, he stacked it on the table next to the fourteen other ones he had supplied.

"Don't you think it is a little too late?" Kitson pondered as he kept his eye trained against the wall. His mind worked fast as he recalculated the times, distances, wind factors, humidity, and target size. Kitson was one of the best snipers at MI6 and probably in the top tier of global snipers. He knew that he could make the more difficult shots and looked at the position he gave to Russell and his target list. Kitson had observed Russell's ability and believed he could adequately perform his part of the plan.

"There is too much politics involved with this mission." Russell looked at his friend and gave him what he heard. "The State Department was informed and vehemently protested any airstrike."

"If your government informs the UN, the mission will be leaked." Kitson was skeptical when it came to covert operations in Africa. Too many had an influence that Kitson believed tainted the issues. "We cannot trust at the UN or in the Liberian government. Someone may have been bribed."

"I agree," Russell replied. "We have no room for errors and absolutely no time to waste." He picked up the magazine clips and tossed them into a large duffle bag. "We need to strike now."

In the makeshift laboratory within the old hangar, Featu was in utter despair and hopelessness. She looked at the tubes that ran out of her veins and into the machines. She knew that her blood was being recycled as it moved in and out of the large machine. She did not understand any of the writing on the side of the device. After everyone had left the hangar, she pulled harder and harder at the restraints. Featu thought of seeing Sam again. She had no one. Featu was a lonely child, and her parents were dead. The only distant relatives lived a more primitive existence. They were from the Mandingo tribe and lived in the remote northern mountains. The Mandingos were descendants of the ancient Mali Empire that ruled a major portion of Africa about four hundred years ago. Featu was tall and slender compared to many Liberian women. From all of the walking she did throughout her life, her legs were solid muscle. Featu turned heads in Liberia by her beauty and could have easily passed as an international model.

While most Liberians were Christian, the Mandingos practiced Islam. Featu was raised by another family when her parents were killed in a cross-border raid by the RUF during the Sierra Leone civil war in the early1990s. The RUF rebels attacked many villages up along the border as easy targets and would steal children to work in their diamond camps. The stories of the RUF's brutality quickly spread from survivors who had escaped captivity. Children were beaten and brutalized by the RUF rebels and forced to work all day long in the blazing sun panning for rough diamonds in the northern Sierra Leone riverbanks. The children were cuffed with wire at the feet and connected to one another with steel linked cables. When a child passed out from dehydration or died, their body would float in the water until they were allowed to leave the panning area at the end of the day. The rumors circulated rapidly from those who had escaped. Featu's adopted parents feared for her safety and sent her away with a missionary who came to administer vaccines. The missionary lady brought Featu to Monrovia and taught her how to be a nurse at an early age.

Featu endured unspeakable suffering growing up in war-torn Monrovia. From the age of eleven, she worked in the missionary clinic. She got her real baptism by fire when the civil war broke out. Casualties from the bombings and automatic weapons fire overwhelmed Monrovia General Hospital. Locals pleaded for help, and wherever they could find someone with any medical background, they took it. Featu learned quickly to stop the bleeding by any means. There was no surgical equipment as the missionary was focused on vaccines. Featu experimented with hot wax, spices, and duct tape to stop the bleeding. She used bandages and lots of them from old garments to hold back the bleeding. Featu learned quickly how to manage an operation to remove gun fragments. The dead were quickly buried in the back in several mass graves to prevent any disease from the rotting flesh. Featu had to help with that task as well. She had many life and death assignments at a very young age that influenced her tremendously to make a difference, for the better in her life.

Featu pulled at her wrists and twisted them. She despised the one Russian scientist who looked like a vampire with his very pale complexion. He was the one who routinely groped her breasts and laughed aloud when he did it. Francesca pulled her arms hard and stopped when she saw the commotion with the Lebanese man who screamed at everyone. She knew the man from the casino where Sam took her for once for a nice dinner. Featu laid back on the pillow and looked at the bright lights that lingered above her head. She thought of Sam. She loved him more than anything. Sam was naïve to think she would be welcomed into his family. Sam told her how much he despised the country club life and the socialites of the Gold Coast. Sam's assignment in Africa was up next month, yet he mentioned that he did not want to leave Liberia without her. Featu thought of life without Sam and sobbed. Featu knew that she was pregnant with Sam's child. She contemplated escape, but how. She was shackled to the bed, and there were many guards with weapons. Ideas raced through her mind. She needed to live. She needed to be with Sam. She needed to have Sam's baby. She needed to survive.

Chapter 29

The future of Liberia was at stake, mainly as thousands of foreigners had already fled. Few foreigners remained. The Camp Hotel, with its secure perimeter and armed security detail, became the one place of refuge. No UN inspectors had arrived to question why the guards were armed, especially with the arms embargo in place. The Piano Bar was allowed to open, yet no one played the piano out of respect for the former musician. Tareeq watched several large fruit spiders walk across the floor. He smacked them with a broom and swept them toward the pile of broken bottles and trash in the center of the room. The tables and chairs were stacked against the wall. He dug out all of the liquor from the storage room. Guests ventured bravely out to the Piano Bar. Tareeq lost track of the money and who owed the hotel. Two local ladies had worked in the office, but one was infected, and the other had not come back. Tareeq had no idea if the one who was infected survived or perished. Information was scarce.

The Lebanese presence in Liberia first started in the 1930s based upon trade throughout the region. The establishment of the Firestone Plantation for rubber exports fueled the flow of foreign investment into Liberia. Shrewd businessmen opened factories by negotiating with local leaders to secure the land under their name. No foreign-born person could own any property outright in Liberia. The founders of the nation decreed this strict rule as a means to ensure American plantation owners would never be able to own land in their newly established free country. Uncle Anwar and Tareeq were part of the new flow of Lebanese to Liberia. As the turmoil in Beirut and Lebanon exploded, thousands migrated to West Africa. Anwar had signed a ninety-nine lease for the land under the Cape Hotel with then Liberian President Samuel Doe. The Cape Hotel was initially built by Germans to house their diplomats as they negotiated rubber contracts with Firestone Rubber plantation in the 1930s. With the outbreak of America's involvement in World War II, Liberia expelled all Germans, and the government took possession. The building fell into severe disrepair. Over the decades, many foreigners attempted to resurrect the grandeur of the Cape Hotel, yet they failed. To get anything accomplished in Liberia's post-war apocalypse was impossible. Anwar was a master negotiator and built solid relationships with many Liberians. When Charles Taylor took over the government, Anwar invited him to a private dinner that was fit for the Queen of England. Anwar knew how to survive. He developed relationships with each U.S. Ambassador, who flowed in and out of Liberia every few years.

Tareeq walked out onto the terrace around the pool. He wore his crisp white suit. Tareeq understood the fear many foreigners had with locals who worked within the hotel. Locals were not trusted, and Tareeq directed them to leave the hotel. Fliers were posted with the new procedures for no direct contact and times when guests would be allowed to go to the restaurant to cook their own meals and most importantly use the pool to relax. In the Piano Bar, Tareeq tried to get the blood spot out of the rug where his Uncle Anwar fell after he was stabbed by one of the Voctrad goons. Tareeq tore up the rug and still could not get the blood out of the wood. The sight of it made him miss his uncle even more.

With most of the rainy season over, Tareeq enjoyed the sunshine. His guests were spread out at different angles and chairs along the pool deck. Eight guests remained. At full capacity, the hotel held two hundred guests. Tareeq had employed a staff of thirty to support the guest's every need. Tareeq reassured the remaining guests that they would all survive the Ebola crisis. Tareeq carried a tray of gin and tonics back and forth. The guests were happy to drink free alcohol, and several had passed out in the bright sunshine. Tareeq repositioned umbrellas to protect the sleeping guests from sunburn.

At the Masonic Temple, Kitson kept a close watch on the computer feeds of satellite imagery and updated Hassan's location. Russell was impressed with Kitson's operational ability. Maps were time stamped with updates. Ike's task was to print aerial photos and match them with the corresponding locations on the large map spread across eight tables. Kitson kept moving back and forth with a magnifying glass as he examined the raw intelligence that was generated. After an hour, Kitson received an MI6 alert that Hassan had used the SIM card to create an international phone call to Syria. The conversation lasted over two minutes and provided an exact location. Whoever Hassan was working for in Syria had to be identified and captured at all costs. The threat to stability in the Middle East rested on this operation, and the future existence of Israel replied upon it. Kitson knew that they had a high probability of success capturing Hassan and destroying the Ebola weapon. The information was time sensitive, and the three of them bolted out of the Masonic Temple.

Ike had stopped the vehicle some distance away from the target's location, which was an abandoned charter fishing business located along a creek that flowed out from the Marshall River. Dozens of waterways existed in and around Monrovia that could be used to get to the Atlantic Ocean quickly. Mansions with massive lawns and boat docks were erected, yet fell into disrepair when the wealthy left Liberia after the recent civil war. Ike remained with the vehicle to protect their means of escape once they captured Hassan. Ike kept the engine running. Kitson and Russell moved into the bush toward the contact.

Kitson sprinted as fast as we could. For a sixty-two-year-old, Kitson could move quickly, but not as fast as Russell. Up ahead, Kitson saw Russell leap over the top of a bush. Russell vaulted into the air. His arms moved in direct motion. The weapon seemed one with him as he swung it through the air. Russell sprinted fast, and Kitson used all of his strength to catch up.

"Don't shoot Hassan," Kitson yelled. "We need him alive." Kitson was out of breath. He stopped for a moment and spoke into his headset.

"Confirmed," Russell said hesitantly. He was out of breath and spoke between breaths. Russell saw the movement ahead and dove toward the ground. Instead of being exposed, he lifted a mirror into the air. He wiggled the mirror to gain a slightly better look. There were several vehicles in the open. Russell's movement did not catch their attention, and he slithered through the brush. Russell moved the sniper rifle along his body and placed into position. He had Hassan dead in his site. Russell played with the trigger with his loose finger. He tapped lightly on the trigger knowing full well how much pressure it would take to pull the trigger.

"Where are you?" Kitson spoke into the headset. He panted heavily and controlled his breathing by doing long exhales.

"Two hundred feet ahead," Russell said. "How do you feel?"

"If I were your age again, I would have been there a long time ago," Kitson responded as a matter of fact. In his earlier years, Kitson was a formidable warrior, yet he never boasted. He never revealed his times from the London marathons that were well under three hours. Kitson never talked about his past. He was a clandestine operative for most of his life. Kitson rarely reflected on the Queen's Medal, one of six ever presented by her Majesty. Kitson moved into the bush very slowly and deliberately. Even for an older operative, Kitson had slick moves and slithered into place. His heartbeat was high and blood pulsed in his veins. He exhaled several long breaths to control his heart rate. Kitson concealed himself in a bush as he spied the target.

"Hassan is on the move." Kitson barked into his headset. "He is the one to the left." Kitson looked into the optical scope attached to the sniper rifle. From two hundred yards, he had a good aim on the target.

"Are you sure he needs to remain alive?"

"We need to know who paid for the attack on Israel," Kitson said, and he warned. "There is more at stake than what had happened here."

Kitson would divulge more at a later time what MI6 had learned in Syria that would toss the Middle East into full-scale war.

"Are you certain the satellite has a lock on him?" Russell inquired as he peered into his optical scope. He was at a closer range than Kitson, who he knew was a better long-range sniper.

"Certain," Kitson replied quickly. He held up his computer that connected to the small satellite dish. The uplink to the satellite was clear and the picture crisp. "Once we take out the thugs, Hassan will be all alone." The plan called for Hassan to be separated from all of his support and he would be an easy capture target.

"There is one more in the car." Russell blurted out. "He is in the backseat. Just saw his head come up."

"Must have been sleeping in the back," Kitson replied. "Looks like they woke him up." Kitson saw Hassan flap his arms ferociously in the air and from the expression on his face he yelled very loudly at the sleeping sentry.
"That gives a total of four targets," Russell replied.

"I'll take the ones close to Hassan," Kitson replied. He knew Russell could shoot; however, he did not want to risk any collateral damage, especially since MI6 wanted Hassan alive.

"Are you positive we have to let Hassan live?" Russell asked again. He trained the rifle's sight on the middle of Hassan's forehead. He really wanted to pull the trigger. One shot would blow his brains out, and Russell believed some redemption.

"There are larger plans for Hassan." Kitson knew his protégé was fast on impulse. Kitson paused for a moment. "Don't worry. I will take the two adjacent to Hassan. You take the one in back and the one getting out of the car." Kitson said. "On the count of one, two."

"Three," Russell replied. Within a millisecond, a fifty caliber round and a short burst of air resonated from the rifle barrel. The eight-inch silencer on the weapon masked the sound and echo of the shot. On the other side of the field, Kitson experienced the same.

Hassan watched in a confused daze as the man he had yelled at in the car emerged in time to have his head blown off. Fragments of skull flew in the air as the man's body fell to the ground. Hassan was bewildered. He looked to his left and right as he watched the other two bodyguards fall. Blood erupted from their chests as they were struck. Hassan dropped to the ground. He looked around, got up, and ran for his life. Hassan looked at the car's ignition and saw the keys were in place. He slid into the front seat and started the vehicle. Hassan hugged the car's floor and pushed his left hand on the gas pedal.

Kitson watched for movement. He knew that they needed him alive. It would be very easy for him to shoot the gas tank and explode the vehicle. Kitson understood that from an intelligence standpoint there was more at stake. He was not allowed access to the ongoing mission in Syria. Kitson was informed by MI6 leadership that Hassan was a high value target and wanted for crimes against humanity based upon what he did in Damascus.

"Go for the tires," Kitson offered.

"I got the rear," Russell said as he was in the best position for those shots. Within two seconds, all four tires exploded from the impacted rounds. Hassan pushed upon the driver's side door and rolled to the ground. He quickly lifted his body upwards and ran toward the trees. Russell watched through his scope and aimed at Hassan's back. He spoke into the headset as he rested his finger on the trigger.

"He's headed for the creek!" Kitson yelled at the top of his lungs.

"I can wound him." Russell had four more shots.

"Take the shot," Kitson replied.

"Confirmed," Russell replied. He moved the scope site from the middle of Hassan's back toward his legs. He fired and saw Hassan drop to the ground. "Hit."

"Good show," Kitson replied. "Do you see him?"

"Not yet," Russell replied. He kept the scope trained along the bushes, yet he did not see Hassan raise his body. Russell continued. "I don't want to fire into the bush as I may kill him."

"Do you hear that?" Kitson shouted. Several hundred feet from their position, a boat's motor had started. "Crap, he's got a motorboat on the creek," Kitson shouted as he stood up. "Go!"

"I'll get him," Russell replied. "You check and make sure none of them are alive still, so I don't get shot in the back."

"Roger," Kitson said as he moved into the open. He kept his weapon at the ready just in case. Kitson checked for vital signs and confirmed Hassan's men were dead.

Like something out of an action movie, Russell jumped over the hood of the vehicle. He tossed the weapon into his shoulder and looked toward the creek. Hassan accelerated the speedboat at full throttle into the creek. Russell did not see Hassan as he was on the deck of the boat. Russell shot at the boat's engine. He observed a ricochet round that bounced off the metal of the engine. He fired the last two shots lower to no prevail. Hassan still motored down the creek. Several hundred feet further, he swung the boat into the waterway that connected with the Marshall River. Hassan powered the boat deeper into Liberia toward the Marshall compound.

Russell found Kitson in the open field. He watched Kitson as he leaned over the dead bodies. Kitson looked for identification, and he took several photos of their dead faces.

"We lost him," Russell stated in a cold manner.

"More than likely, he's headed to the Marshall compound," Kitson said. He moved back and forth from the dead bodies. "These two look like brothers or definitely related."

"Do you think they are all Hezbollah?"

"I would bet the London Bridge on it." Kitson looked at the credentials. "It would have been great to interrogate one of them."

"Yeah," Russell replied. "We could have called in Francesca to work one of them over." Russell looked at the dead face. "She would have enjoyed putting her fists in this guy's face."

"So she has anger management issues?"

"No, she just is really pissed at the world, especially the terrorists who killed her mother."

"I can only imagine how much hatred exists in her."

"She had seen a lot of death in her life,"

"What of your son?" Kitson looked at his protégé. The question had been on his mind for a long time. "Would you consider bringing him to America?" He paused and thought about the boy's mother, "And Francesca?" Kitson looked at his protégé. "What of her?"

"I'm not sure." Russell could not look him in the eye. "We come from different backgrounds. Different lives. It was by chance that we met."

"But blood is blood." Kitson paused for a moment. "Am I right?"

"And her father wants me dead."

Russell pulled out the map from his pocket and unraveled it. Roads and access points were circled. The road network outside of Monrovia was very primitive. There were few main roads and a lot of choke points for ambushes. Ike knew the area well and helped Russell draw in the roads that really were no more than a trail.

"So, we have two options," Russell thought as he spoke out loud. "We can try the suicide mission of attacking forty or fifty heavily armed thugs at the Marshall compound, or we can go after the Ebola weapon that will have a lot of armed thugs guarding it as well."

"Make it simple," Kitson said. "Let's just flip a coin." Russell looked surprised at his British Intelligence mentor as he seemed very uncharacteristically cavalier about what mission to take.

"You call it. Heads for Marshall; tails for MacArthur Airfield."

"Tails," Kitson said. The Liberian dollar coin that had the face of President Tubman on the front and the Liberian state seal on the backside. The coin flipped in the air multiple times and landed on the Liberian state seal. Kitson looked at it and replied, "That's a damn good omen."

Chapter 30

The walls of the Masonic Temple were stripped of photos and maps. Kitson dismantled all of the intelligence maps that he worked very diligently to create. In the center of the room, Ike burned important papers. Flames ignited up the building's interior and provided Russell with an added advantage to marvel at the gigantic murals painted on the ceiling. The ornate designs were something that he would never have expected in a third world country. The lavish intricacies displayed the rich history of the Liberian people. Russell opened his notebook and read the anonymous quote he inscribed on the back cover: 'Doped up soldiers robed in the spoils of war – dresses, wigs, construction helmets, and swimming goggles – fired on civilians and rival factions with equal disdain.' Russell thought of the horrific pain endured by the Liberian people. He needed to take action.

Russell stood still, almost at attention as he dialed the direct line into the American Embassy. He patiently informed the U.S. Ambassador of what transpired and his theory around Kamal blowing up the Minister's mansion in Robertsport. Russell dreaded making the call, yet he knew it was the right thing to do. "Without the Defense Minister, we are at a loss," Russell said. There was a long pause as he waited for the U.S. Ambassador to complete her reply. "There are several good candidates, but I imagine the President will want to select someone close." Russell did not want to second guess any decision made. He understood how things got done in Africa. Anyone who controlled the military and weapons was a threat to the Liberian government. "I understand Madame Ambassador," Russell paused for a long period of time as heard an earful. He looked at Kitson. Russell managed to control the smirk on his face. "Yes ma'am, we will wait for further information if it was an accidental explosion or who may have been responsible." Russell looked at the phone that was disconnected on the other end of the line as the Ambassador had hung up on him.

"What did your Ambassador say?" Kitson asked.

"That there's so much panic with the Ebola outbreak that even some of her staff have requested to leave Liberia." Russell saw several armed convoys depart the embassy compound. He continued. "She is reluctant to state Minister Urey was murdered by Al Qaeda."

"What about the threat of Hassan and Checkov building a weapon to attack Israel?"

"She does not believe me that there is an imminent threat," Russell said. "She is so focused on treating the Ebola outbreak that she had no thoughts of an international conspiracy to attack Tel Aviv with a virus bomb." Russell paused for a moment. "And worse, she believes that the explosion and fire at the Presidential Palace was an accident."

"It is hard to fathom." Kitson put some levity to the situation. "Ebola released on Israel would have a devastating impact on Middle East peace process." Kitson paused for a moment and raised his voice. "Israel will retaliate."

"No one believes that an Ebola weapon existed," Russell replied.

"It is hard for me to believe that the technology had existed for sixty years under the Soviets." Kitson passed for a moment and continued. "And no one knew."

"Someone knew," Russell said. "The Israelis had this on their radar for a long time."

"Remember what I used to tell you about Africa?" Kitson asked his protégé. He had been Russell's mentor for over five years.

"Nothing is what it appears to be."

"You can say the same about the Mossad," Kitson looked at Russell. "Have you spoken with Francesca?"

"No," Russell replied. "She's off the grid."

"Can Langley find her?" Kitson inquired. "MI6 has no activity from her on voice recognition software." He paused for a moment. "She's a ghost. No one can track her."

"There's no movement…no signals – nothing," Russell replied. He reflected on Francesca and seeing her again. Their relationship was tenuous at best. He did not know if he could trust the mother of his child or the Israel Mossad trained killer. "She must have a safe house. The Mossad has been operating in Liberia for decades to keep a close watch on Hezbollah."

"She's an unknown entity," Kitson replied. "We have little room for error and cannot wait on her."

"My gut tells me that she will take out Hassan."

"Sniper rifle?"

"More than likely," Russell added. "She can fire long-range shots with the best of them. If she had a lock on his target or where Hassan would be, she would take him out."

"Do you think she already may be at the Marshall compound?" Kitson looked at his watch and thought if Francesca had a sniper's nest near the Hezbollah compound, she could have already taken the shot on Hassan as he arrived the Marshal compound. Kitson knew in his gut that Francesca would be able to make the shot on a moving target such Hassan's speedboat.

"I put a tracking device in her shoe at the bungalow," Russell confided. "And the device went dead within an hour after she departed."

"She must have discovered it."

"More than likely." Russell thought for a moment. "She does not want us knowing her end game. What would be the worst possible situation?

"An explosion."

"Exactly," Russell conjectured more. "Francesca would be the most effective if she had a large bomb to blow up the Marshall compound."

"And the hangar?" Kitson inquired. "She would have to plant two large bombs simultaneously. Even Francesca would have difficulty accomplishing that task."

"Maybe she had help?" Russell wondered if other Mossad agents had snuck into Liberia.

"No," Kitson said firmly. From his years of intelligence service, he understood her mindset. "Francesca is what you yanks call a lone wolf. She would not bring another operative into Liberia, especially this late in the game. We have very little time to eliminate the threat."

"And waiting for a Special Ops team to arrive is out of the question."

"Exactly," Kitson added. "We need to finish destroying all documents in case we do not come back." Russell nodded in agreement. Both of them knew that in the final assault phase of an operation it was utmost importance to destroy any evidence that would link either MI6 or the CIA back to the operation. Neither of them thought of their own safety or life expectancy; however, it was always in the back of their minds on covert operations. Kitson grabbed documents and tossed them into the fire.

Meanwhile, Francesca was on the move and gladly operated alone. She felt safe and secure when she relied only upon herself. The Mossad taught Francesca to kill, not just any type of kill, but a brutal killing. Francesca moved her hand underneath her shirt and rubbed the scar. Her fingers cascaded across the rippled skin tissue that was decimated by the cauterization of her wound. The brutal eight-inch scar across the left side of her abdomen served as a reminder of what happened to her in Paris. She thought about the mother that she never knew. She was such a young girl when a bomb killed her mother. Francesca pulled at her necklace. The small photo showed a happier time when her mother hugged her. There were no photos of her mother in their house, and her father claimed a fire destroyed everything. For many nights, the young girl would look to the stars and wonder about her mother.

The missile with the ten-pound explosive warhead sat idly by her side as Francesca maneuvered the scope back and forth across the airfield. The range designator had established the distance at about two thousand meters. She could make the shot with a sniper rifle, yet she knew that it would be an interim solution. She needed something more impactful, hence the missile. She needed to get inside. Several video cameras were attached to the shoulder holster on her right side. If one got damaged in the assault, she needed a backup device. She looked up at the sky, far to her left. Deep in the sky, she could see a faint trail from a jetliner. The scope did not help much to identify the aircraft.

"Designate four bravo tango," She whispered into the headset. "Five alpha, alpha present on station," She waited for a response. There was no sound. Slowly a crackle of noise emitted into the headset. Francesca looked around at the grove of trees that concealed her presence. The aerial antennae was positioned in a tree, about ten feet high. She did not want to risk detection by climbing higher into the tree. She speculated that ten feet would be high enough. She had no room for error. For a moment she contemplated climbing the tree to raise the aerial antennae higher. The sound got louder.

"Five alpha, alpha," the pilot spoke, "squadron of four bombers in position." Francesca smiled slightly as her request must have been honored. She provided her father with a detailed assessment that outlined not only striking the airfield but also the Hezbollah compound along the Marshall

River. Her father questioned her motives as he believed that perhaps she wanted more retribution for the men who had tortured Russell. Her father continued to question her loyalty to the Mossad or the CIA man who was the father of her son.

"What's time to target?" Francesca looked at her watch.

"Forty-five minutes time to target." The pilot responded. The four long-range bombers comprised the new vision for Israeli defense that was built in South Carolina as part of a covert plan to better equip Israel for a potential strike at an Iranian nuclear facility.

The long-range bombers were stealth design with wide swept wings and the capability to carry a large payload. The planes were designed around the newly sophisticated bunker buster bomb that was rapidly developed as a measure to destroy the hardened and deeply entrenched nuclear facilities outside of Tehran. These weapons were expensive to create and would not be used on this mission. Each bomber carried a payload of twelve five-hundred-pound bombs that had the detonator fuses adjusted to ignite at direct contact. Over the past three weeks, the Israeli pilots had practiced at night and daytime scenarios to mimic the precise payload release based upon the exact rate of speed and elevation. The first two bombers were the eyes for the formation, and the following two would release.

"Mission confirmed." Francesca looked toward the building on the other side of the flight line. She estimated that it would take her five minutes to sprint along the dirt road that bordered the runway.

Most of the road was concealed by high grass that helped conceal her movements from detection. She adjusted her equipment several times. She rechecked the missile controls three more times. The rocket rested idly and was pointed directly at the large hangar. She had forty-five minutes to get to the other side of the runaway, penetrate the hangar building, obtain video of the Ebola weapon, and escape before Israeli bombs obliterated the target. She concealed her escape vehicle with several branches as best she could. She chugged some water and took off in a dead sprint.

Outside of MacArthur Airfield, Kitson and Russell moved slowly into place. Both were adept at covert operations and concealed themselves very well. The bush on the far side of the abandoned airfield was dense and overgrown. The area had not been used for nearly twenty years, yet there was fresh work. Kitson observed over a dozen trees that were recently cut down. There was a smell of tar in the air, and he saw locals who worked on patching the old tarmac. Two Hezbollah thugs supervised several local men. Kitson wondered if the locals were paid as laborers or kidnapped off the street to work for Hassan. Kitson put his scope on the faces of the two security guards and watched them carefully as they smoked cigarettes. Kitson determined that he would wait to take out the guards after the assault started. He looked at his watch and surmised that Russell must have moved into position by now.

Radio silence was instituted just in case the Russians installed an electronic array to catch any open-air communications. Kitson placed the sniper rifle onto a downed log and moved behind the weapon. He used the high-powered scope to dial in close to the target. The hangar was large enough to hold four small engine aircraft. The building was made out of concrete blocks and looked very old. Kitson zoomed in the scope. The steel entry doors looked new and were a sharp contrast to the old rusted, hangar doors. Holes in the large hangar doors were patched with tin sheets. Kitson watched the airfield and stopped when he caught movement out of the corner of his left eye.

"We have movement," Kitson spoke silently in the headset. He raised his scope to his eye and adjusted the lens. "Are you kidding me?" Kitson said in a surprising tone.

"What?" Russell inquired. "Is it a threat?"

"That depends on if we can trust your girlfriend," Kitson spoke in a flat toned voice. "Do you see her?"

"No," Russell said as he shifted his body and moved to a kneeling position from behind the sniper rifle. He picked up the weapon and shifted it toward the dirt road. Through the tall grass, he saw a female move quickly, at a fast pace. "Are you certain?"

"I caught a glimpse of her," Kitson replied. He thought for a quick second and quipped, "How many white women do you see sprinting down a road in Africa near a bunch of bad guys who have a weapon of mass destruction."

"Good point," Russell blurted out. He looked in the general direction and observed her movement. She was quick, something he had never seen. He adjusted the scope to magnify her movements. She was in and out of view through the tall grass. She moved at a dead sprint and disappeared into a small patch of woods. "Gone," Russell replied. It was short and simple. Russell instinctively knew that trouble was coming.

"How far is the hangar?" Kitson asked. "My rangefinder has it at two thousand meters."

"Sounds pretty accurate." Russell pulled his scope from Francesca's direction and shifted it toward the airfield. "It will take a lot to get across that open space in one piece."

"It's far." Kitson thought about his age and speed. He knew perfectly that all missions had inherent dangers, and he did not want to jeopardize success by moving too slow.

"Let me sprint toward her," Russell replied. "You give me about ten minutes to get to the building." Russell looked at the distance. Francesca's last position was nearly a mile away. Russell could run a seven-minute mile, but not a six-minute mile, or so he thought previously. Russell grabbed his weapon and tossed it over his back with the harness attached. He snatched up the bag of explosives and extra ammunition clips. He slipped another harness tight over his shoulders. Russell had heard Kitson say something; however, he was already sprinting toward Francesca. His heart pounded. His legs moved faster and faster. Russell reached deep into his gut and pushed his limits harder. Adrenaline blasted throughout his body. His arms flung upward and downward. His hands formed a knife-like position and cut into the air as he sprinted harder. The weapon and bag of explosives held snug across his back. The sound in his headset was garbled. Russell's mind was laser-focused on sprinting as hard as his body could withstand.

"Are you close?" Kitson asked into the headset. "I have targets lined up." Kitson paused for a moment. He has repeated himself several times with no response. He was losing his patience. "Need to know if we are a go." Kitson blurted out.

"Go!" Russell replied out of breath and with a heavy pull of air into his lungs. Russell bent over his waist. "Go!" Russell caught another breath. "Take out as many as you can." He panted heavily and almost vomited. He breathed deeply again and held it to control his breathing.

Chapter 31

Kitson kept a close watch on any movement from his rifle's scope. His shooting finger lightly touched the weapon. Kitson did not want to fire inadvertently. Kitson controlled his breathing. He had slowed his pulse rate down. Kitson was a superior marksman, and he held a deep breath as he pulled the trigger. Across the airfield, Kitson fired. The Hezbollah sentry at the corner of the building dropped. The cigarette the man smoked was still in his hand. He was the best target. Kitson looked at the front of the building at the next targets. Five men mingled near the front of the hangar. It would be hard to take them all out. He watched carefully and assessed each target. Kitson was ready to fire.

Francesca did not move when she saw Russell sprint quickly past her position. She knew not to make a sound as any noise would be perceived as a potential threat. Francesca remained curled up. She rubbed her finger over the remote trigger. Four blocks of military grade explosive were attached to the brick wall and spaced three feet apart. She wanted maximum shock effectiveness and a large hole. Digital red lights blinked brightly on the explosives. Francesca watched Russell as he ran toward the building.

As Russell approached the hangar, he had flattened his body against the wall. He looked along the hangar's wall to see the five guards outside the front entrance. He surmised that Francesca had not entered as he would have seen dead bodies littered on the ground. Russell leaned his head back away from the building's corner. He looked around the bushes and did not see movement. He looked at the wall and saw the explosives. The blinking red lights caught his immediate attention. His eyes grew large as he now found himself in the explosion zone. Russell let out a deep sigh and said, "Ah shit." He looked back toward the path and saw a curled-up Francesca wave her hand. Russell looked back to the entrance and ran to her. He slid onto the ground next to her.

"Get close to the ground." Francesca directed.

"What the hell are you doing?" Russell asked. She did not reply. Russell added sarcastically. "Glad to see you too."

"Found her," Russell spoke into the headset. He grabbed her arm and asked. "Are we capturing anyone?"

"No," she said haphazardly. "No survivors needed." She raised up the video device. "I need to get video of the machine and blueprints."

"To re-engineer the weapon?" Russell inquired. He knew Israel had a long-standing history of either capturing weapons or stealing weapon designs to help their cause. Francesca did not respond to his inquiry. After a few moments of silence, she triggered her headset to listen to the pilots.

"We have no room for error," Francesca stated. "Israeli airstrike is inbound." Francesca looked at her watch. "ETA is twelve minutes out."

"Are you kidding me?" Russell shot back. "What did you do?"

"It needs to be destroyed."

"With an act of war?" Russell asked. He looked at her and thought for a moment. He knew what the Mossad was capable of. There was no delineation when it came to protecting Israel. Russell clicked on his headset and spoke softly to Kitson. "Evidently, we have an airstrike inbound."

"And I assume it is not either of our countries," Kitson said calmly.

"Courtesy of our strategic partners." Russell quipped.

"We need a better evacuation plan," Kitson stated as he knew they had limited time to vacate the strike zone. "We have a helo hovering about five minutes away in a holding pattern just in case of an emergency."

"Wait one," Russell replied. He looked at Francesca and asked. "What is your extraction plan?"

"Vehicle on the other side of the airfield. It is a two-minute sprint and accelerating away from blast zone will take up to six minutes."

"So basically, we have no time to get the hell out of here," Russell stated as a matter of fact as he looked at his watch.

"Mission first."

"Let's call in the helo," Russell suggested to Kitson. "We need to make sure to get out of this area and fast."

"Get down," Francesca ordered. She counted down until she hit the detonator. "Three, two, one."

The side of the building exploded in a massive fireball. The concussion from the shock wave rung in Russell's ears. He smacked them with his palms to clear the pressure. He watched as Francesca ran toward the building. He lost her in the smoke. In front of the building, the five men were startled by the explosion. Three of them dropped to the ground as their military training took over. The other two, perhaps newer recruits without combat time, looked bewildered at each other. In that moment of hesitation, the one closer to the door watched the head of his peer explode. He stood motionless, not knowing what to do. In the next split-second, he felt unbelievable pain as his chest was blasted by a high-powered projectile. At the other end of the airfield, Kitson quickly chambered another round and aimed at the men on the ground. The next shot was not perfect; however, he took it. Kitson looked into the rifle's scope, breathed, and squeezed the trigger. He watched the round skid over the ground. The guard lifted his body off the ground. Kitson dropped him with a shot to the back. The two remaining survivors crawled out of view as Kitson fired shot after shot at them. Kitson unloaded another ten rounds in their general vicinity in hopes of hitting anything form a ricochet.

Thick smoke loomed in the air. Francesca and Russell rushed at breakneck speed into the large hole. Russell's sniper rifle seemed large and bulky compared to the Uzi sub-machinegun Francesca had. Russell slung the sniper rifle over his shoulder and pulled out a pistol from his right hip. Francesca unloaded a barrage of fire across the room at figures that haphazardly tried to regain their balance from the explosive concussion. Russell looked toward the wall and saw the front door open. He looked at the two guards who picked up missile launchers. Russell fired at them and struck one of them in the shoulder. They returned fire in Russell's general direction. Russell dove under a table. He looked across the floor and saw several more bodies move. He did not wait for them to gain their composure. Russell fired along the floor and hit several Voctrad goons.

By the time Russell crawled under the next table, the two guards had exited the building with a missile launcher. Russell turned back toward Francesca and observed her going over stacks of papers spread out over the table. She grabbed and stuffed documents into her knapsack. Russell saw one of the Russian scientists stand. By the time he could fire at him, Francesca raised her Uzi with her right hand and released a barrage of ten bullets. The Russian dropped to the floor. Russell saw the containment area with the thick sheets of protective glass in place. Francesca sprinted past the containment area and deeper into the hangar. She had the video recorder in one hand and the Uzi in the other. She fired at several targets on the ground, not knowing if they were dead.

The other Russian scientists crouched on the other side of the Ebola weapon. Once they realized the danger was coming to them, they ran toward the back door. Francesca shifted the Uzi toward their general direction and let out a burst of fire. Bullets ripped across their backs, and their bodies tumbled out of the air onto the concrete. Russell fumbled through their pockets. He rolled the bodies over and took snapshots of their faces. Russel would send everything he obtained back to Langley for further analysis.

"We need to go!" Russell shouted at Francesca. "Now!" Russell added, "We need to go now!"

"Plenty of time." Francesca shot back to him in a calm manner. She climbed over the weapon and zoomed the video recorder in and out to capture the details of the weapon's design. She was puzzled by the nozzles and spent more time looking at them. She lifted her arm in the hand and shook the watch on her hand. "Sixty more seconds here."

"There," Russell shouted. Francesca did not pay any attention. She kept the video recorder going. "There is someone inside the chamber." Russell shot the glass door. The glass exploded and fell to the floor. "It's Featu," Russell shouted. He looked at the medical devices attached to her arms and the digital displays.

"Move," Francesca shouted. "Airstrike is seven minutes out."

"We're coming out the front, don't shoot." Russell looked at Francesca. "Help me." Francesca pushed through the half-broken glass door and pulled out a large knife. She sliced apart the lines and freed Featu from her entanglement.

"Now we can go," Francesca replied. "Airstrike, six minutes out."

"We're coming out," Russell shouted as he followed in trace of Francesca. He grabbed hold of the tubes that hung from Featu's body and made sure no blood leaked out.

"Roger," Kitson replied. "Front clear."

Russell tripped over one of the bodies that fell closest to the door. Francesca stepped on the backs of the dead bodies. Russell looked at the vehicles in front. The remote-controlled missile that Francesca had lined up on the three vehicles blasted them apart. Russell saw the other dead guards and the discarded missile launcher tubes on the ground. As he looked up and to his surprise, he saw Francesca stop and stand still.

"Damn," Francesca shouted aloud. She pointed in the direction of where her vehicle once was. It was now a fireball. The guards had zeroed into the smoke plume from the remotely detonated missile and fired in that direction. They got lucky, and Francesca's escape plan was obliterated.

"Let's go with my option." Russell keyed the headset to talk with Kitson. "Looks like we need a ride. How long to the helo?"

"Two minutes to my position...less time to you." Kitson replied. Without waiting for a reply, he pointed at Ike and motioned for him to follow. "We are on our way. I'll radio the helo."

"How long to the airstrike?" Russell asked as they ran.

"Look." Francesca pointed toward the direction of the ocean. There was something in the distance. Russell shifted the sniper rifle from his back and knelt into position to get a better shooters profile. He raised the scope in the direction Francesca pointed and adjusted the scope optics to increase the resolution. Russell could see the outline of inbound aircraft. The aircraft formation was tight, and it was difficult to determine how many were there.

"Kitson!" Russell shouted. "Run faster."

"Roger," Kitson said as he ran as fast as he could. Ike carried most of the equipment in his arms.

Francesca pulled out her satellite phone. She slapped it against her leg and quickly smacked it against the ground. She looked at the hole in the side of the phone. A bullet had grazed her leg and struck the satellite phone. Francesca slammed it against the ground. She had no means to communicate with the pilots to slow them down. She looked at Russell and asked. "How long to your ride?"

"There," Russell pointed and said. "Helo is inbound...coming in from the west...tree top level."

Russell looked in the direction of Kitson and Ike. They were still about a hundred yards from them. The sixty-two-year-old MI6 operative was by far more athletic than any peer his age; however, he looked exhausted. Russell held Featu close to his body. She was limp and difficult to carry. "We need to go to them." Russell shifted his sniper rifle onto his back and shouted. "Let's go." They both dashed at a lightning pace in the direction of Kitson. The helicopter hovered a few inches above the airfield for a rapid departure. Russell and Francesca sprinted harder. They saw Kitson and Ike climb into the helo. As they approached, Ike reached out for Featu while Kitson yelled into the headset for the pilot to lift off.

Russell raised his sniper scope and watched the Israeli jets move into bombing formation. "Move," Russell shouted, "Faster." He did not have a headset to communicate with the helicopter pilots, so he grabbed Kitson's arm. Russell pointed toward the inbound aircraft. Kitson spoke into the headset. Within a moment, the passengers felt the nose of the helicopter move downward. The British Merlin helicopter shifted forward. The British pilots stationed in Sierra Leone were specially trained in extract operations. The helicopter blades pounded against the air.

Russell swung his body out over the edge and into the open air. The Israeli bombers traveled low, at about five hundred feet above the ground. As they moved farther away, Russell observed bombs fall out of the two rear aircraft. Russell shifted his body back into the helicopter harness and grabbed hold of it tightly. The others saw his move, and they braced as well. The explosive shockwave lifted the tail of the aircraft higher and forced the helicopter into a nose dive. The alarm rang out. The passengers hung on tight as the pilots attempted to regain control. For five seconds, the pilots jostled the controls to stabilize the aircraft. It seemed like an eternity. As the helicopter leveled off, Russell leaned back out of the aircraft and saw the large plume of smoke. On the other side of the helicopter, Francesca leaned out to video the aftermath. The plume rose a thousand feet.

Once he was assured of his safety, Russell relaxed his muscles. He thought to himself how he had survived yet another firefight. Russell looked over at Francesca. The wind whipped through her hair as the helicopter's rotor blades swirled overhead and wind flowed through the open doors. Russell held Francesca's hand tightly and leaned over to kiss her, yet stopped as Russell heard Ike scream aloud. Russell did not understand what Ike said as the sound of the helicopter blades blistered the air. Ike motioned for Kitson to give him a hood. Within Ike's hand was the special juju, mythical creature, carved out of elephant tusk that Kitson had purchased in the Monrovia back alley. For Ike, the juju was powerful. Ike was not only terrified of heights, but he had never been in any flying contraption. Everyone knew Ike was a strong fighter as he witnessed horrors during Liberia's latest civil war. Ike's village was fifty miles from the Sierra Leone border. Doped up children soldiers raided his town and shot anyone moving. When they ran out of bullets, they hacked the villagers with machetes. Ike killed eight of the child soldiers with a machete he picked up to fight back. With his entire family was murdered, Ike had nothing until Frank Kitson Jr. had hired him as a driver over five years ago.

As the helicopter banked along the Marshall River, Francesca grabbed Russell's arm and pointed forward. Kitson informed the pilot to lower to treetop level. The British Merlin helicopter dropped from two thousand feet to less than one hundred. The pilot guided the aircraft directly up Marshall River toward the Hezbollah compound. Russell spotted Monkey Island and glanced to see if he noticed any chimpanzees along the water's edge and saw none. The pilot banked the helicopter to the left so Russell and Francesca could get a better view from their side. Speedboats were upside down in the river. Most were ablaze. The Israeli jets unleashed a barrage of automatic weapons fire on the marina. There was nothing left that would float. Up ahead Russell saw thick clouds of smoke. The helo circulated above what remained of the Marshall compound, otherwise better known as Hezbollah target A89GH3 by the Israeli air operations center.

Russell surmised that there was a slim chance for any survivors. More importantly, if there were any survivors, it would send a strong signal to Hezbollah that their families were not safe when it came to threatening Israel's existence. Russell watched Francesca video tape the carnage.

"Hassan?" Russell shouted over the noise of the helicopter in Kitson's general direction. "He must be dead."

"What?" Kitson shouted back as he removed his headset.

"Hassan," Russell yelled louder. "More than likely he's dead."

"Hard to say," Kitson yelled back at the top of his lungs. "He could have gotten another boat and escaped to the freighter offshore." Kitson looked back toward the ocean in the distance. The freighter was out of sight, yet he knew it was about five miles from land. "We'll keep a trace on him." Kitson put the headset back on.

Kitson requested the pilot to hover over the site at a higher altitude just in case any survivors fired at them. From his vantage point, Kitson could not tell if there were any survivors. The aftermath was horrific. From the information Tareeq had obtained, the Marshall compound housed forty male fighters and another two hundred family members. Russell wondered what they must have thought when the observed four large aircraft fly up the river - what were their final thoughts when they saw the aircraft's bay doors open, and the bombs fall out. Russell watched Francesca as she snapped more photos. There appeared to be no survivors. Francesca's face was cold, expressionless. She did not smile or ever offer any sign of sorrow. Russell knew that this was her war – a lifetime in the making – something she would readily give her life. He knew at all costs; Israel would destroy their enemies. On this mission, Liberia's MacArthur Airfield and the Hezbollah compound located in Marshall were annihilated.

Chapter 32

The remaining twenty-minute flight to Roberts International Airport was uneventful. Russell looked out toward the ocean and reflected on the mission. Once again, he had escaped death by sheer luck. He admired the beauty of crystal blue waves that somersaulted over one another. Russell watched Francesca as she seemed mesmerized by the scenery as well. From the time Russell had first met Francesca at the Cape Hotel, close to five years ago, his life had been turned upside down. Russell fell in love with a trained killer. He had not been allowed to see or talk with his son for a long time. Francesca's father, a senior Mossad official, wanted him dead.

The pilot descended the aircraft to tree top level on final approach. Russell observed a group of children who ran and waved at the aircraft. Russell waved back with his free hand. The children were resilient. From what Russell observed in Liberia, the last civil war coupled with the Ebola carnage had decimated Liberian society. The war cost four hundred thousand Liberian lives and approximately one million citizens displaced out of a population of just three million. The Ebola outbreak added another eight thousand deaths to date.

As the helo landed, the passengers received inquisitive stares as they landed in the isolated Ebola quarantine area. The flight operations crew, who monitored the aircraft arrivals and departures, ran out of the control tower to see the commotion. No one knew what to say to Russell, Kitson, Francesca, or Ike as they walked away from the helicopter. More significantly, many were shocked as Russell carried a limp body. Featu's arms hung in the air, and she appeared dead. In the medical tent, the foreign doctors wore the full, bulky decontamination suits. Russell recognized Sam as he tore off his protective face shield and ran toward them.

"Noooo," Sam yelled. The decontamination suit bogged him down and looked awkward as he moved as fast as possible. Sam yelled out again. "Noooo." He panted and wrapped his hand around her wrist to check for a pulse. "Is she dead?" Sam attempted to rip her from Russell's arms.

"She'll make it," Russell shouted at him. Sam would not listen. He was focused on her face. With his free arm, Russell shook Sam and repeated himself, "She'll make it."

"Oh, dear God." Sam shifted his arms underneath Russell's to get control of Featu's body, so she did not fall to the ground. Again, and again, he repeated himself. "Oh, my Featu…Oh, my Featu."

"She's dehydrated and emaciated." Kitson tried to reassure Sam. "We've found her. She'll be alright."

"Featu what have they done to you?" Sam asked aloud in a high pitch wail. He carried her as fast as he could toward the medical tents.

"You need to test her to make sure she is not infected," Russell shouted. Sam did not pay attention to anything. "You must test her now!" Russell shouted as Sam rushed her toward an inspection tent.

As the helicopter departed, the blades pounded the air and kicked up dust. Kitson gave a final wave as the pilot headed back up the coast toward Sierra Leone. He saw a sign that read, 'In the midst of poverty, there is human excellence.' Kitson pointed out to the stacks of supplies and the influx of U.S. military personnel. "When you Americans commit, you really commit." Kitson slapped Russell's back and added. "Good show mate."

"Right," Russell replied with his imitated British accent. "We need to be cleared from the virus before being released." Russell looked at the Military Policemen who moved toward them. They removed pistols from their holsters and stopped about twenty feet from Russell and his entourage.

"Let me find out what is going on." Russell attempted to take a few steps toward the air operations tent; however, the MPs pointed their weapons. Russell looked around at the makeshift hospital and said, "Looks like we're going into quarantine." Russell followed the directions of the MPs as they pointed for them to walk toward the quarantined area.

Inside the decontamination zone, each of them were forced to take off their clothes and shower. Cold water poured from the showers as they walked underneath. Francesca stripped off her shirt and caught the attention of the MPs, not for her chiseled body, but for the eight-inch-deep scar along the right side of her waist. Francesca did not care about her nudity and used the moment to seduce Russell further as he and the other twenty men in the area watched. Ike picked up a towel and lifted it up for Francesca to dry.

"Let's get a drink," Russell said as he pointed toward a makeshift departure area constructed by the Seabees. The foreigners who were cleared to leave Liberia enjoyed beers purchased by the sailors.

"Let's get smashed," Francesca shot back. She poured the contents of the liquor bottle that she did not know into several shot glasses. It was alcohol. She pushed the glass's contents into her mouth.

"Looks like I got a ride out and to a fifteen-day quarantine site somewhere outside of London," Kitson said as he looked at the paper the MP handed him. The British military jet was inbound and had a special compartment to isolate passengers.

"What about Ike?" Russell turned to Kitson and asked. They each looked at one another and knew what would transpire if the Hezbollah found Ike. With the Defense Minister's death and the nuns raising James, Ike had no family. The Robertsport mansion was destroyed. Ike had nowhere to go. Kitson would not let his old friend suffer.

"Ike, would you like to live in England with me?" Kitson asked.

"Bossman, U bring Ike to land of Queen?" Ike had a tear in his eye.

"Of course," Kitson replied with a warm smile.

Russell opened a local beer and took a large swig of the semi-warm contents. The piss warm taste did not matter. It was still beer. Russell gazed across the airfield and contemplated Liberia's existence. West Africa became the central point to transport captured tribesmen from the Congo River region to the new American colonies. The use of slaves was one of the fueling points for the American Civil War and the near collapse of democracy in the New World. To make matters whole again, a few hundred former slaves and six abolitionists journeyed back to West Africa. The abolitionists purchased land from a tribal king that formed the geographic boundaries of today's Liberia.

Doctor Abuja waved vigorously as he saw Russell and Kitson. He walked briskly toward them as best as he could in the protective spacesuit. He stopped a few feet away from Kitson and Russell as he did not know if they were infected.

Doctor Abuja took multiple blood samples from several survivors and sent them in a vacuum sealed, locked container to the remote CDC facility in New Mexico. He was granted several armed UN guards to travel with the blood samples.

"How is it out there?" Doctor Abuja asked.

"Not good. Ebola has raged beyond Bushrod Island and into Monrovia." Kitson stated as a matter of fact. "Hospitals are overloaded. Bodies are left in the streets."

"What about the evil Russians?" Doctor Abuja asked. "Checkov?"

"Don't know," said Kitson, "The last we heard from our surveillance team was he departed the Jordanian Hospital in a speedboat and no one had seen him since. We looked all over for him. He must have left the country."

"Are we safe?" Doctor Abuja asked.

"With fifty Marines guarding the camp here," Russell pointed around, "You betcha."

"The Russians who remained at the Jordanian Hospital will all be dead within the next day." Doctor Abuja said in a soft tone. He was lucky to have escaped the Jordanian Hospital. Kitson had locked the doors with chains so none of Checkov's men would escape.

"You are safe here," Russell assured him.

"Ebola will continue to rage in Monrovia," Kitson said. He looked at the tent area that contained over a hundred foreigners. Locals were quarantined at the BTC compound. Massive tents were erected on the parade field. There were no toilets, and large holes were dug in the grass. The once pristine field was torn apart. The bungalows were used by government officials. They remained inside and would not open the doors out of fear of that throngs of their citizens would overtake them. There was no interior security within the BTC compound. All of the military guards moved to the perimeter wall to make sure no one escaped. Those who attempted to climb over the wall were shot. No doctors dared enter the compound. The appalling smell lingered in the air as over four thousand Liberians packed into the thirty-acre compound. Horrific images had returned to the BTC compound to add to the horrendous history.

"More medicine has arrived." Doctor Abuja pointed in the air at the U.S. military transport planes that circled high above.

"Ebola will always remain a threat in Africa." Russell proclaimed.

"I have the solution." Doctor Abuja said quietly as he leaned in close. "The solution to not only treating Ebola but preventing the disease from ever developing in the bloodstream."

"Really," Kitson said. He had lived in and out of Africa for about twenty years of his intelligence career and understand the impact of Ebola firsthand. "Can the antidote be developed on a large scale?"

"It would take a large investment." Doctor Abuja added. "Millions of dollars, but it could be done." He looked at tents that housed infected patients. "We could eradicate Ebola just like they did with Polio."

Russell recalled in his research how the CIA had conducted a pandemic analysis twenty-five years prior. Langley realized a major Ebola outbreak would be catastrophic. A sheer desire to treat Ebola upon infection was fostered. Research for the cure became sporadic over the next two decades. Success proved limited – until Doctor Abuja arrived at a remote Air Force base in the Nevada desert.

"How's Major Forleh?" Russell inquired.

"Slight head injury," Doctor Abuja responded, "but stable."

"Can we see him?" Kitson asked. Doctor Abuja nodded and escorted them to the other part of the isolate medical area for the few locals.

"How are you?" Kitson asked as he looked at Major Forleh and added. "You look much better."

"They beat me." Major Forleh said. "The Russians wanted information about the Minister, my boss. I told them nothing."

"The Minister is dead," Kitson stated, as a matter of fact.

"Yes, I heard," Forleh said. "The paper says it was a fire."

"That wasn't the case," Kitson replied.

"Sensational news generates fear." Major Forleh replied. He paused for a moment and added. "Fear causes violence."

"I could not agree more," Russell replied. He looked at the Liberian officer who had a hard life. Forleh survived the brutal civil war. He had evaded the bullets shot by doped up children, many of them younger than him at the time. He wanted to make a difference. When candidates for the new Liberian Army were requested, Forleh was one of the first to raise his hand.

"What of the Hezbollah terrorists?" Major Forleh inquired. "We will have a hard time bringing them to justice. They have much money, and from the rumors, most have left Liberia."

"London reported that Hassan had just placed a satellite call, so we know that he is still alive, but don't worry." Kitson put his hand on Forleh's shoulder and assured him. "Hassan will be taken care of." Kitson looked up at Russell and added. "It may take us a few months or even a year, but we will bring Hassan to justice."

"Hassan will be taken out," Russell interjected. The sound of a jet as it landed surprised them as restrictions in place for any inbound flights.

"That looks like our ride," Kitson said as the British military jet landed. Kitson shook hands with Major Forleh.

"See you soon," Russell shook hands with his mentor. The Ebola operation had lasted four months, and it ended with a brief thirty-second farewell, such was the existence in covert operations.

"Hopefully not too soon," Kitson said. "Ike and I need to go fishing" Ike smiled and waved goodbye.

After the British aircraft came to a complete stop, several men departed and handed Kitson and Ike decontamination suits. They would travel inside the plane in the bulky spacesuits. Before they entered the aircraft, Kitson turned and waived both arms in the air. Ike smiled broadly, and he appeared happy for once.

Russell had not heard from Langley about his next move and wondered if the Ambassador got involved in halting his departure. Russell wanted out of Liberia, so he did not have to explain Israeli jets just decimated a major Hezbollah terrorist cell.

Within a few moments, two MPs came over to Francesca and handed her a piece of paper. She excused herself to get cleaned up. Russell drank another beer as he waited. He looked at the giant mural on the side of the building that stated, "The Love of Liberty Brought Us Here." Russell thought of the pain Liberians had witnessed, yet another horrific event in a long history of violence. The Ebola outbreak crippled Liberia again.

"What about us?" Francesca asked as she returned refreshed. She leaned in close. "What about us, Tom Russell of the American Central Intelligence Agency?" Francesca smiled with those brilliant white teeth.

"Do we have a future?" Russell inquired. He sensed Francesca kept a secret eye on his affairs, regardless of the three-thousand-mile distance.

"Perhaps," Francesca replied. "If not for us ... for our son."

"When are you leaving Africa?" Russell asked.

"That plane should be mine." Francesca watched the El Al jetliner as it landed and taxied toward their general direction. She knew that her father had sent the aircraft. "I am leaving Africa."

"What of us?" Russell asked. "You're Mossad, and I'm CIA. Outside of covert ops, we have nothing in common." He paused for a moment and asked, "What would keep us together?"

"The adrenaline rush," Francesca replied with a smile.

"The missions?" Russell looked at her. She was stunningly beautiful even without a shower. She tied her hair in a knot, and her halter-top revealed her chiseled body.

"Yes, the missions," Francesca replied.

"And after the missions are over?" Russell asked. For the past five years, he had an on-again and off-again romance with one of the deadliest spies in the world. "What do we do after all of the operations are over?"

"Grow old together," Francesca replied. "I love you Tom Russell of the American CIA." Francesca stood up and kissed him on the lips. As Francesca walked across the tarmac, she did not turn. Russell watched as two women in decontamination suits emerged from the aircraft.

When she mentioned that they should spend their lives together, Russell had no response. Being with her was a deadly mission in itself. Francesca was immensely seductive, incredibly lethal, and many wanted her dead. For Russell, she was the mother of his child.

Francesca climbed the aircraft stairs. She stopped at the entrance and looked back toward Russell. She smiled with those brilliant white teeth. Even from a distance, her beauty caught his attention. Russell walked closer and then stood motionless. He did not know what to do with the mother of his only child. He had considered abducting Dominic, yet he knew that Francesca would hunt him down. No place in the world would be safe, not even in America. Russell yearned to see his son again. He did not know if he loved or hated her. There were few normal parts of their relationship. For the most part, they were shot at when they were together.

The one thing Russell did not realize was that Francesca had received new orders to recruit Russell to betray America.

# # #

About the Author

WWW.ANTHONYCFABIANO.COM

Anthony Fabiano has studied counter-insurgency doctrine extensively and incorporated his knowledge into novels based in Africa to highlight some historical epic failures.

Rising from the Marine Corps enlisted ranks to graduate from the U.S. Naval Academy, Anthony Fabiano retired from the Marines after 26 years of military service as a Lieutenant Colonel. He served two tours in Iraq and traveled widely throughout the Middle East. Additionally, as a member of U.S. Central Command staff, he traveled to Afghanistan and Pakistan. In January 2010, he led 54 U.S. military advisors into Liberia; the first ever joint team to do so, becoming the premier mentoring program in Africa. In Liberia, he observed a nation brutalized by fourteen years of civil war that left over 400,000 dead and more than one million displaced. His real-world experience with counter-insurgency doctrine helped to transition the new Armed Forces of Liberia into a military organization that respects civil authority and the Rule of Law. After retiring from the military, he has conducted extensive research on counter-insurgency operations and helped raise awareness of the issues facing Africa today. In his novels, he brings readers a realistic version of the new world order after the decline of the Soviet Union, the growth of the international black market for weapons of mass destruction, the plight of former child soldiers abandoned by society, and the rise of fanatical religious extremism.

Read the other books in the series:

Madness in Liberia

In a fourteen-year span (1989 to 2003), two catastrophic civil wars ripped apart Liberia. A nation formed by freed American slaves with a dream of justice and seeking the liberties that all people deserve became instead a nightmare land ravaged by a despot's crimes against humanity. President Charles Taylor is thrown out of power, yet his diabolical son attempts to wreak havoc and return to control. A small team of Marines led by Major Tom Russell is sent in to collect information on Taylor's war crimes and quickly becomes entrapped in a deadly game where there are no rules…only the madness that is consuming Liberia.

Crisis in the Congo

Tom Russell is back in Africa to track down illegal uranium shipments that originated out of the Congo. In the former Belgian colony, a nation haunted by its past and the brutality of a ruthless thirty-two-year reign by Joseph Mobutu, Russell is shocked at the arrival of his girlfriend, an Israeli Mossad agent who is after a missing atomic weapon. With the help of a retired couple, husband and wife ex-CIA operatives, Russell manages to navigate a corrupt government and extreme danger to strike a blow against an international arms syndicate and eliminate a massive stockpile of high-grade uranium destined for the black market.